ALSO BY JOHN GARDNER

The Resurrection

The Wreckage of Agathon

Grendel

The Sunlight Dialogues

JASON
AND
MEDEIA

JASON
AND
MEDEIA

JOHN GARDNER

ALFRED A. KNOPF
New York
1973

Copyright © 1973 by John Gardner

All rights reserved under International and Pan-American
Copyright Conventions. Published in the United States by
Alfred A. Knopf, Inc., New York, and simultaneously in
Canada by Random House of Canada Limited, Toronto.
Distributed by Random House, Inc., New York.

Library of Congress Cataloging in Publication Data

Gardner, John Champlin, (date)
Jason and Medeia.

1. Jason—Romances. 2. Medea—Romances.
I. Title.
PS3557.A712J3   811'.5'4   72-11021
ISBN 0-394-48317-0

Manufactured in the United States of America

Published June 21, 1973
Second Printing, July 1973

TO JOAN

ACKNOWLEDGMENTS

This poem was made possible by financial gifts from my friends Marilyn Burns, Ruby Cohn, and Duncan M. Luke and by grants from Southern Illinois University and the National Endowment for the Arts. I thank William H. Gass for permission to borrow and twist passages from his *Fiction and the Figures of Life,* and Gary Snyder for permission to borrow and twist two of his translations from the Cold Mountain series. Parts of this poem freely translate sections of Apollonios Rhodios' *Argonautica* and Euripides' *Medeia,* among other things.

And so the night will come to you: an end of vision;
darkness for you: an end of divination.
The sun will set for the prophets,
the day will go black for them.
Then the seers will be covered with shame,
the diviners with confusion;
they will all cover their lips,
because no answer comes from God.

MICAH 3:6–7

JASON
AND
MEDEIA

I

I dreamed I awakened in a valley where no life stirred, no cry
of a fox sparked up out of stillness; a night of ashes. I was sitting
in a room that seemed a familiar defense against darkness, but decayed,
the heavy old book I'd been reading still open on my knees. The lamp
had burned out long ago; at the socket of the bulb, thick rust.
All around me like weather lay the smell of the abandoned house,
dampness in every timber, the wallpaper blistered, dark-seamed,
at the window, the curtains mindlessly groping inward, and beyond,
gray mist, wet limbs of trees. I seemed to be waiting for someone.
And then (my eyes had been tricked) I saw her—a slight, pale figure
standing at the center of the room, present from the first, forlorn,
around her an earth-smell, silence, the memory of a death. In fear
I clutched the arms of my chair. I whispered: "Dream visitor
in a dreaming house, tell me what message you bring from the grave,
or bring from my childhood, whatever unknown or forgotten land
you haunt!" So I spoke, bolt-upright, trembling;
but the ghost-shape, moonlit figure in mourning,
was silent, as if she could neither see nor hear. She had once
been beautiful, I saw: red hair that streamed like fire,
charged like a storm with life. Alive no longer. She began
to fade, dissolve like a mist. There was only the moonlight.
                                                    Then came
from the night what I thought was the face of a man familiar with books,
old wines, and royalty—dark head slightly lowered, eyes
amused, neither cynical nor fully trusting: cool eyes set
for anything—a man who could spin a yarn and if
occasion forced him, fight.
                          Then I saw another shade,

3

a poet, I thought, his hair like a willow in a light wind,
in his arms a golden lyre. He changed the room to sky
by the touch of a single string—or the dream-change rang in the lyre:
no watchfulness could tell which sea-dark power moved first.
If I closed my eyes, it seemed the song of the man's harp
was the world singing, and the sound that came from his lips the song
of hills and trees. A man could revive the dead with a harp
like that, I thought; and the dead would glance back in anguish at the grave,
torn between beauty's pain and death's flat certainties.

(This was a vision stranger than any a man ever saw.
I rose and stepped in close. There came a whistling wind.
My heart quaked. I'd come, God knew, beyond my depth.
I found a huge old tree, vast oak, and clung to it, waiting.)

And now still another ghost rose up, pale silent mist:
the mightiest mortal who'd ever reached that thestral shore,
his eyes like a child's. They seemed remote from me as stars
on a hushed December night. His whitened lips moved,
and I strained forward; but then some wider vision stirred,
blurring my sight: the swaying shadow of a huge snake,
a ship reeling, a room in a palace awash in blood,
a woman screaming, afire . . .
                                        The sea went dark. Then all
grew still. I bided my time, the will of the moon-goddess.

A king stood scowling out over blue-green valleys. He seemed
half giant, but enfeebled by age, his sinews slackening to fat.
In the vast white house behind him, chamber rising out of
chamber, nothing moved. There was no wind, no breeze.
In the southwest, great dark towers of cloud were piled high,
like summercastles thrown up in haste to shield ballistas,
archers of ichor and air, antique, ignivomous engines,
tottering in for siege, their black escarpments charged
like thunderheads in a dream. Light bloomed, inside the nearest—
there was no sound—and then, at the king's left side appeared
a stooped old man in black. He came from nowhere—leering
sycophant wringing his crooked-knuckled hands, the skin
as white as his beard, as white as the sun through whitecaps riding
storm-churned seas. The king stood looking down at him, casual,

believing he knew him well. "My lord!" the old man said,
"good Kreon, noblest of men and most unfortunate!"
He snatched at the hem of the king's robe and kissed it, smiling.
I saw that the old man's eyes and mouth were pits. I tried
to shout, struggle toward them. I could neither move nor speak.

    Kreon, distressed, reached down with his spotted, dimpled hands
to the man he took for his servant, oft-times proven friend,
and urged him up to his feet. "Come, come," the king said, half-
embarrassed, half-alarmed. "Do I look like a priest?" He laughed,
his heart shaken by the sudden worship of a household familiar.
He quickly put it out of mind. "But yes; yes it's true, we've seen
some times, true enough! Disaster after disaster!" He laughed
more firmly, calming. His bleared eyes took in the river
winding below, as smooth and clean as new-cut brass,
past dark trees, shaded rocks, bright wheat. In the soft light
of late afternoon it seemed a place the gods had blessed,
had set aside for the comfort of his old age. Dark walls,
vine-locked, hinted some older city's fall.

                                     He tipped
his head, considered the sky, put on a crafty look.
"They say, 'Count no man happy until he's dead, beyond
all change of Fortune.' " He smiled again, like a merchant closing
his money box. "Quite so, quite so! But the axiom has
its converse: 'Set down no man's life as tragedy
till the day he's howled his way to his bitter grave.' " He chuckled,
a sound automatic as an old-man actor's laugh, or a raven's.
He'd ruled long, presiding, persuading. Each blink, each nod
was politics, the role and the man grown together like two old trees.
Then, solemn, he squeezed one eye tight shut, his head
drawn back. He scowled like a jeweller of thirty centuries hence
studying the delicate springs and coils of a strange timepiece,
one he intended to master. He touched the old slave's arm.
"The gods may test their creatures to the rim of endurance—not
beyond. So I've always maintained. What man could believe in the gods
or worship them, if it were otherwise?" He chuckled again,
apologetic, as if dismissing his tendency
toward bombast. "In any case," he said, "our luck's changing.
I give you my word." He nodded, frowning,
hardly glancing at the husk from which the god peeked out
as the rim of a winecup peeks from the grave of the world's first age.

The spying, black-robed power leered on,
wringing his hands in acid mockery
of the old servant's love.
                              Whatever shadows had crossed
the king's mind, he stepped out free of them.
Tentatively, he smiled once more, his lips like a woman's,
faintly rouged, like his cheeks. His bald head
glowed like polished stone in the failing light. A breeze,
advancing ahead of the storm, tugged at his heavy skirts
and picked at his beard. "It's difficult, God knows," he said,
"to put those times behind us: Oidipus blind and wild,
Jokasta dead, Antigone dead, high-chambered Thebes
yawning down like a ship in flames . . . Don't think I haven't
brooded aplenty on that. A cursed house, men say;
a line fated to the last leaf
on the last enfeebled branch. It's a dreadful thought, Ipnolebes.
I'm only human. I frighten as easy as the next man.
I won't deny that I've sat up in bed with a start, sometimes,
shaking like a leaf, peering with terrified, weeping eyes
at the night and filling the room with a frantic rush of prayers—
'Dear gods, dear precious-holy-gods . . .' —Nevertheless,
I can't believe it. A man would be raving mad to think
the luculent powers above us would doom us willy-nilly,
whether we're wicked or virtuous, proud or not. No, no!
With all due respect, with all due love for Oidipus
and the rest, such thoughts are the sickness of faulty metaphysics."
   The king stared at the darkening sky, his soft hands
folded, resting on his belly. Again he closed one eye
and reached for the old slave's arm. "I do not mean to malign
the dead, you understand. But working it through in my mind
I've concluded this: the so-called curse has burned itself out."
He paused, thought it over, then added, as if with a touch of guilt,
"No curse in the first place, actually. They were tested by the gods
and failed. Much as I loved them all, I'm forced to say it."
He shook his head. "They were stubborn. So they went down raging to the grave
as Oidipus rages yet, they tell me, stalking the rocks
of his barren island, groping ahead of himself with a stick,
answering cries of gulls, returning the viper's hiss,
tearing his hair, and the rest. Well, I'm a different breed
of cat. Not as clever, I grant—and not as noble, either—

but fit to survive. I've asked far less than those did.
I ask for nothing! I do my duty as a king not out of
pride in kingship, pleasure in the awesome power I wield,
but of necessity. Someone must rule, and the bad luck's mine.
Would Kreon have hanged himself, like poor Jokasta? She was
unfortunate, granted. But there have been cases, here and there,
of incest by accident. She set her sights too high, it seems.
An idealist. Couldn't bend, you know. And Antigone the same.
All that—great God!—for a corpse, a few maggots,
a passing flock of crows! Well, let us learn from their sad
mistakes. Accept the world as it is. Manipulate
the possible.
              "Strange . . .
                          "I've wondered sometimes if the gods were aware
at all of those terrible, noble deeds, those fiery orations—
Oidipus blind on the steps, Antigone in the tomb, Jokasta
claiming her final, foolish right to dignity."
He covered his mouth with his hand and squinted. He said, voice low:
"Compare the story of the perfect bliss of ancient Kadmos,
founder of the line, with Harmonia, whose marriage Zeus
himself came down to attend. King Kadmos—Kosmos, rightly—
loved so well, old legends claim,
that after his perfect joy in life—his faultless rule
of soaring Thebes, great golden city where for many centuries
nothing had stirred but the monstrous serpent Kadmos slew—
the gods awarded him power and joy after life. Zeus filled
his palace with lightning-bolts, and the well-matched pair was changed
to two majestic serpents, now Lady and Lord of all
the Dead. So, surely, all who are good get recompense.
If Oidipus did not—hot-tempered and vain—or haughty Jokasta . . .
—But let it be. I don't mean to judge them, you understand.
They behaved according to their natures. Too good for the world." He nodded.
   The wind came up. The sky overhead was as dark-robed
as the god. Old Kreon pursed his lips as if the storm
had taken him unawares. A spatter of rainfall came,
warm drops, and the king hiked up his skirts and ran, his servant
close behind, for shelter under the portico.
The trees bent low, twisting and writhing, their parched leaves
swaying like graygreen witches in a solemn dance. The sky
flashed white. A peal of thunder shook the columned house,

7

the stamping hoof of Poseidon's violent horse above,
and rain came down with a hiss, splashing the flagstones. The king
breathed deep, a sigh, stretched out his arms. "Rain!"
It was as if the gods had sent down rain for his pleasure. "God
bless rain!" The king and his servant laughed and hugged themselves,
watching it fall and listening, breathing the charged air.

Inside the king's vast house a hundred servants padded
softly from room to room, busy at trivial chores,
scrubbing, polishing, repairing—the unimportant lives
reamed out of time by the names of kings.
Slaves, the children of far-famed palaces broken by war,
moved through the halls of Kreon's palace carrying flowers,
filling the smoke-black vases that darkened the royal chambers,
driving away the unpleasant scents of humanness—
sweat, the king's old age, the stink of beloved dogs,
stale wine, chamberpots, cooking. Eyes on the floor, young men
of fallen houses from Africa to Asia moved
silently opening doors to admit the lightning smell—then,
eyes on the floor, soundless as jungle birds, moved on.
The rumble of thunder, the dark murmur of rain, came in.
A young blond slave with eyes as gray as the North Sea
paused in the grillwork shadow of columns, his head lowered,
peering intently, furtively, out toward distant hills
where shafts of sunlight burst, serene, mysterious,
through deep blue glodes; the shafts lit up the far-off trees,
the rims of the hills, like silver threads in a tapestry.
He stood unmoving except for one hand reaching out,
as if for support, to a great white marble chair afire
with figures—goddesses, nymphs, dryads, unicorns,
heroes of ancient tales whose names were clouded in mists
long before the sculptor carved the stone. The figures
burgeoned from one another—arms, legs, wings, limp horns—
as if the stone were diseased, as if some evil force
inside it meant to consume the high-beamed room with shapes,
fat-bellied, simpering, mindless—shapes to satisfy
a civilization hip-deep in the flattery
of wealth and influence, power to the edges of the world. The slave
moved his hand, as if in pain, infinite disgust,
on fat breasts sweetly nippled, polished buttockses,

the dwarf-pear little penises of smiling boys.
The distant shafts of sunlight dimmed, died out; the hills
went dark. In the gray garden, rain drummed steadily
on the rude, unadorned coffin carved from gray-black rock
to house a dead king's bones, forgotten founder of a city,
ancient pessimist locked away safe in the earth's stiff heart.
No rune revealed the monarch's name;
no gravid wordshape hinted which god he trusted in.
　　The old slave dressed in black, Ipnolebes, dear to the king—
his eyes were mortal now—appeared at the columned door.
"Amekhenos," the old man called. The fair-haired slave
looked down, drew back his hand. Whatever smoldered in his mind
was cooled, for the time. He turned, waiting, to the old man.
"Take more wine to the king's guests, Amekhenos."
The young man bowed, withdrew. The old man watched him go,
then turned to his business, supervision of the kitchen slaves
at work on the evening meal. Wherever the old man walked,
slave girls scrubbed or swept more busily, their whispering ceased,
laments and curses—silenced not by fear, it seemed,
but as if all the household were quickened by something in the old man's face,
as if his character carried some wordless meaning in it.
To a boy he said, "Go help Amekhenos with the wine." Without
a word, quiet as an owl in the hall, the boy ran off.

　　Travellers were gathered in the dark-beamed central room of the palace,
men from farther away than the realm of Avalon,
men who brought gold from Mesopotamia, silks from Troy,
jewels from India, iron from the foot of the Caucasus.
They sat in their fine apparel, kings and the minions of kings,
drinking from golden bowls and exchanging noble tales
of storms, strange creatures, islands enveloped in eternal night;
they told of beasts half bird, half horse, of talking trees,
ships that could fly, and ladies whose arms turned men to fish.
They told of the spirits and men and gods in the war now raging
on the plains of Ilium. The kings and Corinthian nobles laughed,
admired the tales and treasures, awaiting their host's return.
The time for exchange was near. The strangers itched for canvas,
sea-salt spray in their beards, the song of the halcyon,
sweeter to sea-kings' ears than all but the shoals of home.
Kreon would hardly have slighted such men in the old days,

they said. They'd burned men's towns for less.
                                        The lords of Corinth
smiled. The king was old, and the wealthiest Akhaian alive.
It gave him a certain latitude, as one of the strangers
saw more clearly than the rest. He spoke to his neighbors—a fat man,
womanish-voiced, sow-slack monster of abdomens and chins—
a prominent lord out of Asia known as Koprophoros.
His slanted eyes were large and strangely luminous,
eyes like a Buddha's, an Egyptian king's.
His turban was gold, and a blood-red ruby was set on his forehead.
I heard from one who claimed to know, that if he stamped his foot
the ground would open like a magic door and carry him at once
to his palace of coal-black marble. He wore a scimitar
so sharp, men said, that if he laid the edge on a tabletop
of solid oak, the blade would part it by its own weight.
I laughed in my hand when I heard these things, yet this was sure:
he was vast—so fat he was frightening—and painted like a harlot,
and his eyes were chilling, like a ghost's.
                                        He said:
"Be patient, friends, with a good man's eccentricity.
We all, poor humble traders, have got our pressing affairs—
accounts to settle, business mounting while we sit here
cross-legged, stuffing our bellies like Egypt's pet baboons,
or fat old queens with no use left but ceremony.
And yet we remain." He smiled. "I ask myself, 'Why?' And with
a sly wink I respond: 'His majesty's daughter, you've noticed,
is of marrying age. He's not so addled in his wits, I hope,
as not to have seen it himself.' " The young man chuckled, squinted.
"I'll speak what I think. He's displayed her to us twice at meals,
leading her in on his arm with only a mump or two
by way of introduction. Her robe was bridal white
impleached with gold, and resting in her golden hair, a crown
of gold, garnets, and fine-wrought millefiori work.
Perhaps he deems it enough to merely—'venditate'—
not plink out his thought in words. These things
are delicate, friends. They require some measure of dignity!"
    They laughed. The creature expressed what had come into all their minds
at the first glimpse of Pyripta. What he hinted might be so:
some man whose treasures outweighed other men's, whose thought
sparkled more keen, or whose gentility stood out

white as the moon in a kingdom of feebly blinking stars,
might land him a lovelier fish than he'd come here baited for—
the throne of Corinth. Even to the poorest of the foreign kings,
even to the humblest second son of a Corinthian lord,
the wait seemed worth it. For what man knows what his fate may bring?
But the winner would not be Koprophoros, I could pretty well see,
whatever his cunning or wealth. Not a man in the hall could be sure
if the monster was female or male—smooth-faced as a mushroom, an alto;
by all indications (despite his pretense) transvestite, or gelded.
And yet he had come to contend for the princess' hand—came filled
with sinister confidence. I shuddered, looked down at my shoes, waiting.

And so the strangers continued to eat, drank Kreon's wine,
and talked, observing in the backs of their minds the muffled boom
of thunder, the whisper of rain. Below the city wall,
the thistle-whiskered guardians watching the sea-kings' ships
cursed the delay, huddled in tents of sail, and cursed
their fellow seamen, hours late in arriving to stand
their stint—slack whoresmen swilling down wine like the hopeful captains
packed into Kreon's hall. The sea-kings knew their grumbling—
talked of that nuisance from time to time, among themselves,
with grim smiles. They sent men down, from time to time,
to quiet the sailors' mutterings; but they kept their seats.
The stakes were high, though what game Kreon meant to play
was not yet clear.

The Northern slave, Amekhenos, moved
with the boy from table to table, pouring Cretan wine
to the riveted rims of the bowls, his eyes averted, masked
in submissiveness. The boy, head bent, returned the bowls
to the trestle-tables, where the strangers seized them with jewelled hands
and drank, never glancing at the slaves—no more aware of them
than they would have been of ghosts or the whispering gods.

The sun
fell fire-wheeled to the rim of the sea. King Kreon's herds,
dwindling day by day for the sea-kings' feasts, lay still
in the shade of elms. The storm had passed; in its green wake
songbirds warbled the sweetness of former times, the age
when gods and goddesses walked the world on feet so light
they snapped no flower stem. The air was ripe with the scent
of olives, apples heavy on the bough, and autumn honey.
Already the broadleafed oaks of every coppice and hurst

had turned, pyretic, sealing their poisons away for the time
of cold; soon the leaves would fall like abandoned wealth. Below,
the coriander on the cantles of walls and bandied posts
of hayricks flamed its retreat. The very air was medlar,
sweet with the juice of decay. The palace of Kreon, rising
tier on tier, as gleaming white as a giant's skull,
hove dreamlike into the clouds, the sea-blue eagles' roads,
like a god musing on the world. As far as the eye could see—
mountains, valleys, slanting shore, bright parapets—
the world belonged to Kreon.
                              The smells of cooking came,
meat-scented smoke, to the portico where Kreon stood,
his hand on his faithful servant's arm, his bald head tipped,
listening to sounds from the house. The meal was served. The guests
talked with their neighbors, voices merging as the sea's welmings
close to a gray unintelligible roar on barren shoals,
the clink of their spoons like the click of far-off rocks shifting.
   "Old friend," the king said thoughtfully, looking at the river with eyes
sharpened to the piercing edge of an evening songbird's note,
"all will be well, I think." He patted the slave's hard arm.
"We'll be all right. The fortunes of our troubled house are at last
on the upswing. Trust me! We've nothing more to do now but wait,
observe with an icy, calculating eye as tension
mounts—churns up like an oracle's voice. We'll see, my friend,
what abditories of weakness, secret guile they keep,
what signs of virtue hidden to the casual glance. Remember:
No prejudgments! Cold and objective as gods we'll watch,
so far as possible. The man we finally choose we'll choose
not from our own admiration, but of simple necessity.
Not the best there, necessarily—the mightiest fist,
the smoothest tongue. Our line's unlucky. The man we need
is the man who'll make it survive. Pray god we recognize him!"
He smiled, though his brow was troubled. It seemed more strain than he needed,
this last effort of his reign, choice of a successor. He stood
the weight of it only by will. He opened his hands like a merchant
robbed of all hope save one gray galleon, far out at sea,
listing a little, but ploughing precariously home. "What more
can a man do?" he said, and forced a chuckle. "Some
may well be surprised when we've come to the end of these wedding games.
We two know better than to lay our bets on wealth alone,

honor like poor Jokasta's, or obstinate holiness,
genius like that of King Oidipus—the godly brain
he squanders now on gulls and winds and crawling things.
Yet some man here in this house . . ." The king fell silent, brooding.
"And yet there's one man more I wish were here," he said.
He pulled at his nose and squeezed one eye tight shut. "A man
with contacts worth a fortune, a man who's talked or fought
his way past sirens, centaurs, ghosts, past angry seas . . .
a slippery devil, honest, not overly scrupulous,
flexible, supple, cautious without being cowardly,
a proven leader of men . . . 'the man who brought help,' as they call him,
for such is the meaning of his name." The slave at his elbow nodded,
smiling. His eyes were caves. King Kreon wrinkled his forehead
and picked at his silvery beard like a man aware, dimly,
of danger crouching at his back.

                                 Just then, from an upper room,
a girlish voice came down—Pyripta, daughter of the king,
singing, not guessing that anyone heard. Wan, giant Kreon
raised one finger to his lips, tipped up his head. His servant
leered, nodding, wringing his fingers as if the voice
were sunlight falling on his ears. She sang an ancient song,
the song Persephone sang before her ravishment.

> *Artemis, Artemis, hear my prayer,*
> *grant my spirit the path of the eagle;*
> *in high rocks where only the stars sing,*
> *there let me keep my residence.*

When the song ended, tears had gathered in the old king's eyes.
He said, "Ah, yes"—rubbing his cheeks with the back of his hand.
"Such beauty, the innocent voice of a child! Such radiance!
—Forgive me. Sentimental old fool." He tried to laugh, embarrassed.
The god feigned mournful sympathy,
touching an ash-gray cheek with fingers gnarled like roots.
Kreon patted his servant's arm, still rubbing his streaming
eyes and struggling for control. He smiled, a soft grimace.
"Such beauty! You'd think it would last forever, a thing like that!
She thinks it will, poor innocent! So do they all,
children blind to the ravaging forces so commonplace
to us. They live in a world of summer sunlight, showers,
squirrels at play on the lawn. They know of nothing worse,

and innocently they think the gods must cherish them
exactly as they do themselves. And so they should! you'd say.
But they don't. No no." He rolled up his eyes.
"We're dust, Ipnolebes. Withering leaves. It's not a thing
to break too soon to the young, but facts are facts. Depend
on nothing, ask for nothing; do your best with the time
you've got, whatever small gifts you've got, and leave the world
a better place than you found it. Pass to the next generation
a city fit for learning, loving, dying in.
It's the world that lasts—a glorious green mosaic built
of tiles that one by one must be replaced. It's that—
the world, their holy art—that the gods love. Not us.
We who are old, beyond the innocent pride of youth,
must bend to that, and gradually bend our offspring to it."
He sighed, head tipped. "She asks for freedom,
lordless, childless, playing out life like a fawn in the groves.
A dream, I'm sorry to say. This humble world below
demands the return of the seed. Such is our duty to it.
The oldest oak on the hillside, even the towering plane tree,
shatters, sooner or later, hammered by thunderbolts
or torn-up roots and all by a wind from Zeus. On the shore,
we see how the very rocks are honed away, in time.
Accept the inevitable, then. Accept your place in the march
of seasons, blood's successions. —In the end she'll find, I hope,
that marriage too, for all its pangs, has benefits."
    He smiled, turned sadly to his slave. "It's true, you know. The song
that moved us, there—bubbled up feelings we'd half forgotten—
I wouldn't trade it for a hundred years of childhood play.
The gods are kinder than we think!" The servant nodded, solemn.
    Kreon turned away, still sniffling, clearing his throat.
"Carry a message for me, good Ipnolebes.
Seek out Jason—somewhere off by himself, if that
proves feasible—and ask him, with all your skill and tact
—with no unwarranted flattery, you understand
(he's nobody's fool, that Jason)—ask, with my compliments,
that he dine in the palace tomorrow night. Mention our friends,
some few of whom he may know from the famous days when he sailed
the *Argo*. Tell him—" He paused, reflecting, his eyebrows raised.
"No, that's enough. —But this, yes!" His crafty grin
came back, a grin like a peddler's, harmless guile. "Tell him,

as if between you and himself—tell him I seem a trifle
'miffed' at his staying away, after all I've done for him.
Expand on that as you like—his house, et cetera."
The king laughed, delighted by his wit,
and added, "Remind him of his promise to tell more tales sometime.
Mention, between the two of you, that poor old Kreon's
hopelessly, sottishly caught when it comes to adventure stories—
usual lot of a fellow who's never been away, worn out
his whole long life on record keeping, or sitting in judgment,
struggling to unsnarl tortuous tangles of law with further
law." He chortled, seeing it all in his mind, and beamed,
clapping his plump dry hands and laughing in wheezes. It was
delicious to him that he, great Kreon, could be seen by men
as a fat old quop, poor drudge, queer childish lunatic.
The river shone like a brass mirror. The sky was bright.
"Go," said Kreon, and patted his slave's humped back. "Be persuasive!
Tomorrow night!"

        He turned, still laughing, lifting his foot
to move inside, when out of the corner of his eye the king
saw—sudden, terrible—a silent shadow, some creature in the grass,
glide down the lawn and vanish. He clutched at his chest in alarm
and reached for Ipnolebes. The stones were bare. "Dear gods,
dear precious holy gods!" he whispered. He frowned, blinked,
touched his chin with his fingertips. The evening was clear,
as green as a jewel, in the darkening sky above, no life.
"I must sacrifice," he whispered, "—pray and sacrifice."
He rubbed his hands. "All honor to the blessed gods," he said.
His red-webbed eyes rolled up. The sky was hollow, empty,
deep as the whole world's grave.

        King Kreon frowned, went in,
and stood for a long time lost in thought, blinking, watching
the frail shadows of trembling leaves. His fingertips shook.

2

In Corinth, on a winding hillside street, stood an old house,
its stone blackened by many rains, great hallways dark
with restive shadows of vines, alive though withered, waiting—
listening for wind, a sound from the bottom of the sea—climbing
crumbling walls, dropping their ancient, silent weight
from huge amphoras suspended by chains from the ceiling beams.
''The house of the witch,'' it was called by children of the neighborhood.
They came no nearer than the outer protective wall of darkening
brick. They played there, peeking in from the midnight shade
of olive trees that by half a century out-aged
the oldest crone in Corinth. They spied with rounded eyes
through the leaves, whispering, watching the windows for strange lights,
alarming themselves to sharp squeals by the flicker of a bat,
the moan of an owl, the dusty stare of a humpbacked toad
on the ground near where the vines began.
                                    He saw it, from his room
above, standing as he'd stood all day—or so I guessed
by the way he was leaning on the window frame, the deep-toned back
of his hand touching his jaw. What he thought, if anything,
was locked in his mirroring eyes. Great Jason, Aison's son,
who'd gone to the rim of the world and back on nerve and luck,
quick wits, a golden tongue—who'd once been crowned a king,
his mind as ready to rule great towns as once it had been
to rule the Argonauts: shrewd hero in a panther-skin,
a sleek cape midnight-black. ''The man who brought help.'' No wonder
some men have had the suspicion he brought it from the Underworld,
the winecup-crowded grave. His gray eyes stared out now
as once they'd stared at the gleaming mirror of the gods, the frameless

sea. He waited, still as a boulder in the silent house,
no riffle of wind in the sky above. He tapped the wall
with his fingertips; then stillness again.

Behind the house, in a garden hidden from strangers' eyes
by hemlocks wedged in thick as the boulders in a wall, a place
once formal, spare, now overrun—the vines of roses
twisting, reaching like lepers' hands or the dying limbs
of oaks—white lilies, lilacs tilting up faceless graves
like a dry cough from earth—his wife Medeia sat,
her two young sons on the flagstones near her feet. The span
the garden granted was filled like a bowl
with sunlight. Seated by the corner gate,
an old man watched, the household slave whose work was care
of the children. Birds flashed near, quick flame: red coral, amber,
cobalt, emerald green—bright arrows pursuing the restless
gnat, overweening fly. But no bird's wing, no blossom
shone like Medeia's hair. It fell to the glowing green
of the grass like a coppery waterfall, as light as air,
as charged with delicate hues as swirling fire. Her face
was soft, half sleeping, the jawline clean as an Indian's.
Her hands were small and white. The children talked. She smiled.

Jason—gazing from his room as a restless lion stares
from his rocky cave to the sand where his big-pawed cubs, at play,
snarl at the bones of a goat, and his calm-eyed mate observes,
still as the desert grass—lifted his eyes from the scene,
his chest still vaguely hungry, and searched the wide, dull sky.
It stared back, quiet as a beggar's eyes. "How casually
you sit this stillness out, time slowed to stone, Medeia!
It's a fine thing to be born a princess, raised up idle,
basking in the sunlight, warmed by the smile of commoners,
or warm without it! A statue, golden ornament
indifferent to the climb and fall of the sun and moon, the endless,
murderous draw of tides. And still the days drag on."
So he spoke, removed by cruel misfortunes from all who once
listened in a spell to his oratory, or observed with slightly narrowed eyes
the twists and turns of his ingenious wit.
No great wit now, I thought. But I hadn't yet seen how well
he still worked words when attending some purpose more worthy of his skill
than private, dreary complaint. I was struck by a curious thing:
The hero famous for his golden tongue had difficulty speaking—

some slight stiffness of throat, his tongue unsure. If once
his words came flowing like water down a weir, it was true no longer:
as Jason was imprisoned by fate in Corinth—useless, searching—
so Jason's words seemed prisoned in his chest, hammering to be free.
   A moment after he spoke, Medeia's voice came up
to the window, soft as a fern; and then the children's voices,
softer than hers, blending in the strains of an ancient canon
telling of blood-stained ikons, isles grown still. He listened.
The voices rising from the garden were light as spirit voices
freed from the crawl of change like summer in a painted tree.
When the three finished, they clapped as though the lyric were
some sweet thing safe as the garden, warm as leaves. Medeia
rose, took the children's hands, and saying a word too faint
to hear in the room above, moved down an alleyway
pressed close on either side by blue-green boughs. Jason
turned his back on the window. He suddenly laughed. His face
went grim. "You should see your Jason now, brave Argonauts!
Living like a king, and without the drag of a king's dull work.
Grapes, pomegranates piled up in every bowl like the gods'
own harvest! Ah, most happy Jason!" His eyes grew fierce.
In the street below, the three small boys who watched, in hiding,
hunched like cunning astrologers spying on the stars, exchanged
sharp glances, hearing that laugh, and a visitor standing at the gate,
Aigeus, father of Theseus—so I would later find out,
a man in Medeia's cure—looked down at the cobblestones,
changed his mind, departed. In the garden, Medeia looked back
at the house, or through it. It seemed her mind was far away.
"Mother?" the children called. She gave them a nod. "I'm coming."
They ran ahead once more. She followed with thoughtful eyes.
Her feet moved, hushed and white, past crumbling grave markers.
   A shadow darkened the sky, then passed. At Jason's gate
a mist shaped like a man took on solidity:
Ipnolebes, Kreon's slave. The three boys watching fled.
With a palsy-shaken hand, a crumpled lizard's claw,
he reached to the dangling rod, made the black bronze gate-ring clang.
A slave peeked out, then opened the gate, admitting him.
Jason met him at the door with a smile, an extended hand,
his eyes hooded, covering more than they told. The bent-
backed slave spoke a few hoarse words, leering, his square gray teeth
like a mule's. Lord Jason bowed, took the old man's arm, and led him

gently, slowly, to the upstairs room. The old man's sandals
hissed on the wooden steps.
 When he'd reached his seat at last,
Ipnolebes spoke: "Ah!—ah!—I thank you, Jason,
thank you! Forgive an old man's—" He paused to catch his breath.
"Forgive an old man's mysteries. It's all we have left
at my age—he he!" He grabbed awkwardly for Jason's hand
and patted it, fatherly, fingers like restless wood. The son
of Aison drew up a chair, sat down. At last, his voice
detached though friendly, Jason asked, "You have some message
from the king, Ipnolebes?" The old man bowed. "I do, I do."
His skull was a death's head. Jason waited. "It's been some time,"
Ipnolebes said, a sing-song—old age harkening back—
"It's been some time since you visited, up at the palace. Between
the two of us, old Kreon's a bit out of sorts about it.
He's done a good deal for you—if you can forgive an old fool's
mentioning it. A privilege of age, I hope. He he!
Old men are dolts, as they say. Poor innocent children again."
Jason pressed his fingertips to his eyelids, said nothing.
"Well, so," Ipnolebes said. It seemed that his mind had wandered,
slipped from its track not wearily but in sudden impatience.
He frowned, then brightened. "Yes, of course. Old Kreon's quite put out.
'Miffed,' you might say. He was a happy man when you came, Jason—
the greatest traveller in the world and the greatest talker, too.
You know how it is with a man like Kreon, whole life spent
on bookkeeping, so to speak—no more extended views
than windows give. It was a great stroke of luck, we thought,
when you arrived, driven from home on an angry wind
through no fault of your own." He nodded and clasped his hands.
His eyes moved, darting. The son of Aison studied him.
"That's Kreon's message?" Ipnolebes laughed. "No, no, not at all!
I spoke no thoughts but my own there. Ha ha! Mere chaff!"
The old man's voice took on a whine. "He asks you to supper.
I told him I'd bring the message myself. I'm a stubborn man,
when I like, I told him. A hard devil to refuse." Again
he laughed, a stirring of shadows. Ipnolebes leaned toward him.
"Pyripta, his daughter—I think you remember her, perhaps?—
she too is eager that you come. A lovely girl, you know.
She'll be marrying soon, no doubt. How the years do fly!" He grinned.
Jason watched him with still eyes. Ipnolebes wagged

his head. "He'll be a lucky man, the man that snags
Pyripta. Also a wealthy man—and powerful, of course."
Jason stood up, moved off. He leaned on the window frame.
"Between just the two of us," the old man said, "you could
do worse than pass a free hour or so with Pyripta. You never
know. The world—"
        Jason turned to him, frowning. "Old friend,
I have a wife." Ipnolebes bowed. "Yes, yes. So you do.
So you feel, anyway. Forgive a poor old bungling fool.
In the eyes of the law, of course . . . but perhaps our laws are wrong;
we never know." His glance fled left. " 'Our laws,' I say.
A slave. My care for Kreon carries me farther than my wits!
And yet it's a point, perhaps. Am I wrong? In the strictly legal
sense—" He paused. He tapped the ends of his fingers together
and squinted as if it were hard indeed to make his old mind
concentrate. Then after a moment: "In the strictly legal
sense, you have no wife—a Northern barbarian,
a lady whose barbarous mind has proved its way—forgive me—
more than just once, to your sorrow. The law no more allows
such marriages into barbarian races than it does between Greeks
and horses, say. If you hope to make your Medeia a home,
and leave something to your sons, it can hardly be as a line
of Greeks. If you hope to gain back a pittance of all she's wrecked—
it can never be, if I understand Greek law, as Medeia's
husband, father of her sons. —But I'm out of my depth, of course."
His laugh was a whimper. "I snatch what appearance of sense I can
for Kreon's good."
        Jason said nothing, staring out.
So he remained for a long time, saying nothing. The slave
chuckled. "It's a rare thing, such loyalty as yours, dear man.
She's beautiful, of course. Heaven knows! And yet a mind . . . a mind
like a wolf's. So it seems from the outside, anyway—seems to those
who hear the tales. A strange creature to have on the leash—
or be leashed to, whichever." His chuckle roused the dark
in the corners of the room again, a sound like spiders waking,
the stir of uncoiling sea-beasts dreaming from the deeps toward land.
"Well, no part of the message, of course. I shouldn't have spoken.
Marriage is holy, as they say. What a horror this world would become
if solemn vows were nothing—whether just or foolish vows!
Even if there are no gods, or the gods are mad—as they seem,

21

and as some of our learnèd philosophers claim—a vow's a vow,
even if we grant that it's grounded on no more than human agreement.
Indeed, what would happen to positive law itself without vows?—
even if vowing is a metaphysical absurdity
as it may well be, of course." The old man grinned, shook his head.
"—And yet for a man to be locked in a vow his whole life long—
a marriage vow illegal from the strictly human point of view,
sworn in the ignorant passion of youth, in defiance of reason,
and proved disastrous!—" Ipnolebes closed his heavy-knuckled
hands on the arm of the chair and, with a rasping sigh,
labored up unsteadily out of his seat. Slowly,
inches at a time, he eased his way to the stairs. "Well, so,"
he said. "I've delivered the message. Do come, tomorrow night,
if it seems to you you can do it without impiety.
Oh yes—one more thing." His head swung round. "There are friends of yours
at the palace, I think. Men from the weirdest corners of the world.
Merchants, sea-kings." The old man chuckled, dark as the well
the stairs went down. "All telling travellers' tales—he he!
Monstrous adventures to light up a princess' eyes and awe
a poor old landlubber king. It'll be like old times!"
He peered, smiling, at Jason's back. "You'll come, I hope?"
Jason turned from the window, eyes fixed on Ipnolebes' beard.
"I'll help you down. The stairs are steep." He came and touched
the slave's arm and carefully took his weight. "You'll come,"
Ipnolebes said, and smiled. Lord Jason nodded, the barest
flick. "Perhaps." His eyes did not follow the black-robed slave
to the gate. The street went dark for an instant; a whisper of wind.
    Medeia, standing in the garden with folded hands, looked up
and winced. "Take care, Hera," she whispered. She called the children,
pale eyes still on the sky. "I know your game, goddess."

    On a hill, late that night, in the windswept temple of Apollo
ringed by towering sentry stones, immemorial keys
of a vast and powerful astrolabe, stern heaven-watcher,
Jason stood, black-caped. On a gray stone bench nearby
a blind man sat, at times a reader of oracles
and soothsayer, at times a man of silence. Corinth
glittered below like a case of lighted jewels falling
tier by tier to the sea. The palace, high and wide,
like a jewelled crown at the center of the vast display, shone

like polished ivory. The harbor was light as dawn with sails,
the ships of the visiting sea-kings.
                                    "I know pretty well what he's up to,"
Jason said. "Better than he knows himself, perhaps."
The seer was silent, leaning on the staff of cornel wood
that served as his eyes. Whether or not he was listening,
no one could say. Visions had made his face unearthly,
stern cliffs, crags, the pigment blackened as if by fire,
the thick lips parched. He was one of those from the fallen city
of dark-skinned Thebes, old Kadmos' city: the seer Teiresias
who learned all the mystery of birth and death when he saw, with the eyes
of a visionary, the coupling of deadly snakes. Men said
he paid in sorrows. Heros Dionysos—majestic lord
of the dead, son of Hades, snatched at birth from his mother's pyre—
sent curses from under the ground to the man who had seen things forbidden:
changed Teiresias to a woman for a time, and for seven generations
refused him the soothing cup, sweet sleep of death. He was now
in his last age. Jason turned to him, not to see him
but to keep from looking at the palace. He began to pace, frowning,
bringing his words out with difficulty, by violence of will.
"I'd win his prize. Terrific match, he'd think. Bold Jason,
pilot of the mighty *Argo*, snatcher of the fleece, et cetera . . .
I could do it. Oh, I'm no Telamon, no Orpheus;
but I'd serve old Kreon better than he dreams. These are stupid times,
intermixed bombast and bullshit whipped to a fine fizz.
I may be a better man to ride them out than those
I thought my betters once, my glorious Argonauts.
I never lullabyed bawling seas with my harp, like soft-
eyed Orpheus, or tore down walls with my bare hands
like Herakles. But I've survived my glittering friends—survived
their finest. Favored by the gods, as they say. —Not that I asked
for that. I no more trust the generosity
of gods than I do that of men. I've seen how they twist and turn,
full of ambiguous promises, sly double dealings. They offer
power, then blast you with a lightning-bolt. Or if gods are honest,
as maybe they are, their honesty's filtered by priests and magicians
who may or may not be frauds. How can man trust anything, then,
beyond his own poor fallible reason? I keep an eye out,
keep my wits. If the gods are with me, good. If not,
I stumble on. I play the chancy world like a harp

tuned by a half-mad satyr on a foreign isle, finding
its secrets out by feel. If the music's fierce and strange—
kinsmen murdered, in my bed a woman from the barbarous rim
of the world—don't think I pause, draw back from the instrument
in horror, shame. I play on, not lifting an eyebrow,
fleeing from resolution to resolution.

                                      "So now
I might play Kreon's lust. —Mine too, Medeia would say.
I could smile, ignore her. I've bent too much to that hurricane.
Whose work but hers that I find myself where I am?—great hero,
homeless, hopeless, my towering city in chaos, her ancient
winding streets like interlocked serpents afire in their own
dark blood—and I can do nothing, exiled, ruined for Medeia—
ruined despite all my nobly intoned coronation vows.
Vows indeed! Ask Trojan Hektor his feeling on vows,
forced to defend an old lecher. Ask Hektor's brother. The gods
themselves pit vow against vow as men pit fighting cocks."

   He paused, rubbing his throat and jaw, relaxing muscles
that seemed to grow more constricted with every word.

                                              Then:
"I could still be king there, sharing the throne with a dodling uncle
I never hated, whatever he thought of me. But it wasn't
room enough for the daughter of mighty Aietes, Lord
of the Bulls, Keeper of the Golden Fleece. So here we are,
blood on the soles of our feet, heads filled with nightmare-visions,
guilt more chilling than the halls of the dead.
My friends on the *Argo* would laugh, in the winds of hell, if they heard it.

   "It might be comforting . . . Kreon's child. A gentler princess,
as slight, by Medeia, as these hills next to the Caucasus. . . ."

   He pursed his lips, jaw muscles drawn in the semi-dark
of temple columns, flickering torches; his eyes were suddenly
remote, as if even casual mention of those windy days
on strange seas, strange shores, could make them rise in his mind
more real than the quiet night he loomed in now. He closed
his eyes, breathed deep. The blind man bent his head, as if
to listen to Jason's mind sheared free of words. Jason
turned abruptly to look at the palace, then away again.
"At one quick stroke I could win not only the throne of Corinth—
huge old city with all its wide, deep-grounded walls—
but all my power back home. That's all they've asked of me:

Renounce the witch and her murder of Pelias; abandon Medeia,
and Argos is yours—now Corinth as well. Why not? No wife
at all, a prize of war that I treated too well, a bedslave
grown too mighty to be tamed like Theseus' Amazon.
Betrayal, perhaps; but the guilt would be trifling beside that guilt
that brings King Pelias' ghost back night after night to stalk
my rest—hooded like a cobra, silent, eyes as mad
as Argos left without a king. And if I do nothing, what then?
Get up, eat, take a walk, eat, stare out a window,
eat again. . . . Surely, whatever my promises,
no mere woman can hold me to that! 'Stay clear of the palace!'
A law. Who'd dare disobey the great, fierce daughter of Aietes?"
He paused, musing. "There are laws and laws. I told my tales
for Kreon, kind old benefactor. But I'd watch the girl
as I told of those terrible battles, curious islands, long nights
rolling in the arms of queens. She had a special blush
she saved for me. There were times when she touched my arm as if
by accident. I encouraged it—pressed it. I could no more pass up
a thing like that than I could pass up a cave, an unknown city,
in the old days. It meant nothing, God knows—except to Medeia.
One more conquest. —Winning means more than it should to me,
no doubt. The usual case of the overly reasonable man
who's turned his cheek too often. —And yet I resisted, in the end.
Heaven knows why." He studied the night. "I make up theories.
I tell myself I resist for Medeia's sake. 'Offend
the king and our last hope's gone, we're wandering exiles again.'
I piously mumble: 'Beware of wounding Medeia's pride.'
    "—All the same, whatever the reason,
I dodged the limetwig, slyly evaded his pretty Pyripta
before the old man was aware himself what he planned for me.
So Pelias comes, nights; stands in the shadows like a dead tree—
solemn old ramdike trailing vines, mere daddock at the core—
demanding something—the prince's head in his hands, Akastos
whom I loved once—loved as I loved myself, I'd have said.
Guilt-raised ghosts.
                "I know, I think, what they want of me.
Climb back. Redeem your home through Corinth's power. Atone.
My mind stretches toward it, trembling, and all at once
I'm afraid. Beyond old Pelias' ghost and that severed head
there's darkness, an abyss. —And yet what is it I fear, I wonder?

Is conquering Jason the slave at last?" He paused, lips pursed,
and glanced at the seer. "The night has a growl of winter in it.
Stars like the flicker of corpse-candles, a sparkle of frost
on the bronze lich-gate. Over soon. Grain of the valleys
winnowed, garnered . . . whatever claims we've made on the season
silenced, settling in the bin; on the snowed-in storehouse walls
no lamps but dreaming bats. And for those who've made no claims—"
Again he paused, reflecting, staring at the ground. At last:
"If I went my way I could make Medeia rich, respected;
if not a queen, then mother, at least, of kings—no cost
but a night, now and then, alone in her golden bed. That would not
wreck her, I think. In any case, let this chance slip,
let some old enemy of ours snatch Kreon's throne—and where are we
then? This too: If I try and lose, that's one thing.
But to let some fat fool win it by default—
                              "No, plainer than that.
She's an Easterner, and a woman. She reasons with her chest, the roots
of her hair. I should know too well by now where such reasoning leads
—her brother murdered, betrayed to confound Aietes' ships;
my uncle carved, strained, boiled by his daughters' love; and us
adrift, horrible to men. Late as it is, I should seize
my duty as husband and father—the hope that lies in Akhaian,
masculine brains, detached, remote from the violent instincts
of child-bearing and giving suck, what women share
with the lioness. I've left our destiny too long
in witchcraft's hands." He paused, glanced at the blind Theban.
"Say what you're thinking."
                    The blind man sat like stone, the light
of torches stirring on his cheek. His sunken eyes stared out
at darkness beyond the harbor. "Men come for my help in prayer,"
he said, "or for reading of oracles. What right have I
to advise?"
            "But say what you think."
                              The old black Theban sighed,
continued looking at the night. "The end is inevitable,"
he said. His eyebrows, silver and thick as frost on rock,
drew up, and he groped for Jason's hand. He found and held it.
"You want no advice from me, and even if you did, the end
is destined. I need no help of signs to see that much,
heavy as I am with experience. For seven generations

I've watched the world's grim processes. I saw the teeth
of the dragon Kadmos slew rise up as fierce armed men; I saw that perfect king and
        his queen transmogrified
when Lord Dionysos—power that turns spilt blood to wine,
unseen master of vineyards—awarded them mast'ry of the dead.
And I've seen things darker still, though the god has sealed my eyes.
All I have seen reveals the same: Useless to speak.
Well-meaning man—" He frowned, looking into darkness. "You may
see more than you wish of that golden fleece. Good night."
                                                      But Jason
stayed, questioning. "Say what you mean about the fleece. No riddles."
"Useless to say," the blind man sighed. He shook his head.
But Jason clung to his hand, still questioning. "Warn me plainly."
Again the blind man sighed. "If I were to warn you, Jason,
that what you've planned will hiss this land to darkness, devour
the sun and moon, hurl seas and winds off course, kill kings—
would you change your course, confine yourself to your room like a sick
old pirate robbed of his legs?" Jason was silent. The black seer
nodded, frowning, face turned earthward. "There will be sorrow.
I give you the word of a specialist in pains of the soul and heart,
as you will be, soon. Let proud men scoff—as you scoff now—
at the idea of the unalterable. There are, between
the world and the mind, conjunctions whose violent issue's more sure
than sun and rain. So every age of man begins:
an idea striking a recalcitrant world as steel strikes flint,
each an absolute, intransigent. The collision sparks
an uncontrollable, accelerating shock that must arc through life
from end to end until nothing is left but light, and silence,
loveless and calm as the eyes of the sphinx—pure knowledge, pure beast.
Good night, son of Aison." And so at last Lord Jason released
the black man's hand and, troubled, turned again to the city.

   The white stars hung in the branches above Medeia's room
like dewdrops trapped in a spiderweb. The garden, below,
was vague, obscured by mist, the leaves and flowers so heavy
it seemed that the night was drugged. Asleep, Medeia stirred,
restless in her bed, and whispered something, her mind alarmed
by dreams. She sucked in breath and turned
her face on the pillow. The stars shone full on it: a face so soft,
so gentle and innocent, I caught my breath. She opened her eyes

27

and stared straight at me, as though she had some faint sense of my presence.
Then she looked off, dismissing me, a harmless apparition
in spectacles, black hat, a queer black overcoat . . .
    She came to understand, slowly, that she lay alone,
and she frowned, thinking—whether of Jason or of her recent dream
I couldn't guess. She pushed back the cover gently and reached
with beautiful legs to the floor. As if walking in her sleep, she moved
to the window, drawing her robe around her, and leaned on the sill,
gazing, troubled, at the thickening sky. Her lips framed words.

>"Raven, raven, come to me:
>Raven, tell me what you see!"

There was a flutter in the darkness, and then, on the sill by her white hand,
stood a raven with eyes like a mad child's. He walked past her arm
to peek at me, head cocked, suspicious. And then he too
dismissed me. She touched his head with moon-white fingertips;
he opened his blue-black wings. They glinted like coal. "Raven,
speak," she whispered, touching him softly, brushing his crown
with her lips. He moved away three steps, glanced at the moon,
then at her. He walked on the sill, head tipped, his shining wings
opened a little, like a creature of two minds. Then,
in a madhouse voice, his eyes like silver pins, he said:

>"The old wheel wobbles, reels about;
>One lady's in, one lady's out."

He laughed and would say no more. Medeia's fists closed.
The raven's wings stretched wide in alarm, and he vanished in the night.
    On bare feet then, no candle or torch to light her way—
her eyes on fire, streaming, clutching old violence—
Medeia moved like a cold, slow draught from room to room,
fingertips brushing the damp stone walls, her white robe trailing,
light as the touch of a snowflake on dark-tiled floors. She came
to the room where her children slept, in one bed, side by side,
and there she paused. She knelt by the bed and looked at them,
and after a time she reached out gently to touch their cheeks,
first one, then the other, too lightly to change their sleep. Her hair
fell soft, glowing, as soft as the children's hair. Then—tears
on her cheeks, no sigh, no sound escaping her lips—she rose
and swiftly returned to her room. The two old slaves in the house—
the man and a woman—stirred restlessly.

.   .   .

　　　　　　　　　　　　　　　　There Jason found her,
lying silent and pale in the moonlight. He kissed her brow,
too lightly to change her sleep, then quietly undressed himself
and crawled into bed beside her. Half sleeping already, he moved
his dark hand over her waist—her arm moved slightly for him—
and gently cupped her breast. He slept. Medeia's eyes
were open, staring at the wall. They shone like ice, as bright
as raven's eyes. The garden, sheeted in fog, was still.
A cloudshape formed. It stretched dark wings and blanketed the moon.

3

I was alone, leaning on the tree, shivering. I listened to the wind.
Below the thick, gnarled roots of the oak there was no firm ground,
but a void, a bottomless abyss, and there were voices—sounds
like the voices of leaves, I thought, or the babble of children, or gods.
I made out a shadowy form. The phantom moved toward me,
floating in the dark like a ship. It reached to me, touched my hand,
and the tree became an enormous door whose upper reaches
plunged into space—the ring, the keyhole, the golden hinges
light-years off. Even as I watched the great door grew.
I trembled. The surface of the door was wrought from end to end
with dragon shapes, and all around the immense beasts
there were smaller dragons, and even the pores of the smaller dragons
were dragons, growing as I watched. Slowly, the door swung open.
I had come to the house of the gods.

   Above the cavern where the dark coiled Father of Centuries
lay bound, groaning, in chains forged by everlasting fire,
Zeus sat smiling, serene as the highest of mountaintops,
his eyes like an eagle's, aware of the four directions. Beside him—
stately, magnificent, dreadful to behold—Hera sat, draped
in snakes. Above her lovely head, like a parasol,
a cobra flared its hood. It stared with dusty eyes
through changing mists. I tightened my grip on my guide's hand.
"Goddess, porter, whatever you are," I whispered, "shield me!"
"Be still," she said. I obeyed, trembling, straightening my glasses,
buttoning up my coat.
                    The queen of goddesses
had beautiful eyes, as benign and warm as the eyes of the snake

were malevolent. Her face was radiant with life, seductive,
as sensuous as the brow of Zeus was intellectual.
The thrones were joined by an arm of gold, and on that arm
Zeus rested his own. The queen's arm lay on the king's,
and their fingers were interlaced. On Zeus's shoulder, a prodigious
birdlike creature perched, half-lion, half-eagle, watching
the snake. "What can all this mean?" I asked. My guide touched her lips.
Suddenly the hall was filled with a teeming sea of gods.
Some were like monsters, some had the shapes of trees or waterfalls;
some were like bulls, others like panthers, elephants, monkeys,
and some were like men—like kings, queens, beggars, saintly hermits.
One came in on a litter of finely wrought ebony set
with centaurs of ivory and silver—a beautiful goddess in a robe
of scarlet, open at the front to reveal great pendulous breasts.
The mortals, her slaves, wore flowers in their hair—the white hair tangled,
matted like the hair of mad women. They wept and moaned
as they walked, limping, half-naked, ragged. Their ankles clinked
and jangled with tarnished jewelry; the perfume they wore
yellowed the air like woodsmoke. Their chalkgray feet were crooked,
their eyes were dim, and beneath the stiffening paint, their faces
were cities destroyed by fire. But whether the bearers were women
or men, I could not guess. Quick fluttering sparrows flew
like swirling leaves in a graveyard, screeching. My shadowy guide
smiled and inclined her head.
                              "Not all gods here are wise,"
she said. "They have all their will, all that a creature can desire:
They feel no hunger, no thirst, no weariness, no fear of death,
no pain or sorrow or lonely old age. But the grinding force
of life still burns in them, endlessly restless, driving, devouring—
the force that blazes in the eyes of the half-starved lion or swells
the veins of the terrified deer. They can never be rid of it.
Some, desiring in a state where nothing is left to desire,
sink to the sickness of ennui and wallow in vast self-pity
like hogs in mire. Some puff up their power, and delight
in smashing the will of the weak. A few, like Zeus, grow wise.
But very few. Observe how the rest crawl through their days.
At times, to break the tedium, the gods feast.
At times, to break the tedium, the gods fast.
At times they quarrel like dogs. At times they smile and kiss.
At times they sue to the king with cantankerous demands. Watch."

32

The goddess in scarlet approached the throne of Zeus and, descending
from her litter, kneeled before him. "O mighty Lord," she said,
"hear the prayer of your sorrowful Aphrodite! Cruelly
the Queen of Olympos mocks me and makes me a laughingstock!
I'm ashamed to be seen among gods. They smirk and ogle, point at me,
whisper behind my back. I filled Medeia's heart
with love, stirred Jason to manly desire, arranged a pairing
fit to be remembered through endless time and to the farthest poles
of space. But Hera has overwhelmed me with her treachery,
cluttering his heart with desires more base, so that all I've done
is nothing, a cloud dispersed! O Great God, Lord of Thunder,
make him shake off this wickedness!" Her cheeks were bright
with anger, her dark eyes flashed; her flowing black hair gleamed
as if even that were in a rage. Yet out of respect for Hera,
or remembering that Hera was Zeus's wife, she controlled herself.
She stretched out her white left arm, her right hand daintily pressed
to her breast, just over the roseate nipple, as if to quell
the terrible quopping of her heart. "Have I ever denied her power—
her supreme rule over all things physical: ships, rivers,
forests, banquets, marriage beds? She fills the world
with beauty, goodness, the excitements of danger. At her command
Ares stirs up the terrors and joys of war. At a word
from her, the gods lure men to the highest pinnacles of feeling—
treasure-hunting, kingdom-snatching. By her pale light
alchemists pawn away all they own to untomb the gold
in lead, the wolf hunts the lamb, the shepherd attacks the wolf,
the adder joyfully strikes at the shepherd's heel. But Lord,
O holy father of gods and men, I've earned some place
in all that hungry rush! Imagine her kingdom with all
my power shut down—no joy in the world but the shoddy glint
of wealth, stern labor, knowledge-grubbing—no gentle eyes
to drip their sweetness on rich men's rings, no loving hands
to smooth the pain from the farmer's back when his long day ends,
no dazzled maiden to flood the alchemist's sulphurous rooms
with the light of her music, her rainsoft fingers on his arm! If my work
is meaningless, say so. I'll trouble your halls no more!" Bright tears
welled in her eyes and her bosom heaved. Her lips were taut.
The ghastly creatures attending her gave out goatish wails.
    Hera's face turned slowly to the king's. "Beautiful performance,"
she said, and smiled. The king said nothing. Dark Aphrodite

glared, her glance like a dart of fire, and the muscles of her face
trembled like the face of the plains when earthquakes crack their beams.
   A gentler goddess came forward then, a gray-eyed goddess
with a crown like a city on a shining silver hill. At her side
philosophers stood, their lean backs bent under thick, smudged scrolls,
their eyes rolled up out of sight; behind her, nervous kings,
each with his own set of tics (quick lip-jerks, twists, winks, nods,
features overcome from time to time by a sudden widening
of the eyes, like shocked recognition); then fat merchants, wiping
their foreheads, clucking, wincing with distaste, their tongues in motion
ceaseless as the sea, wetting their thick, chapped lips; behind
the merchants, poets and musicians, all looking wry at the smell
of the merchants, making ingenious jokes at the merchants' garish
or grandly funereal dress. —But when, from time to time,
a merchant, philosopher, or king keeled over, slain by the light
or brushed by a careless god, the poets and musicians would praise
the nature of man, abstracted to green, magnificent song,
their eyes like waterfalls.
                         The gray-eyed goddess kneeled
at Zeus's feet and, speaking softly, eyes cast down,
she said, "My Lord, Almighty Ruler of the Universe,
most just, most wise, I pray you, do not forget the needs
of Corinth, Queen of Cities. I have tended her lovingly,
cherished her, guided her gently through stunning catastrophes.
Throne after throne I have watched kicked down through the whimsical will
of malicious, barbarous gods—gods who amuse themselves
like boys pulling wings off butterflies. Yet I've kept her pillars,
shrine of the arts, seat of all taste and nobility.
Preserve my work! Give Jason the throne—for the city's sake.
Surely a city means more in your sight than one mere woman!
Pity Athena as she'd have you pity our beloved Aphrodite!
Grant my request, and grant Aphrodite some other gift
still dearer to her."
                    Hera smiled, but the gray-eyed Athena
maintained her mask of innocence. Those who attended her
bowed, heavy with solemnity, and tapped their scrolls,
their money-boxes, crowns, and harps. Aphrodite's cheek
burned dark red. Zeus said nothing.
                                   Her head bent
as if in supplication to the Father of the Gods, Aphrodite

rolled her eyes toward her sister. "Don't play games with me,"
she whispered, "immortal bitch! How wonderfully reasonable
you always make your desires sound! Do you think they're fooled,
these gods you play to? They know what you're after. Power, goddess!
You want your way no matter what—no matter who you walk on.
But you can't come right out and say it, can you. That wouldn't be civil,
and the lovely Athena is *nothing* if not civil!—Well, so are
sewers! indoor toilets!" She trembled with rage. Athena
smiled, as calm and serene as the moon above roiling, passionate
seas. Suddenly the goddess of love burst into tears,
wept like a shepherdess betrayed. The gray-eyed goddess of cities,
magnificent queen of mind, shot a quick glance at Zeus, then widened
her eyes as if in amazement. "Why Aphrodite!" she exclaimed,
"my poor, poor love!" She gathered her sister goddess gently
in her arms like a child, and Aphrodite cried on Athena's breast.
Hera smiled.
       But the brow of Zeus was troubled. He looked
from the love-goddess to Athena. "Enough!" he said. The hall
grew still. The stillness expanded. The eyes of the Father God
were like thunderheads. After some minutes had passed, he said,
"You're clever, Athena. You'd outfox a gryphon. Yet even so,
you may be wrong, and Aphrodite right. You talk
of cities, of how they're more important than a single life.
But the city in which that's true would be not worth living in.
I've known such cities. One by one I've ground them underfoot,
slaughtered their poets and priests and planted their vineyards to salt.
You pleaded against such a city yourself for Antigone, goddess!
Has it slipped your mind? 'Where the dead are left to the crows,' you said,
'where a life means nothing, let the whole white hovel be crows' fodder.'
Justice demands that I grant Aphrodite's wish." He was silent.
   Then Hera turned to him. Her eyes flamed. "And my wish, sir?"
she hissed. "I knew I was a fool to leave my business to Athena!
How can mere reason compete with *that?*" She pointed. Aphrodite
covered her bosom, blushing. "I agree,
it's wrong to make cities more important than the people who live in them.
Cities exist to make possible the splendid life—the life
of mind and sense in harmony, fulfilled to the utmost. Good!
But what of Jason's life? But that doesn't matter, of course. Not to you!
Not with *her* there, pleading with her big pink boobs! What counts with you,
O mixed-up Master Planner? You reason by whim, like the rest of us,

for all your pompous, grandiose pretensions. Fact!
You purse your lips, you muse in beatific silence, you nod,
and you do what you damn well please! Well not to me, husband!
I want what I want, and I'm not putting elegant names on it."
Hardly moving, Zeus glanced at her. The queen's lips closed.
    Then no one spoke for a long time. The attendant gods
shifted uncomfortably, sullen, from leg to leg. Yet more
than a few in that hall, I thought, would have backed her if they dared. Athena
gazed demurely at the floor, as if checking a smile. Zeus sat
with one hand over his eyes.
                         At length, as if contrite,
Athena said softly, "It's fair and just that you upbraid me, Lord.
But my heart spoke truer than my tongue. I gave you, foolishly,
the reasons I thought expedient. But it was not the survival
of the city—not that alone—that I meant to beg of you.
I plead for a good and patient man, a long-suffering man,
one who merits what I ask for him. Aphrodite's madness
has chained him too long. Without the assistance of any god,
he's seen through it. O kind, wise Lord, don't frustrate the climb
of a virtuous man on the rising scale of Good! I claim
no special virtues for cities, but this much, surely, is true:
Virtue tested on rocky islands, country fields,
however noble we call it, is virtue of a lesser kind—
the virtue that governs the hermit, the honest shepherd. The common
bee, droning from flower to flower in his garden, can choose
what's best for him and for his lowborn, pastoral clan. The common
horse can be diligent at work, if his hide depends on it.
The lion can settle his mind to fight, if necessary,
but his virtue, for all his slickness, the speed of his paws, is no more
than the snarling mongrel dog's. It's by what his mind can do
that a man must be tested: how subtly, wisely he manipulates
the world: objects, potentials, traditions of his race. In sunlit
fields a man may learn about gentleness, humility—
the glories of a sheep—or, again, learn craft and violence—
the glories of a wolf. But the mind of man needs more to work on
than stones, hedges, pastoral cloudscapes. Poets are made
not by beautiful shepherdesses and soft, white sheep:
they're made by the shock of dead poets' words, and the shock of complex
life: philosophers' ideas, strange faces, antic relics,
powerful men and women, mysterious cultures. Cities

are not mere mausoleums, sanctuaries for mind.
They're the raw grit that the finest minds are made of, the power
that pains man's soul into life, the creative word that overthrows
brute objectness and redeems it, teaches it to sing." The goddess
bowed, an ikon of humility, and turned to the queen,
stretching an arm in earnest supplication: "O Hera,
Queen of Heaven, center of the world's insatiable will,
support my plea! Speak gently, allure as only you
can allure great Zeus to the good he would wish, himself." She bowed,
and the dew on a fern at dawn could not rival the beauty of the dew
on Athena's delicate lashes. Aphrodite wept aloud,
shamelessly, melted by Athena's words. Even Hera was softened.
As the sea whispers in the quiet of the night when gentle waves
lap sandy shores, so the great hall whispered with the sniffling of immortal gods.
But Zeus sat still as a mountain, unimpressed, his hand covering
his eyes. The gods stood waiting.
                    At last, with a terrible sigh,
he lowered the hand. From the sadness in his eyes, the crushed-down shoulders,
you'd have thought he'd heard nothing the beautiful Athena said. He frowned,
then, darkly, spoke:
                    "All of you shall have your will," he said.
"Aphrodite, your cruel and selfish wish is that Jason and Medeia
be remembered forever as the truest, most pitiful of lovers, saints
of Aphrodite. It shall be so, in the end. As for you, Athena,
dearest of my children for the quickness of your mind—and most troublesome—
you ask that Jason be granted the throne of Corinth, glittering
jewel in your vain array. So he will, for a time, at least.
No king gets more. And as for you, my docile queen—
seductress, source of all earthly growth, terrible destroyer—
you ask that he have all his wish. That he shall, and more. It's done."

   With that word, casting away the darkness which he alone knew,
he called for Apollo and his harp. Apollo came, as brilliant
as the sun on the mirroring sea. He stroked his harp and sang.
The gods put their hands to their ears, listening. He seemed to ignore them.
He looked at Zeus alone, when he looked at anyone,
and Zeus gazed back at him, solemn as the night where mountains tower,
dark and majestic, casting their cold, indifferent shade
on trees and glens, old bridges, lonely peasant huts,
travellers hurrying home. It seemed to me they shared
some secret between them, as if they saw the whole world's grief

as plain as a single star in a winter's sky.

He sang
of the age when great Zeus first overcame the dragons. The halls
of the gods, he said, were cracked, divoted, blackened by fire.
All the gods of the heavens sang Zeus's praise, their voices
ringing like golden bells, extolling his victory.
Elated in his triumph and the knowledge of his power, Zeus summoned
the craftsman
of the gods, Hephaiastos, and commanded that he build a splendid palace
that would suit the unparallelled dignity of the gods' great king.
The miraculous craftsman succeeded in building, in a single year,
a dazzling residence, baffling with beautiful chambers, gardens,
lakes, great shining towers.

Apollo smiled and looked
at Zeus. He sang:

"But as the work progressed, the demands of Zeus
grew more exacting, his unfolding visions more vast. He required
additional terraces and pavilions, more ponds, more poplar groves,
new pleasure grounds. Whenever Zeus came to examine the work
he developed range on range of schemes, new marvels remaining
for Hephaiastos to contrive. At last the divine craftsman
was crushed to despair, and he resolved to seek help from above. He would turn
to the demiurgic Mind, great spirit beyond Olympos,
past all glory. So he went in secret and presented his case.
The majestic spirit comforted him. 'Go in peace,' he said,
'your burden will be relieved.'

"Then, while Hephaiastos
was scurrying down once more to the kingdom of Zeus, the spirit
went, himself, to a realm still higher, and he came before
the Unnamable, of whom he himself was but a humble agent.
In awesome silence the Unnamable spirit gave ear, and by
a mere nod of the head he let it be known that the wish
of Hephaiastos was granted.

"Early next morning, a boy
with the staff of a pilgrim appeared at the gate of Zeus and asked
admission to the king's great hall. Zeus came at once. It was
a point of pride with Zeus that he wasn't as yet too proud
to meet with the humblest of his visitors. The boy was slender,
ten years old, radiant with the luster of wisdom. The king
discovered him standing in a cluster of enraptured, staring children.

38

The boy greeted his host with a gentle glance of his dark
and brilliant eyes. Zeus bowed to the holy child—and,
mysteriously, the boy gave him his blessing. When Zeus
had led the boy inside and had offered him wine and honey,
the king of the gods said: 'Wonderful Boy, tell me the purpose
of your coming.'
                    "The beautiful child replied with a voice as deep
and soft as the slow thundering of far-off rainclouds. 'O Glorious
King, I have heard of the mighty palace you are building, and I've come
to refer to you my mind's questions. How many years
will it take to complete this rich and extensive residence?
What further feats of engineering will Hephaiastos
be asked to perform? O Highest of the Gods'—the boy's luminous
features moved with a gentle, scarcely perceptible smile—
'no god before you has ever succeeded in completing such a palace
as yours is to be.'
                    "Great Zeus, filled with the wine of triumph,
was entertained by this merest boy's pretensions to knowledge
of gods before himself. With a fatherly smile, he asked:
'Tell me, child, are they then so many—the Zeuses you've seen?'
The young guest calmly nodded. 'Oh yes, a great many have I seen.'
The voice was as warm and sweet as milk, but the words sent a chill
through Zeus's veins. 'O holy child,' the boy continued,
'I knew your father, and your father's father, Old Tortoise Man,
and your great-grandfather, called Beam of Light, and his father, called Thought,
and the father beyond—him too I know.
                    " 'O King of the Gods
I have known the dissolution of the universe. I have seen all perish
again and again! O, who will count the universes
passed away, or the creations risen afresh, again
and again, from the silent abyss? Who will number the passing ages
of the world, as they follow endlessly? And who will search
the wide infinities of space to number the universes
side by side—each one ruled by its Zeus and its ladder
of higher powers? Who will count the Zeuses in all of them,
side by side, who reign at once in the innumerable worlds,
or all those Zeuses who reigned before them, or even those
who succeed each other in a single line, ascending to kingship,
one by one, and, one by one, declining?
                    " 'O King,

39

the life and reign of a single Zeus is seventy-one aeons,
and when twenty-eight Zeuses have all expired, one day and night
have passed in the demiurgic Mind. And the span of the Mind in such days
and nights is one hundred and eight years. Mind follows Mind,
rising and sinking in endless procession. And the universes,
side by side, each with its demiurgic Mind and its Zeus,
who'll number those? Like delicate boats they float on the fathomless
waters that form the Unnamable. Out of every pore
of that body a universe bubbles and breaks.'

"A procession of ants
had made its appearance in the hall while the boy was saying this.
In a military column four yards wide the tribe paraded
slowly across the gleaming tiles. The mysterious boy
paused and stared, then suddenly laughed with an astonishing peal,
but immediately fell into thoughtful silence.

" 'Why do you laugh?'
stammered Zeus. 'Who are you, mysterious being in the deceiving guise
of a boy?' The proud god's throat and lips were dry, and his voice
kept breaking. 'Who are you, shrouded in deluding mists?'

" 'I laughed,'
said the boy, 'at the ants. Do not ask more. I laughed at an ancient
secret. It is one that destroys.' Zeus regarded him, unable to move.
At last, with a new and clearly visible humility,
the great god said, 'I would willingly suffer annihilation
for the secret, mysterious visitor.' The boy smiled
and nodded. 'If so, you have nothing to fear. It is merely this:
The gods on high, the trees and stones, are apparitions
in a fantasy. Without that dream in the Unnamable Mind
there is neither life nor death, neither good nor evil. The wise
are attached neither to good nor to evil. The wise are attached
to nothing.'

"The boy ended his appalling lesson and, quietly,
he gazed at his host. The king of the gods, for all his splendor,
had been reduced in his own regard to insignificance.

"Meanwhile another amazing apparition had entered the hall.
He appeared to be some hermit. He wore no clothes. His hair
was gray and matted except in one place at the back of his head,
where he had no hair at all, having lain on that one part
for a thousand years. His eyes glittered, cold as stone.

"Zeus, recovering from his first shock, offered the old man

wine and honey, but the hermit refused to eat. Zeus then asked,
falteringly, concerning the old man's health. The hermit
smiled. 'I'm well for a dying man,' he said, and nodded.
Zeus, disconcerted by the man's stern eyes, could say no more.
Immediately the boy took over the questioning, asking precisely
what Zeus would have asked if he could. 'Who are you, Holy Man?
What brings you here, and why have you lain in one place so long
that the hair has worn from your head? Be kind enough, Holy Man,
to answer these questions. I am anxious to understand.'

               ''Presently
the old saint spoke. 'Who am I? I am an old, old man.
What brings me here? I have come to see Zeus, for with each hair
I lose from my head, a new Zeus dies, and when the last hair falls
I too shall die. Those I have lost, I have lost by lying
motionless, waiting for peace. I am much too short of days
to have use for a wife and son, or a house. Each eyelid-flicker
of the Unnamable marks the decease of a demiurgic Mind. Therefore
I've devoted myself to forgetfulness. For every joy,
even the joy of gods, is as fragile as a dream—a distraction
from the Absolute, where all individual will is abandoned   ˙
and all is nothing and nothing is everything, and all paradox
melts. My friend, I was an ant in a thousand thousand lives,
and in a thousand thousand lives a Zeus, and in others a king,
a slave, a rat, a beautiful woman. I have wept and torn
my hair and longed for death at the graves of a billion billion
daughters and sons; a billion billion of those I loved
have died in wars, plagues, earthquakes, floods. And with every stroke
of catastrophe, my chest has screamed in pain. All these
are feeble metaphors—as I am metaphor, a passing dream,
and you, and all our talk. But this is true: Life seeks
to pierce the veil of the dream. I seek forgetfulness, silence.'
 ''Abruptly, the holy man ceased and immediately vanished, and the boy,
in the same flicker of an eyelid, vanished as well. And Zeus
was in his bed, with Hera in his arms. And he saw, despite his dream,
that she was beautiful. Then Zeus, King of the Gods, wept.
At dawn when he opened his eyes and remembered, Zeus smiled.
He commanded the craftsman to create a magnificent arbor for Hera,
and after that he demanded nothing more of him.''
So the harper of the gods sang, and so he closed.
With his last word, the hall of the gods went dark.

                                                    I was alone.
"Strange visions, goddess!" I whispered, "stranger and stranger!" She was gone.

    Then, like a sea-blurred echo of Apollo's harp, I heard
the music of Kreon's minstrel. Soon I saw Kreon's hall,
the sea-kings gathered in their glittering array, and Kreon himself
at the high table, his daughter beside him, blushing, shy—
like a spirit, I thought: more child than woman. Beside her, Jason
stood with his strong arms folded, muscular shoulders bare,
his cloak a luminous crimson, bound at the waist with a belt
gold-studded, blacker than onyx. Behind him, to his left, stood the shadow
of Hera; at his feet sat Aphrodite, and behind his right shoulder,
lovely as rooftops at dawn, the matchless, gray-eyed Athena.
    "Ipnolebes," Kreon whispered, "command that the meal be brought."
The old king chuckled, patted his hands together, winked.
Ipnolebes bowed and, moving off quickly, quietly, was gone.
The hall waited—dim, it seemed to me: discolored as if
by age or smoke. The sea-kings' treasures, piled high against
walls that seemed, when I first saw them, to be gleaming sheets
of chalcedony and mottled jade, with beams of ebony,
were dark, ambiguous hues, uncertain forms in the flicker
of torches. There were figures of goldlike substance—curious ikons
with staring eyes. There were baskets, carpets, bowls, weapons,
animals staring like owls from their lashed wooden cages. The hall
was heavy, oppressive with the wealth of Kreon's visitors.
The harpsong ended. In a shadowy corner of the great dim room
dancing girls—slaves with naked breasts—jangled their bracelets
and fled. A horn of bone sang out. A silence. Then . . .
as flash floods burst in their headlong rush down mountain flumes
when melting snowcaps join with the first warm summer rains,
sweeping off all that impedes them, swelling the gullies and creeks
to the brim and beyond, all swirling, glittering,—so down the aisles
of Kreon's hall, filling each gap between trestle-tables,
platters held high, hurtling along like boulders and driftwood,
silver and gold on the current's crest, came Kreon's slaves.
Their trays came loaded with stews and sauces, white with steamclouds,
some piled high with meats of all kinds; some trailed blue flame.
A great *Ah!* like the ocean drawn back from the pebbles of the shore
welled through the room. Jason, dark head lowered, smiled.
The huge Koprophoros snatched like a hungry bear at food.

                            42

"They mock me," he whimpered to the man beside him. "They'll change their tune!"
The torches flickered. Kreon patted his hands together.
When I closed my eyes the sound of their eating was the faraway roar
of dark waves grinding over boulders—ominous, mindless.

4

Sunset. She sat in the room that opened on the terrace and garden
watching the red go out of roses, the red-orange flame
drain gradually out of the sky. Leaves, branches of trees,
flowers that an hour before had been sharp with color, became
all one, dark figures etched into dusk. Shade by shade
they became one tone with the night. From Kreon's palace above,
its torchlit walls just visible here and there through gaps
in the heavy bulk of oaks, occasional sounds came down,
a burst of laughter, a snatch of song, the low boom
of table chatter, and now and then some nearer voice,
a guard, a servant at the gates—all far away, bell-like,
ringing off smooth stone walls and walkways, glancing off pools,
annulate tones moving out through the arch of distances.
At times, above more muted sounds, I could hear the drone
of the female slave, Agapetika, putting the children to bed,
and sometimes a muttered rebuke from the second of the slaves, the man.
    Medeia sat like marble, expressionless, white hands clamped
on the arms of her chair. It was as if she were holding the room together
by her own stillness, a delicate balance like that of the mind
of Zeus o'ervaulting the universe, enchaining dragons
by thought. So she sat for a long time.
Then, abruptly, she turned—a barely perceptible shift—
and looked at the door, listening. Two minutes passed.
The breathlike whisper of sandals came from the corridor.
After a time, the old woman's form emerged at the doorway,
stooped, as heavy as stone, her white flesh liver-spotted,
draped from head to foot in cinereal gray, her weight
buttressed by two thick canes. The slave looked in, dim-eyed.

"Thank you, Agapetika," Medeia said.
No answer. But slowly—so slowly I found it hard to be sure
from second to second whether or not she was still moving—
the old woman came forward. "Medeia, you're ill again!"
A moan like a dog's. Medeia got up suddenly, angrily,
and went out to stand on the terrace, her back
to the slave. Another long silence. The sounds coming down from the palace
were clearer here, like sounds through wintry fog: the clatter
of plates, laughter like a wave striking. She said, not turning,
"It's a strange sound, the laughter of a crowd when you've no idea
what they're laughing at." She turned, sighing. "I'm fiercely jealous,
as you see. How dare the man go up and have dinner with the king
and leave me wasting?"
                          The slave did not smile. "You should sleep, Medeia."
She shook her head, refusing her mistress further speech.
The lids of the old woman's eyes hung loose as a hound's. She said:
"When you came to Pelias' city bringing the fleece, your hand
on Jason's arm—the beautiful princess and handsome prince,
lady of sunlight, hero in a coal-dark panther skin—
that time too your eyes were ice. Oh, everyone saw it,
and a shiver went through us. —And yet you'd saved him, and he'd saved you,
and nobody there, no matter how old, could recall he'd seen
a handsomer couple." She closed her eyes and rocked, as slow
as a merchant ship sunk low in the water
when the wind first fills her sails. She said, "Your face was flushed,
and when Jason moved his hand on your arm, the air in the room
turned rich, overripe as apples fallen from the tree—despite
that glacial stillness of eyes. I was heavy with years, life-sickened
already by then. I saw I must end my days in the service
of a lord and lady whose love was a fadge of guilt and scorn,
a prospect evil enough. And little by little, as the tales
of the Argonauts came to our ears, we understood. Such a passion
as Queen Aphrodite had put on you two was never seen
on earth before; not even in Kadmos and Harmonia
was such fire seen. But passion or no, he hated you.
How could he not?—a princely Akhaian, and you'd saved his life
by the midnight murder of your own poor trusting brother! No matter
to Jason that that was your one slim chance. He'd sooner be dead
than safe and ashamed. Worse yet . . . Don't be surprised, lady,
that I dare to speak these things. I can see how it drains your cheeks,

the mention of your brother's murder. No better than you can I tell
which way your anger will strike, at yourself or me. You suck in
breath, and I'm shaken with fear—but my fear is more by far
for you than it is for myself. I've seen how you wince and cry out,
alone. It fills me with dread. You'll plunge into madness, Medeia,
hating what couldn't be helped, wrenching your heart out in secret,
proud—oh, prouder than any queen living—but even at the height
of that fierce Aiaian pride, uncertain,
doubting you merit the friendship of any but the Queen of Death.
You're poisoned, Medeia. Venomed as surely as the ivy burning
from within. I'd cure you if I could, if I knew how to force you to hear me.
Think, child of the sun! Think past the bouldered hour
that dams the flow of your mind. Lord Jason hated you.
Justly, you think? Unselfishly? Is Jason a god?
He'd agreed to your plan—agreed for *your* life's sake, not his.
To save your life, the woman who scattered his wits like a vision—
like the sizzling crepitation of a lightning-bolt—
he'd do what he'd never consider to save himself. No wonder
if after he'd saved what he worshipped, your Jason gnawed his fists
and hated all sight of what proved his weakness. —Jason who once
loved honor, trusted his courage. You taught him his price.''

                                      The slave
was silent awhile. Medeia waited—high cheeks bloodless.
The slave said softly, ''—But time soon changed
all that. Not any intentional act
of yours, Medeia, nor any act of his. Mere time.
We saw how he tensed when you screamed in the pain of your labor, bearing him
sons. Great tears rushed down his cheeks, and his shoulders shook.
In part of his mind—we saw it shaping—he must have seen
that the fault was his, not yours: you showed him what had to be,
and gave him a plan. He'd acted upon it as gladly, that night,
as he'd have changed places with you now. Or the fault was no one's—love
a turmoil prior to rules, and rumbling on beyond
the last idea's collapse. His eyes grew warmer then.
And yours as well. No house was ever more happy, for a time—
the twins babbling in their sunlit cribs, the master and mistress
warmer than sunbeams arm in arm, sitting at the window,
talking and laughing, or sitting in jewelled crowns, on thrones
level with Pelias and his queen's. If troublesome shadows of the past
returned, you could drive them back.

"But soon time changed that too."
Her wide mouth closed, trembling, and her faded slate eyes stared.
"Pelias was a fool; perhaps far worse. And now, at times,
when Pelias would hinder his will, Lord Jason would frown, speak sharply
to you, or to us, or the twins. Your eyes got the she-wolf look.
His slightest glance of annoyance, and up your poison seethed,
old bile of guilt, self-hate, pride, love—black nightmare shapes:
Aphrodite whispered and teased, cruel Hera, and Athena,
gray-eyed fox. *'Seize the throne for him!—Jason's by right!*
Would old Aietes hesitate even for an instant, dismayed
by a sickly usurper of a nephew's lawful place? Strike out!'
I needn't remind you of the rest. Screams in the palace, blood,
the cries of the children awakened in haste when you fled. And now,
for that, from time to time, his eyes go cold."

                                        The slave
came forward a little, tortuously moving her thick canes inch
by inch. "I've lived some while, Medeia. There are things I know.
Give the man time, and he'll come to see, now too, that the fault
was as much his own as yours. Let him be. Be patient, my lady.
No woman yet has defeated a stubborn, ambitious man
by force."

            Medeia turned, smiling. But her eyes were wild.
"I won't win his heart with labor pains again," she said,
"barren as a rock, wrecked as the cities he burns in his wake
with the same Akhaian lust."

                            "Medeia," the old woman moaned,
"leave it to the gods! Let time sift it! Tell me, what wife
in all the ages of the world has seized by her own hand's power
more than the staddle of a grave? Not even the mightiest king
wins more in the end. Consider the tumbled columns of the bed
of the giant Og. His fame is now mere sand, a ring
of stones that startles the wilderness like a ghostly whisper
of jackals crying in the night. My exiled people have
a prophecy for those who trust in themselves. They say:

> *Their horses are swifter than leopards,*
> *fiercer than wolves in the dark;*
> *their horsemen plunge on, advancing from afar,*
> *swooping like an eagle to stoop on its prey.*

They come for plunder, mile on mile of them,
their faces searching like an east wind;
they scoop up prisoners like sand.

They scoff at kings,
they laugh at princes.
They make light of the mightiest fortresses:
they heap up ramps of earth and take them.

Then the wind changes and is gone.
Woe to the man who worships his arm's omnipotence!

I would not wave it away as the noise of a beaten people
shorn of all tools of war but the rattle of poetry.
They were mighty themselves when they sang it first, though humbled now.
Learn to accept! What sorrow have you more great than the fall
of a thousand thousand cities since time began? You have sons.
How can you speak of a ruined womb, Akhaian lust,
when civilizations—races of men with the hopes of gods—
are tumbled to fine-grained ashes, fallen out of history?''
    "Enough!" Medeia said. She turned, in her eyes a flicker
like cauldron light. "Self-pity, you say. So it is. I'll end it,
tear all trace from my heart and stare, dead on, at night
as the tigress slaughters her young, then waits for the hunter's attack.
We're all poor fools, poor witless benoms to startle a crow
in the cast-off grandeur of scullery-slaves. I grant the wisdom
of your gloomy people's prophecy. I howl for justice.
Insane! Where's justice, or beauty, or love? Where grounds for the pride
you charge me with? Childish illusions—not even lies
our parents told, but lies we fashioned ourselves in the playroom,
prettily singing to dolls, dead children of sawed-down trees.
How dare I hoot for love, claim honor owed to me?
Who in the sky ever promised me love or honor? O, the plan
is plain as day, if anyone cares to read. In the shade
of the sweetly laden tree, the fat-sacked snake. Good, evil
lock in the essence of things. The Egyptians know—with their great god
Re, by day the creative sun, by night the serpent,
mindless swallower of frogs, palaces. Let me be one
with the universe, then: blind creation and blind destruction,
indifferent to birth and death as drifting sand. Great gods,
save me from the childish virgin's fantasy, purity of heart,

gentleness, courage in a merely created man! We fall
in love with the image of a mythic, theandric father, domineering
oakfirm tower of strength, and we find, as our mothers found,
the tower is home to a mouse peeking groundward with terrified eyes.
We teach them to act, or act for them. We teach their audaculous hands
the delicate tricks of love-making, teach their abstract
heads the truth about power. They pay us by sliding their hands
up slavegirls' thighs, or turning the tricks of supremacy
on us. And then, when we're ready to shriek and claw, strike back
with the moon-cold anger of the huntress-goddess, absolute
idea of ice, cold flame of Artemis, they come to us
like hurt children, showing the wounds from some other woman
or clever woman's man, and we're won again, seduced
by the only power on earth more cruel, more viciously pure
of heart than woman, ancient ambiguous garden—old monster
Motherhood."
   "Medeia, stop!" The dim eyes widened
and the mouth gaped for air. "Medeia, *child!*" she whispered.
Abruptly, shaken by the word, Medeia was silent. She raised
her hands to her face, then suddenly crossed to the slave and embraced her.
I understood, squinting at the two, that the word had changed her.
I gradually made out why. She'd all at once remembered
what it was to be a child: the inexplicable safety,
the sense of sure salvation adults forget. A fact of reality,
like a house, three sheep in a pasture. In the face of what she knew
she had no choice but acceptance, weeping like a child again.
For all her knowledge of mingled evil and good in the world,
it seemed to her (mysterious, baffling) that she held in her arms
the perishable husk of a truth still pure and imperishable,
eternal as Dionysos drinking and singing in the grave.
"Now, now," the old woman whimpered, weeping. "Now, now, my lady,
no need for sorrow. All will be well. Have faith!"
           "I know,"
Medeia said, and struggled to believe it for a moment longer.
She drew away, forced a smile, and—seeing that the slave
trembled with weakness—led Agapetika to a cushioned bench
with a view of the darkened garden, and helped her down on it.
She frowned, studying the old woman, alarmed by her gasps,
the trembling of the dry, gray hands. "All you say is true," she said.
"I have a kind of proof, in fact—" She paused; then, softly:

"I'll show it to you." Swift, majestic, Medeia was gone
from the room. In a moment she was back, carrying an object wrapped
in skins. She laid it on the carved bench by the window, moved
the tall lamps close to Agapetika's chair, and, taking the package
in her hands again, she carefully unwrapped it. A gleam of gold,
and Agapetika gasped anew. And then it was undone,
with one quick toss unfurled like a dazzling, sunlit flag.
" 'For you,' he told me," Medeia said, " 'because it was won
by both of us. No other woman and no other man
could have done it—though only Argus, child of Athena, could weave
the fleece we two brought home. Make a gown of the cloth, my queen.
A symbol, fit for a goddess, of Jason's love.' —Jason
of the golden tongue, they call him." She brooded. "And yet I was moved."
      We looked—the old woman, Medeia, and I—at the cloth woven
from the golden fleece. It was smooth as silk to the touch, and yet
crowded with figures—peacocks, parrots, turrets and towers,
farmers ploughing their sloping fields under city walls,
and, nearby, soldiers, ladies and lords on splendid barges,
all interlocked with loveknots and (curious lace) sharp bones.
The scenes kept changing, like tricks of light, and our three heads
bent close, almost touching. We looked so hard that our eyes crimped
like the eyes of a man who's stared for a minute at the sun. Old roads
drew us mysteriously inward, plunging into forests so thick
no thread of light broke through where the groaning limbs interlocked.
We came to a clearing, a wide black river tumbling, roaring
at our feet, and across it waterfalls crashed out of terrible heights,
gray cliffs that went up like a falling man's grasp, through brooding clouds;
and the falls, striking, sent out such shocks that the ground where we stood
shivered like the outstretched wing of a soaring hawk. The path
led on—wound inward to a cave like the nose in an ancient skull,
on the far side of the torrent. But the bridge was gone. We were stopped.
Strain as I might, my eyes could pierce no further through
the deceiving mists of the cloth.
                        Then, stranger still, I thought,
I heard faint whispers stirring, rising from the tapestry:
the threads of the cloth, it seemed to me, were singing. They sang:

Argus wove me, craftily wrought my warp and woof
with magic more than Medeia makes, and misery more,
and mystery more. And more than he meant I melt in me

and wider than Argus' wisdom wrought I work my wyrds,
my secret words. For wealth and weal he wove in the warp
(ingenious antic engineer by his ancient art!)
but bonefire, bane, and burning blood he buried in the woof,
buried in the woof as the bobbin drove; for his dark brains burned,
and little his lore of the lower lusts that lurk in love,
lurked in his love for the lady and lord he labored for.
(Woe lay within him when Argus wrought my warp and woof,
the warp and woof of my web so wisely, wickedly wrought.)
Argus wove me, weary old Argus, weary old Argus who wished them well.

I stared at Medeia. She'd heard some other song, perhaps.
Or each of us heard what he knew. For the fat old woman wept
and covered her face with her gray hands, shaking in sorrow.
The room went dark. I reached out suddenly to touch the two women,
hold them a moment longer and warn Medeia. I'd watched
too long as the timid outsider, even as I did in my own life,
thirty centuries hence. "Medeia!" I called. No answer.
Only the moan of the universe turning on its weary wheels.
My hands closed on nothing. She was a dream. "Medeia,"
I whispered. Useless. The long sigh of the galaxies
slowly exhaling, dimming, drifting through darkness. Dreams.

5

The great hall gleamed. Koprophoros spoke, the dark-eyed king
with the womanish voice, great rolls of abdomens and chins.
The ruby glowed on his forehead like blood on fire, and the gold
of his turban, his robes, his scimitar, was bright as the sun.
The meal had been carried away long since, the jugglers returned
to their rooms to count their coins. The slaves moved silently
from table to table, pouring wine. Old Kreon sat
with his chin resting in his hands, observing carefully.
His beloved slave, Ipnolebes, standing beside him, watched
with eyes like dagger holes, his arms folded. He seemed
carved out of weathered rock. Jason gazed at the table—
forehead resting on his hand, his wide shoulders low—
listening thoughtfully, biding his time. Could it be because
I knew the story—children murdered, Corinth in flames—
that the game seemed to me suddenly ominous, a conflict of demons?
Whatever the reason, I felt cold wind run down my spine.
The fat man, harmless as he seemed, comically clowning, filled me
with superstitious alarm.
                            "My noble lords," Koprophoros
began, bowing profoundly, "alas, you see before you
a fool. How dare I deny it?" He clenched his fists, mock tragic,
and let out a terrible noise, an enormous sigh. He winked—
winked as if someone had pulled some secret string in his back.
"I do my best," he said, and gave us a sheepish smile,
"but you see how it is. The gods have, in their infinite wisdom,
dealt me a belly like a whale's, fat breasts like a woman's, a face
androgynous to say the least. I manage as I can!" He chuckled.
He began to pace back and forth, above the seated crowd,

shaking his head and wincing, making morose faces.
Mechanically each footstep picked up his tonnage from the last.
He stretched his arms in Pyripta's direction and shivered with woe.
"I labor for dignity. Alas! Sorrow! I seem, at best,
some poor old goof who's arrived at the wrong man's funeral
and hasn't the courage to sneak to the house next door! —Ah, well,
the gods know what they're doing, I always say." He rolled
his eyes up almost out of sight, then leered, mischievous, goatlike,
goatlike even to the horns, the folds of his turban. He looked
like the whalish medieval demon-figure Beëlzebub,
in brazen armor, sneeping out jokes at God. "It has
advantages, my ludicrous condition. Who'd believe
a lump like me could argue religion with priests, split hairs
on metaphysics with men who make it their specialty—
men of books, I mean, who make scratches on leaves or hides
and read them later with knowing looks, appropriate belches,
foreheads wrinkled like newploughed fields? I do, however—
to everyone's astonishment. 'We in fact may have
misjudged this creature,' they say, and look very solemn, and listen
with ears well-cocked henceforth—and they get their money's worth!
I have theories to baffle the wisest sages!" He leered, looked sheepish,
snatched up a winebowl, drank. "I've a theory that Time's reversed,"
he said then, rolling his coy, dark eyes at Pyripta. She blushed.
"A stunning opinion, you'll admit, though somewhat absurd, of course."
He shrugged, slid his glance to the king. When he winked, old Kreon smiled.
"Then again, I know all the ancient tales of the scribes, and can tell them
hour on hour for a year without ever repeating myself,
tale unfolding from tale like petals from a rosebud, linked
so slyly that no man alive can seize the floor from me,
caught in my web of adventures (ladies, ensorcelled princes,
demons whose doors are the roots of trees) . . . A womanish skill,
you'll say—and I grant it: a skill more fit for a harem eunuch;
nevertheless, a skill I happen to possess—such is
my foolishness, or the restlessness of my clowning mind.
    " 'How,' you must surely be asking, 'can this rank lunatic
have power befitting a god's—the rule of a kingdom as wide
as Indus was, in the old days?' " He sighed and shook his head,
deeply apologetic. "I must tell you the bitter truth.
All my art, my theology, my metaphysics
have earned me nothing! I could weep! I could tear out my hair!" He became

54

the soul of woe. "I reason, I cajole, I confound the wisest
with holy conundrums like these: 'If Zeus is absolute order,
or pure intellect, and the Lord of Death is essential confusion
(that is to say, Chaos), what, if anything, connects the two,
and how can each know the other exists? If Zeus can muse
on all that exists, does Zeus exist?' —But at last my enemies
are convinced (ah, woe!) by mere trivia." Suddenly
he bent, grinning, and with only his teeth, raised up an oak chair
large as a throne—it was carved from end to end with figures—
and, fat neck swelling, he lifted it over his head. With fists
like steel, he cracked and snapped off, one by one, its thick
clawed feet. He laid them on the table like spoons. Then, taking the seat
of stone in his hands, he snapped it like kindling. He spat out the rest
—the back and the cumbersome arms—and then, most amazing of all,
he sucked in breath, belched fire from his mouth like a gasoline torch,
snatching the legs up and lighting them one by one, then hurling them
high in the air, a four-spoked wheel of flame. It turned
faster and faster. Mouths gaping, we saw that he no longer touched them—
the fire-wheel spinning on its own, high over the trestle-tables.
Even the three goddesses, I thought, were baffled by the trick.
Quick as the blink of an eye, the fire-wheel vanished. There was
no sound in the darkened hall.
                         Then all the sea-kings roared,
applauding, beating the flagstone floor with their staffs and shouting,
some crying out for another such trick, while some demanded
that he do that same one again, so that people could watch it more closely;
nothing's more pleasant than discovering the secret rules of things.
How strangely he smiled!—but immediately covered his mouth with his hand.
Then, grinning mournfully, lifting his eyes like a man much grieved
but eternally patient, Koprophoros said, "No more tricks yet.
Dramatic illustration, merely, dear friends. For such is the tiresome
base of my power and wealth. I grant, it's more interesting
to men like ourselves, that Time is reversed." He smiled, his dark
and luminous eyes full of scorn for us all. "But the world is the world."
He sighed profoundly, fat head tipped like a praying priest's,
his fat little hands with their hairless fingers pressed together
at his chest. "I thank the gods," he said, "for my marvelous gifts—
my innate sense of justice, my vast learning, my qualities of soul.
But those, alas, are at last mere private benefits.
The one firm way a man can be sure of his time for thought

is his talent for breaking skulls—the art of punching people,
or getting one's army to. Here below, I'm grieved to say,
the power for good and the power for evil are identical.
The idea of the moral erodes all ethics. Here (though of course
we hope it's otherwise elsewhere) gentle old Zeus is the boss
of the Hades and Hekate gang." Now the mournful smile was back.
"I am, let me hasten to add, a profoundly peaceable man.
Inside this enormous hulk blooms the heart of a lilac!—However,
tyrants don't listen to, so to speak, rime or reason. What is it
to tyrants that *hope* and *soap* are mysteriously linked? One gets
one's throne the other way. Well-a-day! Alack!" He smiled,
suddenly innocent as a girl except for those goathorn folds,
and he bowed. The tables clapped. The king was delighted, it was clear,
and so was Pyripta, smiling down at the tablecloth.
I felt a minute, brief twinge of alarm about *hope* and *soap*.
    He was nobody's fool, Koprophoros. He left no doubt
that he knew how to handle a man as he'd handled the chair, though he took
no special pleasure in violence—unless as art.
He bowed and bowed, as neatly balanced as a dancer, kissing
his fingertips, face sweating.
                            Then tall Paidoboron
stood up, the king of a silent land to the north, where the gray
Atlantic half the year lay still as slate, and icebergs
pressed imperceptibly, mournfully, groaning like weird old beasts
on the dark roads of whales. It was a country known
to Greeks as the Kingdom of Stone. Strange tales were told of it:
a barren waste where no house boasted ornaments
of gold or silver, and no one knew till Jason came
of stains or dyes or of any color but the dim hues
on the skins of animals there, or the grays and browns in rocks.
The towns of that kingdom were few and far between, as rare
as trees on those dim gray hills, and in the largest towns
the houses kept, men said, no more than a hundred souls—
bleak men bearded to the waist and dressed in wolfskins; women
tall and stern and beautyless, like stiff, bare pines.
The houses and barns, the streets, the walls along country roads
were stone, as gloomy as the sea. They knew no culture there
but raising sheeplike creatures—winged like eagles, but shy,
as quick on their feet and as easily frightened as newts. Yet they knew
the second world to the west, for the Hyperboreans owned

great-bellied, stone-filled ships that could sail forever, slow,
indestructible as the stone rings high in their hills. And they knew
more surely than all other men, of the turning of planets and stars:
geometers, learned astronomers, they spent their lives
shifting and rearing enormous megaliths, age after age,
the oldest kingdom in the world. They knew the alchochoden
of every man and tree, knew the earthly afterclap
of all conjunctions, when to expect the irrumpent flash
of crazily wandering comets, could tell the agonals
of stars no longer lit, old planets shogged off course
by accidents aeons old. They came themselves, they claimed,
from the deeps of space, noctivagant beings shackled to earth,
dark shadow of oaks and stones, for some guilt long forgotten.
They waited and watched the heavens as a prisoner stares at fields
beyond his cell's square bars. They studied the wobbling night,
and if some faraway star went wrong they sacrificed
an eldest son to it, and made it right.
                              The king
spoke softly, as if some god were speaking out of him—
a man no more made of flesh and blood than Koprophoros, I'd swear:
stiff as a puppet, a figure in some old electrical game
at the penny arcade, mindlessly obstructing—such was the impression
the black king gave with his ponderous, vaguely funereal manner;
and yet there was anger in his manner too, such old-man fury
at all Koprophoros spoke, I could hardly believe it was not
some hellish joke between them. Solemn as death, he said:
"You advertise your talents, my bloated friend, as if
you intended to put them on sale. No doubt you'd soon find a buyer!"
He smiled, full of scorn for the listening crowd. "How nice to think
a man can outfox the fates by his clever wits, outbox
the wind, outgrapple the fissures that open when earthquakes strike!
Mere childish dreams. Forgive me for saying so. We've stood—
my kingdom—a thousand years. We dreamed like you, at first,
a thousand thousand years ago. But stone cliffs
collapsed on us, seas overran us, monsters crawled
from the deep and claimed our herds. And winds—such violent winds
as you've never seen thus far in these playful hills—so dark
they blanked out sun and moon for seven full years, so thick
they snatched away all our breath like tons of earth falling—
cliffs and seas, monsters from the deep, and those terrible winds

taught us our power was not what we first supposed. A man
can kill a man, if he will, or some beast less than a man,
some beast that shares, in its own way, our humanness—
hunger, the rage to rule, our pleasure in thought. (I have seen
elderly wolves sit thinking, smiling to themselves.) But a man
can tyrannize nothing beyond himself, his own frail kind.
If you've smiled at bears who pompously, foolishly lord it over
lesser bears but shake like mice at the tucket and boom
of heaven, then smile at Koprophoros! How many storms
have you tilted up like a chair and deprived of its legs?" He laughed,
the cackle of an old, old man. The black of his hair was dye,
I understood only now. His face was wrinkled like a mummy's.
Surely, I thought, the man's long years past fathering a child!—
yet here he stands, contending for a wife! (No one in the hall,
or no one besides myself, it seemed, was amazed.) He said:
"I shiver and shake at your leastmost leer, O dangerous friend,
but the hills are cool to both of us, and the thunder laughs.
You hold your throne by discreet and tasteful violence.
As for me, I hold mine—apart. I sit in dreary silence
no man envies, no man steals. What little I need
to eat I plant myself and harvest alone. For talk,
for the stimulation of other men's minds, I have old hymns
and a thousand years of figures carved in stone. I go on,
and my race goes on, the prey of no one but the gods. To a man
new to his glories, blind to the ghostly stelliscript,
knowing not whence he comes or whither he goes—immortal
as the asphodel, he thinks—that may seem a trifling thing,
a man full of hope, unaware of the gods' deep scorn of man,
a founder like you, Koprophoros." He moved his gaze
from table to table slowly. It came to rest at last
on Kreon. The old man sat leaning forward, watching intently,
waiting as if in alarm. Paidoboron smoothed his beard,
as black and thick as the fur of a bear in winter. He said:
"If I were, for instance, the last king in a doomed line,
I'd run to the rim of the world, taking any child I had,
and I'd house myself in stone, and I would propitiate
the gods, my surest foe, with prayers and deodands."
His words died away to silence in the rafters of the hall. The stillness
clung like a mist, as though the black-bearded Northerner
had silenced the crowd by a spell.

Then fat Koprophoros spoke,
rising from his seat, bowing, all grace, to the princess and king.
The deep-red jewel on his forehead gleamed like fire through wine.
Symbols of the soul, those jewels, I remembered. But the blood-red light
trapped inside fell away and away into nothingness
like magnitude endlessly eating its shadow, consuming all space.
"He speaks with feeling," Koprophoros said, then suddenly cackled.
"A man without interest in the throne of busy Corinth and all
her wealth! Pray god we may all be as wise when we're all as poor
as Paidoboron!" He beamed, unable to hide his pleasure
in his own sly play. The princess laughed too, the innocent peal
of a child, and then all the great hall laughed till it seemed that the very
walls would tumble from weakness. Paidoboron, grave, said nothing.
His eyes were fierce. Yet his fury, it seemed to me again, rang false.
I glanced at the goddesses, reclining at ease near Jason, on the dais.
If the two kings were engaged in some treachery, the goddesses too
were fooled by it.
            The chief of the Argonauts watched the Northerner
as though he had scarcely noticed Koprophoros' trick. He said
when the laughter in the hall died down, "Tell me, Paidoboron,
why have you come? I knew you long ago, and I know
your gloomy land. Koprophoros has his joke, but perhaps
his nimble wits have betrayed him, this once. What wealth can a man
bring down from a land like yours? And what can Corinth offer
that you'd take even as a gift? I know you better, I think,
than Koprophoros does. There's no duplicity in you, no greed
for anything Kreon can give. Yet there you stand."
                                    Paidoboron
bowed. "That's true. Even so, I may have suitable gifts
for a king." He said no more, but smiled.
                            Jason laughed,
then checked himself, musing. "You've seen something in the stars, I think,"
he said at last. Paidoboron gave him no answer. "I think
the stars sent you—or so you imagine—sent you for something
you've no great interest in, yourself." He tapped his chin,
thinking it through. Suddenly I saw in his eyes that his thought
had darkened. He said: "If Zodiac-watchers were always right,
we'd all be wise to abandon this hall at once." He smiled.
    Kreon looked flustered. "What do you mean?" When Jason was silent,
he turned to Ipnolebes. "What does he mean?" The slave said nothing.

The old king pursed his lips, then puffed his cheeks out, troubled.
"Fiddlesticks!" he said. Then, brightening: "Wine! Give everyone here
more wine!" The slaves hurried in the aisles, obeying.

                                       But Jason
pondered on, and the sea-kings watched him as Kreon did,
Time suspended by Jason's frown. The game was ended,
I thought, incredulous. He'd understood that the fates themselves
opposed him, through Paidoboron.

                            Then one of the shadowy
forms beside him vanished—Hera, goddess of will,
and the same instant a man with a great red beard stood up,
and a chill went through my veins. His eyes were like smoke. The man
with the red beard snapped, "One thing here's sure. We're all engaged,
whatever our reasons, in a test. It's ungenteel, no doubt,
to mention it. But I never was long on gentility.
These kings don't loll here, day after day, some showing off
their wares by the walls, some flashing their wits at the dinnertable,
for nothing. I say we get on with it." He glared from table
to table, red-faced, his short, thick body charged with wrath.
Kreon looked startled and glanced in alarm at Ipnolebes.
"Jason," the red-bearded man said fiercely, pointing a finger
that shook with indignation, "if you mean to play, then play.
If not, pack off! Make room for men that are serious!"
Jason smiled, but his eyes were as bright as nails. "I assure you,
I had no idea there were stakes involved, and I've no intention
of playing for them, whatever they are. I am, as you know,
a beggar here. I leave the game to you, my dissilient
friend, whatever it is."

                       The man with the red beard scoffed,
tense lips trembling like the wires of a harp, his eyes like a dog's.
"We're to understand that Jason, known far and wide for his cunning,
has no idea of what every other lout here, drunk
or sober, has seen by plain signs: Pyripta's for sale,
and we're bidding." He pointed as he spoke, his face bright red with rage,
whether at Pyripta for her calfy innocence, or at Kreon for his guile,
or at devious Jason, no one could tell. Like a mad dog,
a misanthrope out of the woods, he turned on all of them, pointing
at the girl, scorning the elegant forms of their civility.
Pyripta gasped and hid her face, and the blood rushed up
till even her forehead burned red. Like one fierce man, the crowd,

half-rising, roared their anger. He glared at them, trembling all over,
his head lowered, pulled inward like a bull's. "Get him out of here!"
Kreon shouted. "He's drunk!" But when men moved toward him
he batted them off like a bear. Men jerked out daggers and began
to circle him. He drew his own and, hunched tight,
guarding with one arm, rolled his small eyes, watching them all.

    Then Jason rose and called out twice in a loud voice,
"Wait!" The crowd, the circle of men with their daggers drawn,
looked up at him. "No need for this," he said. "A man
in a rage is often enough a man who thinks he's right
though the whole world's against him. I know this wildman Kompsis.
Dog-eyed, fierce as he is, he tells you the truth as he sees it—
sparing no feelings. He may be a rough, impatient man,
a truculent fool, but he means less evil than you think. He's been
a friend to me. Let him be." The men encircling Kompsis
hesitated, then put their weapons away. Red Kompsis
glowered at Jason, angry but humbled. Then he too sheathed
his knife. Men talked, at the tables, leaning toward each other,
and the sound soon filled the hall.

                              Jason sat down. As if
to himself, he said, "How quickly and easily it always comes, this
violence! It's a strange thing. Poor mad mankind!"
"God knows!" said Kreon, his voice shaky. The princess, her face
still hidden behind her hands, was weeping. It was not cunning—
not Jason's famous capacity for transforming all evils
to advantages—that showed on his face.
The son of Aison, whatever else,
was a man sensitive to pain. It was that, past anything else,
that set him apart, made a stranger of Jason wherever he went.
He suffered too fiercely the troubles of people around him. It made him
cool, intellectual. Nietzsche would have understood. If he was
proud, usurped the prerogatives of gods . . . Never mind.
I was moved, watching from the shadows. He was a man much wronged
by history, by classics professors. Jason leaned forward,
speaking to Kreon now, but speaking so Pyripta would hear:
"It's a hard thing, I know myself, for a man to give up
his natural pride. The outrage strikes and stings, and before
you know it, you've turned, struck back. It makes me envy women.
They've got no option of learning 'the art of punching people,'
and as for making fools out of people by abstract talk—

Time and Space, the ultimate causes of things, and so forth—
their quick minds run in the wrong direction, inclined by nature
to thoughts of their children, comforting the weak, by gentleness soothing
their huffing, puffing males. The fiercest of women reveal
their best in arts like those."
                              The table talk died down.
A few of those nearest had caught his allusions to Koprophoros' speech.
    Jason went on, half-smiling, conversational
(but Hera was in him, and Athena; his eyes were sly). He said,
forming his words with care, yet hiding his trouble with his tongue:
"When Pelias scorned me, refused me all honors because, as he put it,
I was 'wild,' not fit to be anything more than a river tramp,
I wanted to strangle the fool. I'd have gotten off cheap, no doubt.
The people are always more fond of their wild young river tramps
than of grand old tyrants who stutter." He laughed, looked down at his hands.
    Like lightning the goddess Hera returned to the red-bearded man.
"You were scared, Jason. Admit it! Or did it seem *uncivil?*"
    Jason laughed again, to himself. Athena poked him.
"No, not scared," he said, and let it pass.
                              Old Kreon
cleared his throat and squeezed one eye shut, tapping his fingers.
"As a matter of fact," he said, "I'd be pleased to hear about it.
We all would, I'm sure."
                         A few of the sea-kings clapped, then more.
Pyripta glanced at him, blushing, unaware of the gentle touch
of dark Aphrodite's fingertips on her wrist—for the goddess,
fickle, perpetually changing, could never resist a chance
to prove herself. (Yet even now, no doubt, her concern
was mainly for Medeia.) Still Jason frowned and thought.
                                              In the end
they prevailed upon him—and though he insisted he felt like a fool
to be launching a tale so cumbersome (it was late, besides:
by the stars it was almost midnight now) he began it. The slaves
passed wine, and those who had nothing to do collected in doorways
or stood by the treasured walls, listening. More than a few
in Kreon's hall had heard those fabulous tales of the *Argo,*
strange adventures from the days of the princes' exodus,
some in one version, some in another, no two agreeing;
and more than a few had heard about Jason's storytelling,
celebrated to the rim of the world.

                              Reluctant as he was
to speak, his eyes took on a glint. He knew pretty well—
Hera watching, invisible, over his shoulder, crafty—
that whether or not he was playing for the throne, the sighing princess,
he meant to make fools, for his sport, of fat Koprophoros
and the Northerner, shrewd as they seemed. As he spoke, he smiled. Near the roof
an owl was perched, stone-silent, with glittering eyes. A lizard,
light as a stick, peeked from the wall, then darted back.
Nearby, the slave Amekhenos, with the boy beside him,
leaned on the door to listen, head bowed. He too, I thought,
had things he could tell, one day, when the time was right for it.

    The house lower on the hill was dark save one dim lamp
that bloomed dully in its shade like a dragon's lidded eye.
The female slave Agapetika kneeled at the rough-carved shrine
of Apollo the Healer, in the corner of her room. Not like Helios—
rising and setting in anger, rampaging in the Underworld,
sire of dragons, zacotic old war-monger—not like Helios
was the god of poesy, lord of the sun.
                              In her larger room,
high-windowed, dim, Medeia lay troubled by gloomy dreams.
The cloth lay in the moonlight singing softly, faint
as the song of mosquitoes' wings, the sleeping children's breath.
Argus wove me, weary old Argus, weary old Argus who wished them well.

6

"It was Pelias shipped us out. I might have murdered him
and seized my father's kingdom back, and might have been thanked for it.
Nobody cared for his rule. But he was my uncle, and I had
my cousins to think of, also my father's memory, he who'd
given my throne to Pelias, or so old Pelias claimed,
backed by his toadies, I being only a child, unfit,
a ruffian to be watched, required to prove my kingliness.
I seethed, not deaf to the whispers in Iolkos. More than age,
men hinted on every side, had hustled my father to his grave.
It was possible. They wrestled, those two half-brothers, from birth,
contending in anger for the place of greater dignity,
whether the line of Poseidon or of Lord Dionysos should rule.
If Pelias seemed a timid man, consider the weasel:
he does not suck in air and roar like the honest, irascible tiger, or stamp
his hoof in annoyance, like the straightforward horse;
nevertheless, he has his way—soft-furred as the coney,
more calculating, more subtle and swift than a jungle snake,
richer in mystery, conceiving his young through his ear, like a poet.
My father, old women claim, gave my uncle Pelias his limp—
a man more direct than I, my father; rough, red-robed,
beard a-tremble in the fury of long-forgotten winds . . .
    "Shifted to a smoky old house with my mother, I kept my quiet;
watched him when he came to call with his curkling retinue,
watched the cowering, sequacious mob as the old cloud-monger
stammered the state of the kingdom, stuttered his counsellors' thoughts,
balbutiating the world to balls of spit. I watched
with the eye of a cockatrice, but when he smiled, smiled back,
pretended to scoff at the rumors. I would not tangle with him,

at least not yet. Like those who crowded the streets, I beamed,
shouted evoes at his rhetoric. Things might be worse.
He hadn't seen fit to imprison us yet 'for our own protection'—
a gambit common enough. Yet I was in prison, all right.
To an eagle the widest of volaries is not yet sky.
Men came to me in the night with suggestions. I refused to hear them.
Sibyls brought me the riddlings of gods, how they signalled in the dust,
mumbled through thunder. I'd give no ear to their stratagems.

   "For all he said of my wickedness—I was fifteen then—
I preferred to wheel and deal. So, having nothing, only
the dry crumbs Pelias dropped, I made my bargain with him.
I'd sail the seas, bring back whatever my crew and I
could steal, and leave it for him to decide what worth it was.
I wouldn't be the first great lord, God knew, who'd gotten his start
marauding. I gathered my crew together, and with the first fair wind,
we sailed. We were lucky. Good breezes most of the way, good hosts . . .

   "We learned quickly. If men came down to us with open arms,
glad to see strangers, eager to hear of our sea adventures,
we made ourselves their firm friends—praised them to the skies,
fought beside them if they happened to have some war in progress,
drank with them, gave them our shoulders later when they stumbled, climbing
to bed. And when the time for leaving came, they'd give us
gifts, the finest they had—they'd load up our boat to the gunnels,
throw in a barge of their own—and we'd stand on the shore with them, moaning,
tears running down our cheeks, and we'd hug them, swearing we'd never
forget. When we sailed away we'd wave till the haze of land
was far below the horizon. They were no jokes, those friendships.
Sooner than anyone thought, I'd prove how firm they were,
when all at once I had need of the men I'd fought beside,
sung with half the night, or tracked down women with—
princes my own age, some of them, or second sons,
nephews of kings, like myself, with no inheritance
but nerve—courage and talent to spare—and their old advisors,
sea-dog uncles, friends of their fathers, powerful fighters
who'd outlived the centaur war, seen war with the Amazons,
and now, like dust-dry banners in a trunk, waited, their glory
dimmed.

      "So it was with friends. But if, on the other hand,
we landed and men came down at us with battle-axes,
stones and hammers, swords, we'd repay them blow for blow

67

till the rock shore streamed with blood—or we'd row for our lives, and then
creep back when darkness came, invisible shadows more soft
of foot than preying cats, and we'd split their skulls. We'd sack
their towns, stampede their cattle in the vineyards till not one vine
stood straight; and so we'd take by force what they might have made
more profitable by hurling it into the sea before
we came. Yet it wasn't the best of bargains on either side.
Both of us paid with lives, and more than once we lost
a ship. Besides, the booty we snatched and hauled aboard
was mediocre at best—far cry from the hand-picked treasures
given with love by friends. Sometimes when the sea was rough
the loot we'd loaded on the run would clatter and slide, and our weight
would shift, and we'd scratch for a handhold, watching the sea comb in.

  "We learned. We were out three years. When we turned at last for home,
we had seven ships for the one we'd started with. I'd earned
my keep, I thought: a house like any lord's, at least,
and some small say in my uncle's court. I figured wrong.
Sour milk and rancid honey it was, in the eyes of Pelias.

  "The king had gotten the solemn word of an oracle
that he'd meet his death through the works of a man he'd someday see
coming from town with one bare foot. It was soon confirmed.
Just after we landed, I was fording the Anauros River, making
for town and the palace beyond, when I lost one sandal in the mud.
It was stuck fast, gripped as if by the hand of old Hades
seizing at a pledge. The river was flooded—it was a time of thaw—
so I left it there. Pelias was giving a great banquet
for his father Poseidon and the other gods—or all but Hera—
when I came where he sat, his lords and ladies all crowded around him,
dressed to the nines, like a flock of exotic birds—long capes
more brilliant than precious stones, deep blue, sharp yellow, scarlet—
eating and laughing, plump as the mountainous clusters of grapes
the slaves bore in. I bowed to him, dressed in the panther-cape
already famous for midnight strikes, unexpected attacks
from rooftops, pits of dungeons. I bowed, most dignified—
except, of course, for that one bare foot. He looked not exactly
gratified that I'd made it. He looked, in fact, like a man
who's gotten an arrow in his back. Pelias threw out his hands,
tiny chins trembling, and said, 'J–J–J–*Jason!*' And said
no more. He'd fainted. It was three full days before I could see him.

  "Well, no reason to stretch it out. I sat by his bed,

68

summed up my winnings, and waited to hear what he thought it all worth.
I heard, instead, about the golden fleece. I had the m–makings
of a king, he said. He continually squeezed his hands together,
winking. I thought he'd gone crazy. 'J–J–J–*J*ason, b–boy,
you've got the m–makings of a king.' He was gray and flabby, like a man
who's been sitting in a dimly lit room for a full half-century.
His legs and arms were spindles, the rest of him loose, like a pudding,
his large head wide and flat, wrinkled like an embryo's.
In his splendid bedclothes—azure and green and as full of light
as wine falling in a stream in front of a candle flame—
he looked like a slightly frightened treetoad, blinking its eyes,
cautiously peeking out from a spray of peacock feathers.
You would not have thought him a child of Poseidon the Earth-trembler,
but demigod he was, nonetheless, and dangerous.
  "I waited, laboring to figure him out. I dropped the idea
of craziness. He was sly, vulpine. The way he made
his eyes glint when he mentioned the fleece, and wrung his hands
and made me bend to his pillow, to let him poke at me,
conspirators in a cunning scheme—I knew the old man
was sane enough. He was pulling something. Yet this was the plan:
Bring him the golden fleece, and he'd split the kingdom with me,
half and half. I could see at a glance what he wanted, all right,
though I wasn't quite sure of the reason—not then. But half the kingdom!
I looked down, hiding my interest, adding it up. I said:
'You seem to forget the difficulties,' and watched him closely.
'No d–d–d–*diff*iculties!' he said, and splashed out his arms,
then wiped his mouth. 'None for a muh–muh–man like you!'
I waited. He grinned like a monkey. Then after a while he sighed,
allowed that it might be a long way, allowed that there might
be 'snakes' (he glanced at me) 'snakes and suh–suh–so on.' He sighed.
'And if I . . . refuse your offer?' He sighed again, looked grieved.
'You're young, J–Jason. P–popular.' He looked out the window.
And I understood. 'You think I'll reclaim my father's throne
despite all the horrors of civil war. But if, by mischance—'
'J–Jason!' he exclaimed. His eyes were wide with shock. I laughed.
He snatched my hand, and, sickly as he looked, his grip was fierce.
He wept. 'J–Jason, I wish you w–well,' he said. And he did—
as Zeus wished Kronos well when he had all his bulk in chains,
or as Herakles wished for nothing but peace to the slaughtered snake
or the shredded, mammocked tree when he tore off the apples of gold.

'Suppose you had the suh–certain word of an oracle,' he said,
'that a suh–certain man was going to k–k–k–kill you. What would
you do?' I nodded. 'I'd send him to fetch the golden fleece,'
I said. Old Pelias squeezed my hand. 'Go and f–fetch it.'
And so I agreed. Pelias had known I'd agree, of course.
What Pelias couldn't know was that I'd beat those odds.
It meant two things—the perfect ship and the perfect crew.
I could get them. That very day I checked with the augurers,
playing it safe. No signs were ever better; and though
I had, like any man of sense, my doubts about
how much a squinting, cracked old priest—with reasons of his own,
could be, for seeing what he did—how much such a man could know
by watching a few stray birds, still, I was excited. I was
a most devout young man, in those days. Goodness in the gods
was a rockfirm fact of experience, I thought. And so I told
the king that as soon as I'd gotten my ship and crew together
I'd sail.

    "It was Argus who built the ship—old Argus, under
Athena's eye. He built it of trees from her sacred groves,
beech and ironwood, towering pines and great dark oaks
that sang in the wind like men, a vast, unearthly choir—
and Athena showed him herself which trees to cut. When the beam
of the keel went in, old Argus smiled, his long gray hair
tied back with a thong, and the beam said, 'Good! Nice work old man!'
When he notched the planks and lowered them onto the chucks, the planks
said, 'Good! Nice fit!' He carved the masts and shaped them with figures
facing in all the four directions, and after he'd dropped them,
slid them with a hollow thump to the central beam, they said,
'That's fine! We're snug as rocks!' Then he built the booms and wove
the sails. The black ship sang, and Argus had finished it.
    "I gathered the crew.
                    "I can't deny it: there never was
in all this world or on any world a mightier crew
than the Argonauts. Sweet gods, beside the most feeble of the lot,
I seemed, myself, a mildly intelligent hedgehog! I gathered
Akhaians from far and near—all men of genius, sons
of gods—
                    "And the first, the finest of them all, was Orpheus.
He was borne by Kalliope herself to her Thracian lover Oiagros,

high on the slopes of Pimplea. Even as a child, with his music
he enchanted the towering, frozen rocks and the violent streams,
and to this day there are quernal forests on the coasts of Thrace
that Orpheus, playing his lyre, lured down from Pieria,
rank on rank of them, coming to his music like soldiers on the march.

"The next I chose was Polyphemon, son of Eilatos, out of
Larissa. He was, in his younger days, a hero in the ranks
of the incredible Lapithai who warred with the centaurs once.
His limbs by now were heavy with age, but he still had the same
fierce heart.

"The next was Asterios, son of an endless line
of travellers, explorers, river merchants, a man who could trade up
wools and linens to priceless gems. And Iphiklos was next,
my mother's brother, who came for the sake of our kinship. Then
Admetos, king of Pherai, rich in sheep. Then the sons
of Hermes, out of Alope, land of cornfields; with them
Aithalides their kinsman. Then, from wealthy Gyrton,
Koronos came, the son of Kaineos—strong as a boulder,
though he wasn't the man his father was. In Gyrton they say
the old man singlehanded beat the centaurs back,
and after the centaurs rallied and overcame him, even
then they couldn't kill him. With massive pines they drove him
down in the earth like a nail. He was still alive.

"Then Mopsos,
powerful man whom Apollo had trained to excel all others
in the art of augury from birds. He knew when he came, he said,
that he'd meet his end in the Libyan desert.

"Then Telamon
and Peleus, sons of Aiakos, fathers in turn of sons
as awesome as they were themselves—the heroes Aias and Akhilles,
now chief terrors of Troy.

"And after the two great brothers,
from Attica came Butes, son of Teleon,
and Phalerus, famous for their deadly spears. (Theseus,
finest of the Attic line, was out of business. He'd gone
with Peirithoös into the Underworld, and was kept there, chained,
a prisoner deep in the earth.)

"Then out of the Thespian town
of Siphai, Tiphys came. He was a mariner
who could sense the coming of a swell across the open sea

and knew by the sun and stars when storms were brewing, six
weeks off. Athena herself had sent him to join us—she
who'd supervised the building of our ship.

                       "Then Phlias
came, Dionysos' son, who lived by the springs of Asopos—
child of the black-robed god who was my father's father.
Phlias was a dancer, a tiger in battle. He never learned speech.
  "From Argos came Talaos and Areion, and powerful Leodokos.
  "Then came Herakles. He'd heard a rumor of the expedition
when he'd just arrived from Arcadia. It was the famous time
when he carried on his back—alive and thrashing—the monstrous boar
that fed in the thickets of Lampeia. As soon as Herakles heard it,
he threw down the boar, tied up its feet, and left it squealing—
loud as a hurricane—blocking the gates of the great market
at Mykenai. His squire, Hylas, that beautiful boy
whom Herakles loved like a son—or like a god—came with him,
serving as keeper of the bow. He was like a breeze, like rain.
You see them sometimes, boys like Hylas, and you pause, as if
snatched out of Time, stunned for an instant. It's as if you've come
suddenly, turning a familiar corner, to a world more calm,
more innocent than ours, and there at the door of it,
a deity, childlike, all-forgiving; you find yourself
thrilled to what's best in yourself, a spring not yet corrupt,
and as religion wells in your chest— a strange
humility—something else sweeps in, a curious sorrow,
deep, mysterious despair. Such gentleness, such trust,
such beauty of eyes and limbs . . . It was as if I knew even then,
the instant I saw him, that something terrible awaited him,
patient as a wolf, and knew that after the beautiful boy
was gone, strange things would happen to us—smoke-black darkness,
murderous winds, waves that ground at our ship like monstrous
teeth . . . Impossible to say what I mean. He was like a sign
of the best possible in nature, and his very goodness made him . . .
  "But enough. Let me think who else there was.

                       "There was Idmon the seer.
Of all the heroes of Argos, Idmon was the last to come.
Like Mopsos, he knew by his own birdlore that for him the trip
meant death; yet the poor devil came, for his reputation's sake.
A coward's coward, I used to call him. He was terrified
at the very idea that he ever might fly in terror.

                    "From Sparta
Aitolian Leda sent us the mighty Polydeukes,
king of all boxers, and Kastor, master of the racing horse.
She'd borne them as twins in Tyndareos' palace, and loved them so well
she swallowed her fear like bitter wine and allowed them to go
as they wished. No wonder Zeus had loved her, a girl like that,
and planted in Leda's womb the most beautiful woman on earth!
    "From Arene the sons of Aphareos came, Lynkeus and Idas.
They were both brave men and as powerful as bulls—yet I hesitated
before I'd take them on board. Idas was crazy. He talked
pure gibberish at times, and foamed at the mouth. When sane,
he was quarrelsome, insolent, a chip on his shoulder as big as a tree.
But Lynkeus wouldn't have joined without him; and Lynkeus had
the finest eyesight in the world. As easily as you and I
see distant eagles, Lynkeus could see things underground.
Yet Idas' vision was keener still, I learned in the end.
His beads were of human bone, and his cheek bore lion scars,
and scorning, shaming, mocking was all he loved; yet he was not
mad, exactly. Like leopards they watched the world, those brothers,
though Idas fooled you. The man had the eyes of a sleeping dragon.
    "From Arcadia, Kepheus and Amphidamas came, two sons of Aleos,
and their older brother Lykourgos sent us his twelve-foot boy
Ankaios. He had to stay home, himself, to care for his aging
father—a testy, sly old devil, as we saw for ourselves.
The old man didn't approve of allowing a boy so young
to sail with us, whatever his size, and when argument failed
to sway Ankaios' father, old Aleos chewed his gums
and schemed. Ankaios arrived at the ship in a bearskin, waving
a two-edged axe in his right hand. His grandfather'd hidden
his equipment in a corner of the barn, still hoping to the very last
he'd keep his baby home.
                  "Augeias also came,
whose father was the sun; and Asterios and Amphion,
from Pelles' city on the cliffs. And Euphemos followed them,
the fastest runner in the world—the boy Europa, daughter
of Tityos, bore to Poseidon. He was a man who could run
on the rolling waters of the sea so fast his invisible feet
weren't wet by it. —But Zetes and Kalais were faster in the sky,
the two sons of the North Wind, whom Oreithyia
bore to Boreas in the wintry borderland of Thrace. He'd brought her

from Attica. She was whirling in the dance on the banks of the Ilissos
when he snatched her from earth and carried her away to Sarpedon's Rock,
near the flowing waters of Erginos, where he wrapped her up
in a dark cloud and raped her. It was an astounding thing
to watch those sons of hers soar up into the sky, the sea-blue
eagles' road! The wings on each side of their ankles whirred
and spangles of gold burst through like sparks from the dusky feathers,
and they shot away. Their black locks whipped on their shoulders and backs,
but their faces were steady as arrowheads in flight.
                                                    "The last
we took with us was Argus, gentle old craftsman, sly
as Daidalos—but older, richer in ancient lore—
a man who remembered secrets most of the gods had long
forgotten. He was no fighter. In time of war he'd sit
bent over, with his lips drawn tight, his blue eyes violent,
alarmed, as though he'd pierced the forms of the ships we'd burned,
the white bodies of the dead—had pierced the shapes of our destruction,
and saw, beyond them, nothing. And yet he forgave our work,
when breezes had cleaned the air of the stink and smoke, and we'd laid
the dead away. Old Argus didn't much care for us,
destroyers of filigreed halls and high-prowed ships, wasters
of goldsmiths' work, despoilers of cities, the works of mind.
There were times when that gentle scorn of his—a sneer, almost—
inclined us to smash his head for him. But we couldn't, of course.
We needed him—needed his art, if not that calcifying
smile. And Argus came, whatever his distaste, to guard
his masterpiece—to guard, perhaps, whatever work
he could. And because he was curious. Not death itself
would have given the old man pause if he thought he could learn from it.
For all his nobility of mind he was a man consumed
by need to know, need to reduce the universe
to facts.
            "Such was my crew, or anyway the best of it;
all men of genius, sons of the immortal gods.

                                            "The *Argo*
was ready, equipped with all that goes into a well-found ship
when pressing business carries people to sea. We made
our way to the shore where the ship lay grumbling, muttering to herself
to be gone. A crowd of excited townsfolk gathered around us,

tall men, some of them, some of them fine to see; but set
by the best of them all, the *Argo*'s crew stood out like stars
in a dark, beclouded sky. If we weren't a match for Aietes,
Keeper of the Fleece, then nobody was. As the people watched us
hurrying along in our armor, one of them said—a wail—
'Zeus! Pelias has lost his mind! Who'd dare to drive
such men as these from Akhaia? If Aietes dares to refuse
the golden fleece when they ask for it, they can send up his palace
in flames the same day they land. —But the ship must get there first.
I've heard men say there are dangers beyond what a god would face.'

    "The women stood weeping, their hands stretched up in prayer to the gods
for our safe return. There was one, an old servant that I knew. Her eyes
bored into me, and she wailed of my mother with a harsh voice
and a maniac look, pretending she didn't know me. I stood
like a child before her, shaken, rooted to the spot.

                                              " 'Ye gods,'
she moaned, 'poor Alkimede! Thank God *I've* got no son!
Better for her if she'd long since gone to her lonely grave,
wrapped head to foot in her winding-sheet, still ignorant
of this madman's expedition! O that Phrixos had sunk
in the dark waves where Helle died, and the monstrous golden
ram still clamped in his legs! O why was Jason—heartless,
arrogant fool—not born to her dead, to spare her this?
She weeps her eyes out, cries and cries in such black despair
that her sobs come welling too fast for Alkimede to sound them. He might
have buried his mother with his own hands—that much at least
he might have stayed to do for her, having sea-dogged half
his life, far out of her sight, carousing with strangers, fighting
all men's wars but his father's, and his poor old mother worried
sick! She stood as high in her time as any woman
in Akhaia. But now she's left like a servant in an empty house,
widowed, pining in misery after her only son
who cares no more for his mother than he would for a dying dog,
cares for nothing and nobody, only for Jason, apple
of her eye—and apple of his own! Dear gods I wish you could see
how slyly that boy consoles her—and believes every word of it
himself, as if Jason could do no wrong! "Dear mother," says he,
all piety, "do not be grieved that I leave you alone.
We're all alone, we mortals, whether we're near to each other
or far apart. Locked inside ourselves, foolishly, blindly

struggling to do what's right." He moons out the window, sad
as a priest, and she's impressed by it. —Oh my but that boy
can be pretty, when he likes! He kisses her hand and tells her, "Do not
be afraid, Mother. I'm doing what the gods demand. The omens
show it. We used to be rich, Mother. Now that we're poor,
we ought to have learned that nothing counts but the gods' friendship.
Let me serve them; then when you die, you'll die in peace,
whether I'm near or not. You've told me yourself, Mother,
that all there is in the world, at last, is the war or peace
of dying men and the old undying gods. The omens
favor the trip. I must go." And he kisses her cheeks. Ah, Jason!
Cunning buried so deep he can't see it himself! Omens!
Did he ask his friends the augurers what omens they see
for his mother? Or Pelias? Or the city? Would that the birdsongs sang
his death!'

      "And then she was gone; her black shawl vanished in the crowd.
My throat was dry with shame. I was numb. I stood too stunned
to think. If I could have summoned speech that instant, I might
have called it off on the spot, and to hell with the consequences.
But then, from nowhere, a man appeared at my side, a man—
or god, who knows?—hooded till only his beard peeked out.
I thought by the mad-dog hunch of his shoulders, the growl in his throat,
it was crazy Idas, Lynkeus' brother. He touched my arm.
'She never liked you, did she, man.' The words confused me.
I remembered the old woman's slapping me once, and calling out sharply,
another time—I was only a child, and I wasn't to blame for
whatever it was she charged me with. My mind grew clouded.

    "I moved in a kind of daze toward the boat, the streets
of the city behind me, and I racked my brains over whether or not
the woman was right. When I came down to the beach, my friends
were waiting, waving. They raised a shout so loud the gulls
flew higher in sudden alarm. The crew was grinning, their armor
blazing like the sun at noon. They pointed, and I looked behind me,
and lo and behold, Akastos himself was running toward me,
Pelias' son! He'd slipped away from the house while the king
was sleeping, bound to go out with us, whether the old man liked
or not. I seized my cousin in my arms and laughed, and we ran
to the ship. And so I forgot what the old crone said, or forgot
till later, miles from shore.

      "The wind was right, the ship

and the Argonauts both eager to go, and the sooner the better.
I stood on a barrel and waved my arms for attention. I shouted,
and the Argonauts grew quiet. 'Three last details,' I said.
The sea-wind whipped my words away. I shouted louder.
'The first is this. We're all partners in the voyage to Kolchis,
the land where Aietes guards the golden fleece, and we're partners
bringing it home—we hope. So it's up to you to choose
the best man here as our leader. And let me warn you, choose
with care, as if our lives depended on it.' When I
had spoken, they turned like one man toward Herakles,
where he sat in the center of the crowd, and with one voice they called out,
'Herakles!' But the hero scowled and shook his head,
and without stirring from his seat, raising his right hand
like a pillar, he said, 'No, friends, I must refuse. And I must
refuse, also, to let any other man stand up.
The man who wears the pelt of a panther has shown good sense
so far—Jason, Aison's son. Let Jason lead.'
  "They clapped at his generosity and slapped my back,
praising my cunning, swearing that I was the man for the job,
no doubt of it! What can I say? I was flattered, excited.
—But no, the thing's more complicated. I was a boy, remember,
and beloved of the goddess of will, as many things since have proved.
It had never crossed my mind that the crew would turn like that,
as if they'd planned it, and all choose Herakles. —And now
when the giant handed it back to me, and led the clapping
himself, grinning, white teeth flashing, his muscular face
all innocence, so open and boyish that we all smiled too,
what I secretly felt was jealousy, almost rage. It makes
me laugh now. What a donzel I was! But ah, at the time,
how my heart smarted, hearing them praise me like a god! He was
their leader, whatever they pretended. And rightly, of course, he was better,
as plainly superior to me as the sun to a millwheel. And yet
I resented him, and I burned like a coal at their feigned delight,
their self-delusion, in choosing me. I had half a mind
to quit, sulking, and crawl away to some forest and live
like a hermit. Screw them all! At the same time, however,
I wanted to lead them, whether or not I was worthy—I was,
God knew (and I knew) ambitious. All my life I've hated
standing in somebody's shadow. So, with as good a grace
as possible, I blinded myself to the obvious.

I accepted. Orpheus smiled, studying his fingernails.

    " 'Second detail,' I shouted, and cleared my throat—looking
guilty as sin, no doubt. 'If you do indeed trust me
with this honorable charge—' It came to me I was putting it on
a trifle thick, and I hastily dropped the orbicular style.
'We've two things left, and we may as well start on both of them
at once. The first is the sacrifice to the gods—a feast
to Phoibus, for warm, clear days, to Poseidon for gentle seas,
and to Hera, who's been my special friend—thanks to Pelias'
scorn of her. Also an altar on the shore to Apollo,
the god of embarkation. And while we're waiting for the slaves
to pick out oxen from the herd and drive them down to us,
I suggest that we drag the *Argo* down into the water and haul
our tackle on, and cast lots for the rowing benches.'
They all agreed at once and I turned, ahead of them all—
to show my fitness as a leader, I suppose, or escape their eyes—
and threw myself into the work. They leaped to their feet and followed.

    "We piled our clothes on a smooth rock ledge which long ago
was scoured by seas but now stood high and dry. Then,
at Argus' suggestion, we strengthened the ship by girding her round
with tough new rope, which we knotted taut on either side
so her planks couldn't spring from their bolts but would stand whatever force
the sea might hurl against them. We hollowed a runway out,
wide enough for the *Argo*'s beam, and we gouged it into
the sea as far as the prow would reach, deeper and deeper
as the trench advanced, below the level of her stem. Then we laid
smooth rollers down, and tipped her up on the first of the logs.
We swung the long oars inside out—the whole crew moved
like a single man with a hundred legs—and we lashed the handles
tight to the tholepins of bronze, leaving nearly a foot and a half
projecting, to give us a hold. We took our places then
on either side, and we dug in with our feet and put
our chests to the oars. Then Tiphys, king of all mariners, leaped
on board, and when he shouted, 'Heave!' we echoed the shout
and heaved, putting our backs into it, pushing till our necks
were swelled up like a puff-adder's, and our thick legs shook
and our groins cried out. 'Ah!' the *Argo* whispered. '*Ah!*'
At the first heave we'd shifted the ship from where she lay,
and we strained forward to keep her on the move. And move she did!
Between two files of huffing, shouting Akhaians, the craft

ran swiftly down to the sea. The rollers, ground and chafed
by the mighty keel, wheezed like oxen at the ship's weight
and sent up a pall of smoke. The ship slid in and gave
a cry and would have been off on her own to that land of promise
if Herakles hadn't leaped in and seized her, the rest of us shouting,
straining back on the hawsers with all our might. She rocked,
gentle on the tide, singing, and we watched that gentle roll,
and my heart was hungry for the sea.

                           "No need to tell you more.
We piled up shingle, there on the beach, working together
like one man with a hundred hands, and we made an altar
of olive wood. The herdsmen came to us, driving the oxen
and we hailed them, praising their choice. A few of us dragged the great
square beasts to the altar, and others came with lustral water
and barleycorns, and I called to Apollo, god of my fathers,
as I would have called to a man I knew—that's how I felt
that morning, with the *Argo* singing, the men all watching me,
arm in arm—I'd completely forgotten my resentment now;
'O hear us, Lord, Great God Apollo, you that dwell
in Pegaisai, in Aison's city, you that promised
to be my guide! Lord, bring our ship to Kolchis and back,
and my friends all safe and sound! We'll bring you countless gifts,
some in Pytho, some in Ortygia. O, Archer King,
accept the sacrifice we bring you, payment in advance for passage
safe to the fleece and home! Give us good luck as we cast
the ship's cable; and send fair weather and a gentle breeze.'
    "I sprinkled the barleycorns in the fire, and Herakles
and mighty Ankaios girded themselves for their work with the beasts,
the child Ankaios, twelve feet tall, still wearing his bearskin.
The first ox Herakles struck on the forehead with his club, and it fell
where it stood. Dark blood came dribbling from its nose and mouth. The second
Ankaios smote with his huge bronze axe—blood sprayed and steamed—
and the ox pitched forward onto both its horns. The men around them
slit the animals' throats, and flayed them, chopped them up
with swords, and carved the flesh. They cut off the sacred parts
from the thighs and heaped them together and, after wrapping them
in fat, burned them on the faggots. I poured libations out,
old unmixed wine. And Idmon the seer, with Mopsos at his back,
both of them wise in the ways of the gods, watching intently,
smiled and nodded, agreeing as surely as two heads ruled

by a single mind, for the flames were bright that surrounded the meat,
and the smoke ascended in dark spirals, exactly as it should.
'All's well for you,' they said, 'though not for us all, and not
without some troubles, and terrible dangers later.' It was
enough, God knows, for the moment. The crew was jubilant.

"We finished our duties to the other gods in the same spirit.
It seemed to us that they all stood around us smiling, unseen,
like larger figures of ourselves, all arm in arm, as we were,
some with their hands on our shoulders, sharing our joy. Great Zeus,
the very sea and hills, it seemed, locked arms and shared
our joy, our eagerness to go! I wouldn't have given much
that moment for the holy hermit's life in his sullen woods
or stalking the barren island conversing with gulls and snakes
praying, clenching his teeth against the civilities
of man!

"Then we all cast lots for the benches, choosing our oars—
or all of us but Herakles, for the whole crew said,
and rightly, that a giant like that
should take the midships seat, and the boy Ankaios beside him;
and Tiphys, they all agreed, should be our helmsman, the man
who knew when a swell was coming from miles away. It was settled.

"The time of day had come when, after his midday rest,
the sun begins to stretch out shadows of rocks over fields,
and trees are dark at the base but bright above. We'd spent
too long at our preparations. But no use fretting now.
We strewed the sand with a thick covering of leaves and lay
in rows, above where the surf sprawled, gray in the dark. We ate,
and we drank the mellow wine the stewards had drawn for us
in jugs. The men began telling stories, the way men will
when things are going well and there's no more work, and the wine
has made them conscious of the way they feel toward friends, old times,
and the rest. There was nobody there, you'd have thought, who could work
          up a mood
for quarrelling. I lay a little apart from the others,
looking at the sky with my hands behind my head and thinking,
hardly listening to the talk. And after a while, a strange
malaise came over me. All was well for me, the seers
had said, but not for all of us. I thought, briefly,
of my mother. I might never see her again. I wondered which

of my friends would never reach home. It was a queer thing
I was doing. I suddenly wondered why—and saw myself
as a murderer: Herakles, laughing by the fire, huge as a mountain,
beautiful Hylas looking up at him, laughing in a voice
that seemed an imitation of the hero's; Orpheus,
polishing his delicate harp with hands like a lover's . . . Abruptly,
I sat up, trying to check my gloomy thoughts—trying,
to tell the truth, to shake off my sudden, senseless shame.
Idas saw me. As darkness thickened he'd watched, invisible,
except for his eyes. He laughed his nasty, madhouse laugh
and yelled at me, too loud, like a deaf man. 'Jason,' he bawled,
'tell us your morbid thoughts, O Lord of the Argonauts!'
His eyes were wild. 'Is it panic I spy on the face of the warlike
Jason son of Aison? Fear of the dark, maybe?
Lo, we've chosen you keeper of us all, and there you sit,
quiet as a stone! Be brave, good man! We'll all protect you,
now that we've solemnly chosen you—after deepest thought,
you understand, and the most profound reflection!' He laughed.
'By my keen spear, the spear that carries me farther in war
than Zeus himself, I swear that no disaster shall trouble
a hair of Jason's beard, so long as Idas is with him.
That's the kind of ally you've got in me, old friend!'
I couldn't tell if the lunatic meant to mock me or meant
to defend me against some imagined foe. I doubt if he knew
himself. I did know this: with a word, a single wild
assertion, he'd made the night go stony dark as if
he'd closed a door on the gods, and in that selfsame gesture
closed out his friends—perhaps closed out the very earth
at his feet. He lifted a full beaker with both dark hands
and guzzled the sweet unwatered wine till his lips and beard
were drenched with it. The men all cried out in anger at his words,
and Idmon said—it was no mere guess, he spoke as a seer—
'Your words are deadly!—and it's you, black Idas, who'll die of them!
Crazy as you are, you've scoffed at almighty Zeus himself!
Laugh all you will, the time will come—and soon, man, soon—
when you'll roll your eyes like a sheep in flight from a wolf, and no one,
nothing at your back but Zeus!'
                                "More loudly than before, mad Idas
laughed. 'Woe be unto Idas! For he hath drunk of the blood
of bulls. He will surely die! He'll crawl on his belly, eat dust,

and children will kick him in the head! —Come now,
my brave little seer! Employ your second
sight and tell me: How do you mean to escape from poor
mad Idas once he's proved your prophecies lie? I've heard
you prophesied once you'd love some lady of Thrace till your dying
day. Where's she gone now? Snuck off to the woods, Idmon?
Wringing her fingers and moaning and plucking the wild flowers,
timid as a rabbit, hiding from the eyes of men like one of
the god's pale shuddering nuns? I have it on authority
that Zeus is a man-eating spider.' He spoke in fury, with the hope
of raising Idmon against him and cutting him down. I leaped
to my feet—and so did the others—yelling, Herakles in rage,
my cousin Akastos shocked and grieved. Mad Idas' mind
was gone from behind his eyes leaving nothing but smoke, dull fire,
the look in the eyes of a snake before it strikes.
                                        "Then something
happened. We hardly knew, at first, what it was we heard,
but the night grew strangely peaceful, as if some goddess had touched
the sea, the fire, the trees, with an infinitely gentle hand
and soothed them, made them sweet. Orpheus stroked his harp,
singing as if to himself, ears cocked to the sea and stars,
half smiling, like a man in a dream. Then Idas was calm, and recovered,
and the evil spirit left him.
                                        "He sang of the age when the earth
and sky were knit together in a single mold, and how they were
sundered, ripped from each other by terrible strife, how mountains
rose from the ground like teeth. And then, in terror at what
they'd done, and what might follow, they paused and trembled. Then stars
appeared, sent out by the gods to move as sentinels,
and streams appeared on the mountainsides, and murmuring nymphs
to whisper and lull the earth back into its sleep. He told
how, out of the sea, the old four-legged creatures came,
a sacrifice gift from the deeps to the growling shore, and birds
were formed of the earth as a peace-offering to the sky. Then dragons,
cursed race still angry, challenged the gods. King Zeus
was still a child at play in his Dictaian cave. They roamed
the earth, terrifying lesser beasts, alarming even
the gods, an army of serpents who threatened all who'd warred
in the former age—the earth and sea and sky, the roaming
mountains, stalkers in the night. But then the Cyclopes borne

of earth, for love of Hera, earth's majestic mother,
fortified Zeus with the thunderbolt. Then Zeus ruled all,
great god of peace. And all the earth and the arching sky
shone calm and bright as a wedding dress. And the wisdom of Zeus
was satisfied. The craftsman of the gods invented flowers
and green fields, and the world became as one again.
    "So Orpheus sang, but how he ended none of us could say.
We slept. The sea lapped gently, near our feet. And thus
the first night passed, quiet as the legend he sang to us.

    "When radiant dawn with her bright eyes gazed at the towering crags
of Pelion, and the headlands washed by wind-driven seas
stood sharp and clear, Tiphys aroused us, and quickly we shook off
sleep and gulped our breakfast down and ran to the waiting
ship. The *Argo* growled at us, from her magic beams,
impatient to sail. We leaped aboard and followed in file
to our rowing benches. Then, all in order, our gear beside us,
we hauled the hawsers in and poured libations out
to the sea. Then Herakles settled amidships, cramped for space,
huge Ankaios beside him. The ship's keel, underfoot,
sank low in the water, accepting their weight. I gave the signal.
My eyes welled up with tears I scarcely understood myself,
snatching a last quick look at home, and then our oars,
spoonshaped, pointed like spearheads—Argus' sly design—
dug in, in time with Orpheus' lyre like dancers' feet.
The smooth, bright blades were swallowed by the waves, and on either side,
the dark green saltwater broke into foam, seething in anger
at our powerful strokes. The ship lunged forward, riding the roll
that came to us, swell on swell, out of landless distances.
Our armor glittered in the sunshine bright as fire; behind
our stern, our wake lay clear as a white stone path on a field,
or clear except . . . I forget. Some curious after-image,
memory or vision, obscurely ominous. . . . Never mind.
    "All the high gods, it seemed to us, were looking down
from heaven that day, observing the *Argo,* applauding us on;
and from the mountain heights the nymphs of Pelion admired our ship,
Athena's work, and sighed at the beauty of the Argonauts swinging
their oars. The centaur Kheiron came down from the high ground—
he who had been, since my father's death, my friend and tutor.
Rushing to the sea, and, wading out in the gray-green surf,

83

he waved again and again with his two huge hands. His wife
came down with Akhilles, Peleus' son, on her arm and held him
for his father to see. 'Now there's the man to row for us!'
Telamon yelled, Peleus' brother, and Peleus beamed.

"Till we left the harbor with its curving shores behind us, the ship
was in Tiphys' hands, swerving like a bird past sunken rocks
as his polished steering-oar bid. When the harbor receded, we stept
the tall oak mast in its box and fixed it with forestays, taut
on either bow. We hauled the sail to the mast-head, snapped
the knots, unfurled it. Shrill wind filled it out. We made
the halyards fast on deck, each wrapped on its wooden pin,
and thus we sailed at our ease past the long Tesaian headland.
Orpheus sang. A song of highborn Artemis, saver
of ships, guardian of the peaks that lined that sea. As he sang,
fish of all shapes and kinds came over the water and gambolled
in our wake like sheep going home to the shepherd's pipe. The wind
freshened as the day wore on, and carried the *Argo,* swift
and yare as a wide-winged gull.
                              "The Pelasgian land
grew dim, faded out of view; then, gliding on, we passed
the stern rock flanks of Pelion. Sepias disappeared,
and sea-girt Skiathos hove in sight. Then, far away,
we saw Peiresiai, and under the cloudless blue,
the mainland coast of Magnesia, and Dolops' tomb. And then
the thick wind veered against us. We beached our ship in the dark,
the sea running high, and there we stayed three days. At the end
of the third, when the wind was right again, we hoisted sail.
We ran past Meliboia, keeping its stormy rocks
to leeward, and when dawn's bright eyes shone, we saw the slopes
of Homole slanting to the sea close by. We skirted around it
and passed the mouth of the Amyros, and passed, soon after,
the sacred ravines of Ossa and then Olympos. Then, running
all night long before the wind, we made it to Pallene, where
the hills rise up from Kanastra. On we sailed, through the dawn,
and old Mount Athos rose before us, Athos in Thrace,
whose peak soars up so high it throws its shadow over
Lemnos, clear up to Myrine. We had a stiff breeze all
that day and through the night; the *Argo*'s sail was stretched.
But then with dawn's first glance there came a calm. It was
our backs that carried us in, heaving at the oars—carried us,

grinning like innocent fools, to the first of our troubles—Lemnos,
bleaker, more rugged than we thought, a place where murdered men,
ghosts howling on the rocks . . ."

                                  Abruptly, Jason paused,
the beautiful gray-eyed goddess whispering in his ear. He frowned
and looked around him like a man just startled out of sleep. The sky
was gray, outside the windows of Kreon's hall. The king
sat leaning on his hands, eyes vague, as if still listening
though Jason's voice had stopped. At the tables, some were asleep,
some leaned forward like children seated at an old man's knee,
half hearing his words, half dreaming. Pyripta glanced at Jason
shyly, sleepy, but waiting in spite of her weariness.
Then Jason laughed, a peal that startled us all. "Good gods!
I've talked the night away! You're mad to endure it!"
                                      The old king
straightened. "No no! Keep going!" But then he blushed. He knew
himself that his words were absurd, even when others, at the tables,
echoed the request. At the king's elbow, Ipnolebes spoke,
beloved old slave in black, his beard snow-white. He said:
"Good Kreon—if I might suggest it—it's true that it's late, as Jason
says. But it seems to me that you might persuade our friend
to sleep with us here—we have rooms enough, and servants sufficient
to tend to the needs of one more man. And then, when Jason—
and all of us—are refreshed, he could tell us more." The king
stood up, nodding his pleasure. "Excellent!" he said. "Dear Jason,
I insist! Stay with us the night!" The hall assented, clapping,
even fat Koprophoros, for politeness, though
it spiked his spleen that Jason should steal the light from him,
slyly rebuke him with an endless, cunning tale. (But do not think from this
the Asian was easily overcome. His outrage was play,
we'd all soon learn. He knew pretty well what his power was,
and knew what the limit would be for Aison's son.) —Nor was he
alone in seeming distressed. Stern King Paidoboron,
beard dyed blacker than a raven's wings, scowled angrily;
Jason had struck him from the shadows, cunning and unjust, light-footed,
a thousand times. He'd slashed deep, by metaphors,
casual asides too quick for a man to expose, so that
Paidoboron's message was poisoned, at least for now. Nor would
his chance to reply come soon. Gray-eyed Athena's words

in Jason's ear had shown him a stratagem for keeping the floor,
and even now old Kreon was begging him to stay.
                                        But Jason
raised his hand, refusing. He was needed at home, he said;
and nothing Kreon could say would change his mind. At last
he allowed this much: he'd return the following afternoon
and tell the rest—since his noble friends insisted on it.
And so it was agreed. Then hurriedly Jason left his chair
and went to the door, only pausing, on his way, for a dozen greetings
to friends not seen in years.
                        By chance—so it seemed to me,
but nothing in all this dream was chance—the slave who brought
his cloak was the Northerner, Amekhenos. He draped the cloak
on Jason's powerful shoulders without a word, head bowed,
and as Jason moved away, the young man said, "Good night."
Jason paused, frowned as if listening to the voice in his mind,
then turned to glance at the slave. He studied the young man's features,
frowning still, his fist just touching his chin: pale hair,
a Kumry mouth that could laugh in an instant, perhaps in an instant more, forget;
shoulders of a prince, and the round, red face
of a Kelt, and the dangerous, quiet eyes . . . But the memory
nagging his mind—so it seemed to me—refused to come,
and the slave, his eyes level with Jason's, as though he were
no slave, but a fellow king, would give no help. At last
Jason dismissed it, and left. But in front of his house (it was morning,
birdsongs filling the brightening sky), he paused and frowned
again, studying the cobblestones under his feet, and again
the memory, connection, resemblance, whatever it was, would not
come clear.
            The dark house rising above the vine-hung, crumbling
outer walls, the huge old trees, seemed still asleep,
hushed in the yellowing light as an ancient sepulchre.
The feeble lamp still burned at the door. The old male slave,
a Negro stooped and gentle, with steadily averted eyes,
lifted the hooks at the door to let him in, and took
his scarlet cloak. Jason walked on to the central room
which opened onto the garden. His gaze hit the fleece at once—
or he heard it, felt it with the back of his neck before he saw it—
and it seemed to me that the words of the seer had returned to him
like a shock: *You may see more than you wish of that golden fleece.*

He crossed to it quickly and kneeled to touch it, then drew back his hand,
snatched it away like a man burned. And then, more gently,
thinking something I couldn't guess, he touched it again.
Did the fleece have for him, I wondered, the meaning it had for Medeia?—
love sign, proof that despite the shifting, deceiving mists
of their lives together, he knew her worth—understood her childlike
needs as well as he understood, I knew from his tale,
his own? He raised it in his hands and went over to stand with it
by the fireplace. There was no fire, but the wood was piled
in its bin; the lamp stood waiting. With a jolt, I understood.
He meant to destroy the thing, outflank his destiny.
The same instant, I felt Medeia's presence with us.
She stood at the door, in white. In panic, I searched her face
to see if she too understood. But I couldn't tell. No sign.
She watched him fold the cloth and lay it on the carved bench.
They went up. I found myself shaking. Who remembers the elegant speeches
he makes to his wife, the speeches she laughingly mocks herself,
but clings to more than she thinks? If I were Jason and saw
the fleece, and remembered the words of the blind old seer of Apollo,
I too, blindly—like a mad fool, from the point of view
of the old, all-seeing gods . . . I checked myself. They were phantoms,
dead centuries ago if they ever lived. It was all
absurd. I remembered: *The wise are attached neither to good
nor to evil. The wise are attached to nothing.* I laughed. Christ send me
wisdom!

       Still trembling, I went to the door, then out to the garden
to walk, examine the plants and read the grave-markers.
I could hear the city waking—the clatter of carts on stones,
the cry of donkeys and roosters, the brattle of dogs barking.
I sat for a long time in the cool, wet grass, and as
the day warmed, and the children's voices came down from the house—
soft, lazy as the butterflies near my shoes— I fell asleep.

7

Kreon beamed—propped up, plump, on scarlet pillows—
wedged in, hemmed on all sides by slaves, some feeding him,
some manicuring his nails, some waving
fans, great gleaming plumes. His cheeks and bare dome dazzled,
newly oiled and perfumed, as bright as the coverture
of indigo, gold, and green. The pillars of the royal bed
were carved with a thousand liquid shapes: fat serpent coils,
eagles, chariots, fish-tailed centaurs, lions, maidens . . .
Writhing, twisting, piled on top of one another, the forms
climbed up into the shadows beyond where the sunlight burst
like something alive—a lion from the golden age—past spacious
balconies, red drapes.
                            "He was magnificent!"
the king said. The slave in black, standing at his shoulder,
smiled, remote. "Poor Koprophoros!" the king exclaimed,
and laughed till the tears ran down. The slave by the bed laughed with him.
"And poor Paidoboron," he said, and looked more sober for an instant;
but then, unable to help himself, he laughed again.
You'd have sworn he was ten years younger today, his cares all ended.
His laughter jiggled the bed and made him breathless. The dog
at the door rolled back his eyes to be certain that all was well,
his head still flat on his paws. When the fit of laughter passed,
the old king patted his stomach and grew philosophical.
"Well, it's not over yet, of course." Ipnolebes nodded,
folded his hands on his beard. King Kreon lowered his eyebrows,
closed one eye, and pushed out his lower lip. "Make no
mistake," he said, "that man knows whom he's speaking to—
'This for the princess, that for the king; this for the Keltai,

88

this for the Ethiopians.' " He closed his left eye
tighter still, till the right one gleamed like a jewel. "And what
does he offer for Kreon and Ipnolebes?" Abruptly, the bed
became too little span for him. He threw off the cover—
slaves leaped back—reached pink feet to the floor and began
to pace. They dressed him as he walked (somewhat frailly, eating an apple).
"This, certainly, whatever else: the trick of survival
may not lie, necessarily, in heroic strength
or even heroic nobility, heroic virtue—
consider Herakles and Hylas, for instance. The world's complex.
There's the more serious side of what's wrong with Koprophoros.
Graceful, charming, ingenious as he is (we can hardly deny
he's that), his faith's in himself, essentially. The strength of *his* muscles,
the force of *his* intellect. We know from experience, you and I,
where that can lead. Oidipus tapping his way through the world
with a stick, more lonely and terrible, more filled with gloom
than Paidoboron himself. Or worse: Jokasta hanging from a beam.
Or Antigone." He paused and leaned on the balustrade that overlooked
the city, the sea beyond, the visitors' ships. "Antigone,"
he said again, face fallen, wrecked. He raised the apple
to his mouth and discovered he'd eaten it down to the pits. He was silent.
He stared morosely seaward. Ipnolebes stood head bowed,
as though he knew all too well what molested his master's thought.
The king asked, testy, his eyes evasive, "Tell me, Ipnolebes,
what do the people say now about that time?" The slave
stiffened, disguising his feelings, then quickly relaxed once more,
grinning, casually picking at his arm. But if there was cunning
in what he said, or if some god had entered his spirit,
no one there could have known it. "My lord,
what *can* they say?" he said at last. "No one was wrong . . .
it seems to me . . . though what would I know, mere foolish old slave?"
Kreon turned his bald head slightly, lips pursed, eyebrows
low, dark, thick as a log-jam. His neck was flushed—old rage
not yet burned out. Ipnolebes said: "With Oidipus blind,
self-exiled, Queen Jokasta dead, the city of Thebes
surrounded, you had no choice but to seal the gates. That stands—"
He paused, looked baffled for a moment, "That stands . . . to reason. And of course
Antigone had no choice but to break your law, with her brothers
unburied, food for vultures. So it seems . . . It was
a terrible time, yes yes, but no one . . . ." His voice trailed off.

Kreon's mouth tightened. "I should have relented sooner. I was wrong.
To think otherwise . . . Would you have me consider our lives mere dice?"
Ipnolebes wrung his hands. "I'm a foolish old man, my lord.
It seems improbable . . ." "If it's true, then Koprophoros' way's the best:
Seize existence by the scrotum! Cling till it shakes you loose,
hurls you out with an indifferent horn toward emptiness!
I refuse to believe it's true!" But his eyes snapped shut, and he whispered,
"Gods, dear-precious-holy-gods!" I looked at Corinth's towers,
baffled by the sudden change in him. I looked, in my vision,
at the parks, academies, sculptured walkways, houses of the people
(white walls, gardens, children in the streets)—a city as bright
as Paris, greener than London, as awesome in its power for good
or evil as rich New York; and suddenly I knew what shattered him:
Thebes on fire. (*Berlin, San Francisco, Moscow, Florence . . .*
New York on fire. Babylon is fallen, fallen . . .)

The slave shook his head,
rueful. "My lord, what got you back onto this? We should think
of the present, be grateful for the gifts the generous gods give now!"
    For a long time Kreon was silent, looking at the sea. Below him
the city, blazing in the sunlight, teemed with tiny figures
moving like busy insects through the streets. The tents
of the marketplace were shimmering patches of color. By the walls
stood hobbled donkeys, loaded with goods—bright cloth, rope, leather,
great misshapen bags of grain, new wineskins, implements;
above it all, like the tinny hum that rises from a hive,
the sound of the people's voices buying and selling, begging,
trading—people of every description, thieves, jewellers,
shepherds driving their bleating sheep and goats, sailors
up from the ships in the harbor, zimmed and clean-shaved spintries—
shocking as parrots—and prostitutes, old leathery priests . . .
    The old king pointed down at them, touching Ipnolebes' arm.
"See how they live off each other," he said. "Shoes for baskets,
honey for wine, filigree for gold, a few pennies
for a prayer. Picture of the world—so Jason claims. Picture
of the *Argo,* gods and men all 'arm in arm,' so to speak:
no one exactly supreme. If Antigone and I had been
like that, more willing to give and take . . ." Ipnolebes scowled
but kept his thoughts to himself. When Kreon glanced at him
he saw at once that something festered in the old slave's mind.
"Don't keep your thoughts from me, old friend," he said. His look

had a trace of anger in it. Ipnolebes nodded, avoiding
the king's eyes. His gnarled hands trembled on the white of his beard
and it came to me that, for all their talk of friendship, they were
slave and master. Ipnolebes touched his wrinkled lips
with two bent fingers and mumbled, as if to himself, "I was thinking—
trying to think—the old brain's not what it used to be, my lord—thinking . . .
from Aietes' point of view . . . how he felt
when the *Argo*—every man at his task, the south wind breathing
his steady force in the sails—came gliding to the Kolchian harbor
to steal the fleece, burn ships, seduce his daughter—destroy
his house." Suddenly he laughed—the laugh of a halfwit harmless
slave. King Kreon looked at him, his small eyes wider,
glinting. "Aietes was wrong," he said. "The gods were against him."
Ipnolebes nodded, looking at the ground. "They must have been.
But what was his error, I wonder?" King Kreon glanced away.
"Who knows?" he said. "Tyranny perhaps. Or he slighted some god—
who knows? It's none of our business." He closed his mouth. It became
a thin, white line, perspiring at the upper lip. "Who knows."
He shot a glance at Ipnolebes, but the old man's face
was vacant. His mind had wandered—a trick of Athena, at his back—
and Kreon pressed him no more. Ipnolebes excused himself,
mumbling of work, and the king released him, frowning slightly.
When the slave was gone, he stood on the balcony alone, thinking.
All around him, gods stood watching his mind work,
slyly disguised as crickets, spiders, a lone eagle
ringing slowly sunward, on Kreon's left.

                          Below,
Ipnolebes paused on the stairway, listening. A frail old woman,
slave from the south, was singing softly:

          "On ivory beds
          sprawling on divans,
          they dine on the tenderest lambs from the flock
          and stall-fattened veal;
          they bawl to the sound of the minstrel's harp
          and invent unheard-of instruments of music;
          they drink their wine by the bowlful, use
          the finest oil for anointing themselves;

and death they do not think of at all;
death they do not sing of at all.
But the sprawlers' revelry is over."

Without a word, Ipnolebes descended, thinking.

On a bridge in the palace gardens, Pyripta stood looking down
at fernlike seaweed, the wake of a swan, the blue-white pebbles
below. She stood till the water was still
and her reflection—pensive, silk-light hair falling over her bosom—
looked back at her. She seemed to be trying to read the face
as she would the face of a stranger. The face said nothing—as sweet
and meaningless as a warm spring day. She pouted, frowned,
experimented with a smile. She glanced away abruptly,
with a frightened look, alarmed by art. I hurried nearer,
picking my way through flowers. Aphrodite appeared beside her,
faintly visible on the bridge, like a golden haze, and touched
Pyripta's arm. The princess stared at the water once more
and sighed, shook back her hair. "I won't," she whispered. "Why must I?
Later! Please, gods, later! I need more time!" The goddess
moved her hand on Pyripta's hair. The girl looked down,
posing, as before. The flowers of the garden rimmed the pool
like a wreath of yellows and pinks. The swans moved lazily,
like words on the delicate surface of a too-calm dream. Above,
on the palace roof, a songbird whistled its warning to the sky,
the encroaching leaves: "Take care! Take care! Take care up there!"
As I raised my foot, stepping over a flower, the garden
vanished.

   I stood in the shadow of Jason's wall. There were vines,
the scent of black earth, old brick. I went to the open window,
cleaned my glasses on the sleeve of my coat and, standing on tiptoe,
peeked through the louvers. He was dressed to go out, standing at the mirror,
his back to Medeia, brushing his long black hair. She said:
"Don't go, Jason." He said nothing, brushing, his arm and shoulder
smooth, automatic as a lion's. He put down the brush and took
his cape from the slave. Except for his eyes, he seemed relaxed.
His eyes had blue-black glints like sparks.
But he swung the cape to his shoulders gently, graceful as a dancer.

"Jason," she whispered, "for the love of God, don't make me beg!"
He turned to the door. She paled. "Don't go," she said. "Don't go!"
She went past him, blocking the door, and her eyes were wild. "Jason!"
He moved her aside like a child and walked from the house. "Jason!"
she screamed, clinging to the jamb. He didn't look back. He walked
to the gate and through it. I hurried after him, amazed, stumbling,
trying to watch Medeia over my shoulder, where she stood
on the steps.
          "Jason, you're insane!" I hissed. I snatched at his arm.
My hand passed through his wrist. Ghosts, I remembered. Shadows.
I kept close to him, whispering. If Medeia had seen me, so could he,
if he'd use the right part of his mind. "I know the whole story!" I hissed,
"the fiercest, most horrible tragedy ever recorded! God's truth!"
I might as well have complained to the passing wind. We came
to the palace steps. There was a crowd gathering. He started up,
three steps at a bound, his cape flaring out behind. At the door
I caught a glimpse of the blond young slave Amekhenos.
Gone before Jason saw him.
          Then, from behind us in the street,
came a thin, blood-curdling wail. *"Jason!"* We stopped in our tracks.
The crowd shrank back. She stood with blood running down her cheeks,
the skin torn by her own nails. "Jason, I warn you,"
she called, and sank to her knees, stretched out her arms to him.
"By the sign of this blood, I warn you—Medeia, daughter of Aietes,
as mighty a king as has ever ruled on earth—come away!"
    He stared, shrinking. I was sick, so weak that my knees could barely
hold me. Her hair was beautiful—red-gold, shimmering with light,
too lovely for earth—but her face was torn and swollen, bleeding . . .
We looked away, all of us but Jason. At last he went down to her
and, gently, he took her hands. After a moment, he said,
firmly, but as if he were speaking to a child, "No, Medeia."
She searched his face, trembling, clinging to his hands. "Go home,"
he said. "I know you too well, Medeia. Not that your rage
and grief are lies. You feel what you feel. Nevertheless,
this once you can't have your way. If you could show what I do
in any way unjust or unlawful—if you could raise
the shadow of a logical objection, I'd change my course for you.
You cannot. Long as we've lived together, you were never my wife,
only the lady I've loved. There's a difference, in noble houses
with large responsibilities. For love of you

94

I fled my homeland, abandoned my throne, sharing the exile
your crimes earned. I was innocent myself—all Argos knew it;
no one more shocked than I when I learned of that monstrous feast.
Ask anyone here." He turned to the crowd, then to her again.
"Now, and partly for your sake, I mean to rebuild my power,
gain back part of what I've lost. Go home and wait for me."
She drew back her hands from his and, touching her lips, said nothing.
Jason too was silent now. He merely looked at her,
then went back up the steps and into the hall. At the doorway
Kreon nodded, wordless. Jason bowed. They went
to their places. The slaves brought dinner in, and soon the hall
was filled to the chine of the wide-ribbed roof with the whisper of eating,
the snarling of dogs over scraps, the hum of the sea-kings' talk.
Jason sat very still. Pyripta watched him. There were
no gods in sight, today. The servants watched like lepers,
moving without a sound between the trestle-tables.
I whispered, "Change your mind, Jason! It's not too late!"

When the time came, he told the story of Lemnos. Said:

"We couldn't know, as we rowed through dusk to that rocky coast,
the terrible things that had happened on Lemnos the year before—
the wrath of the goddess of love. (We might have guessed from the way
the surf crashed in on those shaded rocks, and the way it pulled back
with a groan and a long, dry gasp.)
                                    "There were now no men on the island;
murdered, every last one of them, by their wives—and all
their sons killed too, so that none might rise to avenge the crime.
For a long time the women of Lemnos had scorned Aphrodite
and thought her wiles and tricks beneath their dignity.
(So Medeia would tell me, long after, whose raven spies,
children of Hekate, keep all the past of the world in mind.)
They were not less wise than their men, the women of Lemnos said—
quicker, if anything, with their minds as with their hands. They would
not creep, stoop, cajole, flatter, run up and down
like slaves—sew half the night while their burly masters slept,
legs aspraddle, snoring, farting from wine, in big
soft beds. If women were weaker, was that some fault of their own?
They were human, as human as men, and they meant to be judged as human.
They declared war, held angry council. From this day forth

they'd crackle and cavil at each least hint of tyranny,
traduce each day all pillars, pylons, fenceposts, stocks
of trees, all shapes ophidian, all tripod forms;
inveigh against all dangling things, hurl malisons
on winds not shrill, all shapes not bulbous, torous, paggled
as the belly of a six-months bride. They would bend their masters' knees!
How reasonable it sounds! How just! So it seemed to them,
talking, thinking together when their men were away on raids.
They put on mannish clothes, cut their hair like men, took even
the rough, harsh speech they supposed sure proof of equality.
What could their husbands say? They could curse them, use male force
to whip their women to heel, but how could they answer them?
They accepted, in the end. They were, of course, the flaw in the plan.
They developed a strange, unruly passion for the captured girls
they'd brought from their raids in Thrace—soft concubines who'd not yet
seen their reasonable rights. Sly and hard-headed, cool,
no more likely than other women to blur their desires
(mix up sex and religion, say, as men can do),
they kissed—all girlish tenderness—the chests and arms
and fists they knew by instinct they had to tame. They praised
their lords' absurd ideas; they listened, dazzle-eyed—
secretly making lists—to grandly romantic trash:
bad poetry, stupid theology—altiloquent
designs in the empty air. They got their reward, as women
do for creeping, stooping, cajoling, flattering. They soon were
hauled off to bed. They handled it well, of course, those captives:
slaves eager to do anything—oh, anything!—
for the beautiful, glorious lord. When he was satisfied
and sleeping, they'd move their girlish hands on his buttocks and legs,
and play, all girlish tenderness, with his private parts.
So the men threw off their wives for the girls of Thrace. Ah, *then*
they knew, those women of Lemnos, what it was to be
a woman! They became as irrational as men, but fiercer than men—
unchecked by the foolish poetry, the stupid ideals,
of the more romantic part of the two-part beast. They killed
their husbands, their husbands' mistresses, and all their sons;
learned the truth of insane ideas: men's soft throats flowering
blood—quick flash of white, the bone, then streaming horror;
and whatever they thought at first—however they cringed, all shock
when first they watched the death convulsion no leopard or wolf

would tolerate, if he understood, but only man—
they learned wild joy in the unspeakable: became not human.
Only one old man escaped, King Thoas, father
of Hypsipyle. She spared him—set him adrift across
the sea, inside a chest. Young fishermen dragged him ashore
weeks later, numb and emaciated, at the isle of Oinoe.

    "They managed well, those Lemnian women,
ploughing, tending to their cattle, occasionally putting on
a suit of bronze. Nevertheless, they lived in terror
of the Thracians; again and again they'd cast a glance across
the gray intervening sea to be sure they weren't coming.

                                          "So when
they saw the *Argo* ploughing in toward shore (for all
they knew, the coulter of a ploughing Thracian fleet) they swiftly
put on the bronze of war and poured down, frantic and stumbling,
from the wooden gates of Myrine, shouting, 'Thracians! Thracians!'
It was a panicky rabble, speechless, impotent with fear, that streamed
to the beach.

          "I sent Aithalides and Euphemos
to meet them, treat for terms. Old Thoas' daughter agreed,
in curious alarm—daylight was spent—to grant us anchor
just offshore for the night. My heralds bowed, withdrew.

    "While the two reported, Lynkeus of the amazing eyes,
mad Idas' brother, looked with his predator's stare at the shore,
his sharp ears cocked, sidewhiskers quiet as a jungle cat's,
his dark hands steady on the *Argo*'s rail. His back was round
with closed-in thought and his eerily beastlike watchfulness.
He said, when they finished, "Jason, those people on the shore are women.
And those by the city wall, the same. And those by the trees."
I looked at him. We all did. "It's a whole damn island
of women," he said. Mad Idas, standing at his shoulder, grinned.

    "As soon as the sky was dark enough, I sent our heralds
back, and Lynkeus with them—the runner Euphemos
for quick report, Aithalides, the son of Hermes,
for his wide mind and his all-embracing memory,
gift of his father, a memory that never failed. They went
to a room where Lynkeus said he could see an assembly gathered.
He was right. It seemed the whole city was there.

                                      "Hypsipyle spoke,
who'd called the assembly together. She said, in the ravens' version

(briefer by nearly an hour than that of Aithalides):
'My friends, we must conciliate these foreigners by our
lavishness. Let us supply them at once with food,
good wine, young women, all they may dream of wanting with them
on the ship, and thus we'll make sure they don't press close to us
or know us too well—as they might if need should drive them to it.
Let these strangers mingle with us, and the dark news
of what happened here will fly through the world. It was a great crime,
and one not likely to endear us much to these men—or to others—
if they learn of it. You've heard what I say. If anyone here
believes she has a better plan, let her stand and offer it.'
    "Hypsipyle finished and took her seat once more in her father's
throne. Then her shrivelled nurse, sharp-eyed Polyxo rose,
an ancient woman tottering on withered feet and leaning
on a staff, but nonetheless determined to be heard. She made
her way to the center of the meeting place, raised her head
with a painful effort, and began:
                    " 'Hypsipyle's right. We must
accommodate these strangers. It is better to give by choice
than be robbed. —But that will be no guarantee
of future happiness. What if the Thracians attack us? What if
some other enemy appears? Such things occur!' She shook her finger,
bent like a hook. 'And they happen unannounced. Look how these came
today. One moment an empty sea, and the next—look out!
But even if heaven should spare us that great calamity,
there are many troubles far worse than war that you'll have to meet
as time goes on. When the older among us have all died off,
how are you childless younger women to face the miseries
of age? Will the oxen yoke themselves? Will they trudge to the fields
and drag the ploughshare off through the stubborn fallow? Think!
Will the farm dogs watch the seasons turning, sniffing the wind,
and know when it's harvest time?
                    " 'As for myself, though death
still shudders at sight of me, I think the coming year
will see me into my grave, dutifully buried before
the bad time comes. But I do advise you younger ones
to think. Dry wind like a claw scraping at the rocky hills
by the burying ground, a long slow file of toothless hags,
brittle as beetles, moaning, inching a casket along
in the dry, needling wind. . . . But salvation lies at your feet!

Entrust your homes, your cattle, your lovely city on the hill
to these visitors! Whatever their beauty or ugliness,
they're lovely beside old age, starvation, the silence at the end.'

"They listened, shocked. A few rose up and clapped; and then
on every side, the hall applauded Polyxo's speech.
Hypsipyle stood up again, ghost-white. 'Since you're all agreed,
I'll send a messenger to the ship at once.' She said to Iphinoe:
'Go, Iphinoe, and ask the captain of this expedition,
whoever, whatever the man may be, to come to my house;
and tell his men they may land their ship and come into town
as friends.' With that, the beautiful golden-haired daughter of Thoas
dismissed the meeting and set out in haste for home.

                                        "More swiftly
Euphemos came, racing over the water, to the *Argo,*
and so we were ready for the news Iphinoe brought.

                                        "Blue eyes
cast down, half-kneeling like a dancer, a slave, a suppliant,
she poured out her tale. I hardly listened to the words, wondering
at the clash of appearance and fact. She seemed more soft than ferns
at dawn, more sweet than a bower of herbs and gillyflowers,
clear and holy of mind as sunlit glodes. I stood
bemused, and heard her out. In the end, I said I'd come.
None spoke against it. We stood observing Iphinoe like men
in a trance: the night was silent, not a wave stirring. By the light
of the ship's torches she seemed a celestial vision of beauty
and innocence—and yet we knew—and we stared, numbed,
like a child who's discovered a spider in the fold of a rose. When the girl
was gone, receding like music toward that torchlit shore,
we gathered around Aithalides, who told what he'd seen
and heard, and we turned it over in our minds like a strange coin,
an arrowhead centuries old. And then I went to them.
I hardly knew myself what I meant to do. Avenge
the dead, perhaps. Yet how can a man set his mind to avenge
a crime he can hardly conceive, an act as baffling as the dreams
of camels?

                "Old Argus knew my thought, as usual.
He called me, frowning, and gave me a cloak as I started for town.
The man knew more than it's good for a man to know. The cloak
was crimson, bordered with curious designs that outshone the rising
sun. I remember the old man's look as he pointed them out.

Here the cyclops, hammering out the great thunderbolt
for Zeus, one ray still lacking, lying on the ground and spurting
flame. And here Antiope's sons, with the town of Thebes,
as yet unfortified. Zethos shouldered a mountain peak—
he seemed to find it heavy work—and Amphion walked
behind, singing to his lyre; a boulder twice his size
came trundling after him. Here came Aphrodite, wielding
Ares' formidable shield. It mirrored her breasts. And here
a woodland pasturage, with oxen grazing—in a grove nearby,
herdsmen fighting off raiders. The trees were wet with blood.
And here stood Phrixos with the golden ram, the huge beast speaking,
Phrixos listening, and the whole weird scene so artfully wrought
that all who looked at it hushed for a moment, listening too,
straining for the creature's words. Who knows what all this means?
Argus wove it. Who knows if he knew himself?
                                        "I wore
the mantle, crossing to the city, and the water glowed blood-red
beside me. When I passed through the gates the women came flocking around me,
reddened, demonic in the mantle's glow. They sighed and smiled
and held out flowers that gleamed, as eerie as gardens lit
by burning walls. I kept my eyes on the ground and walked
till I came to Hypsipyle's palace. The double doors with close-fit
panels flew open—panelling of cypress, the beams of the palace
cedar, and all around me the scent of nard and saffron,
calamus and cinnamon, and incense-bearing trees, Oriental
myrrh and aloes—and Iphinoe led me quickly through
the hall and brought me to a polished chair where I sat and faced
the queen. In blood-red stillness that sweet face looked at me.
For all the old artificer's magic, her cheeks were as fair
between their pendants—and her neck in the cup of her necklaces—
as young doves hiding in the clefts of a rock, the coverts of a cliff.
'My lord,' she said, more soft, more gentle than a child, 'why have
you stayed so long outside our city—a city that has lost
its men? They have gone to the mainland to plough the fields of Thrace.'
She kept back tears. 'I'll tell you the truth. In my father's time
they raided there, bringing booty home, and women too.
But cruel and childlike Aphrodite for a long time
had kept her eye on them, and at last she struck. She made
their hearts furnaces, howling, raging with lust—burned out
their wits. They lost all sense of right and wrong, conceived

a loathing for their wedded wives: turned them out of doors and took
their captives into their beds. For a long time we endured it,
hoping their lust would die—but its heat increased. No father
cared at all for his daughter; a cruel step-mother could kill
the girl-child in his sight, and the father would laugh. No brother
cared for his sister as he ought or defended his mother. At last,
at the dark whisper of a god, we resolved to act. One day
when the men sailed home from raiding, we closed our gates against them,
hoping to drive them elsewhere, whores and all. They fought us.'
She paused, lowering her eyes, as though the memory
were even now a source of pain and shame. 'Some died,'
she said, 'some both on their side and on ours. In the end,
they begged from us our male children and left, and so
went back with their women to Thrace. And there they are now, scratching
a livelihood from its snowy fields.' She paused again,
eyes turned aside, maidenly. 'Because of that,
noble stranger, I invite you to stay and settle with us.
All that women can do for men we'll do for you,
beyond your wildest hopes. And you yourself, captain—
robed like a king—my father's sceptre shall be yours alone,
and all you say shall be heard as law on Lemnos.' She raised
her shy eyes, gently pleading, like a girl who's come to her beloved
and stands now naked and trembling, awaiting her loved one's hands,
fearing he'll scoff at her gift as shameful. What could I say?
I could easily think, in the cloak's unnatural light, that all
her words were lies. Yet how could I know? Old Argus wove
the cloth. There was magic in it, the magic of Athena, queen
of cities, builder of the *Argo*. And what did Athena care
for Hypsipyle, the quiet power a man might gain
as king on that lonely island, guarding its old, deep-grounded
walls, defending its women, right or wrong? As for all
Aithalides saw and heard, should I trust the evidence
of another's fallible senses and not my own? A case of
desperate rationalizing, you may say. I grant it.
But I think no man but a fool would have dared to avenge those deaths
with no more case for Hypsipyle's guilt than that. She was
no ordinary beauty, moreover—whatever her sins.
She was fair as the moon, resplendent as the sun; in her gem-rich robes
as dazzling as an army with all its banners flying.
                                        "I rose.

'We need your help, Hypsipyle,' I said, 'and all you can give us.
But the sovereignty I must leave to you—though not from indifference.
An urgent calling forces me on. I'll talk with my men
and come once more to your palace.' I stretched my hand to her
and she took it. A touch like fire. I quickly turned and left,
and countless young girls ran to me, dancing around me, smiling,
kissing my hands, my cheeks, my clothes. They knew what it was
to be women, manless for a year and more. Before I reached
the shore, they were there before me with smooth-running wagons laden
with gifts. They did not find it hard to bring my Argonauts
home with them. Queen Aphrodite, changeable
as summer wind, was in every blade of grass; she shone
in every rock and tree. And so I spent the night
with Hypsipyle, my truncheon under the pillow. And spent
the next night too, and the next. And I could find no sign
of wickedness in those dove-soft eyes, no trace of a lie
on her apple-scented lips. Nor could my men find evil
hidden in the women who led them gently, shyly, home
to bed. They were not racked by nightmares, prodded and pinched
by guilt, hounded by furies. If they were alarmed at times
by images, were their husbands not alarmed before them,
those who'd raided and bloodied the fields of Thrace? Do innocent
sheep not sometimes cringe, ambushed by memory, the same as
wolves?
       "As I lay beside her one night, my left hand under
her head, my right embracing her, she whispered, 'Jason,
are men capable of love?' I glanced at her eyes. They seemed
a child's eyes, baffled and lonely, but far more beautiful
than any ordinary child's. 'Are women?' I asked. Her eyes
formed tears—whether false or honest tears, who knows? I listened.
The night outside our window fell forever, a void.
I heard the dark sea pounding on the land, the dark wind shaking
trees, and I fell into a dream of wheeling birds, old sea-beasts,
monsters crawling on the land on short, dark legs. If we were
centaurs landed on Lemnos, violent murderers,
still I'd be here in her arms, and might be fond of her.
And Thoas' daughter would move her hand on my wiry mane,
my gift to her coiled in her womb. When hot Aphrodite strikes,
sanity shifts to loblogic. My nightmare turned
to numbers bumping in space like rocks in a vortex. I sat up,

staring. She touched my cheek. We slept again, and again
at dawn the fire awoke in me and I took her in my arms
and thought her filled with light. And still the old gray waves
crashed on the rocks, and the rocks took them, hurled them away again,
took them again; and the ghost-filled wind moved through stiff branches,
howled in the battlements, walkways, spindrift parapets,
moon-bruised stone escarpments sinking in tiers to the sea . . .
falling endlessly, hopelessly . . . My mind was a nest
of snakes. There was nothing to avenge, nor was I, in any case,
keeper of Lemnos' dead. Though the very earth cried out,
voice of their blood, for vengeance (the earth did not cry out),
how could all that be my affair? Search where I might,
I saw no certain good, no certain evil, therefore
nothing I dared to attack. It was not that I doubted their guilt,
ultimately. But all the universe howls for freedom,
strikes at the tyrant when he turns his back. Who dares condemn
the goaded bull when, flanks torn, bleeding, heavy of heart,
he sees his moment and, bellowing, charges the farmer's son?
We lead him away to the slaughterhouse with prods of bronze,
twisting the ring in his nose till the foam runs pink; for once
he's tasted freedom, he's dangerous, useless. And so it was
with the Lemnian women. How could they love with a pure heart now,
how put on a contrition devoid of intrinsicate clauses,
secret reservations? And how could we men demand it of them?
What I mean has nothing to do with mastery. Love was dead
on the sad isle of Lemnos. Or so it seemed to me—seemed
to all of us, those who were there. Old Argus waited on the ship
with Herakles. Those two had refused to come with us,
one too wise, the other too stiffly ignorant. So
we stayed. Day followed day, and still we did not sail.
    "That was no pleasant time for Hera, nursing her grudge,
waiting for Pelias to pay for the times he'd slighted her.
She troubled my chest with restlessness, caused me to gaze
moodily out at the window, peer through the lattice, pace
by the sea, debating, stirred by I knew not what. Nothing
made sense. Why fight for a share in the kingdom with Pelias, when here
I was king alone, for whatever it was worth? Why risk Aietes'
rage for a hank of wool when here I had all the warmth
of Hypsipyle—for what it was worth? What was anything worth?
No doubt she made life on Olympos hard enough, that queen.

When her patience wore out, she came in the shape of a lizard, a spider,
a bird—who knows?—and whispered dreams into Herakles' head
where he slept, sullen, on the ship, held back by the rest of us.
    "Then Herakles spoke. Said stupid words, great bloated mushrooms—
Honor, Loyalty, Lofty Mission, Cowardice, Fame—
grand assumptions of his lame-brained, muscular soul. As if
the universe had honor in it, or loyalty,
or lofty mission because, in the mindless knee-bends, push-ups,
hammer-throws of his innocence, he believed in them.
We could not look him in the eye or give him answer. He had
the power to take off our heads as children tear off branches
in a nut orchard, if he chose to think that 'honorable.'
Was I willing to die for Hypsipyle? Would she for me?
You've lived too long, no doubt, when you've learned that time takes care
of grief. We were young, but many had lived too long. So that
we said, rational as curled, dry leaves in an angry wind,
we'd go. And prepared our gear.
                            "When the women got word of it
they came down running, and swarmed around us like bees that pour
from the rocky hive when the meadows are jewelled with dew and the lilies
are bloated with all bees need. Hypsipyle took my hands
in hers and said, 'Go then, Jason. Do what you must.
Return when you've captured the fleece. The throne will be waiting for you,
and I will be waiting, standing summer and winter on the wall,
watching, surviving on hope. Believe in my love, Jason.
Set my love like a seal on your heart, more firm than death.
Swear you'll return.' I said I would. She didn't believe it,
nor did I believe she'd wait. We kissed. 'The gods be with you,'
I said. She studied my face. 'Don't speak of the gods,' she said.
'Be true to me.' She guided my hand to her breast. 'Remember!'
    "And so we sailed. My gentle cousin Akastos wept
for fair Iphinoe—they were both virgins when we'd first arrived.
'I'll love her till the day I die,' he said. 'Listen to me, Jason.
I see the defeat in your eyes. They say what Idas says:
God is a spider. But I say, No! Beware such thoughts!
God is what happens when a man and woman in love grow selfless,
or a man feels grief for his friend's despair, or his cousin's—grieves
as I do for you.' He turned his head, embarrassed by tears,
and Phlias the mute, Dionysos' son, reached out and touched him.
'I'm only a man. I can't undo all the evils of the world

or answer the questions of the staring Sphinx who sits, stone calm,
indifferent to time and place, his kingly head beyond
concern for the love and hate that his lional chest can't feel.
I can't undo your scorn for words, whether Herakles' words
or mine. But I can say this, and be sure: I'll love Iphinoe
and swear that my gift is by no means uncommon, as you may learn
by proof of my love for you. Scorn on, if scorn gives comfort.'
I understood well enough his depth of devotion. I felt
the same for him. How could I not? Those violent eyes,
that scrawny frame in which, in plain opposition to reason,
he'd stand up to giants, God knew. And be slaughtered.
                                                    "I let it pass,
watching the sea-jaws snap at our driving oars. So Lemnos
sank below the horizon and, little by little, sank from
mind. The *Argo* was silent. Tiphys watched the prow,
steering through rocks like teeth. Above, no two clouds touched.
The sky was a sepulchre. It did not seem to me, that day,
that gods looked down on us, applauding. No one spoke. We sailed.
Ankaios said—huge boy in a bearskin—'Who can say
what his fate may bring if he keeps his courage strong?' I laughed.
Akastos' jaw went tight. I understood, understood."

    Jason paused, frowning. He decided to say no more.
So the day went, by Jason's gift, to Paidoboron,
mournful, black-bearded guest from the North. And yet the day went
to Jason, too. From him those gloomy sayings came,
sayings darker, I thought, than any Paidoboron spoke.
Kreon said nothing when the tale was done, but stared at his hands
on the table, looking old, soul-weary, as if he'd been there.
As Jason rose, excusing himself to go home—it was late—
the king stopped him. "You've given us much to think about,
as usual. It's a tale terrible enough, God knows.
It's filled my mind with shadows, unpleasant memories.
My philosophy's been, perhaps—" he paused, "—too sanguine." He looked
at Pyripta. Her gentle eyes were shining, brimming with tears
for Lemnos' queen. She had not missed, I thought, what Jason
meant by that talk of betrayal. Were they not now asking the same
of him—betrayal of Medeia? And was he not toying with it?
"Consider, Pyripta!" the tale cried out. But she was a child,
and the demand strange. It came to me that she was beautiful.

Not handsomely formed, like Medeia, and not voluptuous,
but beautiful nevertheless—a beauty of meaning, like a common
hill-shrine, crudely carved, to the gentlest, wisest of gods,
Apollo, avenger of wrongs. The king said, glancing up,
"You'll return and tell us more? We'd be sorry to be left in this mood."
He said nothing, I noticed, of Jason's staying in the palace, this time.
Jason was looking at the princess, seeing her as I had seen her.
No wonder, I thought, if he longed to escape from Medeia's stern eyes
to those—unjudging, filled with innocent compassion. "If you wish,"
he said. The old king squeezed his hand. Pyripta smiled.
"Come early tomorrow," she said. She seemed surprised that she'd spoken.
    That morning, seven of the sea-kings made small trades—rich ikons,
jewels and tapestries—and left. The omens were bad.

                                                    Medeia
naked on her bed—old Agapetika beside her—stared
at nothing. For a moment, like Jason, I thought she was dead. The slave
shook her head, too grieved for speech. He called a physician.
The doctor examined her, listened to her heart, looked solemn. She would
be well, he said, though the lady might lie in this deathlike carus
for days—perhaps three or four, perhaps a week. He saw
her face but did not inquire concerning the scratches. Jason
closed the door on her softly, going to his sons. He took them
from the old man's care and held them a moment. Then they went out
and walked in the early morning air, though he hadn't yet slept. I sat
beside her, touching her hand, watching the shadows of the garden
travel across her face. Her slave had cleaned the wounds.
They'd leave no scars. Her scars were deeper. Poor innocent!
My hands moved through the cloth when I tried to cover her.

    Kreon, looking at the city, showed his age. His fingers
shook. "The game has changed," he said. Ipnolebes—standing
bent, morose, beside him—peered into memories: tongues
of flame exploring curtains, the silent collapse of beams,
hurrying men in armor, old women screaming, their shrieks
soundless in the roar of fire. (I saw what Ipnolebes saw—
trick of the dead-eyed moon-goddess. "End it, my lord," he said.
But Kreon frowned. "The gods will see to the end when it's time.
Our man has begun a voyage on what he took to be
familiar seas, and found the world transformed. By chance—

the accident of an angry woman, a scene on the street—
Athena's ship is transmogrified, and all of us with it.
Get off if you can! The pilot's eyes have changed; the world
he sailed, all childish bravura, has grown more dark. Shall we
pretend that his darkened seas are a harmless phantasy?
I don't much care for nightmare-ships. No more than you do.
But I do not think it wise to flee toward happier dreams,
singing in the dark, my eyes clenched shut, if the nightmare world
is real. Somewhere ahead of us, the throne of Corinth
waits for her king's successor—law or chaos. Towns
are not preserved, I fear, by childish optimism.
Alas, my friend, he's turned the *Argo*'s prow to the void.
We'll watch and wait, follow him into the darkness and through it."
    So the old king spoke, nodding to himself. Then went
to bed. Ipnolebes sighed, went down to his own small couch.
"Hopeless," I whispered, bending close to the old slave's ear,
for surely he, at least, had the wits to hear me. "Darkness
has no other side. Turn back in time!" The slave
slept on, snoring. I stared at the hairy nostrils, peeked
at the blackness beyond the fallen walls of teeth, then stepped back,
shocked. There was fire in his mouth: the screams of women and children.
"Goddess! Goddess!" I whispered. But the walls of the dream were sealed,
dark, deep-grounded as birth and death. I heard their laughter,
dry and eternal as the wind. No trace of hope.

8

He said:
"Faith wasn't our business. Herakles' business, maybe;
sailing the cool, treacherous seas of the barbarians.
Or faith was Orpheus' business—singing, picking at his lyre,
conversing with winds and rain.
                              "We beached at Samothrace,
island of Elektra, Atlas' child, where Kadmos of Thebes
first glimpsed his faultless wife. The stop was Orpheus' idea.
If we took the initiation, learned the secret rites,
we might sail on to Kolchis with greater confidence,
'sure of our ground,' he said. I smiled. But gave the order.
I knew well enough what uncertainty he had in mind,
on my back the sky-blue cape from Lemnos' queen, a proof
of undying love, she said; and all around me on the *Argo*,
slaves of Herakles' strength, if not of his idiot ideas;
betrayers, as I was myself, of vows of faithfulness.
Trust was dead on the *Argo,* though no one spoke of it.
We had at least our manners . . . perhaps mere mutual compassion.
    "We glided in where the water was dark, reflecting trees,
the steering-oar turning in Tiphys' hands like a part of himself,
the rowers automatic, the laws of our nautical art in their blood.
And so came in to our mooring place, where vestal virgins
waited in the ancient attire, and palsied, white-robed priests
stood with their arms uplifted, figures like stone. We waded
in, and told them our wish. They bowed, then moved, formulaic
as antique songs, to the temple. And so that night we saw
the mysteries. Impressive, of course. I watched, went through
the motions. Maybe, as the priests pretended, the land had mysterious

powers; and maybe not. All the same to me. Sly magic,
communion with gods—it made no difference. Tell me the fire
that bursts, sudden and astounding, in the huge dark limbs of an oak,
lighting the ground for a mile, is some god visiting us,
and I answer, 'Welcome, visitor! Have some meat!' Politely.
What's it to me if the gods fly to earth, take nests in trees?
Black Idas scornfully lifted his middle finger to them,
daring their rage. Not I. I wished the gods no ill.
No more than I wished the grass any ill, or passing salamanders.
Herakles pressed his forehead to the ground and wept, vast shoulders
swelling with power, a gift of the holy visitor, he thought.
I wished him well, though I might have suggested to the hero, if I liked,
that terror can trigger mysterious juices in the fleeing deer,
and the scent of blood makes lions unnaturally strong. More tricks
of chemistry. But live and let live. Idmon and Mopsos,
the *Argo*'s seers, were respectful. Professional courtesy, maybe;
or maybe the real thing. Of no importance. Orpheus
watched like a hawk. As for myself, I made the intruder
welcome, since he was there, if he was. I might have been happy
to learn the principles of faith between men—husbands and wives,
fellow adventurers—or the rules of faith between one man's mind
and heart, if any such rules exist. I'd been, all my life,
on a mission not of my own choosing (the fleece no more
than an instance), a mission I was powerless to choose against. Such rules
would perhaps have been of interest. But they did not teach them there.
Elsewhere, perhaps. I'll leave it to you to judge. We learned,
there, that priests can do strange things; that worshippers have
a certain stance, expressions, gestures submissive to reason's
analysis—as the worshipped is not. We learned what we knew:
politeness to gods is best. Then sailed on, over the gulf
of Melas, the land of the Thracians portside, Imbros north,
to starboard.
        "We reached the foreland of the Khersonese,
where we met strong wind from the south. We set our sails to it
and entered the current of the Hellespont. By dawn we'd left
the northern sea; by nightfall the *Argo* was coasting in the straits,
with the land of Ida on our right; before the next day's dawn,
we'd left Hellespont behind. And so we came to the land
of Kyzikos, King of the Doliones.
                "Kyzikos had learned,

by the sortilege of a local seer, that someday a band
of adventurers would land, and if not met kindly, would leave
his city on fire, the best of his soldiers dead. He was not
a friendly man—his dark eyes snapped like embers breaking—
a man in no mood, when we landed, to waste his time on us.
He was newly married that day to the beautiful and gentle Kleite,
daughter of Percosian Merops, to whom he'd paid a dowry
fit for the child of a goddess. Nevertheless, when word
of our landing came, he left his wife in the bridal chamber,
mournfully gazing in her mirror, pouting—baffled, no doubt,
that the man cared more for strangers' talk than for all her art,
all the labor of her tutors. But the young king bore in mind
the words of his seer, and so came down, all labored smiles,
and after he learned what our business was, he offered his house and
servants and begged us to row in farther, moor near town.
From his personal cellar he brought us magnificent wine, and from
his own vast herds, fat lambs, the tenderest of weanlings, plump
and sweet with their mothers' milk. We went up to dinner with him.
    "I asked, as we ate with him: 'Tell us, Kyzikos: what will we meet
that we ought to be ready for, north of here? What strange peoples
live between here and Kolchis, tilling the fields, or hunting?'
The handsome young king thought, then said: 'I can tell you of all
my neighbors' cities, and tell you of the whole Propontic Gulf;
beyond that, nothing.' He glanced at his seer. 'Your crew should be warned
of one rough gang especially—the people who keep
Bear Mountain, as we call it here, the wooded, rocky rise
at the tip of our own island. We'd've had hard going with them,
living so close, if Poseidon weren't a shield between us,
father of our line. They're a strange people, lawless, blood-thirsty—
true barbarians; nothing at all like us, believe me!
They no more understand our civilized laws of hospitality
than cows know how to fly. Great earthborn
monsters, amazing to look at. Each of the beasts is equipped
with six great arms, two springing from his shoulders, four below—
limbs coming out of their hairy, prodigious flanks. They look
like spiders, in a way, but their bug-eyed heads are the heads of men,
and their hands, except for the hair, are constructed like human hands.
Their penises are long and double, and the cullions hang
like barnacles on a ship just beached, dark tumorous growths.
Ravenous feeding and raping are all those monsters know.

Stay clear of them, that's my advice. No god ever talks
to that fierce crowd; no priest advises their violent hearts
to gentleness, respect for what the gods love.'

       "I pressed him,
asking what lay still further north. He told me all
he knew. At last, thanking Kyzikos a thousand times
for his kindness, we went to our beds. I saw him speaking with his seer,
smiling happily. We were, the seer was telling him,
the ones. Or so I found later.

     "In the morning, I sent six men
to climb to the higher ground, in the hope of learning more
of the waters we'd soon be crossing. I brought the *Argo* round,
edging the shore of the island, heading north, to meet them.
 "We'd badly underestimated the earthborn savages.
Watchful as they were, my men didn't see them sneaking around
from the far side of the mountain, slipping through the trees like insects,
and then suddenly hurtling away down the slope like pinwheels,
arm under arm, crashing like boulders through the brush. They reached
the wide harbor and, working like lightning, began to wall up
its mouth with stones, penning my men up like cows. Luckily,
Herakles was there with the six. He snatched out arrows,
bent back his recurved bow and, fast as a man could count,
brought down seven monsters. At once, the others turned,
hurling their jagged rocks, a hundred at a time. He fell,
and their huge rocks piled around him like a Keltic tomb. Ankaios,
giant boy, gave a wail, a bawl like a baby's, and ran
to help. Then almost as fast as they fell, he snatched up the rocks
that buried Herakles, and hurled them back, heaving them wildly.
We fled in terror for the open sea as the great stones came,
tumbling slowly like elephants driven off a cliff, making
a rumbling sound as they passed us, inches from our sails. Then Koronos,
son of Kaineos whom the centaurs could not kill, ran down
and helped Ankaios, weaker than the boy but cooler, saner.
And now the rest got their spirits back—the mighty brothers
Telamon and Peleus got arrows in their bows,
and Butes' spear that never missed struck down the monsters'
chief. The monsters charged them with all their fury, and more
than once; but the brutes were done for, squealing like apes gone mad,
pissing and shitting as they died. On our side, we hadn't lost
a man—by no means Herakles! When they rolled the stones

from his face they found him grumbling, angry that his tooth was chipped.
We on the *Argo* rowed in.
                              "When the long timbers for a ship
have been hewed by the woodsman's axe and laid out in rows on the beach
and lie there soaking till they're ready to receive the bolts, and the carpenters
move among them, checking them, nodding with cool satisfaction,
dropping a comment from time to time on the beauty of the thing,
the beauty that only a craftsman can understand—no art,
no way of life seems finer; and so it was with us
that day as we walked the beach, studying the fallen monsters,
stretched out, roughly in rows, on the gray stone beach. Some sprawled
in a mass, with their limbs on shore and their heads and chests in the sea;
some lay the other way round. We observed how the arrows had struck,
how heads had been crushed, how this one had made the mistake of running,
how that one had stood at the wrong time, and this one, stupidly,
had pulled the spearshaft out and had needlessly bled to death.
Then, arm in arm, like men charged with some lofty purpose,
proud of our art, and rightly, we boarded the ship. Behind us
vultures settled on the corpses—came down softly, neatly,
dropping like a hushed black snowfall out of the ironwood trees.
    "We loosed the hawsers of the ship, caught the breeze, and forged ahead
through choppy waves. We sailed all day. At dusk, the wind
died down, then veered against us, freshened to a gale, and sent us
scudding back where we came from, toward our hospitable friends
the Doliones. We came to an island in the dark and landed,
hastily casting our hawsers around high stones. Not a man
on all the *Argo* guessed that this was the very land
we'd left, the isle of Kyzikos. As for the bridegroom-king,
he leaped from his bed at the alarum and rushed to the shore with his men,
bronze-suited, armed; and, thinking his troubles were past—the threat
the seer had warned him of—he struck at once, believing us
raiders—Macrians, maybe—but in any event, unwelcome,
flotsam jacked from the sea. We met, and the clash of our implements
boomed in the dark, leaped like the roar when a forest fire
pounces on brushwood, blowing its bits sky-high. We pushed them
back, back, back, to the walls of the city—Herakles
and Ankaios moving like great black towers, blocking out stars
ahead of us, the rest of us following like the widening belly
of a ship, our swords and spears flashing out in the dark like oars.
They fled through the gates and heaved against them, straining to close them.

We lashed torches to our spears and hurled. The city went up
like oil. Ye gods but we were good at it! Mad Idas shrieked,
dancing with a female corpse. Leodokos, strong as a bull,
pushed in the palace doors and we saw white fire inside.
And then one struck at my left, and I whirled, and even as the spear
plunged in, I saw his face, his helmet fallen away:
Kyzikos! He sank without a word, and when his muscles jerked
and his head tipped up, there was sand in his open eyes. Too late
for shamed explanations now; too late to consider again
the warning of the seer! He'd had his span: one more bird caught
in the wide, indifferent net. Nor was he the only one.
Herakles killed, among lesser men, brave Telekles and
Megabrontes; Akastos killed Sphodris; and Peleus' spear
brought down Gephyros and Zelos; Telamon brought down Basileus;
Idas killed Promeus, and Klytius, Hyakinthos, called
the Good. And there were more—the men Polydeukes killed,
fighting with his fists when his spear had snapped, and the men who were killed
by Kastor, and those that the boy Ankaios killed. There are stones
on the island, marked with their names—brave men known far and wide
for skill, unfailing courage.
                        "So the battle ended, unholy
error. We hurried through fire and smoke, helping the people,
moving them up to the hills, above where the city burned.
For three days after that we wept with the Doliones,
wailing for the king, his young queen, and their beautiful palace—
crumbling walls, charred beams. Then built him a splendid cairn
that moaned in the wind like a widow sick with sorrow, made
by Argus' subtle craft. And we gave him funeral games
and all the noble old ceremonies that men hand down
from age to age—solemn marches as angular
as the priests' hats; dances darker and older than the hills;
poems to his virtue, the beauty of his queen.
                                    "For twelve days then
there was murderous weather—high winds, thunderstorms, soot-black rain,
the angry churning of the sea. We couldn't put out. At last
one night as I slept—my cousin Akastos standing watch,
reasoning out, full of anguish, the whole idea of war,
its pros and cons (wringing his fingers, hammering the rail),
the old seer Mopsos watching and smiling—a halcyon
came down and, hovering above my head, announced, in its piping

voice, the end of the gales. Old Mopsos heard it all
and came to me. He woke me and said: 'My lord, you must climb
this holy peak and propitiate Hera, Mother of the Gods,
and then these gales will cease. So I've learned from a halcyon:
the seabird hovered above you as you slept and, lo! so it spoke!
The queen of gods rules all this earth, the sea, and snow-capped
Olympos, home of the gods. Rise up and obey her! Be quick!'
   "With one eye part way open, I studied the graybeard loon.
His eyewhites glistened, as sickly pale as the albumen
of an egg, and his heavy lips, half hidden in beard and moustache,
shook. He was serious, I saw. I rubbed my eyes with my fists,
laboring up out of dreams. Then, seeing he gave me no choice,
I leaped up, feigning belief, and I hurried from cot to cot,
waking the others, rolling my eyes as seemed proper, telling
the news, how Mopsos had saved us, he and a halcyon.
None of them doubted. Mopsos nodded as I told them the story,
backing up all I said. And so, within that hour,
we started work. The younger of the men led oxen out
from the stalls and began to drive them up the steep rock path
to the top of Bear Mountain (the spider people asleep at its foot,
sending skyward the unpleasant scent of sixteen-day-old
death). The others loosed the *Argo*'s hawsers from the rock
and rowed to the corpse-strewn harbor. Leaving four on watch,
they too climbed through the stench. It was dawn. From the summit you could see
the Macrian heights and the whole length of the Thracian coast:
it seemed you could reach out and touch it. You could see the entrance
          to the Bosporos
and the Mysian hills, and in the opposite direction the flowing waters
of Aisepos, and the city on the plain, Adrasteia.
                              "In the woods
stood a hundred-year-old vine with a massive, shaggy trunk,
withered to the roots. We chopped it down; then crafty Argus
hacked out a sacred image of the queen of gods, long gray hair
flying as he wheeled his axe. He skilfully shaped it, gray ears
cocked to the whisper of Athena. When he finished, we set it up
on a rocky eminence sheltered by dark, tall oaks, and made
an altar of stones nearby. Then, crowned with oakleaves (night
had fallen now, the dark storm howling around us), we
began the sacrificial rites. I poured libations out,
shouting to the goddess to send those flogging winds away.

Mopsos and Orpheus whispered. Then, at Orpheus' command,
the Argonauts, in all their armor, circled the fire
in a high-stepping dance, beating their shields with their swordhilts, drowning
the noise of the Doliones, far below us, still mourning
their king. More wildly than the storm mute Phlias danced, their leader.
Louder and louder their armor rang in the night, and the flam
of drums. I could hardly hear myself, yelling to Hera—much less
hear the howling of the winds, the howl of the mourners. Then—
strange business!—the trees began shedding their fruit, and the earth at our feet
magically put on a cloak of grass. Beasts left their lairs,
their burrows and thickets, and came to us wagging their tails. Nor was
that all. There had never been water—there was neither spring nor pool—
before that time on Bear Mountain. Now, though no one touched
a spade, a stream came gushing from the earth, a stream that flows
even now, called Jason's Well. And so, it seems, the goddess
heard us. We finished our rites with a feast—all this according
to ritual. By dawn, the wind had dropped. We could sail.
    "Old Mopsos said—we were standing in the woods alone, when the rest
had walked back down to the harbor—: 'My son, you did that well!
Never have I witnessed a more auspicious flush of signs!
Such miracles! Surely the goddess Hera loves you, boy!
Surely the crew of the *Argo* is in divinely favored
hands!' I bowed. He studied me, picking at his lip. He said,
eyes wicked, grinning in spite of himself. 'You're unimpressed.
Some trick, you imagine? You think the goddess of will (all praise
to her name) may not have been here with us?' Then I too smiled.
'We made a good deal of noise,' I said, and avoided his eyes;
'If I were a mountain, a stormy sky, and were shaken to the heart
by noise like that, I might do almost anything—goddess
or no goddess.' The old seer chuckled, crazy-eyed.
'Shrewd observation,' he whispered, bending close. 'Bravo!
All very well for a big ignoramus like Herakles
to shudder and shake at magic tricks. We know better, you and I!
Mopsos, king of all augurers, marching to his death—and for what?
And Jason, robbed of his Lemnian beauty, forced on a senseless,
pointless mission—abandoning his mother to ignominious
death, wasting his wonderful oratory ("Jason of the Golden
Tongue," as they say) outshouting cacophonous winds and drums:
pawn of the fates, murderer of friends that he meant no harm to,
weary wanderer in a faithless world (alas! lack-a-day!)—

no wonder if the racket that shakes Bear Mountain to her deepest stones,
the clatter that whisks away winds—has no faintest effect on him!
What has the son of Aison to do with the goddess of will?
—Jason, who's gazed into the Pit!' He cackled, delighted with himself.
'Are we brutes? Are we Balls on Inclined Planes? Are we mindless?—noseless
to the stink, everywhere, of Death? Let Philosophy set it down
that love is illusion, from which it follows, the gods are illusion,
which proves in turn that Mother Nature, who gives such joy,
is an old whore earning her keep!' Then suddenly: 'How do you feel?'
He stared, intense, his eyes so bright you'd have thought some demon
had entered him. *How do you feel?* I thought about it.
I felt like a man renewed. It was completely senseless.
How can the mind know all its mechanics and scoff at aid,
cold-blooded, and yet be aided? Nevertheless, I was
a man reborn. It was stupid. 'Me *too!*' old Mopsos said,
cackling, doing a dancestep, lunatic joy. 'We've had us
some *times!*' he said. 'We've done us some *deeds!!* Old Hera's *in* us!!!'
He paused. 'Whatever that may mean.' He winked, then aimed
his staff at a tree. It was filled, suddenly, with fire. He aimed
at a rock: it burst into feathers, screeched, flapped off. 'So much
for the quacks on the isle of Elektra!' he said. Then, sobering,
adjusting his robe and beads—the robe was none too clean—
he bowed, taking my arm. And so we returned to the ship,
all dignity, solemnly walking in step. And so sailed on.
Idmon, younger of the seers, came over to my rowing bench.
'Pick a halcyon, any halcyon,' he said. He winked.

"Faith wasn't our business. Herakles' business, maybe.
Sailing the cool, treacherous seas of the barbarians . . ."

9

"The wind dropped down to nothing. We rowed—'in a spirit of friendly
rivalry,' mad Idas said, rolling his eyes, making fun of God knew
what. Still, that's what we did, each trying to shame all others.
The windless air had smoothed out the waves on every side;
the sea was asleep. We rowed, driving the singing ship,
swift as a skate, by our own power. It seemed to us—
skimming the sea like a gull, a wingèd shark—not even
Poseidon's team, the horses with the whirlwind feet, could have overtaken us.
But later, when the sea was roughened by the winds that
blow down rivers in the afternoon, we wearied and relaxed,
and we left it to Herakles alone to haul us in, our muscles
shaky with exhaustion, throats burned raw by panting. Each stroke
he pulled sent a shudder through the ship. His sweat ran rivers down
his face and dripped from his nose and chin to his wide chest
and belly, tightened like a fist. Young Hylas beamed at him, watching,
and old Polyphemon, son of Eilatos, grinned, shaking
his hoary head, and swore that not even in his prime, when he fought
with the Lapithai, striking centaurs down with his bare fists,
had he or any other man pulled oars with the power
of Herakles. 'It looks as if by himself he'll bring us
to the Mysian coast!' the old man said. Herakles grinned,
or tried to, his face contorted with the effort of his rowing. But then,
as we passed within sight of the Rhydakos and the great barrow
of Aigaion, not far from Phrygia, Herakles—ploughing
enormous furrows in the choppy sea—snapped his long oar
and tumbled sideways, clear off the bench. He looked up, outraged,
the handle of the oar in his two hands, the paddle end sweeping
sternward, away out of sight. We laughed. He was angrier yet,

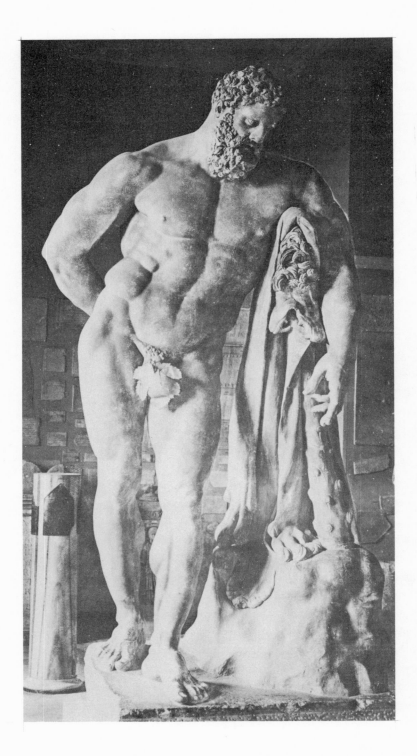

sitting up, speechless and glaring. We took up the rowing as best
we could, weary as we were. Even now he could hardly speak,
a man not used to idleness.
                              "We made our landfall.
It was dusk; the time of day when the ploughman, thinking of his supper,
reaches his home at last and, pausing at the door, looks down
at his hands, begrimed and barked, and curses the tyrant belly
that drives men to such work. We'd struck the Kianian coast,
close to Mount Arganthon and the famous estuary
of Kios. Luckily, tired as we were, the people greeted us
kindly, supplying our needs with sheep and wine. I sent
a few of the Argonauts to fetch dry wood, others to gather up
leaves from the fields and bring them to the camp for bedding; still others
I set to twirling firesticks; the rest of us filled
the winebowls, getting them ready for the usual sacrifice
to Apollo, god of landings.
                              "But Herakles, son of Zeus,
left us to work on the feast by ourselves and set out, alone—
attended by unseen ravens, the night's historians—
for the woods, anxious before all else to make himself an oar
to replace the one he'd broken. He wandered around till at last
he discovered a pine not burdened much with branches, and not
full grown—a pine like a slender young poplar in height and girth.
When he saw it would do, he laid his bow and quiver down,
took off his loinskin, and began by loosening the pine's hold
with blows of his bronze-studded club. Then he trusted to his own power.
Legs wide apart, one mighty shoulder pressed against the tree,
he seized the trunk low down with his hands and, pulling so hard
his temples bulged, face dark with blood, he tore up the pine
by the roots. It came up clods and all, like a ship's mast torn
from its stays, the wedges and pins coming with it, when sudden fashes
break without warning as Orion sets in anger. When he'd rested,
he picked it up, along with his bows and arrows, loinskin
and club, and started back, balancing the tree on his shoulder.
    "Meanwhile Hylas had gone off by himself with a bronze ewer,
looking for a hallowed spring where he might get drinking water
for the evening meal. Herakles himself had trained the boy
in the business of a squire. He'd had the boy since the day he struck down
Hylas' father, Theiodamas, king of the Dryopians.
Not one of Herakles' nobler moments. They were a lawless tribe,

the Dryopians, fornicating with one another's wives,
maddening themselves by the use of strange distillations and roots,
scornful of the gods. Unable to find any honest quarrel,
Herakles went to the king one day when he was ploughing, and began
an argument concerning an ox. One moment the king was laughing,
scornful and clever, enjoying the contest; the next he lay dead
in the fallow, his skull caved in. He felt no guilt about it,
Herakles. He took the child from the basket beside
the field and brought it up, made the boy his servant—trained him
as a shepherd trains up a loyal, unquestioning dog.

                                                  "Soon Hylas
discovered a spring, tracing the swift stream upward in the dark
past moonlit waterfalls, majestic trees—it was not the nearest
of the springs he might take water from; but he was young, after all,
and the night was beautiful, filled with the sound of cascades; immense
ramose old trees, motionless, brooding on themselves. He could stand
on the shelf of rock overlooking the dark, still pool and feel
he was the only boy on earth. To his left the torrent fell away,
swifter than you'd guess, swirling and rippling, murmuring something
that was almost words, and he must have felt that if he made his mind
quite still—more still than the dark—he might, any moment, know
what it said. In the forest beside him, bats were a-flutter; owls
swept silently down the wide avenues of trees; a stately
hart stood quiet as a sapling, watching. A fox crept, sniffing,
in the brush.

                    "There was in that spring a naiad. As Hylas drew near
she was just emerging from the water to sing her nightly praise
to Artemis. And there, with the full moon shining on him
from a cloudless sky, she saw him in all his radiant beauty
and gentleness. Her heart was flooded with desire; she had to
struggle to gather up her shattered wits. Now the moonling leaned
to the water to dip his ewer in, and as soon as the current
was rattling loudly in the ringing bronze, she threw her left arm
firmly around his neck and eagerly kissed his lips;
her right hand snatched his elbow, and down the poor boy plunged,
sinking with a cry into the current.

                                      "Old Polyphemon, son
of Eilatos, was not far off. He'd left our feast to search out
Herakles and help him home with his burden. When he heard
the cry he rushed in the direction of the spring like a hungry wolf

who hears the bleating of the distant flock and, in his suffering, races
down to them only to find that the shepherds have beaten him again,
the sheep are safe, enfolded. He stood on the bank and roared—
the reboation rang down the gorge from cliff to cliff
to the broadening holm below, where the river was wide and deep—
and he searched the night with his dim eyes; he prowled the dark woods,
groaning in distress, roaring again from time to time;
but there came no answer from the boy. He drew his heavy sword
and began to search through the place more widely, on the chance that Hylas
had fallen to some wild beast or been ambushed by savages.
If any were there, they'd have found that innocent easy prey.
Then, as he ran along the path brandishing his naked sword,
he came upon Herakles himself, hurrying homeward to the ship
through the darkness, the tree on his shoulder. Polyphemon knew him at once,
and he blurted out, gasping: 'My lord, I must bring you terrible news!
Hylas went out after water. He hasn't come back. I fear
cruel savages caught him, or beasts are tearing him apart. I heard him
cry.'
    "When Herakles heard those words the sweat poured down
his forehead and his dark blood boiled. In his fury, he threw down the pine
and rushed off, hardly aware where his feet were taking him.
As a bull, maddened by a gadfly's sting, comes up stampeding
from the water-meadows, hurls himself crazily, crashing into trees,
sometimes rushing on, stopped by nothing—the herd and herdsmen
forgotten now—and sometimes pausing to lift up his powerful
neck and bellow his pain, so Herakles ran, that night,
sometimes pausing to fill the distance with his ringing cry.
    "But now the morning star rose over the topmost peaks,
and with it there came a sailing breeze. Tiphys awakened us
and urged us to embark at once, take advantage of the wind. We scrambled
to the *Argo* in haste, pulled up the anchoring stones and hauled
the ropes astern, all swiftly in the shadowy dark. The wind
struck full; the sail bellied out; and soon we were far at sea,
beyond Poseidon's Cape.
                    "But then, at the hour when clear-eyed
dawn peers out of the east, and the paths stand plain, we saw
we'd left those three behind. No wonder if tempers flashed!
We'd abandoned the mightiest and bravest Argonaut of all! What could
I say? It was my mistake. I'd make plenty more, no doubt,
before this maniac mission had reached its end. —All this

for a shag of wool, the right to make dropsical courtiers bow,
smile with their age-old hypocrisy—or dark-lumped urchins
stretch for a cure of the king's evil. I tried to speak
but couldn't. I covered my face with my hands and wept. Mad Idas
chuckled. Catastrophe suited him, confirmed his ghastly
metaphysics.
            "But huge Telamon was rabid, uncle
of Akhilles—a man with a temper like that of the boy who sits
this moment, if what we hear is true, chewing his knuckles,
stubborn in his tent on the blood-slick plain of Troy. He said:
'Who are you fooling with your crocodile tears, sly son of Aison?
Nothing could suit you better than abandoning Herakles.
You planned the whole thing yourself, so that Herakles' fame in Hellas,
if we make it back, can never eclipse your own. But why waste
breath on you! We're turning around, and damned if I'm asking
permission of the man who helped with your stinking plot.' As he finished,
Telamon leaped at Tiphys' throat, his eyes ablaze
with anger. In a minute we'd all have been fighting our way back to Mysia,
forcing the ship through the rough sea, bucking a stiff and steady
wind. But then the sons of the North Wind, Zetes and Kalais,
shot quick as arrows between the two, and checked Telamon
with a stinging rebuke. 'Traitor! Mutineer!' Kalais shouted,
'Are *you* now seizing the command the Argonauts chose by vote?
Have northern seas made the *Argo* a ship of barbarians,
where loyalty's muscle, and keeping faith to old vows is a matter
of size?' Poor devils! A terrible punishment was coming to them
when Herakles learned that their words cut short our search. He killed
the North Wind's sons when they were returning home from the funeral games
for Pelias; and he made a barrow over them, and set up the famous
pillars, one of which sways whenever the North Wind
moves across it, struggling to dig up his sons. —But all that was
later.
            "The wind grew stronger, bringing up clouds; harsh sea-waves
hammered at the *Argo*, slammed at our gunwales till the magic beams
of Athena's ship were howling in fury at Poseidon. Orpheus
played, but the sea wouldn't hear. Then Idmon, younger of the seers,
stood up, wild-eyed, and clinging to the mast, he yelled out, 'Listen!'
We listened, and heard . . . God only knows. But as if in a dream
I saw a hand six paces broad rise up from the water
and grasp the *Argo*'s side, and the ship was still as a stone

despite the terrible wind, the churning, pitch-dark waves.
Then a voice heavier than thunder said: 'Hear me, Argonauts!
How dare ye, in proud defiance of Almighty Zeus,
purpose to carry fierce Herakles to Kolchis? His fate
assigns him Argos, where he's doomed to serve Eurystheus,
accomplishing for him twelve great tasks; and if, in the few
remaining, he happens to prevail, he shall go back to Zeus, his father.
Forget regret. As for Polyphemon, it is his fate
that he found a famous city among the Mysians, where the Kios
disembogues to the sea. He will die, when the gods see fit,
far from his home, in the broad land of the Khalybes.
As for Hylas, a nymph has taken him—too much in love
to ask permission of the bold and glorious Argonauts.'
So he spoke. The thunderheads rumbled as if in a laugh. The huge hand
sank. Dark water swirled around us, broke into foam,
tumbled past rails and coamings and hurled us on.
                                        "Then Telamon
came to me, weeping, and clutched my hand and kissed it, saying:
'Forgive me, lord. Do not be angry if in a foolish moment
I was blinded by love for dear friends lost. The immortal gods
know best, I hope. As for my offense, may it blow away
with the wind, and let us two, who have always been friends, be friends
again.'
          "I said nothing for a long time, the gods' laughter—
soft and dangerous as thunder on the open sea—still ringing
in my ears. It seemed that only I, of all the Argonauts,
or only Idas and I (I saw the madman's eyes),
fully understood that our grand mission was insanity—
and Akastos, perhaps, my cousin, Pelias' son. (He sat,
thin arms folded, staring full of sorrow at the grinding sea.)
It seemed to me that we alone had grasped the message
of the voice that came from the storm: *Love truth, love loyalty
so far as it suits our convenience.* I'd lose still more of them.
Such was the prophecy of the seers on the day we'd left. I'd watch them,
one by one, drift off, slip past recall. And if
I told them now it was all a mistake—those glory-seekers
gathered from all Akhaia (Telamon's brother Peleus,
waving proudly to his son, brought down to see us off
by Kheiron's wife, old Kheiron beaming, waving his two
huge arms; Hylas, beaming at his hero; Herakles rowing,

the muscles of his face like knots) . . . But I was still their captain,
the one will that resolves the many, even when the many
are mad. Sense may emerge at last, in human labors,
or may not. Meanwhile, there must be order, faith in the mission;
otherwise, deadly absurdity. I couldn't afford
mere humanness, the comfort of admitting confusion. I would
lose more that way. The eternal gods can afford whimsy.
Not us. Not I, as captain.
                    "I got control and said:
'Good Telamon, you did indeed insult me grievously
when you accused me, here before all these men, of wronging a loyal
friend. They cut to the quick, those heartless words of yours.
But I don't mean to nurse a grudge against you. It was not some flock
of sheep, some passel of worldly goods you were quarrelling about,
but a man, a beloved comrade of your own. I like to think
if occasion arose you'd stand for me against all other men
as boldly as you did for him.' Then, not too hastily,
like a man setting his rankling wrath aside, I embraced him.
He wept fiercely, like the child he was. And I too wept,
moved by the childlike heart in that towering warlord. Orpheus
studied his golden instrument, knowing my mind too well.
    "I learned later that all turned out in Mysia exactly
as the voice in the storm foretold. Polyphemon built his city;
Herakles resumed the labors he'd dropped in haste at the gates
of Mykenai—but before he left, he threatened to lay
all Mysia waste if the people failed to discover for him
what had become of poor Hylas, alive or dead. The Mysians
gave him the finest of their eldest sons as blood-bond hostages
and swore they'd continue the search.
                    "So much for the steadfast faith
of Herakles.
            "All that day, through the following night,
gale winds carried us on. When the time for daybreak came
there was no light. The wind died suddenly, as if at a sign
from Zeus. The sky went green. There was hardly air enough
to breathe. No man on board had the strength to row. We sat,
soaking in sweat, praying to all the gods we knew.
There were voices—sounds from the flat sea, from passing birds,
the greenness above us: *Where's Herakles? Where's Hylas?* We started,
prayed with our parched lips to the sixteen powers of the sea.

It was unjust—insane. 'What do they want of us?' I asked the seers.
'Where's Herakles? Where's Hylas?' they said, but in voices not
their own. We waited—how many days I couldn't say.
My cousin Akastos sat at my side, on watch, as if
to guard me from some grim foe outside, though he knew pretty well,
like Idas, like Phlias with his hand on my shoulder, where my enemy lurked.

"In that senseless calm, Orpheus remembered Dionysos: sang
how Zeus once put on his darker form, the dragon shape
of Zeus Katachthonios, called Hades, whom he himself expelled
from heaven, and went in that evil form to the shadow of Hera,
the serpent Demeter, deep in the earth, whom Hera hated
and who *was* Hera, though both of them had forgotten. In her
he planted Persephone, later his Underworld queen, by whom
Hades-Zeus had his son Dionysos, who was born many times,
always unlucky. At times he was torn apart by Titans,
at times by animals, at times by women gone crazy with wine
and lust. Once, leading virgins on a violent, drunken hunt,
he captured his quarry and, tearing it apart alive, discovered
in amazement and terror that the beast had a dark human face and horns,
that is, it was himself. It was he who invented wine,
crown of his father's creation—Dionysos' glory, and his ruin.

"Like Dionysos, the founder of Thebes was midnight black;
his queen was white as snow. Because their marriage was perfect,
Zeus came down to their daughter Semele in the guise of a man
and fed her the heart of his once-again-slain son. Queen Hera
saw that the girl was pregnant, and in jealous rage forced Zeus
to visit Semele in his true celestial form—a thunderbolt.
The girl was consumed, but not before Zeus had snatched his child,
whom he sewed into his thigh and carried to the time of delivery
and then returned to Kadmos and Queen Harmonia.

"Though the matchless couple had seemed so flawless they could never die,
in time they grew old and short of breath. Then the child Dionysos
cried out in sorrow to Zeus. The father of the gods came flashing
out of heaven, and in smoke and flames the two were transmogrified, changed
to a dragon and a monstrous snake, now rulers of the dead, chief thanes
of Dionysos. Thus began Hera's rage at Thebes, and the sorrows
of Kadmos' line: Oidipus weeping blood, Jokasta
hanged, Antigone buried alive.

                              "So Orpheus sang
the age-old riddle of things, and it seemed that the still sea listened.

127

"Then, for no reason, there was air again, and the sail bellied out,
and the ship began to move. Toward noon, we spotted land.

"As we beached the ship, a huge old man came out to us,
his arms folded on his chest, his gray beard brustling from his chin
like a bush. Without even bothering to ask what race we were
or what had brought us to his shore, he said: 'Listen, sailormen:
There's something you should know. We have customs here, in the farming
         country of the Bebrykes.
No foreigner daring to touch these shores
moves on, continuing his journey, until he's first put up
his fists to mine. I'm the greatest bully in the world, you'll say—
not without justification. I'm known, throughout these parts,
as Amykos, murderer of men. I've killed some ten of my neighbors,
and here I am, remorseless, waiting to kill, today,
one of you. It's a matter of custom, you see.' He shrugged as if
to say he too disliked it; and then, cocking his head,
wrinkling his wide, low brow, he said: 'The world's insane.
It used to fill me with anguish when I was a boy. I'd stare,
amazed, sick at heart, at the old, obscene stupidity—
the terrible objectness of things: sunrise, sunset;
high-tide, low-tide; summer, winter; generation, decay . . .
My youthful heart cried out for sense—some signpost, general
purpose—but whatever direction I looked,
the world was a bucket of worms: squirming, directionless—it was nauseating!'
He breathed deeply, remembering well how it was. He said:
'I resolved to die. I stopped eating. For a number of weeks
(I kept no count; why should I?) I spurned all food as if it were
dirt. And then one day I noticed I was eating. It seemed mere
accident: my mind had wandered, weakened by my fast,
and *pow!* there I was, eating. Absurd!
But after my first amazement, I saw the significance of it.
The universe had within it at least one principle:
survival! I leaped from my stool, half mad with joy, ran howling
out to the light from my cave, leading all my followers.
"I *exist!*" I bellowed. "Us *too!*" they bellowed. We ate like pigs.
But soon, alas, we were satiated. Though we rammed our fingers
down in our throats and regurgitated, still, the feast
was unappetizing. They looked up mournfully to me for help.
For three long weeks, in acute despair, I brooded on it.

And then, praise God!, it came to me. My own existence
was my first and only principle. Any further step
must be posited on that. I examined my history,
searched voraciously night and day for signs, some hint
of pattern. And then it came to me: I had killed four men
with my fists. Each one was an accident, a trifling event
lost, each time, in the buzzing, blooming confusion of events
that obfuscate common life. But now I remembered! I seized it!
Also, I seized up the follower dodling nearest to me—
meaningless dog-eyed anthropoid, source of calefactions,
frosts, random as time, poor worm-vague brute existent,
"friend" in the only sense we knew: I'd learned his name
by heart. By one magnificent act, I transmuted him.
I defined him: changed him from nothing-everything he was before
to purpose—inextricable end and means. I seized him, raised
my fists, and knocked him dead; and this time I *meant* it. No casual
synastry. My disciples were astonished, of course. But when
I explained to them, they fell, instantly, grovelling at my feet,
calling me Master, Prince of the World, All-seeing Lord.
On further thought, I came to an even higher perception:
As the soul, rightly considered, consists of several parts,
so does the state. It follows that what gives meaning and purpose
to the soul may also give meaning and purpose to the state. I needn't
describe the joy that filled my people on learning this latest
discovery of (if one may so express oneself)
their Philosopher King. To make a long story short, we began
a tradition—a custom, so to speak. Namely, no foreigner touching
these shores is allowed to leave without first putting up his fists
to mine. Regrettably, of course, since you're so young.' He shrugged.
'Who's ready?—Or, to shift to the general: Who's your sacrifice?'
He waited, beaming, pleased with himself—his enormous fists
on his hips. None of us spoke. We simply stared, dumbfounded,
the old man's crazy philosophy bouncing in our heads. At last
Polydeukes stepped forward, known as the king of all boxers.
It seems he'd taken Amykos' boasts as a personal affront.

   " 'Enough!' he said, eyes fierce. 'No more of your polysyllabic
shadowboxing. I am Polydeukes, known far and wide
for my mighty fists. You've stated your rules—your ridiculous law—
and I stand here ready, of my own free will, to meet them.'

                                                    "The king

frowned darkly, not out of fear of our brilliant Polydeukes,
but annoyed, it seemed, by some trifling verbal inaccuracy.
'Free will,' he said, and laughed. '*I* made the ridiculous rules,
not you. *I* have free will, not you. You bump against
my laws like a boulder bumping against a wall.'

         " 'Not so,'
Polydeukes said, voice calm. 'I choose to meet you. A man
may slide with the current of a mountain stream or swim with it.
There's a difference.' Old Amykos stammered in rage. In another minute
they'd have started in without gloves, unceremoniously,
but I intervened with persuasive words. They cooled their tempers,
and Amykos backed away, though even now he glared
at Polydeukes, his old eyes rolling like the eyes of a lion
who's hit by a spear when they hunt him in the mountains and, caring nothing
for the crowd of huntsmen hemming him in, he picks out the man
who wounded him and keeps his furious eyes on him alone.

   "Polydeukes was wearing a light and closely woven
cloak, the gift of his Lemnian wife. He laid it aside.
The fierce old man threw down his dark double mantle with its
snake-head clasps. They chose a place—a wide, flat field,
and the rest of us then sat down, two separate groups.

         "In looks,
no two could have been more opposite, the old man hunchbacked,
bristled and warted like an ogre's child, the younger straight
as a mast, bright down on his cheek. He seemed no more than a boy,
but in strength and spirit he was hardening up like a three-year-old bull.
He feinted a little, seeing if his arms were supple after all that
rowing, the long hot span in the calm. He was satisfied,
or if not, he kept it hidden. The old man watched him, leering,
eager to smash in his chest, draw blood. Then Amykos' steward,
a man by the name of Lykoreus, brought rawhide gloves,
thoroughly dried and toughened, and placed them between them, at their feet.

   " 'We'll cast no lots,' old Amykos said. 'I make you a present
of whichever pair you like. Bind them on your hands, and when
I've proved myself, tell all your friends—if you've still got a jaw—
how clever I am at cutting hides and . . . staining them.'

   "With a quiet smile and no answer, Polydeukes took the pair
at his feet. His brother Kastor and his old friend Talaos came
and bound the gauntlets on. The old man's friends did the same.

   "What can I say? It was absurd. They raised their heavy fists,

and the gibbous old man came leering, all confidence, drooling in his beard,
his eyes as wild as a wolf's, and went up on his toes like someone
felling an ox, and brought down his fist like a club. Polydeukes
stepped to the right, effortlessly, and landed one lightning
blow just over the old king's ear, smashing the bones
inside. The crazy old man looked startled. In a minute he was dead,
twitching and jerking in the wheat stubble. We stared. No match
at all! We hadn't even shouted yet—neither we nor they!
    "The Bebrykes gave a wail, an outraged howl at something
wider than just Polydeukes. They snatched up their spears,
their daggers and clubs, and rushed him as if to avenge themselves
on the whole ridiculous universe. We leaped up, drawing
our swords, running in to help. Kastor came down with his sword
so hard that the head of the man he hit fell down on the shoulders,
to the right and left. Polydeukes took a running jump
at the huge man called Itymoneus, and kicked him in the wind
and dropped him. The man died, jerking and trembling, in the dirt.
Then another came at him. Polydeukes struck him with his right,
above the left eyebrow, and tore the lid off, leaving the eyeball
bare. A man struck Talaos in the side—a minor wound—and Talaos turned on him,
sliced off his head like a blossom from a tender stem. Ankaios,
using the bearskin to shield his left arm, swung left and right
with his huge bronze axes, and the brothers Telamon and Peleus,
Leodokos and I behind them, jabbed through backs and bellies,
limbs and throats with our swords. They scattered like a swarm of bees
when the keeper smokes them from the hive. The remnants of the fight fled inward,
bleeding, spreading the news of their troubles. And that same hour
they found they had new and even worse troubles. The surrounding tribes,
as soon as they learned that the fierce old man was dead, gathered up
and flooded in to attack them, no more afraid of them.
They swarmed to the vineyards and villages like locusts, dragged off
cattle and sheep; seized women and children, to make them slaves;
then set fire to the barns. We stood and watched it all,
almost forgetting to snatch a few sheep and cows ourselves.
The ground was bloodslick, the sky full of smoke from the burning villages.
We watched in shock. Who'd ever heard of such maniacs?
We walked here and there among them, rolling them over on their backs
to pick off buckles, swords with bejewelled hilts, new arrows,
and, best, the beautifully figured bows that no one can fashion
as the craftsmen among the Bebrykes could do, in their day.

A splendid haul.

        "But Polydeukes sat staring seaward—
black waves quiet as velvet, under a blood-red sky—
brooding. He pounded his right fist into his flat left hand
again and again. I touched his shoulder. 'Stupid,' he hissed,
never shifting his eyes from the sea. 'God damned old clown!'
'Ah well,' I said. 'And all that talk!' he said. '—Free will,
survival! I ought to have taken his big black teeth out one
by one! I ought—' 'Ah well,' I said. His eyes were as calm,
as ominous green as the sky those days when the air went dead.
'If Herakles were here,' he said, 'you know what I'd do?'
I shook my head. 'I'd kill him,' he said. 'Or try.' He grinned,
but his eyes looked as crazy to me as the eyes of the man he'd killed.
'He wouldn't approve. You're supposed to be his friend,' I said.
'I'd smash in his brains for good. "Defend your head or die!"
I'd tell him. And no mere joke. Because I *am* his friend.'
I let it pass. Boxers are all insane, I thought.
Like everyone.

        "Late that night, when the Argonauts
were all sitting in a crowd on the beach, gazing at the fire,
Orpheus sang a song of the wonderful skill and power
of Polydeukes' fists. He sang of the age-old hunger of the heart
for some cause fit to die for, some war certainly just,
some woman certainly virtuous. He sang the unearthly, unthinkable joy
of Zeus in his battle with the dragons. Then sang
of Hylas, gentler than morning, gazing at his father's killer
with innocent love and awe. As he sang, the hero of his song,
Polydeukes, rose, bright tears on his cheeks, and left our ring
to walk alone in the woods, get back his calm, we thought.
That was the last we saw of him."

IO

          ·   Then Jason told
of Phineus; spoke like a man in a dream. The sea-kings listened,
leaning on their fists. Not a man in the hall even coughed. They sat
so still you'd have thought some god had cast his spell on them.
Old Kreon stared into his wine, blood-red in its jewelled cup,
and even when Jason's tale scraped painful wounds—the fall
of Thebes, the tragedy of Oidipus—the king showed nothing.
His daughter Pyripta twisted the rings on her fingers and sighed.
Surely the chief of the Argonauts must be aware, I thought,
how queer the tale as he told it now must seem to them.
The Asian, fat Koprophoros, smiled. He did not mask
his pleasure at seeing the Argonaut show his quirky side.
Athena leaned close to the left shoulder of Aison's son,
warning him, struggling to guide him, her beautiful gray eyes flashing;
Hera leaned close to his right, her lithe form moving a little,
weaving like a snake. The story was not what they'd hoped for at all,
this version turbulent with unresolved doubts, key changes not
familiar, chords that clashed, a version of well-known tales
gone crooked, quisquous, trifling matters better off forgotten
blown up out of proportion, and matters of the keenest interest
dropped, passed over in silence as if from obsessive concern
with moments that made no sense. That was no way to win
a throne. Not even Paidoboron, indifferent to thrones,
would wander off like that. Athena and Hera looked flustered,
losing control. Sweet Aphrodite, fond, dim-witted,
hovering over Pyripta, was close to tears—so filled
with pity for the hero as he teased the story of his life for meaning,
she dropped all thought of Medeia, for the moment, and charged the heart

of the princess with tender affection, innocent compassion for the man.

He said:
      "At dawn we stowed the ship with our booty, loosed the
hawsers, hauled up sail, and pushed toward Phineus' land,
riding the swirling Bosporos, driven by wind. The day
was ordinary except for this: around mid-afternoon
a wave came in out of nowhere, and even Tiphys, who knew
the ways of seas and rivers like the back of his hand, was amazed,
watching it come, a gray wall high as a mountain, sweeping
clouds along. It hung, full of menace, directly above
our sail, and we dived for hand-holds—all but Tiphys—and waited
for the end, the shriek of the ship breaking up. We felt—nothing!
no change, the great wave rolling on south, and behind it the river
calm, as quiet as a pool. 'What happened?' I yelled at Tiphys.
Our hearts were pounding like sledges. He said he had no idea.
'Impossible!' I said. 'You know the sea like your own mind.
A prodigy like that, there must be some good reason for it!'
But Tiphys could tell us nothing. 'Perhaps some god,' he said,
pushing his long yellow hair back. 'Maybe some joke.' He shrugged.
Mad Idas grinned, showed all his twisted teeth, and farted.
      "The next morning we put in across from Bithynia;
anchored offshore from the mansion of Phineus the seer. He had
the greatest prophetic gift of anyone living, a man
who knew not merely by flickers, an insight here and there,
but knew by steady intuition—or so men said—as much
as Apollo knew, who knew all Zeus's mind. He won
great wealth by it, but also unspeakable misery.
      "We'd heard, before we landed, nothing of that. We went up,
eager to visit with the prophet whose reputation stretched
farther than merchants travelled, to the ends of the earth. The old man
felt our presence before we came. For days he'd felt
us coming. He rose from his bed—none saw it but one aged raven—
groped for his staff of olive wood, and, feeling his way
by the sootblack wall, his old feet twisted and shrunken beneath him,
he hunted his door. He trembled—age and weakness—and his head
kept jerking, twisting to the side, then up, his horrible blind eyes
searching. At the door he fell, siled over and tumbled, banging
his bald, bruised head on the steps, and down he went like a corpse
to the bottom, all without a whimper, because he'd known he'd fall.

He lay awhile unconscious. He had no friend, no servant
to care for him; not even a dog would live in the same house with Phineus.
    "After a while the seer came to
and groped around in the dust for his staff, and at last found it
and painfully climbed back up it and onto his feet, trembling,
jerking his head, and then, moving slowly, inch by inch,
labored toward his gate and the two stone steps that opened
on the road. There too, as he'd known he would, he fell. And there
we found him lying with his face in the dirt, his legs twisted up
like a child's knot. There were trickles of thin, pink blood in his beard
where he'd broken teeth. My cousin Akastos rushed up to him
and meant to lean over him, listen to his heart, but then drew back
with a look of disgust. And now we too were near enough to smell it:
vultures' vomit, the stink of death on a hot day,
blunt as the kick of a mule. We stood well back from him,
gagging, breathing through our mouths, just keeping our dinners down.
And then—horrible!—the creature we'd taken to be dead for days,
rotting on the road, moved his hand a little—a hand as pale,
as darkly veined as the stomach of a butchered cow. It was caked,
like all his revolting body, with dirt. Where the hand went back
to the dark of his filthy robe, which had fallen over it,
the wrist was like two gray sticks. Then Phineus turned his head,
opened his milkwhite eyes as if to stare straight at us,
and called out: 'Argonauts, welcome! You've come to my rescue at last!'
He moved his tongue around his mouth, then wiped his hand, spitting dust
and blood. 'From the Harpies, I mean,' he said. Then widened his eyes
and let out a croak, like a man who's suddenly remembered something,
a source of pain and rage. We stared in amazement. The old man's
body shrank up, then jerked out stiff, shrank up, jerked out,
and we thought he was dying again. But then he lay limp, and tears
made streaks on his stubbled cheeks. 'O murderous gods,' he said,
and then for perhaps ten minutes Phineus sobbed and sometimes
pounded the road with his fists. At the end of that time he clutched
his belly, looked furious, and spoke. 'I'd forgotten you wouldn't know.
I'd forgotten I'd have to go through with you now the whole insipid
tale. Even though it's a fact that you people will save me, because
it's fated—like everything: endlessly, drearily, stupidly, cruelly
fated—I'm forced to go through dull motions, politely pleading,
cajoling, explaining, telling you my tedious history;
and I'm forced to listen to your boring responses, predictable even

136

to a man not gifted with second sight.' He pulled himself together
and labored up onto his knees, groping with his staff, stifling
the angry imprecations of his swollen heart. Then:
'Believe me, I'd far rather die, and I would have died long ago
if the will of mortals were a match for the will of the gods. But alas!
they've got us all by the bellies. They throw a crumb, a bone,
keep us alive, howling with hunger, and keep us too weak
to raise our daggers to our wrists, crawl down to the river . . . But enough.
Let's get on with it, play out our parts! If I may forestall
your question, Jason, son of Aison—' I cleared my throat.
He stretched out his hands to stop me. 'Don't ask!' he implored. 'Don't drag
it on and on and on! The answer to your question is:
I'm a victim of curses. Not only has a fury quenched my sight—
an affliction bitter enough, God knows—and not only am I
forced to drag through the years far past man's usual span,
aging, withering, no end in sight—but worse than that,
Harpies plague me—eaglelike creatures with human heads.
When my neighbors, or strangers from across the sea, come here to my house
to ask of the future, or of hidden things, and leave me food
as payment, no sooner is the food set out on my plate than down
from the clouds—dark, swifter than lightningbolts—those Harpies swoop
snatching the food from my fingers and lips with their chattering teeth.
At times they leave me nothing, at times a gobbet or two
to keep me alive and screaming. They imbrue with their sewage stench
all they touch. I would rather die than consume the stuff
those Harpies leave—so I rant to myself. But my belly roars,
tyrannical; I submit. Yet this one curse will pass,
if my name is Phineus. The Harpies will soon be driven away
by two of your number, the lightswift sons of the Northern Wind.
It has taken place already in the mind of Zeus.'

                                                   "So he spoke.
We stared in pity and disgust. Then Zetes and Kalais, sons
of the wind, went closer, gagging from the stench but generous;
and the noble Zetes reached for the foul, filth-shrivelled hand
and said, 'Poor soul! There's surely no man on earth who bears
more shame, more sorrow than you! Heaven knows, we'll help if we can.
But first, tell us—' Before he could finish, the old man cringed.
'I know, I know! What's the cause? you'll ask. Have I done some wrong?
Have I rashly offended some god by, for instance, misusing my skill?
If you help me and foil the justice of some great god, will he turn

on you? Say no more! I give you my vow, it's your destiny.
No harm will come! I swear by Apollo, by my own second sight,
by my cataracts, by the home of the dead—may the powers of Hades
blast me to atoms if I die! No ultion will fall on you,
no vengeful alastor seek you out by decree of the gods.'
   " 'Very well,' Zetes said. And now the brothers backed off from Phineus,
ready to faint from his stink. At once, we prepared a meal
for the poor old seer—the last the Harpies were to get. And Zetes
and Kalais took up their watch, knees bent, a short way off
from the prophet who squatted by the steps. Before he could reach for a morsel,
down came the Harpies. They struck and were gone with no more warning
than a lightning flash—the meal had vanished—and we heard their raucous
chattering far out at sea. It seemed the whole world had turned
to stench. But Zetes and Kalais too were gone, we saw—
vanished like ghosts. They nearly caught them—touched them, in fact.
But just as their fingers were closing on the creatures' throats, the sky
went white, and a voice said: 'Stop! The Harpies are the hounds of Zeus!
Don't harm them! They'll trouble your friend no more, swift sons of Boreas!'
And so the brothers turned back, and the curse was ended.
                                                  "We cleansed
the old man's house with sulphur fire, and washed him in the creek,
then picked out the finest of the sheep we'd gotten from Amykos
and made them a sacrifice to Zeus. We set out a banquet in the hall
and sat with Phineus to eat. He ate like a man in a dream,
astounded, baffled by the sweetness of life.
                                          "When we'd eaten and drunk
our fill, the old man, sitting among us by the fireplace, said:
'Listen. I can tell you many things. Not all I know,
but a good deal. I was a fool, once. I used to tell people
the whole nature of the universe. Deeper and deeper
I plunged into things long-hidden, until for some strange reason
(which I understand) those Harpies came, called down from the sky
(not "sent," mind you: *called*—called down as surely as if
I'd raised my hands and cried, "Harpies, snatch away my food!"). Since then I've
learned my place, so to speak, or learned my weakness, which is
the same: my strength. As the glutton eats till it kills him, the visionary
sees. (My father, by the way, had a truly amazing eye
for omens, though nothing like mine. But I'd rather not speak of that.)'
He glanced past his shoulder, furtive, then smiled again and gazed
at the flames with his chalk-white eyes. 'I could tell you many things,'

he said again, and smiled. His corrugate hands and cheeks
glowed in the firelight, shining with joy of life like the eyes
of a lover. We waited. He said, 'I knew a man one time
who suffered in a somewhat similar way. He murdered his father
and married his mother, unwittingly. It was a classic case.
I spoke to him many years afterward. I said, "Come, come, Oidipus!
Surely you recognized the man you killed! Surely, in the hindmost
corner of your mind you saw your image in his face and remembered
his shadow between your mother's breast and you." The king
considered me—or considered my voice (he was blind)—then answered,
"Doubtless, Phineus. Clearly I was fooled, one way or another:
if not by reality, then clearly by something in myself. There are shadows
more than we dream, in the ancient cave of the mind—dark gods,
conflicting absolutes, timeless and co-existent, who battle
like atoms seething in a cauldron, each against all, to assert
their raucous finales. Gods illogical as sharks. We roof
their desperate work with the limestone and earth of reason, but the roof
has cracks: as seepages, springs, dark meres push through earth's crust,
those old, mad gods burst through the mind's thick floor, mysterious
nightmares, twitches, accidents perverting our gentlest acts.
I've made my peace with them." I saw that events had made him
wise. I said: "Perhaps the old man was not your father,
merely another of reality's tricks." He smiled. "Perhaps.
I've heard much stranger things. I've learned that the primary law
of Time and Space is that nothing is merely what it is. The seed
of the flower harbors the poison of the flower. I've watched old lions
pause, befuddled by warring instincts, surrounded by huntsmen.
I've watched my own soul—strange drives forcing me higher and higher
to goals I can barely discern, and one of them is beauty of mind,
true majesty; and one of them is death. I am, I've found
a rhythm, merely: a summer and winter of creation and guilt.
I'm the phoenix; the world. Thanatos and Eros in all-out war,
the chariot drawn by sphinxes, one of them black, one white:
one pulls toward joy, the other toward total eclipse of pain.
With all that, too, I've made my peace. I've fallen out of Time.
I stumble, a blind man guided by a stick. After all this—sick,
meaningless, old—I've lost my reason at last: gone sane."
I said nothing, humbled by the wisdom Oidipus had won—and not by
gift: by violence and grief. I could have expanded what he knew.
I did for others. But I bowed, retired in silence. I have said

to kings that their hope is ridiculous—the hope that someday
kingdoms, heroes, philosophers, laws, may end forever
the natural state—the jungle of the gods in all-out war—
the secret whispers of the buried man, the violence of seas,
benthal stirrings of the blind, pythonic corpse of Atlantis,
the earth in upheaval, thundershouts, whirlwinds, foxes snapping
at the rooster's heels, or the silent victories of termites, spiders,
ants. I have said to other men that the natural state
is final. The forces that crack the efficient crust of mind
crack nations: no hunger, no evil wish to seduce or kill
is lost in the sky god's brain. This darkling plain we flee
toward love is the darkling plain toward which we flee. But why
say all these things to him? I left him groping, stumbling
stone to stone, as we all move stone to stone, each step
catching the balance from the last, or failing to catch it, tumbling us
humbly home to the dust. Don't ask of a man like Oidipus
programs, plans for improvement, praise of nobility. (What are,
to him, great deeds of heroism? A matter of glands,
nerves, old patterns of reaction:—a slight deficiency
of iodine in the thyroid (I speak things long-forgotten),
a sadistic aunt, a bump on the back of the head, and the hero's
a coward.) Every tragedy is fragmentary,
a cut of Time in the cosmic whole, the veil without which
nothing. A man's inability to flee his father's guilt,
his city's, his god's. A man's coming to grips with his own
unalterable road to death. Don't look to the gods for help
in that. For the purpose you ask of them, they were never there.
Earthquakes, fires, fathers, floods make no distinctions:
the good survive and suffer, discover their truths and die,
like the wicked. Indeed, if anyone has the advantage, it seems
the violent, crafty, unprincipled, who seize earth's goods
while the pious stretch out their arms in prayer, and leave empty-handed.
I could tell you, Argonauts . . . Dark, unfeeling, unloving powers
determine our human destiny. The splendid rewards,
the ghastly punishments your priests are forever preaching of,
have no real home but the shores of their violent brains. Learn all
your poisons! There's man's peace!' The old seer smiled and sighed,
gentle as a kindly grandmother. The firelight flickered
soft on his forehead and cheeks as he leaned toward it, stretching
his hands to it. We studied him, polite.

"At last I said:
'Phineus, these are strange words of yours. You tell us tales
of doom, inescapable senselessness, yet all the while
you smile, stretching your hands to the comfort of the fire.'
" 'That's true;
no doubt it's a trifle absurd.' But he nodded, smiling on.
'I was sick to the heart, fighting reality tooth and nail,
staggering, striking—and, behold!, you've made me well. My mind
made monsters up, and all the self-understanding in the world
could no more turn them back than weir down history.'
He paused; then, abruptly, 'I must muse no more on that.' He turned
his head, listening to the darkness in the room behind. We began
to smell something. His face went pale. And then, once more,
he smiled, remembered our presence, remembered the fire. He said:
'Life is sweet, Argonauts! Behold us, each of us drinking down
his own unique sweet poison! May each see the bottom of the cup!
As for myself, I can say this much with good assurance: I will not
last much longer, now that the Harpies have left me. The balance
is gone. Death's not far hence, the death I carry within me.
One grants one's limits at last—one's special strength. One sinks
and drowns there, tranquil, no more at war with the universe,
and therefore dying, like poison sumac become too much
itself, unstriving, released at last into anorexy.
—No, no! No alarm, dear friends! No distress! It was a great service!
There is no greater joy, no greater peace, my friends
than dying one's own inherent death, no other. The truth!'
He paused, looked back at the darkness again with his blind eyes.
He smiled. His smile came forward like a spear. 'I will tell you more:
You ask me: How can you smile, reach out to the warmth, knowing all
you know? Let me tell you another thing about Oidipus.
He knows where he is—where humanity is: in the tragic moment,
locked in the skull of the sky: the eternal, intemporal moment
which lasts to the last pale flash of the world. There tragic man,
alone, doomed to be misunderstood by slumbering minds,
exposed to the idiot anger of hidden and absent forces,
nevertheless stands balanced. In his very loneliness,
his meaningless pain, he finds the few last values his soul
can still maintain, drive home, construct his grandeur by:
the absolute and rigorous nature of its own awareness,
its ethical demands, its futile quest for justice, absolute

truth—dead-set refusal to accept some compromise,
choose some sugared illusion!' His face was radiant.
He wrung his hands; his voice was unsteady. He was deeply moved.
What could I say? It was not for me to pose the question.
We were guests. He might be of use to us. I was glad, however,
when Idas asked it. Sweat drops glistened on his ebony forehead
like firelit jewels.
     " 'Why? —Why soul? Why values? Why greatness?
Why not "Not love: just fuck"?'
        "Old Phineus turned his face,
with a startled look, toward Idas. 'I will tell you more,' he said.
 " 'We should sleep,' I broke in. 'It's a long trip, and dawn near at hand.'
 "The stink in the room was suddenly thick as a dragon's stench.
 "All that day, far into the next night, Phineus talked.
I rose, we all did, tiptoed out. By the following morning
the stink was more than we could bear. There was some dark meaning in it.
No matter. Aietes' city was still a long way north,
and that was where we were aimed. We'd gotten used to it,
rowing, at one with the cosmos, as if we'd emerged from something.
So old comedies end, the universe and man at one.
Incorporation, purgation, harmony restored. Well,
it wasn't exactly like that. We had no complaints, rowing
hard against an eastern wind. Some famous old tale . . . Never mind.
Exhaustion was the name of the game.
       "Then came the stranger. I dreamed
(it was no mere dream) a terror beyond all the wildest fears
of man. I dreamed Death came to me and smiled, and said:
'Fool, you are caught in an old, irrelevant tale. I will speak
strange words to you, a language you won't understand. When you do,
too late! Such is my wile. I will tell you of horror beyond
belief; you won't believe, and so it will come. That is
my trick. I will tell you: *Fool, you are caught in irrelevant forms:*
existence as comedy, tragedy, epic. The heart divided,
the Old Physician who cures the world by his ambles pie;
the magician cook (Hamburger Mary), "Eternal Verities,"
the world as the word of the Ausländer. Those are the web I'll
kill you by. And neither will you believe my power,
or if you believe, imagine it. When I speak of death,
you will think of your own; poor limited beast. What man can't face
his paltry private death? The words are, first: *Trust not*

to seers who conceive no higher force than Zeus. And next:
Beware the interstices. There lies thy wreck. Remember!
I sat up, trembling in the dark, still ship; I cried out, 'Wait!
Who are you?' And then all at once the shore was sick with light:
there were cities like rotten carcases black with children dead;
there were women, befouled, deformed by mysterious burns; and the burnt ground
glowed, a deadly green. 'My name is Never,' he said.
'My name is: It Cannot Be. My name is Soon.'
I saw his eyes and cried out. Then I was alone. It was dark.
I racked my wits for the meaning. Old Mopsos had theories. Said:
'You've listened too much to old Phineus, Jason, with all his talk
of dark, opposing forces—Love and Death. You've conceived
the final war, the ultimate goal of humanity.'
'Then it isn't true?' I asked. He sighed. 'Who knows? Who cares?
Don't think about it. It's millennia off. The dream's mere chaff.'
I wasn't convinced. I could change the outcome. Why send, otherwise,
the terrible vision to me? He smiled when I asked him that.
'Write it down that truth is whatever proves necessary.
Write down the dream as a dream. You created your goblin, Jason,
fashioned him out of your own free-floating guilt and the babble
of Phineus. Go back to sleep, take a friend's advice. —Go to sleep
and don't give your fears more rope.' He turned away. I gazed
through darkness, listening. All still well; no cause for alarm;
nothing afoot but the wind, as usual—endlessly walking,
darkening into the void . . . Then, far away, a flash,
a sun, and the shock of it sent out astounding, sky-high waves,
and as the first approached our ship I broke into a sweat; but then
the great wave struck, moved past, and nothing had happened. Illusion!
I got up, looked in at the darkness of water, and calmed myself.
All well. Nothing afoot. —And yet I was sure, again,
the vision was no mere dream. I stood at the start of something,
in some way I hadn't yet learned; and I might yet change its course.
In my mind I saw myself clambering over the side, slipping down,
soundlessly sinking in the water. I dreamed I'd done it. Peace . . .
    "Make a note. The dark of the buried gods has suicide in it,
black form seeking to crack the efficient crust. I would not
crack. I lay down again and, this time, nothing. Darkness.
And so sailed on, putting the Bithynian coast behind us.
Self-destruction was the name of the game. I wasn't playing.
We sailed on, sliding northward, the *Argo* silent in the night.

II

"I suppose the truth of the matter is that I was bored, simply. As you've seen in everything I've said, I was an ambitious young man—a born leader, I wanted to believe—and fiercely impatient. Think how it must have been with me, hour after hour, mile after mile, river after river. I wanted that fleece closed in my fist, Pelias praising me, the people all wildly shouting 'Hats off!' Perhaps more. No doubt of it. A small, dull kingdom, mere farming country . . . I had glories more vast in the back of my mind than Pelias' kingdom, my fever's rickety stepping stone. Yet all I burned for, all my wolf-heart hungered for, was outrageously far away. No wonder if at Lemnos I nearly gave up on it. Blind from a vision that even at the time was too bright to get a good picture of, I must slog on now through laborious skirmishes with barbaric fools, wearily manipulate my Argonauts (men big as mountains, worrisome as gnats), moil on north, outfox old Aietes, outfox his snake . . . I've seen shepherds at home sit all day long on a single rock, staring out at hillsides, wide green valleys. Well enough for them! As for me, I wanted a ship that would outrace an arrow, fighters beyond imagination. I wanted the unspeakable. I was hardly aware of all this, of course. But I knew well enough that the hours dragged and the adventures were less in the living than I would make them in the telling, later. (If I were a mute, like Polydeukes, I too would abandon the night to Orpheus' lyre.) I lost men, lost time, and in secret I shook my fists at the gods tormenting me. Whatever my strength, compared to the strength of Herakles, whatever my craft compared to that of old Argus or Orpheus, I was a superman of sorts: I could not settle for the reasonable. The Good, pale as mist, would be that which even I would find suitable to my dignity, satisfying food for my sky-consuming lust. The fleece, needless to say, would not suffice. The risk—the clear and present danger—was that nothing would suffice.

"And so the nightmare voice came to me—ghostly hint that I was caught

up in more than anyone knew, some grandiose ultimate agon. If the crew was caught up, to some extent, in these same weird delusions . . .

"However, it is also true that the place was strange, uncanny . . . and true (we've begun to learn to see) that explanation is exhaustion: The essence of life is to be found in frustrations of established order: the universe refuses the deadening influence of complete conformity. Though also, needless to say . . .

"How can the mind accept such a pointless clutter of acts,
encounters with monsters, kings, strange weather—no certainty, even,
which things really occur, which things are dreams? I've barely
hinted at the sights we saw, dull shocks to our sanity.
I've told many times how we slipped through the Clashing Rocks, and have been
believed; but who would believe me now, if I said to you
we slipped in and out of Time, hurled crazily backward and forward?
A man learns how much truth he can get away with. Suppose
I leaned toward you, like this, abandoning dignity,
and moaned, eyes wide: Oh friends, the worst of it all was this:
Time swept over us in waves: one moment the hills were green,
the next, crawling with cities, the next, black deserts where things
like huge black insects belched out smoke and devoured one another.
Suppose I reported that, sailing through fog, we heard dreadful moans,
terrible deep-throated bellows we took to be sea-monsters,
and all at once we'd see lights coming at us—no common torches,
but lights blue-white as stars—and even as we gazed at them,
shaking in terror, believe me, we saw they were eyes—the eyes
of enormous drifting beasts. And sometimes the lights would vanish
and the huge sea-beasts would sink, as if for a purpose, like whales.
Suppose I told you I saw whole seas of dead men floating—
women and children as well—a smell unbelievable—
corpses from shore to shore, and ship prows parting them.
You'd soon grow uneasy, I think. You'd call me a tiresome liar,
and rightly. Then only this: we were riding in eerie waters,
countries of powerful magic. And the strangest part was this:
all that we saw, or thought we saw, was of no importance.
At times the river was poison. At times the sky caught fire.
At times the land we passed seemed virgin wilderness,
and the river birds would land on our ship as if never yet
attacked by the implements of man. The world was a harmless drunk.
"A ship that reeked of incense drifted by us, filled

with sleepy people, eerie music, children in rags
or naked, as some of the adults were naked. They smiled gently,
listlessly waved and jabbered in some outlandish tongue,
human livestock packed in rail to rail on the sailless
ship. They did not mind. Some coupled publicly,
staring nowhere. They filled us, God knows why, with anger.
Even Athena's magic ship was changed, beside
that rotting barque from the world's last age. The planking sang:
    " 'For men, not earth, the time has run out. Though oceans die,
meadows and fields, green hills, they hold no grudge against
their murderer. They drift through time in their long slumber,
secretly waiting, like beasts asleep in caves. Deep space
bombards the poisoned seas with bits of life, and the seas
grow whole again, renew themselves like a heart awakening.
Algae forms along shores. Great, dark, ungainly beasts
dream from the deeps toward land, and out of the slime of blood
and bone—witless, charged with sorrow like a dying horse—
mind comes groping, tentative, fearful, sly as a snake
and as quick to love or strike. So spring moves in again,
as usual, and flowers are invented, and wheels and clocks,
and tragedies, and eventually, as the mind grows old,
familiar with its quirky ways, even comedy is born again—
fat clowns strutting, alone and ridiculous, shaking their fists
at mirrors and fleeing in alarm, to teach that the joke on them
is them. So autumn comes again, as usual:
Splendid triumph of color, when every tree turns philosophical
and the seas, dying, past all repair,
provide mankind with jokes. (All consciousness is optimistic,
even a frog's. Otherwise who would evolve the handsome prince?)
So plankton dies, and the whales turn belly up,
become one world-wide stench of decaying symphonies;
the grass withers. Starvation; plague. A silent planet
again, for a time; drifting boulder pocked with old cities
till space sends life. And once more goggle-eyed creatures gaze
amazed at the brave new world with goggle-eyed creatures in it,
as usual. And all that past minds dreamed or wrote,
feared, predicted with terrible insight—all mind loved
and mocked—is vanished like snow, cool archaeology.
Cheer up, sailors! The wind of time was always dark
with ghosts, pacing, angrily muttering to be born.'

                                                    "The death-ship
vanished, and a moment later, the music; finally the smell.
We talked, held councils; but obviously we could make no sense
of senselessness, and so, in the end, pushed on. And had
adventures, each more lunatic than the last. Not even
Orpheus knew how to twist the thing toward reason, impose
some frame. In any case, I can tell you, it wasn't courage
that kept us going. It wasn't sweet curiosity.
For reasons we hadn't understood at the time—nor did we now—
we'd launched this expedition, and so we continued. They did not
love me for it now. Muttered and grumbled.

                                        "As I say,
we passed the Clashing Rocks. Never mind the details. Two great black
boulders that rose from the sea like a pair of jaws, and snapped
at any who passed between. The prank of some playful god
in the First Age, before the gods grew 'serious.'
A prank deadly for men, though one can see, in a way,
the entertainment value. We'd been forewarned of them
by Phineus—one of his endless, tedious meanderings.
We followed instructions—hurled in a dove, by which we learned
the pace of the thing . . . Never mind. We rowed for our lives, and made it,
and saw the stone jaws lock, to move no more. Ironic.
We could have sailed through at ease, like merchants, chatting, if we'd known their
time was almost out. But in any case, we made it,
and travelled senselessly on.
                                "Then Tiphys spoke, overpleased
at how slyly his oar had steered us through—fatuous,
unctuous with success . . . unless already the mortal fever
was in him, befuddling his wits, and some subliminal fear,
intuition of silence, now stirred his soul to noise. He said,
pompous and hearty, too jovial: 'I think, Lord Jason,
we can safely say all's well! The *Argo*'s safe and sound,
and so are we! For which we may thank pale-eyed Athena,
who gave our ship supernatural strength when Argus drove in
the bolts. The *Argo* shall never be harmed. That seems to be Law.
And so, since heaven's allowed us to pass through the Clashing Rocks,
I beg you, put off all worries. There can be no obstacle
this crew can't easily surmount!'
                                "Our brilliant pilot, I thought,

is a dolt. I turned my head, looked back at the two great rocks,
now motionless, then glanced at him, one eyebrow raised.
But the next instant it struck me that Tiphys' words could be turned
to use. I frowned and steeled myself for the necessary
dullness, and, sighing, taking him gently to task, I said:
    " 'Tiphys, why do you comfort me? I was a blind fool,
and the error's fatal. When Pelias ordered me out on this mission
I should have refused at once, even though he'd have torn me limb
from limb. It was selfish madness which even in selfish terms
has turned out all to the bad. Here I am, responsible
for all your lives—and no man living less fit for it!
I'm wracked by fears, anxieties—hating the thought of the water,
hating the thought of land, where surely hostile natives
will claim some few of our lives, if not the majority.
It's easy for you, good Tiphys, to talk in this cheerful vein.
Your care is only for your own life, whereas I, I must care
for all your lives. No wonder if I never sleep!' So I spoke,
playing the necessary game (and yet I confess, I enjoyed it,
querning the world to words)—and the whole crew rose to it,
or all but one. 'No man,' they cried, 'in the whole world
could vie with Jason as fitting lord of the Argonauts!
It's surely that very anxiety which wrecks your sleep
that steers the *Argo* safely past every catastrophe!
Never doubt it, man! We'd rather be dead, every one of us,
than see you harmed by Pelias!' With old unwatered wine
they drank my health and sent up such shouts that the sea-wall rang
and I nearly shouted myself. But Orpheus looked toward shore,
not drinking. I ignored the matter. 'My friends,' I said, 'your courage
fills me again with confidence. The resolution
you show in the face of these monstrous perils has made me feel
I could sail through hell itself and be calm as a god.' Thus I
played Captain, kept their morale up. I needn't deny I enjoyed it.
Was it my fault the Argonauts—even the slyest
(Mopsos and Idmon, for instance)—had natures a flow of words
could carry away like sticks? And was it my fault that words
were my specialty? I ask you, what other choice did I have?—
though Orpheus watched me, scorned me, keener than the rest at spying
craft (a wordsman himself, though one of a very dissimilar
kind). He said in private, later, avoiding my eyes,
tuning his lyre with fingers as light as wings, 'Come, come!

"Limb from limb," Lord Jason! This is surely some new Pelias—
the stuttering mouse turned lion!' 'I do what I must,' I said.
'Would you have me tell them the truth—that life itself, all our pain
is idiocy?' He feigned surprise. 'You think so, Jason?'
I knew his game. Play innocent, defensive. Draw out your man,
give him the rope to hang himself. And I knew, too,
his arrogance. It's easy for the poets to carp at the men
who lead, the drab decision-makers who waste no time
on niceties—pretty figures merely for aesthetics' sake,
rhymes for the sake of rhymes. They see all the world as forms
to be juxtaposed, proved beautiful—no higher purpose
than harmony, the static world proved lovely as it is.
But what world's static? We create, and we long for poets' support,
we who contract for whatever praise or blame is due
and get the blame—ah, blame that outlasts our acts by centuries!
   "I said: 'My friend, we're booty hunters. We've come this far,
murdered and lost this many men—the friendly king
of the Doliones, Herakles, Hylas, Polydeukes,
and the rest—for nothing but a boast, an adventure of boys. It's time
we turned those crimes to account. I think it's easy for you
to be filled with pompous integrity. My job's more dull.
Whatever high meaning our journey may have—or lack of meaning—
my job is to carry us through. That means morale, poet.
That means unity, brotherhood!' Orpheus smiled, ironic,
avoiding my eyes, and not from embarrassment, it seemed to me,
but as if to glance for a moment in my direction would be
bad art, misuse of his skills. He glanced at Argus, instead,
our sly artificer, who smiled. They have a league, these artists:
a solid front in defense of their grandiose visions of the real,
destroyers of sticks and stones. I was angry enough, God knows.
But that, too, went with the job.
                              "He said: 'Your pilot's sick.'
I studied him, puzzled. He looked at his lyre. 'Your beloved Tiphys
is sick, at death's very door. Does that make you "anxious," Captain?
Does it make you a trifle remorseful of your fine facility
for turning all passing remarks to the common good?' What could
I say? What would anyone say, in my position? I glanced
at Tiphys, standing at the oar. The wind rolled through his hair,
his eyes were alert. He looked like a fellow who'd live six hundred
years, Queen Hera's darling. I glanced back at Orpheus.

'I don't believe it.' But the devil had shaken me, no lie. And he spoke
the truth, as we all found later. Meanwhile Orpheus played,
catching the rhythm of the oars, and little by little, gently,
all but imperceptibly, he increased the tempo.
We passed the river Rhebas and the peak of the Colone, and soon
the Black Cape too, and the outfall of the river Phyllis
where Phrixos once put down with the golden ram. Through all
that day and through all the windless night we labored at the oar,
to Orpheus' hurrying beat. We worked like oxen ploughing
the dark, moist earth. The sweat pours down from flank and neck,
their rolling eyes glare out askance from the creaking yoke,
hot blasts of breath come rumbling from their mouths, and all day long
they plough on, digging their sharp hooves into the soil. So we
ploughed on, goaded by the lyre. (I understood well enough
his meaning. So poets too can govern ships. That was
no news.) Near dawn—at the time of day
when the sun has not yet touched the heavens, though the darkness fades—
we reached the harbor of the lonely island of Thynias
and crawled ashore exhausted, gasping for air. All at once
the lyre was still, and the man at the lyre looked up, strange-eyed,
and lo and behold, we saw the god Apollo striding
like a man. His golden locks streamed down like swirling sunlight,
his silver bow half blinding. The island trembled beneath
his feet, and the sea ran high on the grassy shore. We stood
stock-still and dared not meet his eyes. He passed through the air
and was gone.
          "Then Orpheus found his voice. 'O Argonauts,
let us dedicate this island to holy Apollo, lord
of peace, and song, and healing, and let us sing together
and swear our lasting brotherhood, and build him a temple
to be called the Temple of Concord as long as the world may last.'
We did so—poured libations out and, touching the sacrifice,
swore by the solemnest oaths that we'd stand by one another
forever. A moving ceremony. I did not say
as much as I thought to Orpheus after he'd ended it.
    "We travelled on, young Orpheus stroking his lyre as though
it counted for more than the sails. And did he expect to stir up
rancor in me by his proof that art may also serve
morale? Then that was a difference between us. I use what means
I can to achieve my ends; I no more resented his help

than the wind's. If the quality of acts concerns him, the smell and taste,
the moment to moment morality of it, let him take care
of those. What he'd done to show me up, make a fool of me,
was just what I'd sought myself. So who was the fool? But I
was Captain, and not required to give explanations.
                                                    "And so
we came to the river Lykos and the Anthemoeisian
lagoon. The *Argo*'s halyards and all her tackle quivered
as we flashed along; but during the night the wind died down,
and at dawn we moored at the Cape of Akherusias,
a towering headland with sheer rock cliffs that blindly stare out
across the Bithynian Sea. Beneath the headland, at sea level,
a solid platform of smooth-swept rock where rollers endlessly
break and roar; at the crown of the headland, plane trees rising
stretching their great, dark beams to blot out the sun. We went in.
I watched our pilot. He was restless, too silent. I remembered the words
of Orpheus. I took Idmon aside, younger of the seers,
and spoke to him. Said: 'Idmon, look over at Tiphys, there.
Tell me what you see.' He turned his head away quickly, refused
to hear. Then he said, 'If you've come for hopeful news, you've come
to the wrong man. There is no hopeful news—not on that
or anything.' He tipped his face. He was weeping. I frowned,
baffled again, and left him. How could I have guessed what grief
the poor man had on his mind? We had work, in any case—
the usual repairs, the usual gathering of wood and leaves. . . .
    "On the landward side, the vaulting sea-naes sloped away
to a hollow glen, a cave with overhanging trees and rocks,
the Cavern of Hades. From its pitchdark hollows an icy breath
comes up each morning, covering rocks, trees, ferns with sparkling
rime that clings three hours, then melts in the sun. We listened.
A rumble like voices, the far-off murmur of rollers breaking
at the foot of the cliff, the whisper of leaves as the wind from the cave
pressed by, and perhaps some further voice, like a voice in a dream,
a memory. We stood at the mouth of the cave looking down
at darkness, musing. Shoulder to shoulder we stood, peering in,
Ankaios, the boy in the bearskin; old Mopsos; wise old Argus,
artificer; huge Telamon; Orpheus; Tiphys (his breathing
was short and quick); myself, all the others. . . . We stood peering in,
shoulder to shoulder, each one of us, that instant, alone,
thinking of his personal dead, his private death. But Idas

152

widened his eyes, leered wildly, whispering, 'Ghosts!' He clung
to my arm, clowning even here. I shook him free. My cousin
Akastos touched my shoulder to calm my wrath.
                                                "Not long
thereafter, one of our number would go down through that door
alive, in search of his love, as Theseus had gone already
for a friend, when both of them were young. It's said that Orpheus
willingly moved past Briareos, with his hundred whirling arms,
moved past the terrible nine-headed Hydra and the great flame-breathing
dragon, encountered the colossal giant Tityus,
whose great, black, bloated body sprawled across nine full acres,
and came to the midnight palace of Lord Dionysos himself,
prince of terror, bull-god, huntsman whom nothing escapes.
Majestically then, without words, a mere nod, old Kadmos the Dark
granted what he asked, but after the nod set this condition:
The harper must lead the way, and Euridike follow—a woodnymph,
gentlest, most timid of all creatures, a heart more quickly alarmed
than a deer's (not two men living have ever seen her kind:
they vanish in a splinter of light at the sound of a footfall). She must follow,
and the harper never look back. (How like the gods, I thought,
when I learned of it, to end his pains with a joke.) But he agreed.
No choice, of course. Began his slow way back through the dimness,
stepping past pits where blue-scaled snakes rolled coil on coil,
their hatchet heads hovering, floating, the whole dark trogle alive
with rattling and hissing and the seething of the sulphurous pits. He listened,
harping the guardian serpents to sleep—the horned cerastes,
the basilisk with its lethal eyes—and he heard her step,
timid, behind him, and so, chest pounding, continued. Moved past
terrors to make a man sick—much less a nymph, coming after him,
alone. And still he gazed forward. Imagine it! Shrieks, screams, cackles,
flashes of light, sudden forms, quick wings, sharp hisses of air,
bright skulls (*Was that my Euridike's scream?*) . . . How the gods must
        have howled,
rolled in the dirt on their bellies. —However,
he'd agreed, one capable of death, therefore of dignity,
and so, solemn in the Funhouse (behind him the beautiful woodnymph,
white arms reaching, yellow hair streaming in the cavern's wind,
eyes like a fawn's), he moves past grisly shapes, indecent
allegories—*Grief, Avenging Care,* and (look!) there's
Pale Disease, the back of his hand to his forehead (woe!),

and lo, there's *Melancholy Age,* his hand on his pecker, shrunk
to a stick. Step wider, Orpheus! That's *Hunger* there!
Snaps like a dog! And by him, *Fear,* trembling, pressed close
to *Pain* and *Poverty* and *Death!* So past them all they moved,
those lovers, and he saw the first faint light of day. They'd made it!
No more horrors, not even a spider, a hornèd ant
between where he stood and the green-edged light of freedom! He turned.
She ran toward him . . . and vanished. He stared in grief and rage
and then, with a groan, remembered. And so he left the Funhouse,
walked out into the light. He died soon after, a wreck.
Go there now and you'll see two shades together, alone
on a flat rock ledge, holding hands. There are sounds of dripping springs,
faint moans farther in, the whisper of spiders walking.

                                                             "A tale
most spiritual, most moving. And yet I'll tell you the truth:
He wouldn't have done it at forty, or even at thirty. He'd have wept
and ordered a monument for her, or started a fund. Shall we say
hooray for youth, inexperience? Shall we grieve our loss,
splendor in the grass, mourn that we've passed twenty-three? I've seen
small boys tease snakes, dive into torrents,
eat poison, planning to survive. The innocent
are fools, and the wise are cowards. Between those two grim lots
we construct, out of paper and false red hair, our dignity.
    "Never mind. We stood by the cave, looking in. Old Mopsos said:
'Shade you'd care to converse with, lord of the Argonauts?'
He was smiling, food in his beard. I shook my head. He turned
to Tiphys, and his smile was wicked now. 'Maybe you then, Tiphys!
Something tells me you're eager to see inside.' But Idmon,
younger of the seers, broke in. 'Old witch, enough of this!'
His voice cracked. He was enraged. Bright tears splashed down his cheeks.
His fists were clenched, and if Telamon hadn't reached out and restrained him—
he and the boy, Ankaios—we might have lost Mopsos right then.
I spoke up quickly: 'We've wood to gather.' We turned away.
And so, at that Cape, we passed six days. Unprofitably.
    "We left two graves on the island. We saw the first night that Tiphys
was not himself—irritable, testy, unable to keep warm
though sweat stood out on his forehead. From old King Lykos' city,
nearby, we called physicians. They came—great fat old mules.
With their fingertips they opened the sick man's eyes, peeked in
and solemnly shook their heads. 'Here's a dying man,' they said.

We watched with him, praying to Apollo, god of healing. But Idmon,
younger of the seers, refused to come close. He knew that his time
had come, and he meant to stay far from the thing, give fate the slip.
He would not walk in the woods with us, nor go where there might be
vipers, spiders, bees. He went out to a wide, low field
and set up an altar to Apollo and, wailing, threw himself over it,
moaning, pleading for mercy; his face and chest were bathed
in tears. Not all his prophetic lore, not all his prayers
could save him. By a reedy stream at the edge of the water-meadow
there lay a white-tusked boar—he was big as an ox—cooling
his huge belly and his bristly flanks in the mud. He lived
alone, too old for sows; an isolate. There young Idmon
went, cutting reeds for his altar fire. The boar rose up
with a jerk, a grunt of annoyance; with one quick, casual tusk,
opened the young seer's thigh. He fell to the ground, shrieking.
Those who were nearest him rushed to his aid. Too late, of course.
The boar had opened his belly now, from the bowels to the chest.
Peleus let fly his javelin as the boar retreated;
he turned, charged again. And now crazy Idas wounded him,
and unsatisfied when the boar went down on his knees, impaled,
Idas threw himself over him, screaming like a boar himself,
seized the boar by the knife-sharp tusks and twisted till he broke
its neck. Moaning, they carried Idmon to the ship, and there,
in Idas' arms, he died. Idas raged, beat the planks with his fists.
He didn't remember then that he'd wanted to kill poor Idmon
once. We dug the grave. Where Tiphys lay, the physicians
talked. One spoke of a curious case. He sat in the corner,
fingers interlaced on his belt, his eyes half shut. He said,
droning, blinking his red-webbed eyes, familiar with death:

'. . . a case of decay of the extremities. On the hands the tipjoints and in part
even the second joints of the fingers were wanting, having rotted off, and
the remaining stumps of the fingers were much swollen and in part nearly
ready to fall off. The right-hand knuckle joint of the youngest child's fore-
finger was already rotting away, and the feet of the two older brothers were
in still a more horrible state. They were mere shapeless masses surcharged
with foreign matter, with several deep, consuming sores going down to the
bone and discharging bloody, putrid water. The children's arms and legs
had lost all sense of feeling below the elbows and knees. Some fellow before
me, in order to ascertain the insensibility of the members, had pierced one

155

boy through the hand up the arm with a long needle to a point where pain was felt, which occurred at the elbow. The patient's exhalations were positively unbearable, the true odor of putrescence. Their digestion was utterly prostrated.'

The other was more metaphysical. He smoothed his beard,
pacing, occasionally rolling an eye toward Tiphys. His heavy
robe trailed on the planking, occasionally snagged. He said:

'. . . deal of nonsense been spoken about death, if you want my professional opinion. For instance, "Dying is the only thing no one can do *for* me." Grotesque banality! If to die is to die in order to achieve some end—to inspire, to bear witness, for the country, or some such, then *anyone at all* can die in my place—as in the song in which lots are drawn to see who's to be eaten. There is no personalizing virtue, so to speak, which is peculiar to *my* death. Or again, they say, "Death is the resolved chord which ends the melody." Sentimental tripe! Hogwash! An end of a melody, in order to confer its meaning on the melody, must emanate from the melody itself, as any fool should be able to recognize. The perpetual appearance of the element of Chance at the heart of each of a given man's projects cannot be apprehended as that man's possibility but, on the contrary, as the nihilation of *all* his possibilities, a nihilation which itself is no longer a part of his possibilities. Death is the end, the putrification, of freedom.'

So they spoke, waiting out the night, doing all they could for us.
However, for all their wisdom, Tiphys died. We dug
a grave, a pit by Idmon's, one more gap in the flow
of Space. I had strange dreams that night. I dreamed I stood
in a silent, twilit land where all was ruled, where there were
pyramids and pillars and porches, colonnades and domes;
and I entered the gates and approached. At the center of the city I found
a great square, with obelisks that quadrasected
the square; between the central two stood a stone crypt,
the grave, I thought, of a person of some importance. But as
I stepped more near, I knew it was no mere mortal's grave.
The door swung open. In the darkness within I saw the corpse—
monstrous, luminous—of a snake. I forget the rest. Orpheus
whispered something, old Argus crooked his finger at me.
I screamed, I remember, and woke with my head in my cousin Akastos'
scrawny arms. I drew away in anger. No reason.

"We slaughtered sheep, our due to the dead; and Argus built
a barrow over their graves. And after all this was done,
and no one among us could think of a further rite, we found
our heaviness more than before. All the Argonauts cast themselves down
by the sea and lay like figures hacked out of stone. I lacked
the heart to move them, and Orpheus gave me no help, prepared
to let all the crowd of them rot for his artist's self-righteousness,
his pleasure in seeing the cool politician helpless. They refused
to eat—no spirit left. So they lay for days, staring,
and I, their captain, with them, awash in Time and the doctors'
words: *the element of chance. Decay of the extremities.*

12

"Ankaios, child in a bearskin, leaned on the steering oar,
all smiles, hell-driving his cargo of half-dead Argonauts.
They knew no more than I. It seemed some god possessed him,
pricked him to whimsy. He'd thrown us aboard, pushed the *Argo* out,
climbed on, drawn down the sail to the wind. He came from a line
of sailing people. Watched his father, his grandfather,
learned their tricks. If the boy lacked judgment—teasing the rocks,
tempting the wind, the waves—we were none the worse for it.
He believed himself indestructible, great Zeus his friend,
as if they'd made some pact between them—and maybe they had,
that moment: a blast from the god's nostrils, and the *Argo*'s sails
were filled, and all our enslaving griefs devoured like stubble:
We were moving again; caught in the mill of the universe—youth
and age, wisdom and stupidity, sorrow and joy—the ancient
balances, wheels of the age-old meaningless grinding. Time
washed over us in waves. Say it was a dream. Behind
our stern a fleet assembled, black ships taller than mountains,
sailless, laboring north as if in their flagship's wake.
We turned to each other, questioning, baffled to discover that here
we were, on the move again, coming more awake, coming more
to life, with each fresh gust. No one could explain. The huge boy
grinned, managing the steering oar as Tiphys alone
could do, or so we'd thought.
                                    "Then up from the magic beams
of the *Argo,* singing at our feet, there came new tones, a majestic
hymn, as if all the choiring trees of Athena's grove,
and all the gods, and all the fish of the sea had come together to sing
their praise of the queen of goddesses.

Hera never sleeps!
She fills the world
with beauty, goodness, danger. At a word
from her the gods lure men to the highest
pinnacles of feeling. By her command
the wolf drags down the lamb, and the shepherd
shoots the wolf,
and the adder joyfully strikes at the shepherd's heel.

She is never spent! She moves
like light, from atom to atom, forever changing
forever
the same.

Queen Hera
consumes the land and sea with beauty
and danger. Stirs
the dragon in his lair (vermilion scaled),
awakens the timorous butterfly,
the many-hued heart of man.

She never rests:
Poseidon is her servant, the Earth-shaker,
and Artemis, huntress;
and Love and Death and Wisdom are all in her retinue.
Sparrows, hawks, bulls, deer, trees, roses—
Hera is in them!

Songbirds whistle on the eaves: Praise Hera!
Exalt her, hills and rivers!
Praise Hera!
Honor her, kingdoms!
Praise Queen Hera!
Honor her all that soars, or walks, or creeps.

Thus sang the *Argo,* Athena's instrument;
and suddenly something was clear: It was not my will resolving
the many wills, and not Orpheus' will, but a thing more complex.
We on the *Argo* were the head, limbs, trunk of a creature, a living thing

larger than ourselves (it was Amykos' idea), a thing puzzling out
its nature, its swim through process. What powered its mammoth heart
was not my will or any other man's, but the fact that by chance
it had stumbled into existence. Confused, diverse desires
hurled the beast north to Aietes' city: my scheme of the fleece,
however important to all of us once, was a passing dream,
less than a ghost of a word in the gloom of the beast's weird mind
(flicker of a bat, frail hint of order, some pious saw).
'We're after the fleece,' the black leviathan could remind itself,
lumbering north, old lightning in its eyes, its monster fins
stretched wide, groping into darkness. But it wasn't the fleece we sought.
Nor anything else. The mind of the beast had no center—had only
its searchingness, its existence. Old Hera was in us—and in
the mysterious ships behind us, travelling in our wake, still following
hungrily, booming, from another time and place. (Say
it was a dream.) We were—and the black-scarped ships behind us were—
the world according to Phineus: cavern of warring gods,
the delicate crust of reason. Thanatos. Eros. And had
no choice, then, but submission: *submit and obey* was the beast's
cruel law. —And if it was tyrannical law, unsubtle as a fist,
it was freedom, too: we were children in the shelter of the kind, mad father's
yard. I had cracked my wits too long on why we were driving
north, affronting all reason. It was merely the creature's will.
It was our business, our custom, our destiny. Too long I'd bathed
in the torrents, streams, still pools of each novel emotion. No more
such lunacy! Sensation, sleep! Imagination,
give up your stolen chair, cold throne of the terat. I was,
I saw at last, the demon's agent, merely—enslaved
as the cords in an orator's throat, or as the Argonauts,
turning in the wind of my words, were tools of my own—or all
but Orpheus. I would overwhelm him as surely as once
we struck down, not out of hate but by force of destiny,
poor Kyzikos, King of the Doliones, or Amykos, famous
boxer who proved inferior and therefore died, as, later,
Polydeukes died of his weakness, excessive humanity, tainted
blood.

   "The ghost fleet gloomed behind us, assenting. And then
it vanished. If there was some meaning in that, we evaded it;
blinked twice, stared fiercely ahead.

        "We'd come to Kallikhorus;

we passed the tomb of Sthenelos, son of Aktor, who fought
with Herakles in his Amazon raid. His dusky ghost
rose up and signalled to the ship in his warlike panoply,
moonlight gleaming on the four plates and the scarlet crest
of his helmet. We brailed the sail. The old seer Mopsos said
we must stay, put the ghost to rest. I was not in a mood to debate,
still half dazed by my insight into the beast we'd become
a part of—Mopsos an impulse, an instinct, a pressure not to be
resisted. I gave the order. We cast our hawsers ashore,
paid honor to the tomb. Libations; sheep. Sang praise of the ghost
invisible except for his armor. And then set forth once more
on the sea. At dawn, came round the Cape of Karambis,
and all that day and on through the night we rowed the *Argo*
north along endless shores. So came to the Assyrian coast,
and took on water, sheep, recruits—three friends of Herakles
stranded by him long since, when he fought with the Amazons.
They bore no grudge, as was right. We took them aboard in haste—
the wind brooked no delay. So, that same afternoon,
rounded the headland that cantled above us like a stone sheltron
guarding the Amazons' harbor. The old men told us a curious
story of the place. They said that once there Herakles
captured the daughter of Ares, Hippolyta's younger sister
Melanippa. He took her by ambush, intending to rape her,
but Hippolyta gave him her own resplendent cestus by way
of ransom, and when he saw her naked, that beautiful virgin—
in later days she was Theseus' queen—the great oaf wept,
all his virtue in his senses. The queen wouldn't lie with him;
the man couldn't think what to do. He might have won, then and there,
his war, but he backed away from her—fled in confusion to the woods—
abandoning the beautiful sisters, his half-wit head full of grandiose
booms, such as Innocence, Honor, Dignity, Virtue. —Not so
when Theseus came. He'd seen a great deal—had walked through Hades
for his friend, when Peirithoös was taken. He knew the meaninglessness of things.
Brought the Amazon forces to check and might, if he wished,
have slaughtered them all. He held back. Observed the naked virgin
on her knees before him, in chains, surrounded by Akhaian guards,
men in great plumes, their war gear gleaming in the tent, and said:
'I'll speak with her majesty alone.' They laughed. Who wouldn't have laughed?—
but Theseus' eyes were cool. The guards withdrew. He said:
'Queen, don't answer in haste. I've won this dreary war,

as you see by the plainest of signs. I could injure you more, if I wished.
Chained hand and foot, you can hardly resist me. I could teach you more
than you dream of humiliation. Yet all I've done—or might
do yet—is nothing to the humiliation of life itself,
this waste where men are abandoned to the whims of gods. I've seen
what games they play with the dead.' And he told of Briareos
with his hundred whirling arms, a beast of prey more terrible,
more ludicrous, to divine minds, than the hurricane
that makes men scurry like squealing rats to shelter, trembling,
whimpering obscenely, clinging to one another's bodies until,
unspeakably, their fear collapses to lust, and under the
screaming winds they couple like dogs in a crate. He told
of the Hydra, from whom the unwoundable dead fly shrieking, bug-eyed,
chased by the thunderous rumble of the laughing gods. Told then
of Tityus, whose obscene weight mocks finitude,
turns heroes' powerful thighs to ridiculous sticks, and told
of pitch-black Prince Dionysos and his soundless dance. 'All this,'
said Theseus, 'I have seen. I can abandon you
to death and all its foolishness, and follow, in time,
as all men must; or we can forestall that mockery
for now. Choose what you will. Either way, I grant you, we're
not much. We've sent our thousands, you and I, to the cave
to wait for us. It hardly matters how long they wring
their shadowy hands and watch. Choose what you will.'
                                                    "The Amazon
laughed. 'Nothing of my virgin beauty? Nothing, O king,
of my fierce pride, my loyalty? Nothing of how, in the hall,
passing the golden bowl, my great robes trailing, I might
adorn your royal magnificence?—Nothing of my breasts, my thighs?'
Theseus sighed. 'I'd serve you better than you think. I have seen
dead women—shadowy thighs, sweet breasts—going out and away
like a sea.'
        "Then, more than by all his talk of Briareos
and the rest, the queen was moved. She said: 'You do not fear
I'll kill you, then, in your bed?' Old Theseus touched her chin,
tipped up her face. 'I fear that, yes.' And so he left her,
and so the war was resolved; she became his queen. The two
became one creature, a higher organism with meanings of its own,
groping upward to a troubled kind of sanctity. (All that
was later. We knew, at the time the old men told the tale

of Herakles, nothing of Theseus' later gains.) I saw,
whatever the others saw, one more clear proof of the beauty
of cool, tyrannical indifference, and the comic stupidity
of Herakles' simpering charity, girlish fright. The future
lies, I thought, not with Herakles, howling in the night for love
of a boy—much less with such boys themselves, sweet scented, lost.
The future lies with the sons of the *Argo*'s officers,
rowing in furious haste past peace, past every peace,
searching out war's shrill storm of conflicting wills.

                                     "We struck
and plundered, then fled that Amazon land, moved on to the shores
of the Khalybes, that dreary race that plants no corn,
no fruit, never tames an ox. They dig in search of iron,
darken the skies with soot. They see no sun or moon,
and know no rest. From a mile offshore you can hear their coughing,
dry as a valley of goats. We took on water and left
in haste. We'd seen too much, of late, of death. Yet they
were men like ourselves, we knew by the eyes in their smudged faces,
blacker than Ethiopians'. Surely they had not
meant to evolve into this! —But we had no heart to pity
or ponder that. Ghost ships passed us. Vast, dark dreams,
troubles in the smoky night. Sometimes the strangers hailed us,
called out questions in a foreign tongue. We bent to the oars,
pushed on. And so we eluded them.

                                 "We passed the land
of the Tibareni, where men go to bed for their wives in their time
of labor. He lies there groaning, with his quop of a head wrapped up,
and his good wife lovingly feeds him, prepares a bath. We passed
the land of the Mossynoeki, where the people make love
in the streets, like swine in the trough; oh, they were a pretty race,
as gentle as calves. When Orpheus sang to them of shame, remorse,
of beasts and men, they smiled, blue-eyed, and applauded his song.
We were baffled; finally amused. We kissed them, women and men,
and left. Let the gods improve them. And so to the island of Ares,
where the war god's birds attacked us. We soon outwitted them.

   "That night old Argus sat on the ground, by the firelight,
studying the wing of a bird, one of those we'd killed. His eyes
were slits. 'Still learning?' I said. The old man smiled and nodded.
'Secrets of Time and Space,' he said. 'The gods are patient.'
I waited. He said no more. His delicate fingers spread

the pinions, brighter than silver and gold in that flickering light.
The bird's head flopped on its golden neck, beak open, bright
eyes wide. They had seen the god himself. Now nothing. I said:
'It's old, this creature?' Argus nodded. 'Old as the world is.
Older than the whole long history of man from Jason down
to the last pale creature crawling in poisonous slime to his loveless
lair, the cave of his carnage.' I stared at him, alarmed. 'Explain.'
Old Argus smiled, looked weary, and made a pass with his hand.
'There are no explanations, only structures,' he said.
'A structured clutter of adventures, encounters with monsters, kings . . .'
He gazed toward sea, toward darkness. 'The mind of man—' he said,
then paused. The thought had escaped him. In the lapping water, the *Argo*
sighed. *You are caught in irrelevant forms.* So I'd heard, in my dream.
Caught, the black ship whispered. I would make the best of it.
Tiphys was dead, our pilot, and Idmon, younger of the seers.
We were left to the steering of a boy, the visions of a half-cracked witch.
We were better off, could be. We knew where we stood.

                                        "There came
a storm, sudden, from nowhere. We cowered in the trees. Mad Idas
whispered, 'Go to it! Show your violence, Zeus! We're learning!
"Submit and obey," says the wind, "for I am a wind from Zeus,
Great Father who beats my head and batters my ass as I
whip yours. Submit and obey! Look upward with cringing devotion
to me just as I do to Zeus, for I am better. Do I
not shake your beard? Crack treelimbs over your head? Sing praise
of Boreas!" ' Idas' moustache foamed like the sea, and his eyes
jerked more wildly than the branches whipping in the gale. His brother,
staring out into darkness, made no attempt to hush him.
'We're learning, still learning,' mad Idas howled. He got up on his knees.
and the gale shot wildly through his robes, sent him out like a flag. 'As you
whip us, great Boreas, we the lords of the *Argo* will whip
Aietes' men—cornhole the king and his counsellors, fuck
great ladies! So much for kindness, the hope of the cow! So much
for equality, soft, nonsensical, sweetness of the whimsical tit!
We're learning!' At a sudden gust, he fell headlong. Lynkeus reached out
and touched him, without expression. The fierce wind whistled in our ears.
Orpheus was silent, daunted. If Idas was wrong, it was not for
Orpheus to say: he was an instrument, merely: a harp to the fingers
of the gods. (And I was by no means sure he was wrong.)

                                        "Then came

dawn's eyes, and we looked out to sea and we saw, to the east and west,
black wreckage. And we saw a beam in the harbor, rising and falling,
and men. As they came toward land, we stripped and went out to them
to help. We drew them to the sandy shore. Four men, half drowned,
clinging to the splintered beam with fingers stiffened into claws.
We laid them down by the fire and fed them. Soon as they could speak,
we asked their race. The sons of Phrixos, they said. (We were not
surprised. We'd heard from Phineus how we'd meet with them,
and all their troubles before.) They came from Kolchis, kingdom
of Aietes, where exiled Phrixos lived. You know the story:
    "The king of the Orkhomenians had two wives.
By the first, he had two sons, Phrixos and Helle. When the first wife
died, and he married the second, that cruel and jealous woman
twisted an old, murky oracle and suggested to the king
that Phrixos be given in sacrifice for the pleasure of Zeus.
The king agreed, but Phrixos escaped with his brother, flying
on a monstrous ram of gold which the great god Hermes sent.
Above the Hellespont, Helle fell off and was lost. The huge ram
turned his head, encouraging Phrixos on, and so
they came at last to Kolchis, and there, on the ram's advice,
Phrixos gave up the ram in sacrifice to Zeus, and gave
the fleece to Aietes, the king, in return for his eldest daughter.
Now the four sons had abandoned Aietes' city to return
to their father's homeland, city of the Orkhomenians,
intending to claim their rights. But Zeus, to show his power,
stirred Boreas up from his sleep and ordered pursuit of them.
The North Wind had softly blown all day through the topmost branches
of the mountain trees and scarcely disturbed a leaf; but then
when nightfall came, he fell on the sea with tremendous force
and raised up angry billows with his shrieking blasts. A dark mist
blanketed the sky; no star pierced through. The sons of Phrixos,
quaking and drenched, were hurled along at the mercy of the waves,
spinning like a top at each sudden gust and flaw. The dark wind
tore off the sailsheets, split the hull at the keel. They caught hold
of a beam, the last of the firmly bolted timbers that scattered
like birds alarmed in the night as the ship broke up. Black wind
and waves were pushing them to shore when a sudden rainstorm burst.
It lashed the sea, the island, and the mainland opposite.
They gave up hope, passed out, still clinging to the beam. So we

discovered them, close to the shore, some whimsical gift or tease
from the gods.

    " 'Whoever you are,' the sons of Phrixos said,
'we beg you by Zeus to provide us help in our need. We are men
on a mission we cannot abandon, not even now, stripped bare,
weakened, ridiculed by winds. We have sworn a solemn vow
to our father, the hour of his death, that we will redeem his throne
and wealth. No easy adventure, beaten as we are, pushed past
despair. Yet the vow's been made, and we will fulfill it if we can.'
 "I glanced at my crew. It seemed they hardly understood what wealth
the sea had sent. No need of a Tiphys or an Idmon now!
We had, right here in our hands, men born and bred in the east,
sailors who knew these streams as we knew the Pegasai,
and they knew the kingdom of Aietes—no doubt had friends among
that barbarous race. We could use these poor drowned rats! I seized
the hands of the man who spoke for them, youngest of the brothers, Melas.
'Kinsman!' I said, and laughed. I turned to the others. 'You
who beg us for strangers' help are long lost kinsmen, for I
am Jason, son of Aison, son of Dionysos, Lord
of the Underworld. Your famous father and my own father
were cousins, and I have sailed with these friends for no other cause
than to seek you out and return you safe to your homeland, with all
the chattel and goods you may rightfully claim as your own. Of all that
more in a while. For now, let us dress you and arm you, and offer
a sacrifice, as is right, to the god of this island.' The crew
brought clothes, the finest we had, and heirloom swords, and we built
an altar and made a great sacrifice of sheep. When that
was done and we'd feasted our fill, I spoke to them again, framed words
to suit their needs and mine, and to please the Argonauts,
indeed, to please even Orpheus, if possible.
  " 'Zeus is most truly the all-seeing god! Sooner or later
we god-fearing men that uphold the right must come to his attention.
See how he rescued your father Phrixos from a heartless woman,
his cruel step-mother, and made him a wealthy man besides.
And see how he saved you yourselves, preserved you in the deadly storm
and brought you directly to those who have come here in search of you!
And finally this: see how he's armed you, not only with swords
but with fighting companions, the mightiest fighters now living—Akastos,
my cousin, and Phlias, my father's half-brother (don't mind those staring

eyes: he has no mind; a dancer)—and Orpheus,
king of all harpers, and Mopsos, king of all seers, and Argus,
famous artificer—' Thus I named them all, and praised them,
praising the god. They listened smiling, heads bowed. I said:
'The sacred vow you have sworn to your dying father gives all
this crew, I think, new purpose. For it cannot be hidden, I think,
loath though I am to speak of it—that we've suffered great losses,
sorrows and pains that have checked us, nearly overcome us. Your vow—'
I paused, as if undecided. 'On board our ship you can travel
eastward or westward, whichever you choose. Either to the city
Aietes rules, or home to your dear Orkhomenos. You'll need
no stronger craft, your own smashed to bits by the angry sea,
never having come, if I remember, even to the Clashing Rocks,
those doors no ship but the *Argo* has ever passed.' I frowned,
pretended to reflect, like a man who's lost his thread. And then:
'However, it seems to me that you may have forgotten something.
Who but Zeus could have brewed up this terrible storm? Must we not
atone, disavow the intended sacrifice to Zeus of Phrixos—
curse, these many years, of all the Akhaian isles, and
mockery of all his justice? And was not the golden fleece
your father's—a prize he gave up to Aietes' might, forgetting
that gifts of the gods are loans? I am not a seer, of course.
I may be wrong. On the other hand, if you served as our pilots,
running no risk but the sea, who knows what peace it might mean
for Phrixos' ghost? This much seems sure: When winds churn waves,
the god of the sky is aware of it. If we help you flee,
against his will, it may be not even Athena can save
her ship. —But the deathbed vow is yours, of course, not ours.'
I spoke it gently, like a slow man thinking aloud. They stared—
the sons of Phrixos—aghast. They knew well enough, no doubt,
Aietes would not prove affable if we dared to steal
that fleece. Young Melas spoke, when he found his voice. 'Lord Jason,
be sure you can count on our help in any other trouble but this!
Aietes is nobody's fool, and anything but weak. He claims
his father was the sun. You'd believe it, if ever you saw him! His men
are numberless, and the fiercest warriors on earth. His voice
is terrifying. He's huge as the god of war. It will be
no easy trick to snatch that fleece. It's guarded, all around,
by a serpent, deathless and unsleeping, a child of Hera herself,
the mightiest beast in the world. Your scheme's impossible!'

168

"The Argonauts paled at his words. Then Peleus spoke. 'My friend,
if all you say is true, and the thing's impossible,
at least we might see this snake, as a tale for our grandchildren.
And yet it may be, at the last minute, we may happen to spot
some oversight in Aietes' careful precautions. I say
we look, then scurry if we must.' At once all the Argonauts
took heart. Mad Idas rolled up his eyes, all piety.
'Men who make vows to the dying should try to fulfill them, if it's
convenient,' he said. We laughed to prevent him from more. I said:
'It's late. We'll talk of this further tomorrow.' The crew agreed.
We slept, Peleus on watch, by my order, lest Phrixos' sons
evade the promised discussion and leave us marooned. At dawn
we persuaded them, sailed east. By dark we were passing the isle
of Philyra. From there to the lands of the Bekheiri,
the Sapeires, the Byzeres, travelling with all the speed
the light wind gave. The last recess of the Black Sea opened
and gave us a view of the lofty crags of the Caucasus,
where Prometheus stood chained with fetters of bronze, screaming,
an eagle feeding on his liver. We saw it in late afternoon,
the eagle high above the ship in the yellow-green light. It was near
the clouds, yet it made all the canvas quiver in the wind as its wings
beat by. The long white feathers of its terrible wings rose, fell,
like banks of highly polished oars. Soon after the eagle passed,
we heard that scream again. Then again it passed above us,
flying the same way it came. So Aietes would scream, I swore,
and all his sycophants.
                    "Night fell, and after a time,
guided by Melas, we came in the dark to the estuary
of Phasis, where the Black Sea ends. Then quickly we lowered sail
and stowed the sail and yard in the mastcage, and lowered the mast
beside them; then rowed directly to the river. It rolled in foam
from bank to bank, pushed back by the *Argo*'s prow. On the left,
the lofty Caucasus Mountains and the city of Aia; on the right,
the plain of Ares and the sacred grove where the snake kept watch
on the fleece, spread coil on coil through the groaning branches of an oak,
the mightiest oak in the world. We stared in wonder, in the moonlight.
I glanced at Orpheus' lyre. He smiled, shook his head. 'Not this one.'
I turned toward Mopsos. 'Fire in the tree, you think?' He laughed.
'And make that creature cross, boy? Not on your life!' The dusky
eyes stared out at us, dreaming, if old snakes dream. I poured

libations out, pure wine as sweet as honey from a golden
cup—a gift to the river, to earth, to the gods of the hills,
to the spirits of the Kolchian dead. Then the boy Ankaios spoke:
'We've reached the land of Kolchis. The time has come to choose.
Will we speak to Aietes as friends, or try him some harsher way?'
Nobody answered him, all of us weighing the power of the snake.

    "Advised by Melas, I ordered my men to row the *Argo*
to the reedy marshes, and to moor her there with anchor stones
in a sheltered place where she could ride. We found one, not far off,
and there we passed the night, our eyes wide open, waiting.
No one asked me now if the thing we were doing made sense.
War proves itself—all reason slighter than a feather in the wind
beside that strange aliveness, chilling of the blood, dark joy.
We'd become what we were, at last: a machine for theft: a creature
stalking the creature in the tree, our multiple wills interlocked,
our multiple hungers annealed by the heat of the great snake's threat.
I whispered my name to myself and it rang like a stranger's name,
the name of a god, an eagle, some famous old Titan's sword.
Behind me, stretching to the rim of the world, ghost armies waited,
silent, nameless, in strange attire, watching for my sign
with eyes as calm as dragons' eyes. The goddess was in us."

13

So he spoke, and the visiting kings sat hushed, as if spellbound, through
those shadowy halls. It seemed to me that his weird vision
of armies behind him, waiting in the wings, stirred all who heard him
to uneasiness. As he ended, the room went strange. The walls
went away like the floor of the sea, yet vast as the great hall seemed,
the goddess showed me chambers beyond, blue-vaulted rooms,
expanses of marble floor like a wineglass filled to the brim
with light, and marmoreal peristyles, each shining pillar
twelve feet wide, the architraves made hazy by hovering
clouds; and in those spacious rooms where no life stirred,
I might not have guessed the existence of all those gold-crowned kings
attending to Jason's tale.
                    I found
a room where slaves were whispering the name
Amekhenos. The goddess showed me
where he crouched in the bowels of the palace peering out, eyes narrowed,
watching the palace guards pace back and forth on the wall,
their queer strut mirrored in the lilypad-strewn lake. The grass
was as green as grass in a painting, the sky unnaturally blue;
the walls of houses below were the white of English cream,
with angular shadows, an occasional tree,
its leaves autumnally blazing. Far to the east, beyond
the sea's last glint, it occurred to me, there were more kings gathered,
brought together by the tens of thousands,
to die for Helen, or honor, or the spoils of war on the plains
of Troy. Beside the guests of Kreon, the numberless host
of Agamemnon's army would seem the whole human race.
Yet beyond rich Troy lay Russia—darkforested Kolchis—and Indus,

and beyond those two lay China, so many in a host that the eye,
even the eye of vision, couldn't gather them in. "Behold!"
the goddess said, invisible all around me. With the word
she darkened the sky, and the grayblue waters became, all at once,
a horde of people on the move, bearing their possessions on their backs,
features ragged with hunger, eyes too large, luminous.
The children walking at their parents' sides or straggling behind
had distended bellies, and I knew by the gray of their eyes that they carried
plagues. I watched them passing—the crowd went out from me
from horizon to horizon, and the dust they stirred
made a cloud so vast that the mightiest rays of the sun were hidden.
Suddenly the cloud was a dragon with a fat-thighed woman on its back,
her chalk-white, hydrocephalic forehead covered all over
with elegant writing, swirls and serifs that squirmed like insects
as I tried to read. The woman had a robe of flowing crimson
and she carried a torch which belched thick smoke like factory smoke.
She rode toward me, and then—from north, south, east, and west—
great louts came lumbering, treading on the people, and made their way,
teetering and reeling, to the huge woman. With her hands, she raised
her skirt and spread her buttocks for them, and roaring, prancing,
they thrust themselves in, and the earth and sky were sickened with filth,
blackened to a towering mass like a writhing, bull-horned god.
I choked and gagged. "Goddess!" I cried out. "Goddess, save me!"
   Gulls darted back and forth above the grayblue water,
mournfully calling. The slaves in the palace were whispering.
And then, baffled, still puzzling at the meaning of the strange revelation,
I was back in the hall of Kreon, where Jason was standing as I'd left him,
silent, and old King Kreon was waiting, the slave beside him,
Ipnolebes. I wondered if all I had seen I'd seen
in Ipnolebes' eyes, or perhaps the eyes of the Northern slave
watching the guards as they strutted, this side of the battlements,
or the slaves who whispered. I shuddered and shook myself free of all that,
or tried to. The curious image held on. The gem-lit, gold-crowned
heads of the visiting kings (there seemed not many of them now)
strangely recalled the numberless hosts of ánhagas,
friendless exiles forever on the move in perpetual night.

   I could see by Kreon's pleasure and the timorous smile of Pyripta
that Jason's story was winning them. Indeed, not a soul
thought otherwise. It seemed no contest now. He'd seized

their hearts and minds by his crafty wit and clung like a bat
to his advantage. His thoughts were dangerous, and they knew it. His scheme,
now clear, was impossible to block. When men sit talking by the fire,
exchanging opinions of interest, discussing
betrothals, curious adventures, and one, by the moving of his sleeve,
reveals a scorpion, all mere trading of civilized insights
stops: Death takes priority. So Jason, spinning
his web of words, closed off all other business. They must hear it through, approve
or not. Yet fat Koprophoros wouldn't give up his hopes
entirely. As Jason waited, the ghastly creature rose,
his eyelids drowsily lowered on his dark and brilliant eyes,
and spoke.
      "My lords, this Jason is rightly renowned for his cunning!
See what he's done to us! Penned us up like chickens in a coop
by his artistry! First he seduces our girlish emotions
with a tale of love—the poor sweet queen of Lemnos!—and wins
our grudging respect by disingenuous admissions of his cruel
betrayal in that grungy affair. But that was mere feinting, test
of the equipment! For behold, having shown us beyond all shadow of a doubt—
so he made it seem—that solemn Paidoboron and I were wrong,
two addlepates, you'd swear—myself no better than a tyrant,
and my friend from the North a coward ('like one of the gods' pale shuddering
nuns' was, I think, his phrase), he uses our chief ideas
to create an elaborate hoax, a dismal drama of anguish
in which he—always heroic beyond even Orpheus!—
encounters monsters more fierce than any centaur—monsters
of consciousness. Have I misunderstood? Is not his tale
of poor young Kyzikos and the Doliones an allegory
attacking all human skills—the skills of sailors, armies,
even augurers?—Skills like mine, like Paidoboron's?
It's a frightening thought, you'll confess, that the essence of humanness—
man's conviction that craft, the professional's art, may save him—
is drunken delusion! We hunch forward in our chairs, ambsaced,
waiting for Jason, who conjured the bogy, to exorcise it.
But ha! That's not his strategy. Pile on more anguish,
that's the ticket! The tales of Herakles and Hylas, and poor Polydeukes.
Human commitment, love of one man for another—that too
goes up, by his trickery, in smoke. Ah, how we suffered for Jason,
watching him through those losses! Who'd fail to award poor Jason
whatever prize is available, guerdon for his sorrows! And while

we wait, we children, for proof that true love exists, as we hoped,
he stifles our life-thirsty souls in old Phineus' winding-sheet!
'O woeful man,' he teaches us, 'all life is a search
for death.' —Is that the fleece for which we blindly sail
chill seas? And yet we believe it, since Jason tells us so,
Jason of the Golden Tongue! And even the skeleton's sickle
is meaningless! So Jason's physicians preach: 'decay
of the extremities,' 'the element of Chance at the heart of all
our projects.' 'Und Alles Sein ist flammend Leid,' we cry.
'O, save us, Jason,' we howl in dismay, 'feed us with raisin cakes,
restore us with apples, for we are sick with loss!' " Koprophoros
gaped, eyes wide. "Are we wrong to think there's a life before death?"
He shuddered. "We wring our hands, cast up our eyes to heaven
whimpering for help. But heaven will not look down. No, only
Jason can save our souls, sweet Golden Lyre. And in
our need, what does he send us? Another great bugaboo!
We're victims: we're groping cells in the body of a monster seeking
its own dark, meaningless end! What man can believe such things?
No man, of course! And soon, when the time is right, be sure
he'll rescue us—when he's twisted and turned us by all his tricks,
baffled our desire, exhausted our will—he'll discover the secret
of joy exactly where he hid it himself, in some curlicue
of his death-cold python of a plot. Nor will we object, if we,
as Jason supposes, are children.
                    "But I think of Orpheus . . ."
The Asian paused, looked thoughtful, his hand on his chin. Then:
"Jason's revealed it himself: there are artists and artists. One kind
pulls strings, manipulates the minds of his hearers, indifferent to truth,
delighting solely in his power: a man who exploits without shame,
snatches men's words, thoughts, gestures and turns them to his purpose—attacks
like a thief, a fratricide, and makes himself rich, feels no remorse:
lampoons good men out of envy, to avenge some trivial slight,
or merely from whim, as a proof of his godlike omnipotence.
His mind skims over the surface of dread like a waterbug,
floats on logic like a seagull asleep on a dark unrippled
sea. But the sea is alive, we suddenly remember! The mind
shorn free of its own green deeps of love and hate, desire
and will—the mind detached from the dark of tentacles
mournfully groping toward light—is a mind that will ruin us:
thought begins in the blood—and comprehends the blood.

The true artist, who speaks with justice,
who rules words in the fear of God,
is like morning light at sunrise filling a cloudless sky,
making the grass of the earth sparkle after rain.
But false artists are like desert thorns
whose fruit no man gathers with his hand;
no man touches them
unless it's with iron or the shaft of a spear,
and then they are burnt in the fire.

                              "My friends,
Orpheus was that true artist! He boldly sang the world
as it is, sang men as they are—a master of simplicity,
a man made nobler than all other men by his humanness.
'There's beauty in the world,' he said, and courageously told of it.
'And there's evil,' Orpheus said, and wisely he pointed out cures.
We praise this Jason's intellectual fable: it fulfills our worst
suspicions. But the fable's a lie." He said this softly, calmly,
and all of us sitting in the hall were startled by the change in the man,
once so arrogant, so full of his own importance, so quick
himself to use sleight-of-wits. The hall was hushed, reproached.
"We may have misjudged this creature," I thought, and at once remembered
the phrase was Koprophoros' own.
                              Jason said nothing, but sat
with pursed lips, brow furrowed, and he seemed by his silence to admit
the truth in Koprophoros' charge.
                              Then Paidoboron rose and said:
"As a man, not as an artist, I would condemn the son
of Aison. His betrayals of men are as infamous as Herakles' own.
His tale seeks neither to excuse or explain them, but only to make us
party to his numerous treasons. We all know well enough
the theme of his tale of Lemnos: as once, for no clear reason
(unless it was simple exhaustion, mother of indifference),
he abandoned the yellow-haired daughter of Thoas—so now, for no
just reason, he'd abandon Medeia for Lady Mede."
                              The wide
hall gasped at that frontal attack. The tall, black-bearded king
stared with fierce eyes at Jason. The lord of the Argonauts
paled, but he neither lowered his gaze nor flinched. King Kreon
glanced at Pyripta in alarm. She opened her mouth as if

to speak, but said nothing, pressing one hand to her heart. The Northerner
said, grim-voiced: "Treason by treason he undermines
morality. He tells of the treason of the Doliones,
how they offer, one moment, a feast, fine wine, and the next moment turn,
forgetting the sacred laws of hospitality,
more barbarous even than the spider people, who were, at least,
within their earthborn natures consistent. Are the Doliones
condemned in Jason's tale? Not at all! They get threnodies!
For even the gods betray, according to Jason, as do
their seers. So Hylas—whom Jason excuses by virtue of his youth
and the soft, warm weather that shameful night—betrays his trust
as squire, goes up to the furthest of the pools. So the Argonauts
all turn, as one, against Herakles. So Phineus
betrays, defying the gods; so Mopsos turns in scorn
on dying men; and so all the crewmen, spurred by the mad
philosophy of Idas, betray the core of humanness, become
a mindless, fascistic machine. Thus cunningly Jason persuades
that treason is life's great norm. He pulls the secret wires
of our angular heads, makes us empathize with his own foul sin,
and bilks us all of the heart's sure right to condemn such sin.
Corrupter! Exploiter! No more such fumets! The world is alive
with laws, and all who defy them will at last be destroyed by them.
Think back on the days of old, think over the years, down the ages.
Are the gods blind? indifferent to evil and stupidity?
They've spoken in all man's generations, and they speak even now:
'You are fat, gross, bloated, a deceitful and underhanded brood,
a nation wealthy and empty-headed. Your hills will tremble
and your carcases will be torn apart in the midst of streets.

> *A great fire has blazed from my anger.*
> *It will burn to the depths of Hades' realm.*
> *It will devour the earth and all its produce;*
> *it will set fire to the foundations of mountains.'* "

The dark king paused, his words still ringing, and his eyes had no spark
of humanness in them, it seemed to me. Jason said nothing.
Then, once more, Paidoboron spoke, more quietly now,
his hoarse, dry voice like an oracle's voice through cavern smoke:
"You've raised up again and again that towering son of Zeus,
fierce Herakles, as the chief of betrayers, suggesting that nought
you've done, or might do, could hold a candle to his perfidy.

Shame, seducer! The ideal of loyalty raged in that man!
Loyalty to Zeus, to Hylas, to his friends. He struck down Hylas'
father from passionate hatred of his evil State—never mind
how cheap his murderous stratagem. He threatened to lay
all Mysia waste out of passionate sorrow at loss of his friend.
And in the same mad rage he murdered the sons of Boreas,
who had loved him weakly, intellectually, and prevented your ship
from turning back when you'd stranded him. Wide-minded Zeus
did not bequeath his wisdom to his son: from Alkmene he got
his brains. But the sky-god's absolutes burned in Herakles
like quenchless underground fire. They do not burn in you.
Impotent, wily, colubrine, you'd buy and sell
all man's history, if it lay in your power. Ghost ships indeed!
Civilization beware if Jason is the model for it!
When feelings perish—the wound we share with the cow and the lion—
then rightly the world will return to the rule of spiders." So
he spoke, and would say no more. And Aison's son said nothing.
I would not have given three straws, that moment, for Jason's hopes.

And then, all at once, came an eerie change. The red-leaved branches
framed in the windows, blowing in the autumn wind, snapped into
motionlessness. Every man, fly, cricket,
the wine that fell streaming from the lip of the pitcher in the slave boy's hand,
hung frozen. It seemed the scene had become a divine projection
on a golden screen. Then, in that stillness, Hera leaped up,
eyes blazing, and, turning to Athena, flew into a rage. "Sly wretch!"
she bellowed. I flattened to the floor. Her voice made the rafters shake,
though it failed to awaken the sea-kings, frozen to marble. Athena
fell a step backward, quaking. I had somehow dropped my glasses,
so that all I could see of the goddesses was a luminous blur.
I felt by the wall, furtive as a mouse, and at last I found them,
hooked them over my ears in haste and peeked out again.
The queen of goddesses wailed: "What a perfect *fool* I was
to trust you even for an instant! You just can't *resist,* can you!
I think you're my true ally, and I listen to Jason's cunning,
and I think, 'That Athena! The goddess of mind is surely Zeus's
masterpiece!' And what are *you* thinking? You're dreaming up *answers!*
You don't *care!* You don't care about *anything!* He stops to take a breath
and your quick wit darts to old Fatslats there, and you inspire him with words
and you ruin all Jason's accomplished! —And *you,* you halfwit—"
She whirled to confront Aphrodite. "You caused the whole thing! You change

your so-called mind and forget about Medeia and make our Pyripta
all googley-poo over Aison's son, and Athena can't help it,
she has to oppose you. It's a habit, after all these centuries."
Aphrodite blushed scarlet and backed away as her sister had done.
"Your Majesty, do be reasonable," Athena said.
Her voice was soft—it was faint as a zephyr, in fact, from fear.
But the wife of Zeus did not prefer to be reasonable.
Her dark eyes shone like a stormcloud blooming and rippling with light.
"Betrayal," she groaned, and clenched her fists. "That's good. That's really
good! You make Paidoboron talk of betrayal, how fine
true loyalty is, and you, you don't bat an eyelash at how
your trick's a betrayal of me! Does nothing in the world count?
How can you do it, forever and ever manufacturing structures,
when the whole vast ocean of Time and Space is thundering aloud
on the rocks, and the generations of men are all
on the run, rootless and hysterical?"

                                        "Your Majesty, please,
I beg you," Athena said. The queen of goddesses paused,
still angry, I thought, but not unaware of gray-eyed Athena's
fear and helplessness. Aphrodite kept quiet, her dark
eyes large. Hera waited—stern, but not tyrannical, at last;
and at last Athena spoke, head bowed, her lovely arms
stretched out, imploring. "You're wrong, this once, to reproach me, Goddess.
I do know the holiness of things. I know as well as you
the hungry raven's squawk in winter, the hunger of nations,
the stench of gotch-gut wealth, how it feeds on children's flesh.
I've pondered kings and ministers with their jackals' eyes,
presidents sweetly smiling with the hearts of wolves. I've seen
the talented well-meaning, men not chained to greed,
able to sacrifice all they possess for one just cause,
fearless men, and shameless, earnestly waiting, lean,
ready to pounce when the cause is right—waiting, waiting—
while children die in ambiguous causes, and wicked men
make wars—waiting—waiting for the war to reach their streets,
waiting for some unquestionable wrong—waiting on graveward . . .
Precisely because of all that I've done what I've done, raised men
to test this lord of the Argonauts. I have never failed him
yet, and I will not now; but I mean to annoy him to conflict,
badger till he racks his brains for a proof he believes, himself,
of his worthiness. I mean to change him, improve him, for love

of Corinth, Queen of Cities. You speak of Space and Time.
No smallest grot, O Queen, can shape its identity
outside that double power: a thing is its history,
the curve of its past collisions, as it locks on the moment. What force
it learned from yesterday's lions is now mere handsel in the den
of the dragon Present Space. And therefore I raise opposition
to Jason's will, to temper it. His anguine mind,
despite those rueful looks, will find some way."

                                                The queen
seemed dubious. It was not absolutely clear to me
that she perfectly followed the train of thought.
But hardly knowing what else to be, she was reconciled.
Gray-eyed Athena, encouraged, and ever incurably impish,
turned to the love goddess. "You, sweet sister," she said with a look
so gentle I might have wept to see it, "don't take it to heart
that the queen of goddesses turns on you in her fury when I,
and I alone, am at fault. If my motives indeed were those
she first suspected, then well might I call to my dear Aphrodite—
sitting graveolent in her royal hebetation, surrounded by all
her holouries—for help. Such is not the case, however.
Let there be peace between us, I pray, as always." So speaking
she raised Aphrodite's hands and tenderly kissed them. The love goddess
sobbed.

                Then everything moved again—the branches in the windows,
the people, the animals, wine in the pitcher. Then Kreon rose.
The roar died down respectfully.

                            "These are terrible charges,"
the old man said, and his furious eyes flashed fire through the hall,
condemned the whole pack. "I've lived many years and seen many things,
but I doubt that even in war I have seen such hostility.
When Oidipus sought in maniacal rage that man who'd brought down
plagues on Thebes—when Antigone left me in fiery indignation
to defy my perhaps inhuman but surely most reasonable law—
not then nor then did I see such wrath as has narrowed the eyes
of Paidoboron and Koprophoros. It's not easy for me
to believe such outrage can trace its genesis to reason! However,
the charge, whatever its source, requires an answer." He turned
to Jason, bowed to him and waited. The warlike son of Aison
sat head-bent, still frowning. At last he glanced up, then rose,
and Kreon sat down, gray-faced. The smile half breaking at the corners

of Jason's mouth was Athena's smile; the dagger flash in his eyes was the work
of Hera. Love was not in him, though his voice was gentle.

                                                    "My friends,
I stand accused of atrocities," he said, "and the chief is this:
I have severed my head from my heart, a point made somehow clear
by dark, bifarious allegory. I have lost my soul
to a world where languor cries unto languor, where cicadas sing
'Perhaps it is just as well.' In the real world—the world which I
have lyred to its premature grave—there is love between women and men,
faith between men and the gods. If you here believe all that,
believe that in every condition the good cries fondly to the good,
and the heart, by its own pure fire, can physician the anemic mind,
I would not dissuade you. Faith has a powerful advantage over truth,
while faith endures. But as for myself, I must track mere truth
to whatever lair it haunts, whether high on some noble old mountain,
or down by the dump, where half-starved rats scratch by as they can,
and men not blessed with your happy opinions must feed on refuse
and find their small satisfactions.
                                    "My art is false, you say.
I answer: whatever art I may show is the world itself.
The universe teems with potential Forms, though only a few
are illustrated (a cow, a barn, a startling sunset);
to trace the history of where we are is to arrive where we are.
There are no final points in the journey of life up out of
silence: there are only moments of process, and in some few moments,
insight. Search all you wish for the key I've buried, you say,
in the coils of my plot, Koprophoros. The tale, you'll find,
is darker than that—and more worthy of attention. It exists.
It has its history, its dreadful or joyful direction. The ghostly allegory
you charge me with is precisely what my tale
denies. The truth of the world, if I've understood it, is this:
Things die. Alternatives kill. I leave it to priests to speak
of eternal things.
                    "And as for you, Paidoboron,
if I claim that the world has betrayals in it, don't howl too soon.
Every atom betrays; every stick and stone and galaxy.
Notice two lodestones: notice how they war. But turn one around
and behold how they lock like lovers embraced in their tomb. So this:
some things click in. Some sanctuaries, at least for a time,
are inviolable. What fuses the metals in the ice-bright ring

of earth and sky, burns mind into heart, weds man to woman
and king to state? What power is in them? That, whatever
it is, is the golden secret, precisely the secret I stalk
and all of us here must stalk. I've told you failure on failure,
holding back nothing. But I still have a tale or two to tell—
meaningless enough in the absence of all I've told already—
that you may not mock so quickly."

                              He was silent. Had he tricked them again,
danced them out of their wits like a prophet of gyromancy?
Athena smiled and winked at Jason. Dark Aphrodite
glanced at Hera for assurance that all was well.

                              Then Kreon
rose again, gazed round. When no one dared to speak,
he turned to his slave Ipnolebes, who nodded in silence.
Kreon rubbed his hands together, furious, and at last
pronounced the matter closed. He dismissed the whole assembly
till the hour of the evening meal, when Jason would resume his tale,
and, taking the princess' elbow in his hand, bowing to left
and right, unsmiling, he descended from the dais. As the two passed
the threshold, the others all rose and followed, and so the hall
was emptied except for the slaves—near the door the Northerner
and the boy. The goddess vanished. The vision went dark. I heard
the nightmare crowd on the move again, in the shadow of the beast,
smothered in the skirts of the prostitute. Then sound, too, ceased,
and I hung in darkness, nowhere, clinging to the oak's rough bark.
A blore of wind, like the breeze at the entrance to a cave, tore
at the ragged tails of my overcoat, sheathed my spectacles in ice.

14

I stood, by the goddess' will, in Medeia's room. Pale light
fell over her, fell swirling, burning on the golden fleece
beside her, and then moved on, moved past the two old slaves
to the door where the children watched. I could not look at them
for pain and shame. Dreams they might be, as old and pale
as ghosts in the cairns of Newgrange, but dream or solid flesh,
they were children, inexplicably doomed. How could I close my wits
on truths so weird? (Who can believe in the spectre who walks
leukemia wards, who stands severe above laughing girls
whose hearts pump dust? Who can believe those pictures in the news
of a million children, senselessly cursed, dying in silence,
caught up in Dionysos' wars, or the refugee camps
of Artemis?) All time inside them . . . And then I did look,
searching their eyes for the secret, and found there nothing. Softly,
my guide, invisible around me, spoke. "Poor dim-eyed stranger,
you've understood the question, at least. Look! Look hard!
Study their eyes, windows of the world you seek and they
have not yet dreamed the price of: the timeless instant. They have
no plans, only flimmering dreams of plans, intentions dark
as the lachrymal flutter of corpse-candles. Their time is reverie.
But already will is uncoiling there. They flex their fingers,
restless at the long dull watch. The garden is filled with birds,
bright sunlight. They remember a cart with a broken wheel, a cave
of vines by the garden wall. They have now begun to be
of two minds. Now love and hate grow thinkable,
sacrifice and murder, mercy and judgment. And now, look close:
with a glance at each other—sly grins, infectious, so that we smile too,
remembering, projecting (for we, we too, were children once,

slyly becoming ourselves, unaware of the risk)—they step,
soundless as deer, to the doorway and through it to their liberty.
Or so they guess, unaware that the house will vanish, and the garden—
and the palsied slaves they've slipped they will find transmogrified
to skulls, bits of ashen cloth, dark bone. And they'll wring their hands,
restless again, and search in children's eyes for peace,
in vain. Yet there is peace. Strange peace: from the blood of innocents.
You'll see. The gods have ordained it." I stared, alarmed at that,
and snatched off my glasses to hunt with my naked eyes for the shade—
she-witch, goddess, I knew not what—but no trace of her.
I turned up the collar of my coat, for the room had grown chilly. And then
she spoke one brief word more: "Listen."
                                        On the bed, eyes staring,
Medeia spoke, ensorcelled—death-pale lips unmoving.
I glanced, alarmed, at her eyes and my glance was held; I seemed
to fall toward them, and they weren't eyes now but pits, an abyss,
unfathomable, plunging into space. I cried out, clutched my spectacles.
The wind soughed dark with words and the pitch-dark wings of ravens
crying in Medeia's voice:

                    "I little dreamed, that night,
sleeping in my father's high-beamed hall, that I'd sacrifice
all this, my parents' love, the beautiful home of my childhood,
even my dear brother's life, for a man who lay, that moment,
hidden in the reeds of the marsh. Had I not been happy there—
dancing with the princes of Aia on my father's floors of brass
or walking the emerald hills above where wine-dark oxen
labored from dawn to dusk, above where pruning-men crept,
weary, along dark slopes of their poleclipt vineyard plots?
I'd talked, from childhood up, with spirits, will all-seeing ravens,
sometimes with swine where they fed by the rocks under oak trees, eating
acorns, treasure of swine, and drank black water, making
their flesh grow rich and sweet and their brains grow mystical.
No princess was ever more free, more proud and sure in the halls
of her father, more eager to please with her mother. But the will of the gods
ran otherwise."
                    The voice grew lighter all at once, the voice
of a schoolteacher reading to children, some trifling, unlikely tale
that amuses, fills in a recess, yet troubles the grown-up voice
toward sorrow. She told, as if gently mocking the tragedy,

of gods and goddesses at ease in their windy palaces
where the hourglass-sand takes a thousand years to form the hill
an ant could create, here on earth, in half an hour. She told
of jealousies, foolish displays of celestial skill and spite;
and in all she said, I discovered as I listened, one thing stood plain:
she knew them well, those antique gods and mortals, though she mocked
their foolishness. I peered all around me to locate the speaker,
but on all sides lay darkness, the infinite womb of space.

She told, first, how Athena and Hera looked down and, seeing
the Argonauts hidden in ambush, withdrew from Zeus and the rest
of the immortal gods. When the two had come to a rose-filled arbor,
Hera said, "Daughter of Zeus, advise me. Have you found some trick
to enable the men of the *Argo* to carry the fleece away?
Or have you possibly constructed some flattering speech that might
persuade Aietes to give it as a gift? God knows, the man's
intractable, but nothing should be overlooked." Athena
sighed. She hated to be caught without schemes.
"I've racked my brains, to be truthful," she said, "and I've come up with nothing."

For a while the goddesses stared at the grass, each lost in her own
perplexities. Then Hera's eyes went sly. She said: "Listen!
We'll go to Aphrodite and ask her to persuade that revolting boy
to loose an arrow at Aietes' daughter, Medeia of the many
spells. With the help of Medeia our Jason can't fail!"

Athena
smiled. "Excellent," she said and glanced at Hera, then away.
Hera caught it—no simpleton, ruler of the whole world's will.
"All right," she said, "explain that simper, Lightning-head."
Athena's gray eyes widened. "I smiled?" Hera looked stern. Athena
sighed, then smiled again. "There is . . . a certain logic
to events, as you know, Your Majesty. Your war with Pelias
has taken, I think, a new turn. If Medeia should fall in love
with Jason and win him the fleece, and if she returned with him
and reigned with him—and Pelias . . ." Queen Hera's eyebrows raised,
all shock. "I give you my solemn word I intended no
such thing!" Then, abruptly, she too smiled. Then both of them laughed
and, taking one another's arms, they hurried to the love goddess.

She was alone in her palace. Crippled Hephaiastos had gone to work early,
as he often did, to create odd gadgets for gods and men
in his shop. She was sitting in an inlaid chair, a heart-shaped box
on the arm, and between little nibbles she was combing her lush, dark hair

with a golden comb. When she saw the goddesses standing at the door,
peeking shyly through the draperies—in their dimpled fingers
fans half-flared, like the pinions of a friendly but timorous bird—
she stopped and called them in. She crossed to meet them quickly
and settled the two, almost officiously, in easy chairs,
before she went to her own seat. "How wonderful!" she said,
and her childlike eyes were bright. "It's been ages!"
                                                    The queen of goddesses
smiled politely, cool and aloof in spite of herself. She glanced at Athena,
and Athena, innocent as morning, inquired about Aphrodite's
health, and Hephaiastos' health, and that of "the boy." She could not
bring herself to come out with the urchin's name. When the queen
of love had responded at length—sometimes with tears, sometimes
with a smile that lighted the room like a burst of pink May sun,
the goddess of will broke in, a trifle abruptly, almost
sternly, saying: "My dear, our visit is only partly
social. We two are facing a disaster. At this very moment
warlike Jason and his friends the Argonauts are riding at anchor
on the river Phasis. They've come to fetch the fleece from Aietes.
We're concerned about them; as a matter of fact I'm prepared to fight
with all my power for that good, brave man, and I mean to save him,
even if he sails into Hades' Cave. You know my justified
fury at Pelias, that insolent upstart who slights me whenever
he offers libations. 'Peace whatever the expense' is his motto.
Even those beautiful images of me he's ordered ripped down
from end to end of Argos, for fear some humble herder
may dare to assert himself as Pelias himself did once,
when his brother was rightful king. I won't mince words: I want
his skull, and I want it by Jason's hand—not just because
he's proved himself as a warrior (though heaven knows he's done so).
Once, disguised as an ugly old woman with withered feet,
I met him at the mouth of the Anauros River. The river was in spate—
all the mountains and their towering spurs were buried in snow
and hawk-swift cataracts roared down the sides. I called out, pleading
to be carried across. Jason was hurrying to Pelias' feast,
but despite the advice of those who were with him, despite the rush
of the ice-cold stream, he laughed—bright laugh of a demigod—
and shouted, 'Climb on, old mother! If I'm not strong enough
for two I'm not Aison's son!' Again and again I've tested
his charity, and he's always the same. Say what you like

about Jason, he does not blanch, for himself or for others."

Words failed
the queen of love. The sight of Hera pleading for favors
from her, most mocked of all goddesses, filled her with awe. She said:
"Queen of goddesses and wife of great Zeus,
regard me as the meanest creature living
if I fail you now in your need! All I
can say or do, I will, and whatever small strength I have
is yours." Her sweet voice broke, and her lovely eyes brimmed tears.
Athena looked thoughtful. She could not easily scorn Aphrodite,
whatever her dullness. You might have imagined, in fact, that the goddess
of mind felt a twinge of envy. She was silent, studying her hands.
She knew nothing, daughter of Zeus, of love; but she knew by cool geometry
that she was not all she might be—nor was Hera.

   Hera spoke, choosing her words with care. "We are not
asking the power of your hands. We would like you to tell your boy
to use his wizardry and make the daughter of Aietes fall,
beyond all turning, in love with the son of Aison. Her aid
can make this business easy. There lives no greater witch
in Kolchis, even though she's young."

Then poor Aphrodite paled
and lowered her eyes, blushing. "Perhaps Hephaiastos," she said,
"could make some engine. Perhaps I could speak to—" Her voice trailed off.
"The truth is, he's far more likely to listen to either of you
than to me. He sasses me, scorns me, mocks me. I've had half a mind
to break his arrows and bow in his very sight. Would that be right, do you think?"
She wrung her fingers, looked pitiful. "As you well know, his father and I
do *everything* for him. And how does he pay us? He won't go to bed,
refuses to obey us, says horrible, horrible things, and in front of company!—
but he's a child, of course. How can he learn
to be loving if *we* don't show love and forgiveness? How can he learn
to have generous feelings toward others if we aren't first generous to him?
Parenthood really is a horror!"

Athena and Hera smiled
and exchanged glances. Aphrodite pouted. "People without children,"
she said, "know all the answers. Never mind. I'll do what you ask,
if possible."

Then Queen Hera rose and took Aphrodite's
milkwhite hand in hers. "You know best how to deal with him.
But manage it quickly if you can. We both depend on you."

She turned, started out. Athena followed. Poor Aphrodite,
sighing, went out as well. She'd never been meant to be a mother.
But too late now. (Married to a dreary old gimpleg—she
who'd slept, in her youth, with the god of war himself! —Never mind.
—Nevertheless, it was a bitter thing to waste eternity
with a durgen, genius or not.) She wiped her eye and sniffed.
She glanced through the world and saw Jason, watchful on the *Argo,* a man
as handsome as Ares in his youth. And she turned her eyes to the palace
of Aietes, and saw where Medeia slept, and suddenly her heart
was warmed. The goddesses were right: they made a lovely couple!
Things not possible in heaven she meant to shape on earth.

   The Argonauts were sitting in conference on the benches of their ship.
Row on row sat silent as Jason spoke. "My friends,
my advice is this—if you disagree, speak up. I'll go
with three or four others, to Aietes' palace and parley, find whether
he means to treat us as friends or to try out his army against us.
No point killing a king who, if asked, would gladly oblige us."
With one accord, the Argonauts approved.
With the sons of Phrixos, and with Telamon, the father of Aias,
and with Augeias, Aietes' half-brother, the captain of the Argonauts
set forth. Queen Hera sent a mist before them, so covered the town
that no man saw them till they'd reached Aietes' house. And then
the mist lifted. They paused at the entrance, astonished to see
the half-mile gates, the rows of soaring columns surrounding
the palace walls, and high over all, the marble cornice
resting on triglyphs of bronze. They crossed the threshold then,
unchallenged, and came to the sculptured trees and, below them, four springs,
Hephaiastos' work. One flowed with milk, another with wine,
the third with fragrant oil; but the fourth was the finest of all,
a fountain that, when the Pleiades set, ran boiling hot,
and afterward bubbled from the hollow rock ice-cold. All that,
they would learn in time, was nothing to the flame-breathing bulls of bronze
that the craftsman of the gods had created as a gift for Aietes. There was also
an inner court with ingeniously fashioned folding doors
of enormous size, each of them leading to a splendid room
and to galleries left and right. At angles to the court, on all sides
stood higher buildings. In the highest, Aietes lived with his queen.
In another Apsyrtus lived, Aietes' son, and in yet
another, his daughters, Khalkiope and Medeia. That moment

Medeia was roaming from room to room in search of her sister.
The goddess Hera had fettered Medeia to the house that day;
as a rule she spent most of her day in the temple of Hekate, of whom
she was priestess.
                    The voice of the narrator softened. I had to close
my eyes and concentrate to hear.
                              "And I was that child Medeia,
a thousand thousand lives ago. And yet one moment
stands like a newly made mural ablaze in the sun. I glanced
at the courtyard and saw, as the mist rose, seven men, and their leader
wore black, and his cape was a panther skin. His hand was on his sword,
and his look was as keen as a god's. Without knowing I'd do it, I raised
my hand to my lips, cried out. In an instant the courtyard was astir—
Khalkiope joyfully greeting her sons, her children by Phrixos,
my father approaching on the steps, all smiles, huge arms extended,
and a moment later his servants were working with the carcase of a bull,
more servants chopping up firewood, and others preparing hot water
for baths. I stared from the balcony, half in a daze. Stupidly,
unable to move a muscle, I watched sly Eros creep in
(none of them saw him but me). In the porch, beneath the lintel
he hastily strung his bow, slipped an arrow from the quiver to the string, and,
still unobserved by the others, ran across the gleaming threshold,
his blind eyes sparkles, and crouched at Jason's feet. He drew
the bow as far as his fat arms reached, and fired. I could
do nothing. A searing pain leaped through me. My heart stood still.
With a laugh like a jackal's, the little brute flashed out of sight and was gone
from the hall. The invisible shaft in my breast was flame. Ah, poor
ridiculous Medeia! Time and again she darts a glance
at Jason, and she cannot make out if the feeling is mainly pain
or sweetness!
                    "How can I say what happened then? In a blur,
a baffling radiance, I moved through the feast. His eyes dazzled,
his scent—new oil of his welcoming bath—filled me with anguish
as blood and the smoke of incense-reckels confound the dead.
        "When they'd eaten and drunk their fill, my father Aietes asked questions
of the sons of Khalkiope and Phrixos. I paid no attention, but watched
that beautiful, godlike stranger. He never glanced once at me,
but myself, I could see nothing else. For even if I closed my eyes,
he was there, like the retinal after-image of a candleflame.
Childish love-madness, perhaps. Yet I do not think so, even now.

We're all imperfect, created with some part missing; and I saw
from the first instant my crippled soul's completion in that dark-robed
prince. He stood as if perfectly fearless in front of Aietes,
a king whom he could not help but know, by reputation,
as one of the world's great wizards, king of an enchanted land,
and no mere mortal, for the sun each night when it took to its bed
did so in Aietes' hall. I knew at a glance that the man
from the South was no skillful magician. His eyes were the eyes of one
who lives by shrewd calculation, forethought, willingness to change
his plans. If my father were suddenly to raise up a manticore
at his feet, the stranger would study it a moment, consider the angles,
converse with it, probably persuade it. There could be no guessing what
that strange prince thought or felt, behind those mirroring eyes;
and all my impulsive, volcanic soul—the ages of Tartar,
Indian and Kelt that shaped us all, as Helios' children,
and made us passionate, mystical, seismic in love and wrath—
went thudding as if to a god to that man for salvation. My face
would sting one moment as if burned; the next, a freeze rang through me.
Make no mistake! The spirit knows its physician, howeverso halt, lame, muddled
the mind in its stiff bed reason! I watched
his smile—self-assured, by no means trusting—and I felt, as never
before, not even as a child, like a wobbly-kneed fool.
                                        "And then
my father was speaking, and shifting my rapt gaze from the stranger
I saw in amazement that my father was shuddering with rage, his huge
fists clenched, his red beard shaking, his eyes like a bull's. 'Scoundrels!'
he bellowed at Phrixos' sons, my nephews. 'Be gone from my sight!
Be gone from my country, vipers in the nest! It was no mere fleece
that lured you—you and these troglodytes—here to my kingdom. You think
I'm a gudgeon who'll snap at a fishhook left unbaited? You want
my throne, my sceptre, my boundless dominions! Fools! Scarecrows!
D'you think you can frighten a king like Aietes with sonorous poopings
of willow-whistles?—cause me to bang my knees together
with the oracular celostomies of a midget concealed
in an echo chamber? Boom me no more of the Argonauts' power,
naming off grandiose names, panegyring their murder of centaurs,
spidermen, Amazons, what-not! I am no horse, no bug,
no girl! If you had not eaten at my table, I'd tear your tongues out
and chop your hands off, both of them, and send you exploring
on stumped legs, as a lesson to you!'

          "The man called Telamon
came a step forward, his thick neck swelling, prepared to hurl
absurd defiance at my father. I knew what would happen if he did.
My father would crush him like a fly, for all his strength. But before
the word was out, the stranger in black touched his shoulder and smiled—
incredibly (what kind of being could smile in the presence of my father's
wrath?)—and broke in, quick yet casual: 'My lord,' he said,
'our show of arms has perhaps misled you. We were fools, I confess,
to carry them in past your gate.'
                    "The voice took my breath away.
It was no mere voice. An instrument. What can I say?
(As my Jason says.) It was a gift, a thing seen once in, perhaps,
a century. Not so deep as to seem merely freakish, yet deep;
and not so vibrant, so rich in its timbre, as to seem mock-singing,
yet vibrant and rich. . . . I remember when Orpheus sang, the sound
was purer than a silver flute, but when Orpheus spoke, it was
as if some pot of julep should venture an opinion. The sound
of the famous golden tongue was the music of a calm spring night
with no hurry in it, no phrenetics, no waste—the sound of a city
wealthy and at peace—a sound so dulcet and reasonable
it could not possibly be wrong. Had I not been in love with him
before, I'd have fallen now. Wasn't even my father checked,
zacotic Aietes? The ear grows used to that voice, in time.
I have learned to hear past to the guile, the well-meant trickery; but even
now when he leaves me on business, and we two are apart for a week,
his voice, when I hear it at the gate, brings a sudden pang, as if
of spring, an awareness of Time, all beauty in its teeth. He said:
'We have not come to your palace, believe me, with any such designs
as our bad manners impart. Who'd brave such dangerous seas
merely to steal a man's goods? But we're willing to prove our friendship.
Grant me permission to help in your war with the Sauromatiae—
a war that has dragged on for years, if the rumors we've gathered are true—
and in recompense, if we prove as loyal as we say we are,
grant us the fleece we ask for—my only hope, back in Argos.'
    "Father was silent, plunged into sullen brooding. (I knew
his look well enough, that deep-furrowed brow, the eyes blue-white
as cracked jewels. He was torn between lunging at the stranger, turning off
that seductive charm by a blow of his fist, or a white bolt sucked
from heaven; or, again, putting the stranger to the test. At last,
his dragon-eyes wrinkled, and he smiled, revealed his jagged teeth.

" 'Sir, if you're children of the gods, as you claim, and have grounds
        for approaching
our royal presence as equals, then we'll happily give you the fleece—
that is, if you still have use for the thing when we've put you to the proof.
We are not like your stuttering turkey Pelias. We're a man of great
generosity to people of rank.' He smiled again. My veins
ran ice.
        " 'We propose to test your courage and ability
by setting a task which, though formidable, is not beyond
the strength of our own two hands. Grazing on the plain of Ares
we have a huge old pair of bronze-hoofed, fire-breathing
bulls. We yoke them and drive them over the fallow of the plain,
quickly ploughing a four-acre field to the hedgerow at either
end. Then we sow the furrows—but not with corn: with the fangs
of a monstrous serpent, and they soon grow up in the form of armed men,
whom we cut down and kill with our spear as they rise up against us on every
side. We yoke our team in the morning; by evening we're through
our harvesting. That is what we do. If you, my good man,
can manage the same, you can carry the fleece to your tyrant's palace
on the same day. If not, then you shall not have it. Make no
mistake: It would be wrong for the grandson of dragons to truckle
        to a coward.'
                "Lord Jason
listened with his gaze fixed on the floor.
For a long time he said nothing, turning it over in his mind.
At last he brought out: 'Your Majesty, right's on your side and you leave
us no escape whatever. Therefore we'll take your challenge,
despite its preposterous terms and although we're aware that we're courting
death. Men can serve no crueler tyrant than Necessity,
a lord whose maniac whims brook no man's reasoning
and no appeal to kindness.'
                "He wasn't much comforted
by my father's sinister reply: 'Go, join your company.
You've shown your relish for the task. Be aware: if you hesitate
to yoke those bulls, or shirk that deadly harvesting,
I'll take up the matter myself, in a manner calculated
to make all other men shrink from coming and troubling their betters.'
    "They left. My heart flew after them. He was beautiful, I thought,
and already as good as dead. I was overwhelmed with pity
and I fled to my room to weep. What did it mean, this grief?

Hero or villain (and why did *I* care which?) the man
was walking to his doom. Well, let him go! I had seen men die
before, and would again. What matter? —But my sobs grew fierce,
tearing my chest for a stranger! 'And yet how I wish he'd been spared,'
I moaned. '—O sovereign Hekate, grant me my prayer! Let him live
and return to his home. But goddess, if he must be conquered by the bulls,
may he first learn that I, for one, will be far from glad of it!'

The voice fell silent. I continued to listen in the dark. Then:

"On the ship, her lean bows virled with silver, black hull bruised
and cracked, resealed with oakum—the scars of narrow escapes;
pounding of the stormwaves, battering of rocks—the crew of the *Argo*
listened in silence to the water lapping, the bullfrogs of the marsh.
    "Then Melas spoke, my cousin, the boldest of Phrixos' sons—
bolder by far than my sister. 'Lord Jason, I've a plan to suggest.
You may not like it, but no expedient should be left untried
in an emergency. You've heard me speak of Aietes' daughter
Medeia, a witch, and priestess of Hekate. If we managed to win
her help, we'd have nothing to fear. Let me sound my mother out
and see if Medeia can be swayed.' The son of Aison laughed
(I forgive him that), and said, 'Things are serious indeed when the one
pale hope of the glorious Argonauts is a girl!' All the same,
he put it to the others. For a time they were silent in impotent despair.
For all their power, there was no man there who could yoke those oxen;
not even Idas was so far riven of his wits as to dream
he might. Melas spoke again. 'Do not underestimate
Medeia. The goddess Hekate has taught her extraordinary skill
with spells both black and white, and with all the magic herbs
that grow on land or in water or climb on the walls of caves.
She can put out a raging forest fire, stop rivers in spate,
arrest a star, check even the movements of the moon. My mother,
her sister, can make her our firm ally.'
                                    "They wouldn't have believed,
but the gods, who watch men enviously, deprived by nature
of man's potential for sorrow and joy, broke in on the Argonauts'
helplessness with a sign. A dove pursued by a hawk
dropped into Jason's lap, while the hawk, with its murderous speed,
was impaled on the mascot at the stern. Immediately Mopsos spoke:
'My lords, we're in Aphrodite's hands. The sign's unmistakable.

This gentle bird whose life was spared is Jason's and belongs
to her. Go Melas, and speak with your mother.' The Argonauts
applauded; and so it was decided. At once young Melas set off.

"Poor Khalkiope! The princess was chilled to the bone with fear.
Suppose Medeia should be shocked and, stiff with the righteousness of youth,
tell all? Suppose, on the other hand, she agreed and, aiding
the Argonauts, should be caught by that half-mad wizard?—Either way
horror and shame and sorrow!
                              "Meanwhile Medeia lay
in her bed asleep, all cares forgotten—but not for long.
Dreams soon assailed her, bleak nightmares of a soul in pain.
She dreamed that the stranger had accepted the challenge, but not in the hope
of winning the golden fleece: his plan was to carry her away
to his home in the South as his bride. She dreamed that she, Medeia,
was yoking the bulls of bronze. She found it easy work,
pleasant as flying. She managed it almost listlessly.
But when all was done, her father was enraged. The brother she'd loved
past all other men stepped in. Old Aietes struck him with a club,
then, horrified, broken, he gave the decision to her: she could do
as she pleased. Without a moment's thought, she turned her back
on her father. Aietes screamed. And with the scream she woke.

"She sat up, shivering with fright, and peered round the walls of her room.
Slowly reality crept back, or something akin to reality:
an airy dream she mistook for memory of Jason. Why could
he not stay home, court Akhaian girls, torment the kings
of Hellas, and leave poor Medeia alone to her spinsterhood?
Tears sprang to her eyes; in one quick motion of mind
and body, she leaped from her bed and, barefoot, rushed to the door
and opened it. She would go to her sister—away with this foolish
modesty! She crossed the threshold, but once outside,
was uncertain, ashamed. She turned, went back into her room again.
Again she came out, and again crept back. Three times Medeia
tried, and three times failed. She clenched her fists in fury
and threw herself face down on the bed and writhed in pain.
Then, lying still, she was aware of the softness of her breasts. She whispered
the stranger's name, and at the magic word—more powerful spell
than any she'd learned from Hekate—her tears came flooding.

"Presently one of the servants, her own young maid, came in
and, seeing Medeia in tears, ran swiftly to Khalkiope,
who was sitting with Melas, considering how they might best win Medeia's

aid. When Khalkiope heard the girl's story, she jumped up, terrified,
and hurried to her sister. 'Medeia!' she cried, 'what's the meaning of these tears?
Has Father told you some awful fate he's decided on
for my sons?'

"Medeia blushed. How hungry she was to give answer!
But her heart was chained by shame. Ah, time and again the truth
was there on the tip of her tongue, and time and again she swallowed it.
Her lips moved; but no words came. Then her mind's eye
saw Jason gazing at the floor before Aietes, slyly preparing
some answer to stall his wrath. Inspired by the image, Medeia
brought out: 'Oh, sister, I'm terrified for your sons. It seems
our father will certainly kill them, and the strangers with them. I had
a terrible vision just now, and I saw it all.'

"It was Khalkiope's turn to weep. The tears ran rivers down her cheeks.
Medeia furtively watched, her heart like a fluttering bird.
'I knew it!' Khalkiope gasped between sobs. 'I've been thinking the same.
That's what brought me to your room. Dear Medeia, I beg you to help me.
First, swear by earth and heaven you won't tell a word of what I say,
but will work with me to save them. By the blessed gods, I implore you,
do not stand by while my precious children are murdered! If you do,
may I be slain with them and afterward haunt you from hell, an avenging fury!'

"With that she burst into tears once more, sank down, and
throwing her arms round her sister's knees and burying her head
in Medeia's lap, sobbed as if her heart would burst. The younger sister, too,
wept long and hard. Throughout all the house
you could hear their lamentations.

"Medeia was the first to speak:
'Sister, you leave me speechless with your talk of curses and furies.
How can I ease your heartache? As God is my judge, Khalkiope—
and by earth and heaven, and by all the powers of land and sea—
I will help you to save your sons with whatever strength or skill
I have.'

"Then Khalkiope said, 'Could you not devise some scheme,
some cunning ruse that will save the stranger, for my children's sake?
He needs you as much as they do, Medeia. Oh, do not be merciless!'

"The girl's heart leaped, her cheeks crimsoned; her eyes grew misty
with joyful tears. 'Khalkiope, dearest, I'll do anything at all
to please my sister and her sons. May I never again see morning
and no mortal see me in the world again if I place any good

ahead of the lives of your sons, my beloved kinsmen. Now go,
and bury my promise in silence. At dawn I will go to the temple
with magic medicine for the bulls.' Khalkiope left, carrying
her news of success to her son. But Medeia, alone once more,
was sick with shame and fear at her daring to plot such things
in defiance of her father's will.

                "Night drew down darkness on the world;
on the ship the Argonauts looked toward the Bear and the stars of Orion.
Wanderers and watchmen longed for sleep. The cloak of oblivion
stilled both sorrow and laughter. At the edges of town, dogs ceased
to bark, and men ceased calling one another. Silence reigned
in the blackening gloom. But sleep did not come to Medeia. More clear
than the bedroom walls, the stars beyond the window frame,
she saw the great bulls, and Jason confronting them. She saw him fall,
the great horns tearing at his bowels. And the maiden's poor heart raced,
restless as a patch of moonlight dancing up and down on a wall
as the swirling water poured into a pail reflects it. Bright tears
ran down her cheeks, and anguish tortured her, a golden fire
in her veins. One moment she thought she would give him the magic drug;
the next she thought, no, she would sooner die; and the next she'd do neither,
but patiently endure. And so, as Jason had done before Aietes,
she debated in painful indecision, her eyes clenched shut. She whispers:
  " 'Evil on this side, evil on that; and I have no choice
but to choose between them. Would I'd been slain by Artemis' arrows
before I had ever laid eyes on that man! Some god, some fury
must have brought him here with his cargo of grief and shame. Let him
be killed, if that is his fate. And how can I get him the drug
without my father's knowledge of it? What story can I tell
that his dragon's eye won't pierce? Then, suddenly panicky, she thought:
'Do I meet him alone? And speak with him? And even if he dies,
what hope have I of happiness? Far blacker evils
than any I toy with now will strike my heart if Jason
dies! Enough! No more shame, no more glory! Saved from harm,
let Jason sail where he pleases, and let me die. On the day
of his triumph may my neck crack in a noose from the rooftree, or may
I fall to the sly bite of poison.' She saw it in her mind and wept:
and saw that even in death she'd be taunted like mad Jokasta,
who bucked in bed with her royal son, and every city,
far or near, would ring with her doom—the wily little whore
who threw away life for a stranger! 'Then better to die,' she thought,

'this very night, in my room, slip out of the world unnoticed,
still innocent.'

        "She ran out quickly for the casket that held
her potions—some for healing, others for destruction—and placing
the casket on her knees, she bent above it and wept. Tears ran
unchecked down her cheeks, and she saw her corpse stretched out in state,
beautiful and tragic. The city howled, and fierce Aietes
tore out his hair in tufts and cursed his wickedness,
he who'd brought his daughter to this sad pass. She was now
determined to snatch some poison from the box and swallow it,
and in a moment she was fumbling with the lid in her sorrowing eagerness . . .
but suddenly paused. Clear as a vision, she had seen death,
at the corner of her eye. An empty room, a curtain blowing,
some dim memory or snatch from a dream . . . There was icy wind
whistling in the walls of her skull, collapsing her chest like the roof
of an abandoned palace. And now the pale child's lip trembled.
She thought of her playmates—more girl than woman—and the scent of fire
in the temple, and of caracolling birds and of newly hatched birds in their nests
in the plane trees, cheeping to heaven. And all at once it seemed
she had no choice but to live, because life was love—every field
and hillside shouted the same—and love was Jason.

        "She rose,
put the box in its place. Irresolute no longer, she waited
for dawn, when she could meet him, deliver the drug to him
as promised. Time after time she would suddenly open her eyes
believing it must be morning, but the room was black.

        "At length
dawn came. Now the tops of the mountains were alight, and now the spring-
green stath where the flamebright river flowed past long-shadowed trees,
and now there were sounds in the peasant huts, the stone and wattle
barns. Medeia was filled with joy, as if risen from the dead,
and her mind went hungrily to meet the light, the smell of new blossoms,
and newploughed ground and the sweat of horses. And she whispered, 'Yes,'
and was ready.

        "She gathered the flamebright locks that swirled past her shoulders,
washed the stains from her tear-puffed cheeks and cleansed her skin
with an ointment clear as nectar. She put on a beautiful robe
with cunning broaches, and draped a silvery veil across
her forehead and hair, all quickly, deftly, moving about
oblivious to imminent evils, and worse to come.

"She called
her maidens, the twelve who slept in the ante-chamber of Medeia's
room, and told them to yoke white mules to her chariot at once,
as she wished to drive to the splendid temple of Hekate.
And while they were making the chariot ready, she took out a drug
from her casket. He who smoothed it on his skin, after offering prayer
to Hekate, would become for that one day invulnerable.
She had taken the drug from flowers that grew on twin stalks
a cubit high, of saffron color. The root was like flesh
that has just been cut, and the juice was like sap from a mountain oak.
The dark earth shook and rumbled underneath her when Medeia cut
that root, for the root was beloved of the queen of the dead.
                                                    "She placed
the salve in the fragrant band that girdled her, beneath her bosom,
and stepped out quickly and mounted the chariot, with two of her maidens,
one at each side. Then she herself took the reins and, seizing
the well-made whip in her right hand, she drove down through
the city, and the rest of her handmaids laid their fingers over
the chariot wicker and, holding up their skirts above
their white knees, came running behind. She fancies herself,
her hair flying, like Artemis driving her swiftly racing
deer over mountains' combs to the scent-rich sacrifice.
Attendant nymphs have gathered from the forests to follow her,
and fawning grove-beasts whimper in homage and tremble as she passes.
So Aietes' daughter sped through the city, and on either side,
beggars, tradesmen, carters, old women with bundles of sticks
made way for her, avoiding the princess' eye.
                                              "Meanwhile,
Jason was crossing the dew-white plain with Melas and the old
seer Mopsos, skillful at omen reading. And thanks to Hera,
never yet had there been such a man as was Jason that day,
clear-eyed, radiant, his mind more swift, more sweet in flight
than an eagle riding on the sky-blue robes of gods. In fact,
his companions, walking beside him, were awed. As they reached the shrine
they came to a poplar by the side of the path, whose crown of countless
leaves was a favorite roost for crows. One flapped his wings
as they passed and, cawing from the treetop, delivered a message from Hera.
'Who is this looney old seer who hasn't got dawkins' sense,
nor makes out even what children know, that a girl does not
permit herself one word about love when the man she meets

brings strangers with him? Away with you, you crackpot prophet,
incompetent boob! It's certainly not Aphrodite that sends
your visions!'

"Mopsos listened to the bird with a smile, despite
the scolding. He turned to Jason and stretched out his arms and said,
'Carry on, Jason. Proceed to the temple where Medeia awaits you.
Praise Aphrodite! Now Melas and I must go on with you
no further. We'll wait right here till your safe return. Good luck!'

"Meanwhile the poor love-sick Medeia was singing and dancing
with her maids—or rather, pretending to. For time and again
her voice would falter and come to a halt. To keep her eyes fixed
on the choir was more than she could do. She was always turning them aside
to search the distant paths, and more than once she was close
to fainting at a sound of wind she mistook for a footfall. But at last
he appeared to her yearning eyes, striding like Sirius rising
from the ocean—Sirius, hound of heaven,
brilliant and beautiful but filled with menace for the flocks. Medeia's
heart stood still; her sight blurred. A flush spread across
her cheeks. She could neither move toward him nor retreat, but, as in
a frightening dream, her feet were rooted to the ground. As songbirds
suddenly hush at an eagle's approach, silent, titanic,
scarcely moving a wing as it rings on invisible winds,
so Medeia's maidens fell silent and quickly disappeared. Then Jason
and Aietes' daughter stood face to face, without a word,
like oaks or pines that stand in the mountains side by side
in the hush when no breeze stirs.

"Then Jason, observing the pallor
on Medeia's face and the quickness of her breath, reached out to take
her hand—white fire shot through her—and said: 'My lady, I'm alone.
Why this terror? I was never profligate, here or at home
in my own country. Take my word, no need to be
on guard against me, but ask or tell me what you wish. We've come
as friends, you and I, and come to a consecrated spot which must not
be mocked. Speak to me: ask what you will. And since you've promised
already to give me the charm I need, don't put me off,
I beg you, with timorous speeches. I plead by Hekate herself,
by your parents and Zeus, whose hand protects all suppliants.
Grant me your aid, and in days to come I'll reward you richly,
singing your praises through the world till your name is immortalized.
Remember Ariadne, who befriended Theseus. She was a darling of the gods

and her emblem is burning in the sky: all night Ariadne's Crown
rolls through the constellations. You, too, will be thanked by the gods
if you save me and all my friends. Indeed, your loveliness
seems outer proof of extraordinary beauty within.'
                                        "So he spoke,
honoring her, and she lowered her gaze with a smile embarrassed
and sweet. Then, uplifted by Jason's praise, she looked him in the face.
Yet how to begin she did not know. She longed to tell the man everything at once.
But she drew the charm from her clove-scented cincture
and dropped it in his hand. He received it with joy. The princess revelled
in his need of her, and she would have poured out all her soul to him,
so captivating was the light of love that filled his gleaming
eyes. Her heart was warmed, made sweeter than the dew on roses
in dawn's first light.
                        "At one moment both were staring at the ground
in deep embarrassment; the next they were smiling, glancing at each other
with shy love. At last Medeia forced out speech:
'Listen. When you have met my father and he's given you
the serpent's teeth, wait for the moment of midnight. Then bathe
in a swift-running river. Afterward, go out in a robe of black
and dig a round pit. There kill a ewe and sacrifice it whole,
with libations of honey from the hive and prayers to Hekate.
After that, withdraw. And do not be tempted to glance behind you,
neither by footfalls and the baying of hounds nor by anything else,
or you'll never return alive. In the morning, melt this charm
and rub it all over your body like oil. It will charge you with strength
and confidence to make you a match for the gods themselves. Then sprinkle
your spear and shield and sword as well. Then neither the weapons
of the earthborn men nor the flames of the bulls can touch you. But you'll not
be immune for long—for one day only. Nevertheless,
don't flinch, ever, from the encounter. And something more: When you
have yoked the bulls and ploughed the fallow (with those great hands
and that great strength, it won't take you long), and the earthborn men
are springing up, watch till you see a good number of them
rising from the loam, then throw a great boulder among them and wait.
They'll fall on it like famished wolves and kill one another.
That's your moment. Plunge in!
                                "'And so you'll be done, and can carry
the fleece to Hellas—a long, long way from Aia, I believe.
But go, nonetheless. Go where you will, go where your fancy

pleases, after you part from us.' She fell silent, staring
at the ground, and hot tears ran down her cheeks as she saw him sailing
home. She looked at him and sorrowfully spoke. 'If ever you reach
your home, don't forget what I have done for you.
As for myself, I'll never forget you.' Medeia paused,
then timidly asked: 'Tell me about that girl you mentioned—
the one who gave help to some hero and later grew famous for it.'
Jason studied her, puzzled by her blush, and then, suddenly,
he understood, and was touched by Medeia's concern for reputation,
her willingness to help him despite her fears. Gently he said:
'Ariadne, yes. Without her assistance, Theseus could never
have overcome the minotaur and made his way back
through the Labyrinth. He bore Ariadne away with him
when he'd met his test, and no other man ever praised the name
of a woman as he did hers. I can only hope that, as
her father Minos was reconciled at last with Theseus
for his daughter's sake, your father will at last be reconciled with us.'

  "He had thought, poor Jason, that talking to the girl in this gentle way
would soothe her. But instead his words filled Medeia with gloomy forebodings,
and bitterness as well. White flecks appeared in her blushing face
and she answered with passion: 'No doubt in Hellas men think it right
to honor commitments. My father is hardly the kind of man
this Minos was, if your story's true. And as for Ariadne,
I cannot claim to be a match for her. Speak to me no more
of kindness to strangers. But oh, do remember when you're back in Iolkos;
and I, despite my parents, will remember you. The day
you forget me and speak of me no more, that day may a whisper come
from afar to me, some parra to tell of it; may the wild North Wind
snatch me and carry me across the dark sea to Iolkos, and I
denounce you, force you to remember that I saved your life. Expect me!
I'll come that day if I can!' Bright tears ran down her cheeks.

  "Jason spoke quickly, smiling. 'Dear lady, you may spare the wandering
winds that task, and spare the bird that arduous flight!
Rest well assured, if you come to us you'll be honored and revered
by everyone there—men, women, children. They'll treat you like a goddess,
since thanks to you their sons and brothers and fathers came home.
And I, I'll build you a bridal bed, and a house we can share
till death. Let that be settled between us.

                          "As she heard his words
the girl's heart leaped. And yet she shuddered at the things she must do

202

to earn the stranger's love. Her maids, who'd been watching from afar,
grew restive now, though they dared not intervene. It was
high time for flight; but Medeia had as yet no thought of leaving,
entranced by Jason's beauty and bewitching talk. As for him,
whatever his passion, he'd by no means lost his wits. He said:
'We must part, Medeia, before we're seen by some passer-by.
We'll meet again. Have faith.' And touching her hand, he retreated
and was gone. Her maids ran forward. She scarcely noticed them.
Her mind benumbed, she got in the chariot to drive the mules,
taking the reins in one hand, the whip in the other, and blindly,
home she drove to the palace. As soon as her feet touched earth
Khalkiope came, pale as marble, to ask what chance for her sons.
Medeia said nothing, heard not a word she spoke. In her room
she sank to the crimson hassock at the foot of her bed, leaned over
and rested her cheek on her left hand, tearfully pondering
the incredible thing she'd done. But whether she wept for joy
or fear, she could not tell.

        "That night, in a lonely place
under open sky, Lord Jason bathed in the sacred river,
drew on his coal-black cape, his famous panther skin,
and dug a pit one cubit deep, and piled up billets,
and spread a slain ewe on the wood. He kindled the fire from below,
poured out libations, called on Hekate, and withdrew. The goddess
heard, from the abyss, and rose. Her form was surrounded by snakes
that slid like spokes from a hub and coiled round the silent oaks
until every twig seemed alive, their serpent eyes like the gleam
of a thousand flickering torches. And the hounds of the Underworld
leaped up, dark shapes all around her, and filled the night with their howls
till the stones in the earth were afraid and the far hills trembled. Then came
more fearsome things—a cry like a girl's, Medeia's, grim joke
of Hades, eternally bored. Then the heart of the Argonaut quaked,
for he knew the cry, and his whole dark body burst out in a sweat
and he paused, but only for an instant, then stubbornly Jason walked on,
and his eyes did not look back. He came to his friends again.

"At dawn old black-eyed Aietes put over his breast the cuirass
the god of war had given him. On his head he set
his golden helmet with its four plates, gift of the sun.
He took up his shield of many hides and his unconquerable spear,
and mounted the well-built battle-car that he'd won from Phaiton.

The Lord of the Bulls took the reins and drove to the contest grounds,
a crowd of Kolchians behind him, hurrying on foot, in silence,
no man daring to challenge Aietes' eye. There soon
came Jason, on his head a helmet of glittering bronze full of teeth
like nails, on his shoulder a sword. His body was naked and shone
like Apollo's eyes. Aietes was troubled, but waited.
                                                    "Then Jason,
glancing around, saw the great bronze yoke for the bulls, and beside it
the plough of indurated steel, built all of one piece. He went up to them,
planted his sword in the ground by the hilt, and laid down the helmet,
leaning it next to the sword. Then stirred to examine the tracks
the bulls had made, and mused, half-smiled at Aietes. And now
from the bowels of the earth, the fuliginous lair where the huge bulls slept,
up they came, breathing fire. Their great necks rippled, as thick
as cliffs, as poised as the arching necks of dragons. They lowered
their heads, eyes rolling, swung up their muscular tails like flags,
and gouged up divots of earth with their knife-sharp brazen hooves.
First one, then the other, the monsters lolled their weight forward,
gathering now for the charge. The Argonauts trembled, watching.
But Jason planted his feet far apart and waited, as firm
as a reef in the sea when it takes on the billows in a gale. He held
his shield in front of him. The bulls, bellowing loudly, came at him.
They struck. He shifted not an inch. They snorted, spewed from their mouths
devouring flame. He was not devoured. Their heat came down
like lightning shocks, like waves of lava. But Jason held.
Seizing the right-hand bull by the tip of its horn he dragged it
slowly toward the yoke, then brought it to his knees with a kick
and, casting his shield aside, he yoked it. And so with the second.
Aietes frowned and mused.
                                        "Then Jason ploughed, his shield
on his back, his helmet on his head, his sword in his hands like a goad,
pricking the great beasts forward. The earth turned black at their fire,
but the furrows turned, the fallow lay broken behind them. He sowed
the teeth, cast them far from himself, taking many a backward glance
to be sure no earthborn demon should catch him unawares. And the bulls,
thrusting their sharp bronze hooves into earth, toiled on till the day
was two-thirds spent. The work of the ploughman was done, the wide field
ploughed. He freed the bulls, shooed them off. They fled across the plain,
bellowing, tossing their heads, still huffing fire. He quenched
the fire in his throat at the bordering river, then waited with his spear.

And now—it was dusk—the earthborn men came sprouting like barley.
The black earth bristled with bucklers, double-headed spears, and helmets
whose splendor flashed to Olympos. They shone like a night full of stars
when snow lies deep and wind has swept off the clouds. But Jason
remembered the counsel of Medeia of the many wiles: picked up
a boulder from the field—a rock four men would have strained to budge—
and staggering forward with the rock in both arms, he bowled it toward them,
and at once crouched behind his shield, unseen, full of confidence.
The Kolchians gave a tremendous shout, and Aietes himself
was astonished to see that great ball thrown. But the earthborn men
fell on one another in a froth, and beneath each other's spearpoints
toppled like pines uprooted in a violent gale. And now,
like a thunderstone out of heaven, pursued by its fiery tail,
the son of Aison came, spear flashing, and the dark field streamed
with blood. Some fell while running, some still half-emerged,
their flanks and bellies showing, or only their heads. So Jason
reaped with his murderous sickle that unripe grain. Blood flowed
in new-ploughed furrows like water in a ditch.
                                        "Such was the scene
the Lord of the Bulls surveyed, and such was his rage and grief.
For he knew well enough whence came this miraculous power in the man.
He went back numbed with fury to the city of the Kolchians.
So the day ended, and so Lord Jason's contest ended.

15

"The witch slept, and in dreams the goddess Hera filled
her heart with agonizing fears. She trembled like a fawn half hidden
in a copse at the baying of hounds. Her eyeballs burned; her ears
filled with a roar like the crashing of a tide. She played again
(it was no mere game) with the thought of some deathwort painless and swift.
Far better that than the vengeance her father would devise. (She'd seen him,
a shadowy form in her sorcelled mirror, seated with his nobles,
preparing his treacherous stroke.) She groaned, awakened in terror,
the shadow of a crow on the moon. She slipped her feet down, groping,
moving in silence to the box where her potions were locked, then paused,
remembering the stranger's words. It was not possible, perhaps—
and yet, perhaps in that kinder world . . . In haste, half swooning,
Medeia kneeled down and kissed her bed, her eyes streaming,
and kissed the posts at each side of the folding doors, and the walls.
She snipped a lock of her hair for her mother to remember her by,
and then, to no one in the darkness, whispered, 'Farewell, Mother.
Farewell Khalkiope; farewell my home, my belovèd brother,
farewell sweet rooms, old fields . . .' She could say no more, sobbed only,
'Jason, I wish you had drowned!' Then weeping like a newly captive
slave torn roughly from her home by the luck of war, she fled
in silence swiftly through the palace. The doors, awakening
to her hasty spells, swung open of their own accord. So onward
barefoot she ran down narrow alleys, her right hand raising
the hem of her skirt, her left hand holding her mantle to her forehead,
hiding her face. Thus swiftly, fearfully, she crossed the city
by lightless streets, and passed the towers on the wall unseen
by the watch. The moon sang down, cool huntress-goddess, grim:
'How many times have you blocked my rays by your incantations,
to practice your witchery undisturbed—your search for corpses,

noxious roots? How many times have you terrified innocents,
raising up devils, the shadow of wolves, along country lanes?
Go then, victim of the mischief god! Seek out thy light,
sweet Jason, life-long heartache! Clever as you are, you'll find
there's deadlier craft than witchcraft stalking the night. Go! Run!'

"Thus sang the moon. But Medeia rushed on, and arrived at last,
at the high earth sconce by the river and, looking across it, caught
the bloom of the Argonauts' bonfire, kept all night, celebration
of victory. She sent a clear call ringing through the dark
to Melas, Phrixos' son, on the further bank. He heard
and recognized her, as Jason did. They spoke to the others.
The Argonauts were speechless with amazement and dread. Three times
she called; three times they shouted back, rowing toward her.

"Before they'd shored or cast off the hawsers, Jason leaped
light-footed from the *Argo*'s deck, and after him Phrixos' sons.
At once she wrapped her arms around Jason's knees, imploring:
'Save me, I beg you, from Aietes' wrath—and save yourselves.
Our tricks are discovered; there's nothing we can do. Let us sail away
before he can reach his chariot! I'll give you, myself,
the golden fleece. I have spells that can bring down sleep on the serpent.
—But first, before all your men, you must call on the gods to witness
your promises to me. You must vow you will not disgrace me when I
am far from home and in no dear kinsmen's protection.' She spoke
in anguish, fallen at his feet. But the words she spoke made Jason's
heart leap high, whether for joy at her beauty—now granted
as a gift to him—or joy at her promise of the fleece, she could not
tell, study his eyes as she might. He raised her to her feet,
embracing her. Then, to comfort her: 'Beautiful princess,
I swear—may Olympian Zeus and his consort Hera, Goddess
of Wedlock, witness my words—that when we're safe in Hellas,
I'll make you my wedded wife.' And he took her hand in his.
She believed him, and said, 'I have nothing to promise in return but this:
I'll be faithful to you. Wherever you go, I will go.'

"So to the ship, and at once, with all speed, to the sacred wood
in hopes that while night still clung they might capture and carry away
the treasure, in defiance of the king. The oars with their pinewood blades
skirled water, awakening the dark. As the boat slid out from shore
like a nearly forgotten dream, Medeia gasped, wide-eyed,
and stretched out her arms to the land, full of wild regret. But Jason,
never at a loss, spoke softly, and her mind was calmed. She turned

like a charmed spirit, and gazed toward the isle of the serpent.

                                 "The *Argo*
glided landwards, the mast tip blazing with dawn's first glance,
and, guided by Medeia, the Argonauts leaped to the rockstrewn, windless
beach—a muffled jangle of war-dress, and then vast stillness.
A path led straight to the sacred wood. They advanced, silent;
and so they came within sight of the mammoth oak, and high
in its beams, like a cloud incarnadined by the fiery glance
of morning, they saw the fleece. They stood stock-still, amazed.
It hung, magnificent, above them, like a thing indifferent
to the petty spleen of Aietes, courage of Jason, or the beating
of Medeia's confounded heart. It seemed a thing indifferent
to Time itself: Virtue, Beauty, Holiness, Change—
all were revealed for an instant as paltry children's dreams,
carpentered illusions to wall off the truth, man's otherness—
eternal, inexpiable—from this. The Argonauts remembered again
Prometheus' screams—first thief of celestial fire; remembered
the whispering ram on the mantle that Argus had made, off Lemnos,
Phrixos listening, all attention, and all who looked on it
listening, tensed for the secret; but the smouldering ram's eyes laughed,
and the secret refused their minds. *Stay on! It's not far now!*
A moral meaningless, outrageous. For a long time they stared,
like mystics gazing at an inner sun, some nether darkness,
pyralises. But now the sharp unsleeping eyes of the snake had seen them,
and the head swung near like a barque on invisible waters. Their minds
came awake again, and even the bravest of the Argonauts shook
till their armor rang, and their legs no longer held them. The serpent
hissed, and the banks of the river, the deep recesses of the wood
threw back the sound, and far away from Titanian Aia
it reached the ears of Kolchians living by the outfall of Lykos.
Babies sleeping in their mothers' arms were startled awake,
and their mothers, awakening in terror, hugged them close. Apophis,
in his sheath of blue-green scales, rolled forward his interminable coils
like the eddies of thick black smoke that spring from smouldering logs
and pursue each other from below in endless convolutions. Then
he saw the witch Medeia rise from the ground and stand,
her hair and eyes like flame, her strangely gentle voice
invoking sleep, a sing-song soothing to his ancient mind;
he heard her calling to the queen of the Underworld—softly, softly—
and as Jason looked up, stretched out flatlings in the shadow of her skirt,

the snake, for all its age and rage, was lulled a little.
The whole vast sinuate spine relaxed, and its undulations
smoothed a little, moving like a dark and silent swell
rolling on a sluggish sea. Even now his head still hovered,
and his jaws, with their glittering, needlesharp tusks, were agape, as if
to snap the intruders to their death like fear-numbed mice. But Medeia,
chanting a spell, sprinkled his eyes with a powerful drug,
and as the magic assaulted his heavy mind, the scent spreading out
around him, his will collapsed. His wedge-shape head sank slowly,
his innumerable coils behind him spanning the wood. Then, rising
on feeble legs, Jason dragged down the fleece from the oak,
Medeia moving her hand on Apophis' head, soothing
his wildness with a magic oil. As if in a trance herself,
she gave no sign when Jason called. He returned for her,
touching her elbow, drawing her back to the ship. And so
they left the grove of Ares.
                    "Magnificent triumph, you may think.
Was Aietes not a devil, and his downfall just? Ah, yes.
But the legend of human triumph coils inward forever, burns
at the heart with old contradictions. The goddess was in us, the anguine
goddess with sleepy eyes.
                    "Victorious Jason, on the *Argo,*
lifted the fleece in his arms. The shimmering wool threw a glow,
fiery, majestic, on his beautiful cheeks and forehead. And Jason
rejoiced in the light, as glad as a girl when she catches in her gown
the glow of the moon when it climbs the welken and gazes in
at her window. The fleece was as large as the hide of an ox, a stag.
When he slung it on his shoulder, it draped to below his feet. But soon
his mood changed. With a look at the sky, he bundled the fleece
to a tight roll and hid it in a place only Argus knew
in the *Argo*'s planking, for fear some envious man or god
might steal it from him. He led Medeia aft and found
a seat for her, then turned to his men, who watched him thoughtfully,
puzzled by the hint of strangeness he'd taken on. He said:
'My friends, let us now start home without further delay. The prize
for which we've suffered, and for which you've labored unselfishly,
unstintingly, is at last ours. And indeed, the task
proved easy, in the end, thanks to this princess whom I now propose,
with her consent, to carry home with me and marry. I charge you,
cherish her even as I do, as saviour of Akhaia and ourselves.

And have no doubt of our need for haste. Aietes and his devils
are certainly even now assembled and rushing to bar
our passage from the river to the sea. So man the ship—two men
on every bench, taking it in turns to row. Those men
not rowing, raise up your ox-hide shields to protect us from arrows.
We hold the future of Hellas in our hands! We can plunge her into sorrow,
we can bring her unheard of glory.' So saying, he donned his arms.
They obeyed at once, without a word. Dramatically, Jason
drew his sword—the same he'd used for goading the bulls—
and severed the hawsers at the stern, abandoning the anchor stones.
Then, in his brilliant battle gear, he took his stand
at Medeia's side, near the steersman Ankaios. And the *Argo* leaped
at the mighty crew's first heave. And still none spoke. They watched him.
And she—I—knew it, and was sick at heart, remembering the song
of the moon. We had done a splendid thing—and I above all,
—was that not true?—forsaking my dragon-eyed father, rejecting
his treachery, turning half-blindly, innocently
to the strange new doctrine, Love. Oh, it was not glory I asked,
throwing myself on the mercy of Jason's Akhaians. I asked
to live, only that, to live and be treated unshamefully.
Yet Jason glanced at the sky, the shore, still thinking of the fleece,
and the ship rode low in the water, it seemed to me, with guilt.
The snake would be waking now, I knew; its dumb wits grieved,
its earth-old spirit shaken. It made no sound.
                                        "We came
to the harbor mouth like a high sentry-gate guarding the port
where my father maintained five hundred of his fastest ships. Inside,
the water was dark, the sun still struggling with the hills. Mad Idas
spoke, eyes rolling, mule-teeth gleaming, spitting in Jason's
ear. 'The *Argo* could slip in and out of there quicker'n a weasel.
Consider what warmth we could get for our chilly bones, out of all
that wood! Recall how we sent up the city of the Doliones—
a city well guarded and wide awake—whereas here there's hardly
an upright creature, discounting the chain-wrapped bollards.' His brother,
catlike Lynkeus, studied the docks, the black-hulled ships.
He pointed the guards out—ten of them. Jason mused, then nodded.
'We'll risk it,' he said, and signalled Ankaios at the steering oar.
The ship veered in, oars soundless all at once, though those on the selmas
rowed more swiftly than before. In the shadow of the sleeping hills
the *Argo* was black as the water, invisible as death except

for the silver virl on her bows, a downswept sharksmile, cruising.
We shot in nearly to the anchor stones of the resined fleet—
I'd hardly guessed their skill, those professional killers of Akhaia,
and my heart thrilled with pride. Then suddenly all was light,
shocking as crimson ruddle on a snow white lamb: their spears
arked through blackness to the tinder of sails like rushing meteors,
like baetyls hurled by infuriate gods. Then men on the ships,
stumbling, half awake, snibbed the hawserlines, struggling to flee
the incineration of the ships struck first—there men with mattocks
and fire-axes struck out, blinded by smoke and steam,
at timbers redder than rubies—but they found no channel for flight,
pleached on all sides by their own burning ships, lost in a forest
of hissing swirls of smoke. Hulls shogged together, sailmasts
clattered to smouldering decks, and still the resin that saved them at sea caught fire,
racing from barque to barque like flame through grass; and above where the moored
　　　ships burned,
ash hung white as mist, then slowly settled, a floating scurf. And now
came the rowing cry, unholy celeusma ringing on the cliffs, and we shot to seaward,
a third of Aietes' fleet—five hundred lean-prowed ships—descending, flaming,
bartizans fallen like collapsed tents, to seek out the harbor floor. Old Argus
stared back, sooty and sweaty, at the sinking ships, and his fists
were clenched. 'Insanity!' he whispered, but no one heard.
　　　　　　　　　　　　　　　　　　　　　　　"As vast
as the sea, numberless as the leaves that fall in autumn from the beams
of trees, the army of Aietes gathered and rushed to the shore,
the king in his chariot of fire drawn, swift as the wind, by the horses
of Helios. Beside him rode Apsyrtus, my brother—
Apsyrtus, golden maned, gentle-eyed as a girl. But already,
driven by gods and the Argonauts, our ship stood far
to sea. In a frenzy, Aietes lifted his hands to Helios
calling his father to witness the outrage. Then howling, half mad,
he cursed his people and threatened them one and all with death
if they failed to lay hands on his daughter: said whether they found her on land
or captured the ship on the high seas, they must bring him Medeia,
for Aietes was sworn to be avenged for that monstrous betrayal. Thus
Aietes thundered. The sun dimmed; the gray earth shook.
But the *Argo* sailed on, protected by a wind from Hera. At once
the Kolchians equipped and launched their remaining ships—an immense
armada despite all the damage we'd done—and out they came,
flight on flight of dark swallows, fleeing catastrophe.

Hera was determined that Medeia must reach the Pelasgian land,
bring doom to the house of Pelias. But the Argonauts' eyes were grim,
their faces stern, for still Lord Jason was strange with them,
no longer himself.
                    "Then young Orpheus abandoned his shield
and took up, instead, the golden lyre with which he could tame
not only trees, fish, cattle, but even the grudge-stiff hearts
of men. Lord Jason looked fierce, but I reached out my hand to him,
touching the border of his mantle, and he kept his silence, waiting.
    "It was strange music for that desperate time: not charging rhythms
urging the rowers to out-do themselves, but music as calm
as the glass-smooth sea untouched by the magical wind from Hera.
One by one the Argonauts—who, heaving at the oars
or proffering shields, had glanced again and again at Jason,
distrustful, stirred by wordless doubt—grew calmer, forgetful
of the secret anger they could not themselves understand. Orpheus
sang of the pride of Zeus and the labor of Hephaiastos,
and how Zeus, awakened from his dream, wept. The lyre fell silent.
Jason stared down, ashamed, yet hardly aware what his shame
might mean. Aithalides spoke, whose memory never slept.
'You cast your eyes to the sky, the shore, and at times, it seems,
toward us, apprehensive. It's a trifling slight, though we should have deserved,
by now, more trust. But for all your care that the fleece be guarded,
you've forgotten the words of Phineus—that we'll sail back home
by a different route. Surely his words were not idle, Jason.
Troubles await us in the route we steer. So the seer foretold.
Turn your mind from its jealousy to that!' The son of Aison,
touched like the rest by the music, showed no anger. He glanced
in my direction for help. But despite the pursuing fleet
and my certain knowledge that I, beyond all the rest, was the quarry,
I could not advise him. The wind blew steadily, plunging us on.
He turned to the old seer Mopsos, bedraggled, smiling like a fool
at some joke. He too was helpless—not a bird in sight. Then, moved
by a god, or by his lunacy—who can say?—mad Idas
crowed like a rooster and lifted one hand from his oar to flap it
like a wing, to mock the seer. With strange attention, the old
man watched. And when Idas fell back laughing, the old man said,
'It's true, yes. Ridiculous . . . but never mind.' And to Jason:
'Imagine a time when the reeling wheel of stars was not
yet firm—when one would have looked in vain for the Danaan race,

for no men lived but the Arcadians, who were there before even
the moon. Egypt was the corn-rich colony of dawn, for the sun
arose, in those dim days, from the south. Dark tales remain,
remembered by migrating birds, old sundials wrong about time,
as earth tells time—remembered by temples whose holy gates
are askew by a quarter turn. Old sea-birds speak of it.
Birds of the farmyard scoff.' He paused,
straining to remember. 'From Egypt, a certain man set out—
there had been some terrible catastrophe, explosions in the ocean,
a continent lost—a man set out with a loyal force
and made his way through the whole wilderness of Europe and Asia,
and founded cities as he went. A few, so birds report,
survive. I have seen myself old tablets of stone containing,
allegedly, old maps. On one there's a river. The priests
of the Keltai, old as their oak trees, call it Ister. I can say
no more, or nothing but this: If the ancient stream still flows,
if the ages have left that forgotten seaway navigable,
our route lies somewhere to the west.' No sooner did his voice cease
than Hera granted us a sign. Ahead of us, a blinding light
shot westward, down to the horizon. The Argonauts sent up a shout,
and away, all canvas spread, our black ship sailed.
                                                    ''One fleet
of Kolchians, riding on a false scent, had left the Black Sea,
between the Kyanean rocks. The rest, with Apsyrtus in command,
unwittingly made for Ister, blindly hunting. —But it was
more than that, I know; was he not my brother? He was no
devil, sorcerer or not. He had hoped to have no part
in capturing me. But the stars at his birth were unkind to him.
They discovered the river and entered it—his heart full of dread—
turned at the first of the river's two mouths, while we took the second,
and so his fleet outstripped us. His ships spread panic as they went.
Shepherds grazing their flocks in the broad green meadows by the banks
abandoned their charge and fled, supposing the ships great monsters
risen from the sea, old Leviathan-brooder, for never before—
or never in many a century—had the Ister been plagued
by ships. Apsyrtus' eyes grew vague. He was of two minds,
fearing for my life, fearing for his own if he incurred our father's
wrath. And so in anguish he set down watchmen as he passed,
to report, by the blowing of horns or flashing of mirrors, if we
on the *Argo* sailed behind him. The message soon came. In sorrow,
he drew up his fleet as a net.

"Ah, Jason, reasonable Jason!
Had not the moon's song warned me?—my light, my life-long heartache!'
But reasonable, yes. If the Argonauts, outnumbered as they were,
had dared to fight, they'd have met with disaster. They evaded battle
by coming to terms with Apsyrtus. Both sides agreed that, since
Aietes himself had said they'd be given the golden fleece
if Jason accomplished his appointed task, the fleece was theirs
by right—Apsyrtus would blink their manner of taking it.
But as for me—for I was the bone of contention between them—
they must place me in chancery with Artemis, and leave me alone
till one of the kings who sit in judgment could decide on the fate
most just—return to my father or flight with the Argonauts.

"I listened in horror as Aithalides told me the terms. I paled,
fought down an urge to laugh. Had they still no glimpse of the darkness
in Kolchian hearts? Could Jason believe that, free of me,
Apsyrtus would sweetly make way for them—rude strangers who'd burned
his father's ships, seduced his sister, set strife between
a brother and sister as dear to each other as earth and sky?
He must carry me home or abandon Kolchis; but once his sister
was off their *Argo,* he'd sink that ship like a stone. —Yet rage
burned hotter by far in my heart than scorn. I trembled, imagining
the tortures that king, old sky-fire's child, would devise for me.
He had loved me well, loved me as he loved his golden gates,
his gifts from Helios and Ares. No need to talk of reason
in Aietes' pyre of a brain. He'd become a man like the gods,
like seasons, like a falling avalanche. Not all the earth could wall out the rage
of the sun's child, Lord of the Bulls.
                                        "And so I could not rest
till I'd spoken with Jason in private. When I saw my chance I beckoned,
getting him to leave his friends. When I'd brought him far enough,
I spoke, and Jason learned to his sorrow what his captive was.
His mind took it in. No spells, no charms would I use on him,
though I might by my craft have had all I wished with ease. Lips trembling,
cheeks white fire, I charged him: 'My lord, what is this plan
that you and my brother have arranged for my smooth disposal? Has all
your triumph fuddled your memory? Have you forgotten all
you swore before heaven when driven to seek out my help? Where are
those solemn oaths you swore by Zeus, great god of suppliants?
Where are the honey-sweet speeches I believed when I threw away conscience,
abandoned my homeland, turned the high magic of gods to the work

of thieves? Now I'm carried away, once a powerful princess, become
your barter, your less-than-slave! All this in return for my trust,
for saving your hide from the breath of the bulls, your head from the swords
of giants! And the fleece! Flattered like a goose-eyed country wench
I granted what should have been sacred, what may be no more, for you,
than a trophy, a tale for carousing boys—but for me the demise
of honor, the death of childhood, disgrace of my womanhood!
I tell you I am your wife, Jason—your daughter, your sister,
and no man's whore. And I'm coming with you to Hellas. You swore
you'd fight for me—fight come what may—not leave me alone
as you diddle with kings. Jason, we're pledged to one another,
betrothed in the sight of gods. Abide by that or draw
your dagger and slit my throat, give my love its due. Think, Jason!
What if this king who judges me should send me to Kolchis—
supposing—incredibly—that my brother keeps his word, refrains
from sheathing you all in fire before he drags me home
to protect his own poor head from my father's rage. Can your mind
conceive the cruelty of my father's revenge? —As for yourself,
if the goddess of will, as you say, is your protector—beware!
When was she kind toward cowardice?' Raising my arms and eyes
to heaven, I cried, 'May the glorious Argonauts reach not Hellas
but Hell! May the fleece disappear like an idle dream, sink down
to Erebus! And even in Hades' realm, may howling furies
drive false Jason from stone to stone for eternity!'
And then, to Jason: 'You have broken an oath to the gods. By your own
sweet standard, Reason, my curses cannot miscarry. For now,
you're sure of yourself. But wait. I'm nothing in your eyes, but soon
you'll know my power, my favor with the gods. Beware of me!'
    "I boiled with rage. I longed to fill all the ship with fire,
kindle the planking and hurl my flesh to the flames. But Jason
touched me, soothing. I had terrified him. 'Medeia, princess,
beware of *yourself!*' And again that voice, still new to me,
had uncanny power. 'You begin with complaints, appeals, but soon
your own blood's heat makes a holocaust. Call back your curses.
It's not finished yet. Perhaps I may prove less vicious than you think.
Look. Look around you at the Kolchians' ships. We're encircled by a thousand
enemies. Even the natives are ready to attack us
to be rid of Apsyrtus as he leads you home to Aietes. If we dare
strike out at these hordes, we'll die to a man. Will it please you more,
sailing back to your father, if all of us are slaughtered, and you

are all we leave them as a prize? This truce has given us time.
We must wait—and plan. Bring down Apsyrtus, and his force—for all
its banners, its chatter of bugles—will clatter to the ground like a shed.'

"My eyes widened, believing for an instant. The next, I doubted.
Was he lying? I was sick with anguish. His look was impenetrable.
I who moved at ease with the primal, lumbering minds
of snakes, who knew every gesture of the carrion crow, the still-eyed
cat, who knew even thoughts of the moon, stared humbly, baffled,
at the alien eyes of Jason. It seemed impossible
that the golden tongue, those gentle hands, could lie. Searching
vainly for some sure sign—his hands on my arms—I felt
a violent surge of love, desire not physical merely,
but absolute: desire for his god-dark soul. I whispered:
'Jason, plan *now*. Evil deeds commit their victims
to responses evil as the deeds themselves. If what you say
is true—if my brother's forces will collapse when my brother falls,
and if that, as you claim, was your hope when you sealed that heartless truce—
then once again, I can help you. Call Apsyrtus to you.
Keep him friendly. Offer him splendid gifts, and when
his heralds are taking them away, I'll speak and persuade them to arrange
a meeting between us—my brother and myself. They'll do it, I think.
They no more wish me sorrow than does my brother. When we meet,
slay him. I will not blame you for it. The murder's our one
last hope.'

"And still Lord Jason's eyes were impenetrable,
studying me. His swordsman's hands closed tighter on my arms,
as if horrified. But at last he nodded, the barest flick,
revealing no sign of his reasons. My anguish was greater than before:
on one side, terror that he scorned me for the plan, seized it merely
as the skillful, methodical killer I knew he was; on the other,
sorrow for Apsyrtus. He'd thrown me up on his shoulders as a child,
had shaken snow-apples down for me from hillside trees.
Despite all that, he would drag me to my father's torture rooms.
Was I more cruel? But my mind flinched back. It was not a question
for reason. There was no possibility of reason, no possibility
of justice, virtue, innocence, on any side.

                                            "So that,
mind blank, heart pounding in terror and self-condemnation, I watched
as Jason in his scarlet mantle, all stitched with bewildering figures,
laid out gifts for Apsyrtus, with the Argonauts' help. Black Idas

watched me, smiling to himself, and soon the trap was set.
I watched Lord Jason debating in his mind the final gift—
the mantle of scarlet that Argus wove, majestic but gloomy—
it sent out a dull, infernal light—or the sky blue mantle
King Thoas gave to Hypsipyle when she wept and spared him,
sending him out on the sea. The son of Aison chose
the blue, hurled it on the pile as if in anger; then,
suddenly smiling, transformed, he came where I stood. The heralds
approached. My mind went strangely calm, as calm as it was
when I charmed the guardian snake. They left with the message. When I
had come to the temple of Artemis—so the message ran—
Apsyrtus must meet me, under cover of night. I would steal the fleece
and return with the treasure to Aietes, to bargain for my life. Such was
the lure. I know pretty well how Apsyrtus received it, sweet brother!
His heart leaped up and he laughed aloud. 'Ah, Medeia!
Brilliant, magnificent Medeia of the many wiles!' He could scarcely
wait for nightfall, pacing restless on his ship and smiling,
beaming at his sister's guile.
               "The sun hung low in the heavens,
reluctant to set, but at last, blood red with rage, it sank.
As soon as darkness was complete he came to me, speeding in his ship,
and landed on the sacred island in the dead of night. Unescorted,
he rushed to the torchlit room where I waited and paced. He seized me
with a cry of joy, proud of my Kolchian cunning. And for all
my grief and revulsion, my murderer's certainty of his imminent death—
tricked for an instant by his smile of love—may the gods forgive me!—
I returned the smile. With his bright sword lifted, Jason leaped
from his hiding place. I turned my face away, shielding my eyes.
Apsyrtus went down like a bull, but even as he sank to the flagstones
he caught the blood in his hands, and as I shrank from him,
reached out and painted my silvery veil and dress. I wept,
soundless, rigid as a column. We hid the corpse in the earth.
Orpheus was there, standing in the moonlight. 'There was no other way,'
I said, rage flashing. He nodded. I said: 'I loved my brother!'
Perhaps even Jason understood, dark eyes more veiled than a snake's.
He took my hand, head bowed. We returned to the Argonauts.
Apsyrtus' fleet was heartsick, divided and confused, when they learned
by local seers, that the prince was gone forever. And so
the *Argo* escaped.
               "Such was our crime, our helplessness.

16

"In Artemis' temple we killed him. The blood-wet corpse we hid
in the goddess' sacred grove. Then Zeus the Father of the Gods
was seized with wrath, and ordained that by counsel of Aiaian Circe
we must cleanse ourselves from the stain of blood, and suffer sorrows
bitter and past all number before we should come to the land
of Hellas. We sailed unaware of that, though with heavy hearts,
praying, the sons of Phrixos and I, for their mother's escape
when news of the murder came to Aietes' dragon-dark mind.
Our fears, we learned much later, were not ill-founded. He lay
on the palace floor for days, shuddering in lunes of rage,
calling on the gods to witness the foul and unnatural deed
committed in Artemis' temple. He'd neither lift his eyes
nor raise his cheek from the flagstones, but wept and howled imprecations,
hammering his fists till they bled. And at last it reached his thought
that she who had seemed most innocent, bronze Khalkiope,
was most at fault. Then soon chaogenous dreams of revenge
were fuming in his serpent brain, the last of his sanity burned out,
and he called her to him.
                              "She knew when the message came what it meant.
She touched her bedposts, the walls of her room, with the air of one
distracted, and since they could grant her no time for parting words,
she left with the guards themselves her sad farewell to our mother.
She looked a last time at the figures of her sons, the work of a sculptor
famous in the East, and tears ran down her cheeks in streams.
Then, walking in the halls with her silent guards, her sandals a whisper
on fire-bright tessellated floors, she prayed for the safety of her sons;
and for all her trembling—most timid of all Aietes' children,
her hair like honey as it rolls from the bowl—she kept her courage,

and came where Aietes lay. He rose up a little on his arms
and hissed at the guards. They backed away as commanded. And then,
though he'd planned slow torture, unspeakable pain for the sly eldest daughter
(so she seemed to him), he was suddenly wracked by such fiery rage
that he hurled his axe, and Khalkiope, with a startled cry,
was dead. A death to be proud of, the sweet gift of life to her sons!
   "We left behind the Liburnian isles, and Korkyra
with its black and somber woods, and passed Melite, riding
in a softly blowing breeze; passed steep Kerossus, where the daughter
of Atlas dwelt, and we thought we saw in the mists the hills
of thunder.
              "Then Hera remembered the counsels and anger of Zeus.
She stirred up stormwinds before us, and black waves caught us and hurled us
back to the isle of Elektra with its jagged rocks where once
King Kadmos struck down the serpent and found his wife. And suddenly
the beam of Dodonian oak that Athena had set in the center,
as keel to the hollow ship, cried out and told us of the wrath
of Zeus. The beam proclaimed that we'd never escape the paths
of the endless sea, nor know any roofing but thunderous winds
till Circe purged us of guilt for the murder of Apsyrtus. And if
in cleansing us by ritual, the heart of Circe
remained aloof, forgiving by law but not by love,
then even in Hellas our lives should be cursed. The beam cried out:
'Pray for your souls now, Argonauts! Pray for some track
to the kingdom of Helios' daughter!' Thus wailed the *Argo* in the night.
The Argonauts hurled up prayers to the gods as the ship leaped on
through dark welms streaming like a wound. O, dark as my soul was the place!
Sick those seas as my body in riotous rebellion—fevers,
chills, mysterious flashes of pain. His ghost was in me,
a steady nightmare, a madness. I vomited, fouling my beauty
in Jason's sight. Not even Orpheus' lyre could check
that sickness throbbing in my head, or the fire in my bowels. They looked
away, one and all, as from Hell itself. I hissed imprecations,
and they listened with white teeth clenched.
                                "And as for the sea, it was
the water of Helios' wrath. No bird, for all its rush,
for all the lightness of its arching wings, could cross that deep,
but mid-course, down it would plunge, fluttering, consumed in flames;
and all around it, the daughters of Helios, locked in poplars,
wailed their piteous complaint, and their weeping eyes dripped amber.

"There sailed the joyless Argonauts, weary of heart, overwhelmed
by stench where the body of Phaiton still burned. At night, by the will
of the gods, we entered an unknown stream whose rock shores sang
with the rumble of mingling waters. So on and on we rushed,
lost in the endless domain of the murderous Kelts. Now storms,
now raging men dismayed us, thinning our company.
My sickness stayed. My hand on the gunnel was marble-white;
my face grew gaunt, rimose. We touched at the kingdom of stone,
the kingdom of iron men, the kingdom of the ants. As dreams
insinuate their unearthly cast on the light of the sick
man's room, making windows alien eyes, transforming chairs
to animals biding their time, so now to the heartsick *Argo*
the world took on a change. The night was unnaturally dark,
crowded with baffling machines we could not quite see. And then
at dawn we looked out, in our strange dream, on motionless banks
where no beast stirred and even the leaves on the trees were still.
No songbird sang, and the clouds above us were as void of life
as stones. We struggled to awaken, but the ship was sealed in a charm.
We waited. Then came to a fork in the stream, a great hushed island,
and the Argonauts, half-starved, rowed in, cast anchor, and made
the long ship fast. As far as the eye could see on the windless
rockstrewn beach, there was nothing alive. The tufts of grass
on the meadow above were still, as if lost in thought.

                                           "On a hill,
rising at the center of the island, there stood a grove so dense
no thread of light came through, and between the boles of the trees
lay avenues. We went there, Lynkeus leading the way
with his powerful eyes. I walked behind him, my hand in Jason's,
and my spirit was filled with uneasiness. I was sure the air—
chill, unstirring—was crowded with thirsty ghosts. We found
no game; it seemed that even the crawling insects slept.

    "Without warning from Lynkeus, we reached a glade and, rising
in the center of the glade, a vast stone building in the shape of a dome.
The gray foundation rocks were carved with curious oghams:
spirals like eddies in a river, like blustering winds—the oldest
runes ever made by man. At the low, dark door of the building
a chair of stone stood waiting. We studied it, none of us speaking.
And suddenly, even as we watched, there appeared a figure in the chair,
seated comfortably, casually, combing his beard. He was old,
his hair as white as hoarfrost. But as for his race, he was nothing

we knew—a snubnosed creature with puffy eyes. His face,
like his belly, was round, and he wore an enormous moustache. He said:
'Ah ha! So it's Jason again!' The lord of the Argonauts stared,
then glanced at me, as if thinking the curious image were somehow
my creation. The old man laughed, impish, a laugh
that rang like bells on the great rock mound and the surrounding hills.
He laughed till he wept and clutched his sides.
                                        "I asked: 'Who are you?
Why do you mock us with silent sunlit isles and laughter,
when Zeus has condemned us to travel as miserable exiles forever,
suffering griefs past number for a crime so dark I dare
not speak of it?' He laughed again, unimpressed by grief,
unmoved by our hunger. 'Mere pangs of mortality,' he said.
'If you knew *my* troubles—' He paused, reflecting, then laughed again.
'However, they slip my mind.' I repeated the question: 'Who are you?'
He tapped the tips of his fingers together, squinting, though his lips
still smiled. 'Don't rush me. It'll come to me.' He searched his wits.
'I'm something to do with rivers, I remember.' He pulled at his beard,
pursed his lips, looked panic-stricken. 'Is it *very* important?'
Suddenly his face brightened and he snapped his fingers. At once—
apparently not by his wish—an enormous sow appeared,
sprawled in the grass beside him, her eyes alarmed. He snapped
his fingers again, looking sheepish, and at once the huge beast vanished.
Again the name he'd been hunting had slipped his mind. Then:
'Spirit of sorts,' he said. 'Not one of your dark ones, no god
of the bog people, or the finger-wringing Germans, or—'
His bright eyes widened. 'Ah yes! I'd forgotten! —We have dealings, we powers,
from time to time. I received a request from the goddess of will.
Abnormal. But isn't everything? —Forgive me if I seem
too light in the presence of woe. We're not very good at woe,
we Grand Antiques. Treasure your guilt if you like, dear friends.
Guilt has a marvelous energy about it—havoc of kingdoms,
slaughter of infants, et cetera. Discipline! That's what it gives you!
(Discipline, of course, is a virtue not all of us value.) However,
Time is wide enough for all. Indeed, in a thousand years
(I've been there, understand. A thousand thousand times I've heard
the joke, and that lunatic punchline) . . . But what was I saying? Ah!
Sail on in peace!—or in whatever mood suits your temperament.
The passage is opened, this once, after all these millennia.
Make way for the flagship *Argo,* ye golden generations! Make way

for purification by fire, salvation by slaughter!' His eyes—
pale blue, mocking, were a-glitter; but at once he remembered himself.
'Forgive me, lady. Forgive an old bogyman's foolishness, lords
of Akhaia.' His smile was genuine now. 'The universe
has time for all experiments. Sail in peace!' He vanished.
And the same instant the sky went dark and we found ourselves
on the *Argo,* on a churning sea. Black waves came combing in,
and mountains to left and right were yawing apart for us,
and the opening sucked the sea in, and like a chip on a torrent
the *Argo* went spinning, careening, the walls half buried in foam,
to the south. I clung to the capstan. I would have been washed away,
but the boy Ankaios abandoned the useless steering oar
and caught my arm and held me till Jason could reach me, crawling
pin by pin along the rail. He held me by the waist, his arm
like rock. So we stood as we fell, dropped down from a dizzying height,
a violent booming around us, as if the earth had split,
and we looked up behind us in terror and saw the mountains close,
and the same instant we struck and were hurled to the belly of the ship.
The *Argo* shrieked as if all her beams had burst, and water
boiled in over us. Then, at Ankaios' shout, we knew
we were safe, the ship was afloat, all her brattice-work firm despite
contusions, a thin, dark ooze. And thus we came, by the whim
of the river spirit of the North, to the kingdom of Circe, daughter
of the sun, my father's sister.
                    "We did not speak of the dream—
the cynical god who could scoff at all human shame and pain.
Did only I dream it? There are those who claim we create, ourselves,
in the dark of our minds, the gods who guide us. Was I in fact
remorseless as the snake who smiles as he swallows the bellowing frog?
Did my dreams create, then, even the dizzying fall of the *Argo,*
that dark-as-murder sky? I dared not speak of the dream,
but the image of the god remained, like the nagging awareness of a wound,—
that and the sunlight in which he sat, with his attention fixed
on his beard. If I closed my eyes, relaxed, I could drift to him again,
abandon all sorrow and guilt forever, as if such things
were childhood fantasy, and only this—his twinkling eyes,
his laugh, his comb, his silent, sunlit glade—were real.
I could step, if I wished, from my sanity to peace. I resisted,
perhaps for fear of Jason.
                    "We came to Circe's isle.

"At Jason's command, the Argonauts cast the hawsers and moored
the ship. We soon found Circe bathing where spindrift rained
on shale. That night she'd been alarmed by visions: the walls of her palace
were wet with blood, it seemed to her, and flames were devouring
the magic herbs she used for bewitching strangers. With the gore
of a murdered man she quenched the flame, catching the blood
in her hands. It clung to her skin and garments. When she awoke, at dawn,
the mood of the dream was still upon her, and so she'd come
to lie in the spray by the pounding surf and be cleansed. As she lay there
it seemed to her in a waking dream that saurian beasts
flopped from the water—beasts neither animal nor human, confused
and foul, as if earth's primeval slime were producing them, testing
its powers in the age before rain, when the terrible sun was king.
As she looked, the creatures took on, more and more, the appearance of men.
She rose, watching them with witch's eyes, and stepped back softly
in the direction of the grave-dark grove and the palace beyond. With her hand
she beckoned, a movement like wind in a sapling. And the Argonauts, trapped
in the power of her spell, came after her. The son of Aison
reached out, touched my hand. He knew—though helpless to resist,
unable to command his men to stay—that Aietes' sister
would prove no friend, her eyes as soulless as my father's, her girlish
beauty as deadly as Aietes' anguine strength. At his touch
I wakened. I gazed around me in alarm, like a life-prisoner
startled from pleasant dreams to his dungeon reality.
They walked like men asleep, smiling. On the terry ahead,
the demonic witch smiled back. She had hair like a raven's, a smile
malicious, seductive, uncertain as the shifting patterns of leaves
on her ghostly face. With the long fingers of her left hand
she touched her breast, then gently, gently, dark eyes staring,
she moved the tips of her fingers to the cloud of hair that bloomed
below. Make no mistake: it was not mere sex wise Circe
lured them with. She promised violence, knowledge like the gods',
forbidden mysteries deeper than innocence or guilt. —Nor think
that I could prove any match for her, witch against witch. Helpless,
in anguish at Jason's appeal for help, I cried out, 'Circe!
Spare them!'

"The queen witch swung her glowing eyes to me
and knew that I too was of Helios' race, for the children of the sun
have eyes like no other mortals. At once, with a curious smile,
she unmade the spell, as though her mind were far away,

and Jason signalled his men to wait, and we two alone
went up with Circe to her palace.
                    "The queen of witches drew on
her sable mantle and signalled the two of us over to chairs
of gold. We did not sit, but went to the hearth at once
and sat among ashes, in the age-old manner of suppliants.
I buried my face in both my hands, and Jason fixed
in the cinders the treasure-hilted sword with which he'd slain
Apsyrtus. We could not meet her eyes.
She understood, smiling that curious smile again,
mind far away; and in reverence to the ancient ordinance of Zeus,
the god of wrath but of mercy as well, she began to offer
the sacrifice that cleanses murderers of guilt. To atone
for the murder still unexpiated, she held above
our heads the young of a sow whose dugs swelled yet from the fruit
of the womb, and slitting its throat, she sprinkled our hands with the blood;
and she made propitiation with offerings of wine, calling
on Zeus the Cleanser, hope of the murder-stained, who seize
in maniac pride what belongs to the gods alone; and all
defilements her attendants bore from the palace.
                    "Then Circe, by the hearth,
burned cakes unleavened, and prayed that Zeus might calm the furies,
whether our festering souls were stained by the blood of a stranger
or a kinsman.
                    "When all this ritual was done, she raised us up
and led us to the golden chairs; and she herself sat near,
facing us. At once she asked us our names and business
and why we had come here as suppliants. For she remembered her dreams,
and she longed to hear the voice of her unknown kinswoman.
I answered, telling her all she asked,
sick at heart, answering softly in the Kolchian tongue.
But I shrank from speaking of the murder of Apsyrtus. Yet Circe knew,
shrewd on the habits of devils and men. And yet in part
she forgave me, for pity. She touched my hair,
watching the flicker of the fire in it,
remembering things.
                    "Then Circe said: 'Poor wretch, you have
contrived, it seems, the unhappiest of home-comings.
You cannot escape for long your father's wrath, I think.
The wrongs you have done him are intolerable, and surely he'll soon

reach Hellas to have his revenge for your brother's murder. However,
since you are my suppliant and niece, I'll not increase your sorrows
by opposing your wishes through any active enmity.
But leave my halls. Companion the stranger, whoever he is,
this foreign prince you've chosen in your father's despite. And do not
kneel to me at my hearth in the hope of my own forgiveness,
though I've granted you, as I must, the ritual of Zeus. If your peace
depends upon Circe's love, you will find no peace.' With that,
smiling past us, solemn eyes unfathomable,
she left us to find our way out however we might. I wept,
my anguish and terror measureless. Then Jason touched
my hand, raised me to my feet, and led me from the hall. And so
in part the demands of Zeus were satisfied. The gods
had forgiven, though Circe had not. Yet soon came reason for hope
that the curse was at least much weakened. If Circe's heart was stone,
not all our kind was so cruel. Or so it seemed to me,
weighing the curse in my mind, on the watch for omens.

                                                   "In the gray
Karaunian sea, fronting the Ionian Straits, there lies
a rich and spacious island, border of the kingdom of the living
and the dead—the isle of the Phaiakians, whose oarless barques
transport men, silent and swift as dreams, from the flicker of shadows
to the sweaty labor of day. There, after months and sorrows,
the *Argo* touched. The king, with all his people, received us
with open arms. They sent up splendid thank-offerings,
and all the island fêted us. The joyful Argonauts
mingled with the crowds and enjoyed themselves like heroes come home
to their own island. But the joy was brief, for the fleet of Kolchians
who'd passed from the Black Sea through the Kyanean Rocks arrived
at the wide Phaiakian harbor and sent stern word to the king
demanding that I be returned to my father's house at once,
without any plea or parley. Should the king refuse, they promised
reprisals bitter enough, and more when Aietes came.
Wise and gentle Alkinoös, king of the Phaiakians,
restrained their furious bloodlust and dealt for terms.

                                                 "Thus even
at the front door of Hellas, my hopes were dashed again,
for a prospect even more dread than capture by my brother had arisen:
capture by Kolchians hostile to me—hostile to all
mankind after endless scavenging months on the sea. I appealed

to Jason's friends repeatedly, and to Alkinoös'
wife Arete, touching her knees with my hands. 'O Queen,
be gracious to your suppliant,' I begged; 'prevent these Kolchians
from bearing me back to my father. If you're of the race of mortals,
you know how the noblest of emotions can lead to ruin. Such was
my case. My wits forsook me—though I do not repent it. I was
not wanton. I swear by the sun's pure light, I never intended
to run from my beautiful home with a race of foreigners,
much less commit crimes worse. For those I have paid, my lady,
startled awake in the dead of night by memory—shrinking
from my new lord's touch, unjustly suspecting disgust in him.
I was a princess, lady, in a kingdom that stretched out half the width
of the world—the colony of the sun. I was initiate
to the mysteries of fire, could speak with the moon, knew life and death,
sterility, conception; I was served by nuns sufficient to throng
this whole wide isle of the Phaiakians. And now am nothing,
a hunted criminal, exiled, condemned to death. Have mercy!
Soften the heart of your lord, and may the high gods grant you
honor, children, and the joy of life in a city untouched
by dissension or war forever.' Such was my tearful appeal
to Arete.
        "But I spoke less timorously to the Argonauts,
besieging each of them in turn: 'You, O illustrious
dare-devil lords—you and the help I gave you in your troubles—
you alone are the cause of my affliction. Through me the bulls
were yoked, and the harvest of earthmen reaped. Thanks to me alone
you're homeward bound, and with the golden fleece you sought. Oh, you
can smile, looking forward to joyful reunions. But for me, your warprize,
nothing remains. I'm a thing despised, a wanderer
in the hands of strangers. Remember your oaths!—and beware the fury
of the suppliant betrayed. I seek no asylum in temples of the gods,
no sanctuary in forts. I have trusted in you alone.
I look up in terror for help, but your hearts are flint. Do you feel
no shame when you see me kneeling to a foreign queen? You were ready
to face all Kolchis' armies and snatch that fleece by force,
before you had *seen* those armies. Where's all your daring now?'
        "The Argonauts tried to calm me, reassure me. But their eyes
were evasive, I saw. I shook with fear. A deadly despair
had come over them, it seemed to me—a wasting disease
of the will. They had heard the insinuations of the sirens, had seen

friends die, and they knew still more must die. They had sailed through the channel
of Skylla and Kharybdis and had begun to grasp the meaning of adventures
past—or the absence of meaning in them. No fire was left
but the wild furnace of my own heart.
                                          "Night came at last
and sleep descended on our company. But *I* did not sleep.
My heart sang pain and rage, and tears flooded from my eyes
and my Heliot mind hurled fire at the ships of the Kolchians,
and fire at the Argonauts' heads and the heads of the Phaiakians,
and fire at the sing-song moon. But the queen of goddesses
blocked my magic. They slumbered on.
                                          "That night in the palace
King Alkinoös and Arete his queen had retired to bed
as usual. As they lay in the dark, in the hearing of ravens,
they spoke of the Kolchian demand. Arete, from the fullness of her heart,
said this to the king: 'My lord, I beg you for my sake to side
with the Argonauts, and save this poor unhappy girl
from Aietes' wrath. The isle of Argos lies near at hand;
the people are neighbors. Aietes lives far away; we know only
his name. And this: Medeia is a woman who has suffered much.
When she told me her troubles she broke my heart. She was out of her mind
when she gave that man the magic for the bulls. And then, as we sinners
so often do, she tried to save the mistake by another.
But I hear this Jason has solemnly sworn in the sight of Zeus
that he'll marry her. My love, let no decision of yours
force Aison's son to abandon his promise to heaven. What right
have fathers to claim their daughters' love as the gods claim man's?
Behold how Nykteus brought the lovely Antiope to sorrow—
Nykteus of Thebes, that midnight monarch whose daughter's beauty
outshone the moon's, so that Helios himself was in love with her.
Behold how Danaë suffered perpetual darkness in a dungeon
because of her father, though Zeus himself was in love with her
and sought her deep in the earth, in the shape of a driving rain.
Behold how Ekhetos drove great brazen spikes in his daughters'
eyes. Old men are mad, my lord. It is hardly love
that moves them, whatever their howls. Love sends out ships to search
new mysteries, not haul back miscreant hearts, bind love
in chains.'
          "Alkinoös was touched by his wife's appeal. He said:
'I could, I think, repel the Kolchians by force of arms,

siding with the *Argo* for Medeia's sake. But I'd think twice
before I dared to defy just sentence from Zeus. Nor would
I hurry to scoff at Aietes, as it seems you'd have me do.
There lives no king more mighty. Far away as he is, he could bring
his armies and crack us like nuts. I must therefore reach a decision
the whole world and the gods above will acknowledge as wise.
I'll tell you my whole intent. If Medeia is still a virgin,
I'll direct the Akhaians to return her to her father. But if she and Jason
have married, I'll refuse to separate them. Neither will I give,
if she carries a child in her womb, that child to an enemy.'
Thus spoke the king of the Phaiakians, and at once fell asleep.
But Arete, pondering the wisdom of his words, rose silently
and hurried through the halls of the palace to find her herald. She said:
'Go swiftly to Jason, and advise him as I shall say.' And she told
the king's decision. And swift as a shadow the Phaiakian went.
He found the Argonauts keeping armed watch in the harbor near town,
and he gave them the message in full.

                              "At once, and with no debate,
the Argonauts set about the marriage rites. They mixed new wine
for the immortal gods, led sheep to the altar that Argus built—
so curiously fashioned that it seemed to be sculpted from a single stone,
though its gem-bright parts were innumerable, and the removal of any
would bring all its glory to ruin—and with their swords they slew
the sheep. And before it was dawn, they made the marriage bed
in a sacred grove. The swift-winged sons of the wind brought flowers
from the rims of the world, and Euphemos, racing on the sea, called nymphs
who came bringing gifts of coral and priceless pearl. The heroes
famous for strength—Koronos, Telamon and Peleus,
and mighty Leodokos, and Phlias, son of Dionysos, and lean
Akastos, whose heart was like a bull's—surrounded the altar in a ring,
guarding the bride and groom and the old seer Mopsos, in white,
from the attack of the Kolchians or demons from under the earth, dark friends
of Helios. And behold, in the sky, snow white in the rays
of the yet-horizoned sun, there appeared an eagle, sign
of Zeus, so that none might carp in future days that the marriage
was false, being made by necessity. They spread on the bed
the golden fleece as a bridal sheet, and to Orpheus' lyre,
the Argonauts sang the hymeneal at the door of the chamber,
and the nymphs of the tide sang with them. And thus the son of Aison
and I, Medeia, were married.

              "Then dawn's eyes lit the land,
old Helios red as a coal; and lightly, his hand on my arm,
Lord Jason slept, at peace. Not I.
                    "The streets now rang,
the whole Phaiakian city astir. On the far side
of the island, the Kolchians were also awake. And Alkinoös
went to them now, as promised, to give his decision in the case.
He carried in his hand the staff of judgment,
the golden staff with which he gave out, impartially,
justice among the Phaiakians. And with him throng
on throng of Phaiakian noblemen came in procession, armed.
Crowds of women meanwhile poured from the city to view
the wide-famed Argonauts; and when they learned our joyful news
they spread it far and wide, and all Phaiakia came
to celebrate. One man led in the finest ram
of his flock; another brought a heifer that had never toiled; still others
brought bright, two-headed jars of wine. And far and wide
the smoke of offerings coiled up blinding the sun. There were golden
trinkets, embroidered robes, small animals in cages—and still
the Phaiakians kept coming. There were casques of chalcedony
and mottled jade, and figures of ebony, and ikons of gold
with emerald eyes. There were baskets, carpets, bowls, weapons,
there were songs not heard since the First Age—mute Phlias danced—
and for seven days more they came, those gentle Phaiakians.

    "And as for Alkinoös, from the moment he gave his judgment
and learned soon after of the marriage, he stood intransigent.
He couldn't be shaken by threats or oaths, and he refused to dread,
beyond the displeasure of Zeus, Aietes' enmity.
When the Kolchians saw that their case was hopeless, they remembered the vow
of Aietes, and feared to return to him. More humble now,
they craved the king's asylum. Alkinoös granted it.
I wept for joy, all danger past. I was sure I would soon
be home. I looked at Jason—that beautiful, gentle face—
and could nearly believe, in spite of myself, that the world was born
anew, all curses cancelled.
                    "But at times in dreams I saw
the merry old god of rivers, who laughed in the North, untouched
by the sorrows that unhinge man. And at other times I dreamed
I stood in the sacred grove of Artemis and searched for something.
It would soon be dawn, the rim of the mountains already on fire.

I must hurry. I must struggle to remember. Whatever it was I sought,
it was near, as near as my heartbeat. I heard a footstep. Or was it?
A swish like the blade of a scythe . . . that I remembered . . . And I
would scream, and Jason would hold me, his eyes impenetrable.

"So the days passed, and on the seventh day
we left the isle of the Phaiakians, the *Argo* loaded
to the beams with Phaiakian treasure. King Alkinoös gave
strong men to replace all those we'd lost from the rowing benches
in our dark wanderings, and Arete sent six maidens with me
to comfort and serve me as once I was served at home. On the shore
King Alkinoös and his queen stretched up their hands and prayed
to the gods for our easy passage and final forgiveness for crimes
committed of harsh necessity; and the people kneeled,
the whole population, weeping. And so we left the place,
sailing for home. I rolled the sound on my tongue. For home.
I started, cried out. For out of the corner of my eye, I thought,
I'd caught a glimpse of the river-god combing his beard, watching us,
terrible god from the beginning of things, who laughed at guilt.
'Jason!' I whispered.

" 'Easy, my love,' said Jason, smiling.
They were all smiling, their eyes like the gods' dark mirror, the sea."

17

I awakened and looked in alarm for Medeia. The voice had ceased
and the winds that tumble and roar in space—so I thought in my dream—
were swallowed to nothing. I clung to the bole of the oak like a bat.
Then came a shimmering light, sea-green on every side,
blurred cloudshapes, moving, like crowds of sea-beasts hemming me in.
The silence changed; it swelled—more swift than a falling tower—
to a boom, sharp voices of angry men. And now, suddenly,
my eyes focussed, or the universe focussed, life crashed in on me:
sweat-dank, bearded sailors milling like bees in a hive,
howling against some outrage, I knew not what. I'd grown
more solid, it seemed. When they bumped me, hurriedly elbowing past,
I staggered. They tromped my feet, jostled me, caved in my hat
with no apology, hardly a glance. Wold-I, nold-I,
I moved with the crowd. Men all around and ahead of me jumped,
clambered for a view, shook fists, shouted. I caught a few snatches.
Someone was dead, murdered by the king, the crew of some ship
arrested by Kreon's police. Some voice of authority bellowed
from a raised platform somewhere ahead of us, but his cries were drowned
by the roar of the mob. I struggled for breath, shouted
for the goddess, but no help came. Some man at my back growled bitterly,
"Corinth is cursed. We were fools to come." Another voice answered,
"Everywhere's cursed." I craned my neck to see who'd spoken,
but they all looked alike, their tanned hides toughened by gale and salt
to the thickness of a twice-baked galley biscuit. At their necks hung daggers
with thong-wrapped handles and serried blades. On their wrists, brass sheaths
ornate with dragons and monsters of the deep. Then someone seized
my shoulder—so fierce that my arm went numb and I shouted—and without
a glance, he shoved me away and down. In horror I felt myself

falling to the mud, my spectacles dangling, precariously hooked
by one ear. I squealed like a rat incinerated,
my mind all terror, my left hand clutching at my spectacles, right hand
stretching to snatch some hold on the sweatwashed back of the giant
in front of me. I fell, sank deep in the mud; the maniacal
crowd came on, stepping on my legs, battering my ribs.
On the back of my left hand, blurry as a cloud, fell a scarlet drop
of blood. "Dear goddess!" I whimpered. I'd surely gone mad. It was
no dream, surely, this jangling pain! A foot sank, blind,
on the four fingers of my thin right hand and buried them;
thick yellow water swirled where they'd been, then reddened with blood.
My mind grew befuddled. My vision was awash.
Then hands seized me, painfully jerked me upward, at the same time
heaving back at the crowd. I gave myself up to the stranger,
clinging still to my spectacles. My rescuer shouted,
struck at the crowd with his one free arm like a wounded gorilla.
We came to a wall, a doorway; he dragged me inside, put me down
on a pile of skins, and scraped the bloodstained mud from my face.
Gradually, my vision cleared. I remembered my spectacles
and, finding a part of my vest still dry,
I wiped them, as well as I could. One lens was cracked like a sunburst,
a small piece missing. The other was whole. My rescuer, seeing
what I struggled to do, though he had no faintest idea what it meant,
brought me water in a jug, poured it on the lenses, then offered
a cloth. When at last I could see again, we looked at each other.
He was young; not intelligent, or so I suspected, his face defeatured
in its lionish, square-jawed frame. His small gray eyes were round
with amazement. I might have been an elf, a merman, a unicorn's child.
Behind him, three women and a man, in the robes of shop-people,
bent at the waist to stare at me. And still, outside,
in the blinding brightness, the rioting sailors pressed and shouted.
The young man turned, following my gaze. Then all at once
some change came over the crowd. There were cries of alarm, loud questions.
The crowd rolled back, retreating from the pressure in front. The women
and the bearded man—his beard came nearly to his knees—came bustling
to the door, peeked timidly out, their silhouettes blocking the light.
They gave sharp yells, all four of them at once, and rushed to us, reaching,
chattering gibberish—some argot Greek or Semitic tongue
I couldn't identify—and pushed us farther from the door into darkness.
I caught a glimpse—as I plunged with them in past bolts of cloth,

calfskins, wickerwork, leather—of Kreon's police force, armed
with naked swords and whips, great helmets like mitres that shone
brass-red. Each time a whip flashed out, some man fell screaming
to the yellow mud, his torn arms clenching his head. Then darkness;
we'd come to a deeper stall, the air full of spices—aloes,
cloves and saffron and cinnamon . . . They whispered
in the language foreign to me. We waited for a long time.
My eyes adjusted to the dimness a little, and I saw the old man
was as thin and ashen as an old wood spoon. His marmoset face
was covered like a cheap plaster wall with bumps and nodes like droppings
of mason's grout; his tiny eyes were like silver coins.
He pulled at his beard with his fingers, watching in secret alarm
(as I watched him) for signs that I might prove dangerous.
His wife was brown and swollen, sullen, the others
buxom and dimpled, country odalisques
with dull, seductive eyes. All four of them watched me in fear,
exactly as they'd watched the crowd, the Corinthian police. I grinned.
The four grinned back, and the man who'd saved me; a glow of teeth
in the cavern-dark of wares. The merchant brought wine. We drank.
    When the streets were quiet, we crept back out, down wynds and alleys
to a silent square—fother by the walls, abandoned winejugs,
wases of straw and faggots, wrecked carts . . . It was dusk. Here and there
men lay still, as if asleep, sprawled out in the mud, on cobblestones,
drawn up onto the stoops of shops that stared at the empty
twilit square like lepers waiting for blessing. We went—
the man who had saved my life and I—to a man who sat
some twenty feet from the door of the shop that protected us.
He sat with his face in his drawn-up knees, as if weeping, or sick.
I touched his shoulder. He fell over slowly, indifferently, dead.
My friend looked at me and nodded. He held out his hand, palm up.
I understood, put my palm on his. He nodded again,
unsmiling; and so we parted.

                        I had no desire now
to climb that hill to Kreon's palace. My body ached
from the soles of my feet to the crown of my head. My clothes were ragged,
damp and bespattered, mud-stained. My right-hand fingers were numb
and misshapen; broken, I believed. However, I climbed as far
as the first of the palace pools, where I meant to wash the blood off,
caked on my hands and face. I studied my reflection, amazed:

hat battered like a tramp's, the pockets of my suitcoat ripped,
my nose grotesquely swollen, the spectacles tilted, bent.
I straightened my glasses as well as I could, then tucked them in my pocket.
In the stone gray sky above, bats circled. The city was still.
Then someone spoke to me. "See it to the end." I wiped the water
from my eyes and looked. He stared gravely at nothing—the ancient
seer of Apollo whom I'd seen, long since, with Jason. I hooked
my spectacles over my ears and looked more closely: a man
so calm he seemed to encompass Time like a vase. He said:
"See it to the end. The gods require it." He turned away,
and I saw only now the boy with him, his guide. I struggled
to speak, but couldn't. I glanced up the hill at the palace, aglow
like the galaxy with torches. When I turned to the seer again
he was moving slowly downhill, leaning hard on the boy. I found
my voice and called, "Teiresias!" He turned, waiting.
I realized in alarm we had nothing to say.

Enveloped
in a mist that hid me from the watch, I climbed to the palace. The crowd
was thinner by half than when last I'd listened to Jason speak.
It filled me with dread. I knew well enough what the reason was.
The best had abandoned the contest, and not because Jason appeared
to be winning. The brutal quelling of the riot, tyrannic use
of the law's whole force on their own long-suffering, disgruntled crews—
and perhaps something more, the murder I'd heard of, the crew arrested—
had turned them to scorn of Corinth and Corinth's prize. Without
a word, I suspected, they'd turned their steps to the harbor and sailed
for home. I was partly wrong, I learned later. There were shouts in the palace,
young kings outraged, old kings quietly astounded at Kreon's
ways. But my guess was right in this: the best who'd come
had abandoned Corinth, prepared to become, on further provocation,
her enemies.
        I moved, among those who remained, to a stairway,
a raised place where I could see. Except for the kings who'd departed
all was the same, I thought—the princess Pyripta in her chair
of gold, with her hand on her eyes (her light-filled hair fell softly,
swirling, enclosing her shoulders as if as protection); Kreon
stern in his place, lips pursed, eyes squeezed half shut; the goddesses
listening, watching like kestrels, except Aphrodite, who sat
half-dreaming, studying Jason and Pyripta. I noticed at last

that Kreon's slave Ipnolebes was missing, as was
the blond Northerner, Amekhenos. But I had no time
to brood much on it. Jason was speaking. His voice was gentle,
troubled, I thought. How much had he seen, in his lordly isolation,
of the day's events? I saw him with the eyes of the young Medeia,
stunned in her father's courtyard. He would have been thinner then,
as big in the chest, less thick in the waist, his gestures tentative,
boyish despite all those daring deeds already. His eyes
seemed hardly the eyes of a power-grabber. What was he, then?
Yet perhaps I knew. His guarded glance at the princess, for instance.
Age-old hunger of vanity, hunger to be loved just one
more time, and just one more, one more—give the lie to death
for an instant. But it wasn't enough for him, the total adoration
of a girl. He must have whole cities' adoration—and he'd had that, once,
rightful prince of Iolkos, the throne his uncle had usurped
and he might have won back, without shame, by bloody deeds; yet chose
the reasonable way, for all his might in arms, for all
his people's love. "Evil deeds commit their victims,"
Medeia had said, "to responses evil as the deeds themselves."
That was the law he'd sought to change.
No wonder if the child of Aietes hadn't understood, had struck—
sky-fire's child—with the pitiless force of her father's father.
And so Lord Jason had lost it all. I remembered again
the crowd of outraged sailors, turning and turning, grinding . . .
My memory seethed with the image, all space astir like grain
in the narrowing flume of a gristmill. Against that ceaseless motion,
Jason stood in the great hall still as a rock, a tree,
as gentle of mind, as reasonable, as firm of will
as the cool, intellectual moon. Ah, Jason knew, all right,
of the riots. Calm, his voice an instrument, he spoke:

"Six weeks the god's wrath banged us shore to shore among foemen,
men who fought naked, cut off their enemies' heads. All that
for Circe's failure to forgive. Old Argus' wonderful engine,
driven as if by its own will, struck rocks and laughed
at the steering oar of Ankaios. I lost there fourteen men
to wrecks and those savage raids. I gave what attention I could
to Medeia—whatever was left, to the needs of my men. She was sick,
hour on hour and day on day, some strange collusion
of body and mind, or a poison shot down from Helios.

I loved her, yes, though her bowels ran black, and at times, in pain,
she raged. I loved her, if anything, more than before that time,
as you love a child you've nursed through the night, alarmed by his trembling,
cooling his forehead in terror of convulsions. Loved her for the shame
that closed her hands to fists, made her jawline clench. A love
that trenched past body to the beauty deeper, the humanness
astounded by love not earned by its outer form. She was,
in her own crazed, blood-shot eyes, a thing despicable, vile;
to me the wealth of kingdoms, dearer than my flesh, her acrid
lips, distilled wild honey, her tangled hair more joy
than goat flocks frisking in the hills. —Yet rage she did; demanded
more than my hands could give, my reeling mind hold firm.
Raged and wept, while claws of rock reached up at us
and savage strangers struck us from every tree and rock
on shore. I clung to my scrap of sanity like Theseus clutching
Ariadne's thread in the Labyrinth. At times I sobbed,
clenched my teeth at the loss of friends. At times, with the help
of Butes, king of the spear, and Phlias and Akastos, kept calm
by fear for me, I heartened my men with words. Mad Idas
mocked, shouted at the winds, demanded that Zeus destroy him.
He beat his chest with his great black fists and slobbered, convinced
that for him, for his slight against Zeus, we endured this punishment.
Once, in the night, he went overboard. Medeia awakened
with a scream, aware of catastrophe.
We saw him at once, and Leodokos, mighty as a bull, went over.
Swimming like a dolphin, he dragged him back to the *Argo,* poor Idas
spluttering, cursing the gods and the skewbald sea.
                                        "So, hurled
by unknown winds and waters, we came to the Sirens' isle.
I shackled my men and Medeia like slaves; myself as well.
Orpheus played, struggling to drown out their song, or untune it.
The sea was calm, full of sunlight.
    "I heard it well enough: music peeling away like a gull
from Orpheus' jazz. Dark cavern music, the music of silent
pools where no moon shines: the music of death as secret
hunger. What can I say? They were not innocents,
those sirens: it was not peace they sang, fulfillment in joy.
Who'd have been sucked to his death by that?—by holy dreams
of isles forever green, where shepherds play their pipes
softly, softly, for girls forever white? It wasn't

gentleness, goodness, the sweetness of age those sirens sang:
the warmth of a family well provided for, a wife
grown old without a slip from perfect faithfulness.
I have heard it said by wise old men that 'history'
is all you have left in the end, the fond memories shared
by a man and a woman who've seen it all, survived it all,
together. There is no nobler reward, they say. Perhaps.
But that was not the unthinkable hope they lured us with.
They sang of known and possible evils driven beyond
all bounds, slammed home like crowbars driven to the neck in great, thick
abdomens of rock. Oh, not like sailors' whores,
who whisper with girlish lust, the nebulous verge of love,
what wickedness they mean. (She arches her back to you,
her breasts grow firm, packed tight with passion, as if they're filled
to the bursting point with milk. She seizes your mouth with hers;
plunged in, you can't break free, clamped in by a fist, her legs
closed on your hips like jaws.) All that, for the moment at least,
is love. They did not sing to us of love. They sang . . .
terrible things. No generous seaport prostitute,
whispering, screaming—whatever her tricks—could satisfy
our murderous, suicidal lust from that day on. Nothing
(by no means islands forever green) could quench, burn out
our need beyond that day. It was pain and death they sang:
terrible rages of sex beyond the orgasm,
blindness, drunkenness bursting the walls of unconsciousness,
the murderer's sword plunged in beyond the life-lock, down
to life renewed, midnight black, imperishable.
Such was the song, cold-blooded lure, of those cunning, sly-
eyed bitches. Orpheus' fingers jangled the lyre, but couldn't
blot from our minds their music's deadly mysticism.
One of our number, Butes the spearman, went overboard,—
snapped steel chains and plunged. We'd have followed him down, if we could.
We couldn't. We strained at our shackles and raged; we frothed at the mouth;
the *Argo* sailed on, and Orpheus played, immune to our wrath
as he was to their song. He took no stock in absolute evil,
or good either. (The god of poets, the Keltai say
is a sow, rooting, rutting with boars, able to converse
with wind.) Orpheus
sighed, endured by his harp-playing.
Which was well enough for him, but what of the rest of us?

"We sailed on, sorrowing, Medeia blaked with a fury that had
no possible vent: fury at the father she loved; at herself;
at me for the murder of the brother whose murder she'd engineered . . .
And so we came to the terror of Skylla and Kharybdis. On one side,
sheer rock cliff, on the other the seething, roaring maelstrom.
We looked, Ankaios sweating. I scarcely cared. My soul
was thick with the torpor of those who have listened to the sirens and failed
to act. Was I half asleep? On the left, rock scarp as steep
as the walls of a graveyard trench, and as certain to grind our dust:
call it death by rectitude. On the right side, turning
like an old constrictor, a woman enraged,—death by violence,
bottomless shame; between—barely possible—death by indifference,
soul-suffocation in the corpse that stinks, plods on. Ankaios
wept, abandoned the steering oar. I called on Asterios,
son of an endless line of merchants. He seized the oar,
tongue between his teeth, his brown eyes luminous.
I laughed—God knows, without joy. And clumsy as he was with the oar,
he knew the line and kept it, who cared for nothing in life
but the clinquant possible of profit tomorrow. The heavy ship
was as easy for him as a lighter by the quay. Short-sighted fool,
valueless, podging, unfit for the company of thinking men,
I give you this: You kept possibilities open, so that,
plodding, stinking, we may yet have time to reconsider—perhaps
oppose you, perhaps turn tradesman and find amusement in it.
    "We came to the wandering rocks. The sky was choked. Hot lava
shot up on every side through spicious, roiling steams.
Great islands loomed around us, rowelled like brustling whales,
sank once more into darkness. The sails were like ruby, like blood.
By the light of explosions from the hills surrounding we chose our channels
—there, and there—the options shot up like partridges,
wide roads, keyholes of daylight, all of them fair, all fine
in the instant's vision of the possible. But the black sky closed
like a curtain, and the steam came swirling again, and the channel was gone,
another one gaping to the right of us, sucking us in—in the distance,
sky. Yes, this then! Good! —But a belch of flame, cascade
of boulders, and the sea was revised once more. Old Argus watched it,
fascinated, too preoccupied for fear. Again and again he glanced
from the tumbling seas to the sky. He shouted,
swinging his eyes to me, shaggy beard splashed red by the sea,
'It's all Time–Space in a duckpond, Jason! See how it moves

by law, yet unpredictably. So the galaxies turn
in their aeviternal spans, some bodies wheeling to the left,
some wheeling right, some rolling head over heels like bears,
a few—like the overintellectual moon—staring, as if
with a mad *idée fixe*, at a single point. It's food
for thought, this sea. It teaches of terrible collisions, the spin
of planets battered to chaos by a dark star drifting free,
the plosion of a sun in the northwest corner of the universe,
flash of a comet, collapse of a cloud of dust. Like colliding
balls, the planets scatter in dismay, then quickly settle
on a new course, new synchysis, and feel secure. Then *CRASH!*
an instant later (as the ends of the universe read their clock)
a new, more terrible collision—new cries of alarm in the heights . . .
We here, who assess durabilities by clicks too brief
for the mind of space to vision except by number theory,
we watch the sun sail west, and we nod, approve the stupendous
rightness of things. "Choose so-and-so," say we, "and we bring on
such-and-such." We frigate the hills with purpose: "This oak,
meaningless before, I delimit as wood for my cart." We move,
secure, never glancing down, on precarious stepping stones,
Mondays and Tuesdays a-shiver in the torrent of Time.' He laughed,
indifferent to grim implications. He meant no harm in life,
Argus, observer of mechanics, creator of machines. A man
who hated war so long as he thought as a citizen,
but fashioned the mightiest engine of war yet built, with the help
of the goddess. A man who lived by order, fashioned by his grasp
of predictables, but observed, cold-blooded, and laughed, that order
was illusion, a trick of timing. Incredible being! Knowledge
was all, in the end; the pawks in the book he'd leave to the future,
if luck allowed its survival. Not so with Orpheus,
whose machine was art, a bit for piercing the surface of things,
advancing nothing, returning again and again to the cryptarch
heart, where there is no progress and each new physical engine
threatens the soul's equilibrium. At the words of Argus
he paled, though I'd heard him express, himself, thoughts twice as grim.
'Not true,' he shouted. He clutched my shoulder, pointed at a glode
where blue burst through with a serenity like violence.
'The gods see more than we mortals dream. I tell you, Jason,
and swear to it too, these seas that fill us with terror are alive
with nymphs, pale nereids sent here by Hera. They leap like dolphins,

running on the reefs and breaking waves, fanning our sails
with the swing of invisible skirts; and the hand of the tiller is the hand
of Thetis herself, sweet nereid wife of Lord Peleus.
Whatever the bluster of the wandering rocks, we need not fear them.
The world is more than mechanics. If that weren't so, we'd be wrecked
long since!' In a sea of choices, none of them certain, I chose
to believe him. We kept her upright, scudding with the wind, accepting
any opening offered. Whatever the reason, we came
to quiet seas and sunlight, for which we thanked the gods,
on the chance they'd had some hand in it. It was not my part
to speculate.
          "We were close inshore, so close that through
the haze on the land we could hear the mooing of cattle and bleating
of sheep. We were drenched, half-starved, stone-numb with weariness,
but according to the boy at the helm, Ankaios, the land was the isle
of Helios. We needed, God knew, no further bavardage
with *him*. And so we continued on and arrived, half-dead,
at the isle of the pale Phaiakians.
                    "There we married,
Medeia and I, our hands forced by necessity.
A fleet of Kolchians, arriving by way of the Black Sea,
drove Alkinoös to a choice. Medeia, by secret dealing
with Alkinoös' queen, outwitted the old man's justice—
for which I was glad enough, no warbling songbird gladder,
for I knew then nothing of the wandering rocks we had yet to face,
that child of the sun and I, back home in Iolkos. She was,
not only in my eyes but even to men who despised the race
of Aia, a woman more fair than the pantarb rising sun,
the moon on the sea, the sky-wide armies of Aietes with all
their trumpets, crimson banners, bronze-clad horsemen. She seemed
as fair beside all others as a dew-lit rose of Sharon
in a trinsicate hedge of thorn, more fine than a silver dish,
the curve of her thighs like a necklace wrought by a master hand.
My heart sang like Orpheus' lyre on that wedding night,
played like lights in a fountain—and whose would not?
                              "We sailed
joyful, Phaiakian maidens attending Medeia, Phaiakian
sailors heaving on the rowing seats left vacant by the dead.
And so came even in sight of Argos' peaks. Mad Idas
danced in a fit of wild joy. The prophecy of Idmon had failed:

the hounds of Zeus had forgotten him, or if not, at least,
had spared him for now, had spared him the doom he'd dreaded most,
a death that dragged down friends. But even as he danced for joy,
his brother, Lynkeus of the amazing eyes, put his black hand gently
on Idas' shoulders, gazing into the sea and beyond
the curve of the gray horizon. Nor was it long before
we too saw it—a stourmass terrible and swift, blackening the western sky,
rushing toward us like a fist. We heaved
at the *Argo*'s oars. Too late! We lurched under murderous winds,
black skies like screaming apes. We struck we knew not where,
hurled by the flood-tide high and dry. Then, swift as an eagle,
the storm was gone. We leaped down full of dismay. Gray mist,
a landscape sprawling like a dried-up corpse, unwaled, immense.
We could see no watering place, no path, no farmstead. A world
calcined, silent and abandoned. Again the boy Ankaios
wept, and all who had learned navigation shared his woe.
No ship, not even the *Argo,* could suffer the shoals and breakers
the tidal wave had hurtled us unharmed past. There was no
return, the way we'd come, and ahead of us, desert, gray,
as quiet as a drugged man's dreams. Poor Idas
sifted our gold and gems, the Phaiakians' gift, and howled
and bit at his lips until blood wet his kinky beard. Though the sand
and sea-smoothed rocks were scorching, our hearts were chilled. The crew
strayed vaguely, seeking some route of escape. Bereft of schemes
I watched them and had no spirit to call them back, maintain
mock-order. When the cool of nightfall came, they returned. No news.
And so we parted again, each seeking a resting place
sheltered from the deepening chill. Medeia lay shivering, moaning,
in the midst of her Phaiakian maidens, her head and chest on fire
with the strange plaguing illness, Helios' curse. All night
the maids, their golden tresses in the sand, cried out and wept,
as shrill as the twittering of unfledged birds when they lie, broken,
on the rocks at the foot of the larch. At dawn the crew rose up
once more and staggered to the sunlight, starved, throats parched with thirst,
no water in sight but the salt-thick sea—the piled-up gifts
of the Phaiakians mocking our poverty—and again set out
fierce-willed as desert lions, in search of escape. And again
returned with nothing to report.
                              "We gave up hope that night.
All that will could achieve, we'd done. We sought out shelters,

prepared to accept our death, the sun's revenge, triumph
of Helios. We listened to the whimpers of the maidens and wept for them,
and secretly cursed the indifferent, mechanical stars.
                                                    "But on
that Libyan shore dwelled highborn nymphs. They heard the laments
of the maids and the groans of Medeia. And when it was noon, and the sun
so fierce that the very air crackled, they came, for pity
of the maidens, doomed unfulfilled, having neither men nor sons,
and stood above me, and brushed my cloak's protection from my eyes
and called to me in a strange voice, a voice I remembered
yet could not place—some shrew with the flat Argonian accent
I'd known as a child.—'Jason!' I looked, saw nothing but the blinding
sun. They cried, 'Pay back the womb that has borne so much.
Call strength from murdered men. Redeem these thousand shames.
Embrace your ruin, you who have preached so much on mindless
struggle, unreasoning hope. Have you still no love?' So they spoke,
voices in the white-hot light. I had no idea what they meant,
whispers of madness, guilt. I slept again, awaiting
death. And then sat up with a start, a crazy idea
tormenting me: the womb was the *Argo* who'd borne us here,
the murdered men not those I'd lost before but those
around me, grounded by the sun; and my ruin was the sun himself:
I must go to the center of the furnace, my only prayer for the men,
the Phaiakian maidens, and Medeia. Oh, do not think I believed
it reasonable! The desert was hotter where I meant to go,
and the *Argo* no weight for men half-starved, no water to drink
on a trip that might take us days, if not all eternity.
Nevertheless, I roused them, fierce, a lion gone mad,
and stumbling, incredulous, they obeyed. I sent no scouts ahead,
and no man there suggested it. Blind luck was our hope,
perhaps blind love, the Argonauts bearing that monstrous ship,
spreading her weight between shoulders meaningless except for this,
their union in a madman's task. In their shadow the maidens walked,
singing a hymn of heatwaves, the pitiless sun, a dirge
for all of us. And so those noblest of all kings' sons,
by their own might and hardihood, lips cracked and bleeding,
carried the *Argo* and all her treasures, shoulder high,
nine days and nights through the death-calm dunes of Libya.
    "I shared the weight till the seventh day. Then Medeia fell,
unconscious, and could not be wakened. So I carried my wife in my arms,

shouting encouragement to the men, reassuring the maidens. The sun
filled all the sky, it seemed to us. But the maidens sang,
struggled to help with the load till they fell, befuddled, giggling
like madwomen. We dragged them on. Told lunatic jokes,
talked with the sun, the sand, a thousand sabuline visions—
and so we came to water. But left the desert strewn
with graves, unmarked by stick or stone. One half my crew
and two of the maidens we buried in the white-hot sand; and not
the least of those who fell there, slaughtered by the heat, was Ankaios,
nobleman robed in a bearskin and armed with an axe. We buried
the twelve-foot child and wept. Our tears were dust. Then set
the *Argo* down in the calm Tritonian lagoon, and searched
for drinking water.
                         "The sky was blinding white, all sun.
It seemed to us that we came to the body of a huge gray snake,
head smashed, by the trunk of an appletree. From the venom sacks down
the corpse was asleep, undreaming, the coils a thicket of arrows,
such deadly poison that maggots perished in the festering wounds.
And close to the corpse, it seemed to us, we saw fiery shapes
wailing, their mist-pale arms flung past their golden heads.
At our first glimpse of the beautiful strangers, majestic beings
in the white-hot light, they vanished in a swirl of dust. Then up
leaped Orpheus, praying, wild-eyed: 'O beautiful creatures, mysteries,
whether of Olympos or the Underworld, reveal yourselves!
Blessed spirits, shapes out of Ocean or the violent sun,
be visible to us, and lead us to a place where water runs,
fresh water purling from a rock or gushing from the ground! Do this
and if ever we bring our ship to some dear Akhaian port,
we'll honor you even as we honor the greatest of the goddesses,
with wine and with hecatombs and an endless ritual of praise!'
No sooner did he speak, sobbing and conjuring strangely with his lyre
than grass sprang up all around us from the ground, and long green shoots,
and in a moment saplings, tall and straight and in full leaf—
a poplar, a willow, a sacred oak. And strange to say,
they were clearly trees, but also, clearly, beings of fire,
and all we saw in the world was clearly itself but also
fire.
        "Then the beams of the oak tree spoke. 'You've been fortunate.
A man came by here yesterday—an evil man—
who killed our guardian snake and stole

248

the golden apples of the sun. To us he brought anger and sorrow, to you release
from misery. As soon as he glimpsed those apples, his face
went savage, hideous to look at, cruel,
with eyes that gleamed like an eagle's. He carried a monstrous club
and the bow and arrows with which he slew our guardian of the tree.
Our green world shrank to brambles and thistles, to sand and sun,
and in terror, like a man gone blind, he turned to left and right
bellowing and howling like a lost child.
And now he was parched with thirst, half mad. He hammered the sand
with his club until, by chance, or pitied by a god, he struck
that great rock there by the lagoon. It split at the base, and out
gushed water in a gurgling stream, and the huge man drank, on his knees,
moaning with pleasure like a child and rolling his eyes up.'

                                           "As soon
as we heard these words we rushed to the place, all our company,
and drank. Medeia—still unconscious, more cruelly punished
than those we'd buried in the sand—I placed in the shadow of ferns
at the water's edge. I bathed her arms and legs, her throat
and forehead, and dripped cool water in her staring eyes. With the help
of her maidens, I made her drink. She groped toward consciousness,
rising slowly, slowly, like Poseidon from the depths of the sea,
until, wide-eyed with terror at some fierce vision in the sun,
invisible to us, she clenched her eyes tight shut, clinging
with her weak right hand to my cousin Akastos, with her left to me.
Mad Idas wept. Doom on doom he must witness, and sad
premonitions of doom, to the end of his dragged-out days. No more
the raised middle finger, the obscene joke through bared fangs;
no more the laughter of the trapped, that denies, defies the trap.
He'd recognized it at last: more death than death, and he rolled
his eyes like a sheep in flight from the wolf, and nothing at his back
but Zeus. Such was the sorrow of Idas, the bravest of men,
now broken.
        "As soon as our minds were cooled, we came to see
that the giant savage of whom the tree had spoken could be none
but Herakles, much changed by his many trials. We resolved
to hunt for him, and carry him back to Akhaia, if the gods
permitted. The wind had removed all sign of his tracks. The sons
of Boreas set off in one direction, on light-swift wings;
Euphemos ran in another, and Lynkeus ran, more slowly,
in a third, with his long sight. And Kaanthos set out too,

impelled by destiny. Kaanthos was one who'd ploughed for his living
and his heart was steady and gentle. He had had a brother once,
a man of whom nothing is known. He found a grazing flock
of goats kept alive by desert thistles, and he sought the goatherd
to ask for news of Herakles, the sky-god's son.
Before he could speak, the herd leaped up with a look of alarm
and threw a stone at him. It struck the poor man squarely on the forehead,
and Kaanthos, astounded, fell, and his life ran out. Nor was that
the least of my men to be lost on sandswept Libya.
As for Herakles, we found no trace. They all returned;
we prepared to set sail for home.
                "And then came Mopsos' time,
foreseen by him from the beginning, thanks to his birdlore. He was
the noblest of seers, for all his peculiarity—
his whimsy, the grime on his fingers, the bits of dried food in his beard—
but little good his wisdom did him when his hour arrived.
   "An asp lay sleeping in the sand, in shelter from the midday sun,
a snake too sluggish to attack a man who showed no sign
of hostility, or fly at a man who jumped back. It meant
no harm to anything alive, though even a drop of its venom
was instant passage to the Underworld. Old Mopsos, chatting
and strolling with Medeia and her maidens, while the rest of us worked on the ship,
by chance stepped lightly, with his left foot, on the tip of the creature's
tail. In pain and alarm, the asp coiled swiftly around
the old man's shin and calf and struck, sinking its fangs
to the gums. Medeia and her maidens shrank in horror. Old Mopsos
clenched his fists in sorrow. The pain was slight enough,
but he knew he was past all hope. He lifted his foot to free
the asp. Already he was paralyzed, numb. A dark mist
clouded his sight, and his heavy limbs fell. In an instant, he was cold,
his flesh corrupting in the heat of the sun, his hair falling out
in patches. We dug him a grave at once and buried him.
Then went down to the ship, full of woe.
                "With Ankaios dead,
no sure helmsman among us, our chances of reaching Akhaia
were slim. But Peleus took the oar, the father of Akhilles,
and we drew the hawsers in. There must surely be some escape
from the wide Tritonian lagoon, we thought. Having no aim,
we drifted, helpless, the whole day long. The *Argo*'s course,
as we nosed now here, now there, for an outlet, was as tortuous

as the track of a serpent as it wriggles along in search for shelter
from the baking sun, peeping about him with an angry hiss
and dust-flecked eyes, till he slips at last through a dark rock cleft
to freedom. And so we too found freedom. Once in the open,
we kept the land on our right, hugging the coast. The sun
was kinder now, though fierce enough. We slept in the shadow
of rocks by day, and drove the *Argo* by the power of our backs
from twilight till dawn's first glance. And so wore out by stages
the curse of Helios."

                  Here Jason paused, looked down,
his dark eyebrows knit. The hall was silent, waiting,
Kreon leaning on his arms, his gaze intent. I could feel
their dread of the man's conclusions.
                          He said: "Except, of course,
that no man—no house—wears out a curse by his own power.
We may with luck propitiate the gods, live through our trials;
but the offense is still in the blood, and our sons inherit it,
and our sons' sons, and shadow progeny arching to the end
of time. I half understood them now, those ghostships riding
the *Argo*'s wake. By some inexplicable accident
we were, ourselves, the point of no turning back. We closed
an age. 'The Golden Age,' men will call it. They'll honey it with lies
and hone for it, with languishing looks, and bemoan their fall
and curse my name and treason. . . . Their curses will not much stir
my dust. I was there; I saw the truth. A childish age
of easy glory in petty marauding, of lazy flocks
on bluegreen hills where every stream had its nymphs, each wood
its men half-goat; where the rightful monarch of a sleepy throne
could be set aside, as was I at Iolkos, and given the choice
of fighting for his right like a long-horned ram dispossessed of his gray
indifferent ewes, or accepting the slight humiliation
and moving on. I changed the rules—declined the gauntlet,
made deals, built cunning alliances, ambitious in secret,
with always one thought foremost: keep to the logic of nature.
Be true, within reason, to friends, with enemies ruthless. Be just,
but not beyond reason. Honor the gods and men and the stones
of the earth, but not to excess. Have faith sufficient to fight;
beware all expectations.
                  "For there is no power on earth

but treaty, no love but mutual consent—whatever the relative
power of those consenting. Not even the gods are firm
of character; much less, then, men. The promise I make,
I make to a man who may change, become anathema to me.
Therefore, be just, recall no vows still meet, but know
we sail among wandering rocks. By these few principles—
some known to me at the start, some not—I organized
the Akhaians. It would be, from that day forward,
powers pitted against powers, the labor of monstrous machines—
at best, a labor for universal good; at worst, perhaps,
exploiters faceless as forests, and the cringing exploited, the forests'
beasts.
        "So riding by night, my hand on Medeia's, I watched
the shadowy ships like mountains that followed in our wake. As before,
Time washed over us in waves. I dreamed it was stars we sailed,
and our oars stirred dust on the moon, or our shadow stretched out, prow
to stern, in the shadows that tremble and float down Jupiter.
At times stiff birds passed over us, roaring, and mountains took fire.
Medeia, watching at my side, said nothing, and whether or not
she understood these visions, I could not guess. I told her
the words I'd heard in my dream, off the isle of Phineus:
You are caught in irrelevant forms. Beware the interstices.
She studied me, child of magic; could tell me nothing. Gently,
I covered her hand. Sooner or later, I knew, I'd grasp that mystery.
I'd pierced a part of it already: it was there at the intersections
of the billion billion powers of the world that the danger lay,
and the hope; the gaps between gods, or men, or gods and men;
the gaps between minds—my own and Aiaian Medeia's. Invisible
gaps at the heart of connectedness, where love and will
leaped out, seek to span dark chambers, and must not fail. I seemed
for an instant to understand her, as when one knows for an instant
a tiger's mind; the next, saw only her face, her radiant,
wholly mysterious eyes. I was not as I was, however,
with Hypsipyle on the isle of Lemnos. It was not mere fondness,
shared isolation that I felt. I put my arms around her
as a miser closes his arms, half in joy, half in fear, around
his treasure sacks—as a king walls in his city, or a mother
her child. As the raging sun reaches
for the pale-eyed, vanishing moon, so Medeia's burning heart
reached for my still, coiled mind; as the moon reforms the light

of the sun, abstracts, refines it, at times refuses it,
yet lives by that light as memory lives by harsh deeds done,
or consciousness lives by the mindless fire of sensation, so I
locked needs with Medeia, not partner, as I was with Hypsipyle,
but part. She returned the embrace, ferocious: a wild off-chance.
Thus as Helios' wrath withdrew we staked our claims,
all our curses smouldering still in our blood.

   "And so we came at last by the will of the deathless gods to Akhaia.

18

"It wasn't easy, sharing the rule with senile Pelias.
All real power in the kingdom was mine. It was not for love
of the stuttering, wrinkled old man that Argus devised the palace
that made us the envy of Akhaia, or built the waterlocks
that transformed barrenness to seas of wheat, or built, above,
the shining temple to Hera that soared up tower on tower,
mirrored by lakes, surrounded by majestic parks. It was not
for love of Pelias that Orpheus brought in the mysteries
of Elektra to Argos, and made our city of Iolkos chief
of the sacred cities of the South. Nor was it for him that Phlias
created the great dance of Heros Dionysos, which brought us glory
and wealth and favor of the god of life and death. I shared
all honors with Pelias, though I'd changed his kingdom of pigs and sheep
to a mighty state; and I did not mind the absurdity of it.
And yet he was a thorn, a hedge of thorn, and I might have been glad to be
        rid of him.
I could move the assembly by a few words to magnificent notions—
things never tried in the world before. I could have them eating
from my hand, and then old Pelias would rise, wrapped head to foot
in mufflers and febrile opinions. His numerous chins a-tremble,
blanched eyes rolling, the tip of his nose bright red, like a berry
in a patch of snow, he'd stutter and stammer, slaughterer of time,
and in the end, as often as not, undo my work with a peevish
No. Nor was he pleased, God knows, to share the rule
with me. He hadn't forgotten the oracle that warned, long since,
that he'd meet his death by my hand. He couldn't decide, precisely,
whether to hate and fear me outright—whatever my pains
to put him at ease—or feign undying devotion, avuncular

pride in my glorious works. At times he would snap like a mongrel,
splenetic, critical of trifles—insult me in the presence of the lords.
I was patient. He was old, would eventually die. His barbs were harmless,
as offensive to all who heard them as they were to me. My cousin
Akastos would roll his eyes up, grinding his teeth in fury
at his father's ridiculous spite. I would smile, put my hand on Akastos'
arm, say, 'Never mind, old friend.' It drew us closer,
his shame and rage at his bumbling father's stupidity.
He had, himself, more honor with the people than his father had,
having sailed to the end of the world with us—a familiar now
of Orpheus, Leodokos, and the mighty brothers
Peleus and Telamon. He'd become, through us,
a friend of the hoary centaur Kheiron, and come to know
the child Akhilles, waxing like a tower and handsome as a god.
What had Akastos to do with a snivelling, whining old man,
Akastos who'd stood at the door of Hades, listened to the Sirens,
braved the power of Aietes and the dangerous Kelts? The old man
hinted that after his death Akastos should follow him
as my fellow king. It was not in the deal; I refused. Akastos
was furious—not at me. And now he seldom came
to the palace, bitterly ashamed. He remained with Iphinoe, at home,
or travelled with friends, supporting their courtships or wars.
                                                            "At times
Pelias would drop his peevishness, put on, instead,
a pretense of cowering love. He'd sit with his head to one side,
lambishly timid, and he'd ogle like a girl, admiring me.
'Noble Jason,' he'd call me, with lips obscenely wet,
and he'd stroke my fingers like an elderly homosexual,
his head drawn back, as if fearing an angry slap. His desire
to please, in such moods, was boundless. He couldn't find honors enough
to heap on me. He gave me gifts—his ebony bed
(my father's, in fact), jewels, the sword of Atlantis—but with each
gift given, his need—his terror of fate—was greater than before.
In the end he gave me the golden fleece itself as proof
that all he owned was mine, I need not murder him.
He was mad, of course. I had no intention of murdering him.
And still he cringed and crawled, all bootlicking love. That too
I tolerated, biding my time.
                        "Not all on Argos
shared or understood my patience. On the main street,

on the day of the festival of Oreithyia—our chariot blocked
by the milling, costumed crowd—a humpbacked beggarwoman
in fetid rags, a shawl hiding all but her hawkbill nose
and piercing eyes—a coarse mad creature who sang old songs
in a voice like the carrion crow's and stretched out hands like sticks
for alms—leaped up at sight of me, raging, 'Alas for Argos,
kingless these many years! Thank God I'm sick with age
and need not watch much longer this shameful travesty!
We had here a king to be proud of once, a man as noble beside these pretenders
as Zeus beside two billygoats!
That king and his queen had a son, you think? He produced what seemed one—
an arrogant, cowardly merchantry-swapper with no more devotion
than a viper. The father's throne was stolen—boldly, blatantly—
his blood cried out of the earth, cried out of the beams and stones
of the palace for revenge. The son raised never a finger. And the mother,
poor Alkimede, my mistress once, was driven from her home
to lodgings fit for a swineherd. There she lived with her boy,
as long as he'd stay. It was none too long. For all her pleas,
for all the great sobs welling from her heart, he must leave her helpless,
friendless in a world where once she'd stood
as high as any in Akhaia. O shameless! Shame on shame
he heaped on her: not on his own but in foul collusion
with the very usurper who seized that throne, he must sail to the shores
of barbarians, and must bear off with him on his mad expedition
the finest of Akhaia's lords! Few enough would return, he knew.
O that he too had been drowned in the river with innocent Hylas,
or fallen like Idmon to a maddened boar, or withered in Libya!
She might have had then some comfort in death, though little before,
wrapped in a winding-sheet wound by strangers, tumbled to her tomb
like a penniless old farm woman. And Jason returned,
joyful with his barbarous bride, and shamelessly joined the usurper,
smiling on half of his father's blood-soaked throne. See how
he preaches justice and reason, preaches fidelity,
trades on his great past deeds to avoid all present risks.
"Do not rave," he raves; "no shame can trouble our city.
Prophesy wealth and wine! The past is obliterated!
Tell us no more about crimes in the tents of our ancestors!
Justice and reason, like tamed lions, have settled in Iolkos."
Where is his justice and reason? Where is his loudly bugled
fidelity? The throne was stolen; stolen it remains.

What of fidelity to fathers and mothers? What of fidelity
to the dead in their winecupped graves?'
                                      "So the old shrew raged, shaking.
Medeia, standing beside me, glared with eyes like ice.
Softly, she said, 'Who is this creature
you allow to berate you in the streets?' I touched her hand to calm her.
'A woman who loved my mother,' I said. Medeia was silent.
It was not till another day she asked, 'Is this accusation
just, that Pelias stole your father's throne?' I thought,
Everything is true in its time and place. But answered only:
'I was young; my father was unsure of me. There were vague rumors . . .
It was all a long, long time ago.' But after that
when I spoke in the assembly or debated plans with my fellow king,
and Pelias had qualms, found reasons for doubt, objected, found cause
for delay, she would watch him with tigress eyes.
                                  "Pelias,
as his mind dimmed with the passing years, grew increasingly a burden.
It's a difficult thing to explain. He interfered with me less.
He grew deaf as a post and nearly blind, his mind so enfeebled
that in the end he relinquished all but a shadow of his former power.
The trouble was, he seemed to imagine that both of us
had abandoned the nuisance of government. Old-womanish, dim,
he'd call me to his bedroom and beg from me stories of the Argonauts,
or he'd tell me, as if we were shepherds with all afternoon to pass,
tedious tales of his childhood. It proved no use to send
his daughters instead, willing as they were—good-hearted, sheltered
princesses with the brains of nits. It had to be me—
myself or Akastos, and Akastos rarely came. I would stoop,
absurd in my royal robes, by the old man's bed, and listen,
or pretend to listen, brooding in secret on Argos' affairs.
The drapes would be drawn, a whim of his daughters, as though he were
some apple they hoped to preserve through the winter in a cool dark bin.
He would stutter like a fond old grandmother, on and on. At times
he'd recall with a start the prophecy, and he'd hastily offer
his cringing act, lading on flattery, protesting his life-long
love. His fingers, clinging to mine, gripped me like a monkey's.
His daughters would listen, drooping like flowers from slender stalks,
and whenever they spoke it was tearfully, with a kind of idiot
gratitude for the affection I showed their belovèd father.
At last he'd sleep; I'd be free to leave the place.

                                        "I'd go
to the wing of the palace I kept with Medeia and the children; I'd pass
in silence among our slaves, and my heart was sullen with suspicion.
Surely, I thought, they must mock me. Jason in his kingly robes,
shouldered like a bull, gray eyes rolling as he sits, polite
as a cranky old shepherd's serving boy, by the bed of Pelias,
hanging on stammered-out words. O shameless coward indeed!
I would stand alone at the balustrade of marble, glare out
at the sea, Orion hanging low, contemptuous.
I was not a coward, I knew well enough,
and it ought not to matter what others supposed.
I governed well—no man denied it. If I wasted time
on a fusty, repulsive old man, I had excellent reasons for it.
I was no Herakles pummelling the seasons
with passionate, mindless fists. Oh, I could admire the crone
who cackled in the streets, full of rage and scorn,
her loves and hates as forthright as boulders in the grass. No doubt
she would, in my place, have struck down Pelias at the first suspicion,
as would Herakles; or failing that, she'd have schemed and plotted—
would never have seemed to accept, as I did, his right to the throne,
or half of it. She'd have schemed and slaughtered, maintained the honor
of Iolkos' noble dead, whatever the cost to the living—
bloodshed of factions, houses in furor, families divided,
chaos for ages to come. I had no doubt that the course
I'd chosen was best, my seemingly shameful compromise.
Absolute passion, absolute glory, was for gods, not men.
I could claim the status of a demigod, but the future was not
with them.
            "Yet glaring out toward sea, resolved on a course
no man of sense could conceivably mock,
I was filled with a dangerous weariness.
More real than the seven-story fall
that gaped below me, more sharp to my sense than the quartz-domed tomb
of Alkimede on its high hill north of the temple of Hera,
or the figure of Medeia at my back, as heavy as bronze with anger—
visions of flight would snatch my mind—the *Argo*'s prow
bobbing like the head of a galloping horse, half smothered in foam,
dark shapes looming out of fire-green water, then vanishing—
the wandering rocks.
            "I was protected once by an old Kelt,

sired by a bear on a moon-priestess, or so he claimed.
We talked, in his shadowy hall, of freedom. His boy sat hunched
by the hearthstone, listening, watching with eyes like a cat's. From the beams
of the old king's walls hung the heads of his vanquished enemies,
and above the fire, nailed firmly to the slats, hung the leathern arm
of a giant. He said: 'I see no freedom in peace and justice.
I see no meaning in freedom that leaves some part of my soul
in chains. I grant, it's a noble ideal, this thing you purpose—
a state well governed, where no man tromps on another man's heel,
the oppressed are aided, the orphan and the widow win justice in the courts,
and each man holds to his place for the benefit of all. But I'd lose
my wind in a state so noble. I'd develop maladies—
mysterious, elusive, beyond any doctor's skill. Like a bat
in a cage, I'd wither, for no clear reason, and die.' The boy
at the hearthstone smiled, sharp-eyed, heart teeming with thought. The king
with mild blue eyes—cheeks painted, startling on that dignified face—
shook his head slowly, amused. 'You speak to me of gentle apes
in Africa and claim their kinship. Let Argus advise us,
who'd studied the world's mechanics for most of a century.
Is that indeed our line?—In this colder land we say
mankind is a child of the cat, old source of our crankiness,
our peculiar solitude—for though we may sometimes hunt in packs,
and share the kill, if necessary, we have never hunted
like brotherly wolves or bears.' He smiled.
'By another legend, the gods made man from the skull of a rat,
that grim and deeply philosophical scavenger who picks, light-footed,
perilously cunning, through houses of the dead, spreads corpses' sickness
to all he meets, yet survives himself and laughs at carnage
and takes bright trinkets from the slaughtered.

                                             " 'Be that
as it may—' The king glanced over at his boy. '—If my blood's essence
is not the gentleness and wisdom of Zeus but, whatever the reason,
has murder in it, as well as devotion and trust like a boy's,
then freedom is not for me what it is for Zeus. The freedom
of the eyes is to see and the ear to hear; the freedom of the soul
is to love and defend one's friends, assert one's power, behead
one's enemies, poison their streams.' He smiled. 'My words appall you.
But come! It was not I who proclaimed the supreme value
of liberty. I might well admire the state you dream of,
where nature's law is replaced by peace and justice—though I would not

visit the place. But do not mistake these noble goods
for freedom.' He reached his hand to my knee and smiled again.
'Your course will no doubt prosper, Jason. Your philosophy has
a ring to it, a nobility of glitter that can hardly fail
to appeal to the collector rat. Ten thousand years from now
men will look back to the Akhaians with pious admiration, and to us,
the treacherous Kelts, as bestial and superstitious, to whom
good riddance. And they may have a point, I grant. And yet you'll not
outlast us, lover of mind. From age to age, while your
spires shake in the battery of the sun, we, living underground,
will gnaw the animal heart, doing business as usual.'
I turned to the boy, a child with the gentleness of Hylas. I'd heard
him sing, and his voice was sweeter than dawn in a wheat-filled valley.
The severed heads of enemies hanging on the hall's dark beams
shed tears at his song, and the greatest of harpers, Orpheus himself,
was silenced by the music's spell. 'You, too, believe all this?'
I asked and smiled. For the Kelts were friends; I was not such a fool
as to hope to convert their mysterious hearts and brains by Akhaian
reasoning. The boy said shyly, 'How can I doubt
what I've heard from the cradle up? This much at least seems true
for both of you: You'd gladly fight to the death for friends,
whatever your theories.' We laughed. That much
was true, no doubt. Medeia smiled and glanced at me.
    "But now, standing at the balustrade and gazing wearily
seaward, I saw all that more darkly. The Keltic king
was righter than I'd guessed. I'd achieved the ideal of government
I dreamed of then: equal justice for all free citizens,
peace in the city. Yet my beast heart yearned, past all denying,
for violence. I envied Akastos, balanced, alive,
on the balls of his feet, riding in that rattling chariot of war
with the army of Kastor, repelling a wave of invaders on the plains
of Sparta. In the silence of the star-calm night, I could hear their shouts,
piercing the hundreds of miles—the snorting and neighing of horses,
the swish of a javelin hungrily leaping, the tumble of weighed-down
limbs.
    "Medeia said, 'Jason?' I turned to her. 'Tell me your thought.'
'No thought,' I said grimly. She said no more. I saw mad Idas
dancing with a corpse by the light of the burning gates of the palace
of Kyzikos. Saw Idmon writhing, his belly ripped open.

Saw the great eagle, with pinions like banks of silvery oars,
sailing to the mountain of Prometheus.
                                        "Hard times those were
for Medeia. She tended to the children, kept track of the household slaves
and hid from me her mysterious illness, or struggled to.
I glimpsed it at times: a tightness of mouth, an abstracted look;
and I remembered her sickness on the *Argo*. For all her skill with drugs,
she couldn't encompass her body's revolt—now menstrual cramps,
sharp as the banging of Herakles' club, and indifferent to the moon,
now unknown organs rebelling in their dens, now flashes of fire
in her brains. I would find her standing alone, white-faced with agony,
her corpse-pale fingers locked and her green eyes glittering, ferocious.
At times in the dead of night she would rise and leave our bed
and, passing silent as a ghost beyond the outer walls,
hooded, a dark scarf hiding her face, she would search the lanes
and gulleys of Argos for medicinal herbs—mecop and marigold,
the coriander of incantation, purifying hyssop,
hellebore, nightshade, the fennel that serpents use to clear
their sight, and the queer plant borametz, that eats the grass
surrounding it, and gale, and knotgrass . . . I began to hear
reports of strange goings-on—a slain black calf in a barrow
high in the hills; a grave molested; a visitation
of frogs in the temple of Persephone. I kept my peace,
watching and waiting. At times when I heard her footfall, quiet
as a feather dropping, and a moment later the closing of a door,
a whisper of wind, I would rise up quickly and follow her.
She led me through fields—a dark, hunched spectre in the moonless night—
led me down banks of creeks that she dared not cross, through groves
of sacred willows as ancient and quiet as the stones of abandoned
towns, then up to the hills, old mountains of the turtle people
who cowered under backs of bone as they watched her pass. She came
to a wide circle of stone, an ancient table of Hekate.
There she would slaughter a rat, a toad, a stolen goat,
singing to the goddess in a strange modality,
older than Kolchis' endless steppes,
and dropping her robe, her pale face lit by pain, she would dance,
squeezing the blood of the beast on her breasts and belly and thighs,
and her feet on the table of stone would slide on the warm new blood
till the last undulation of the writhing dance. Then she'd lie still,
like a bloodstained corpse, till the first frail haze of dawn. Then flee

for home. She'd find me waiting in the bed. She suspected nothing.
Little as I'd slept, I'd awaken refreshed,
would plunge into work as I did in the days when the *Argo*'s beams
groaned at the hammering of waves or shuddered at the blow of sunken
rocks. Pelias, weeping on the pillow, would stutter the fruit
of his senility, clinging to my hand. 'Beware of puh–*pride, my son.
My suh–son, beware of offending the g–g–g–gods.*' His daughters'
heads hung pale as cornflowers; their pastel scarves
fluttered in the flimsy wind of their love and awe. I could bow
and smile, unoffended, as alive in the stink of his sickness as I was
in the field of Aietes' bulls.
                      "On other occasions, when she left
to haunt the wilderness in search of some cure for her malady,
I rose up, silent, and walked to the chamber of a certain slave
and slipped into bed beside her, my hand on her mouth. I did not
love her, make no mistake, a cowering, mouse-shy creature
as repulsive to me as Pelias was in his feeblest moods.
But I'd lie beside her, exploring the curves of her body with my hands,
caressing her soft, damp fur, and at last would mount and pierce her,
twist and stab till she cried out in pain and fright. Again
and again, through the long still night I'd use her, driving like a horse;
she'd weep—once dared like a fool to strike me. I laughed. When dawn
crept near, I'd return to my own room, and when Medeia came,
slyly I would make love to her. We'd awaken refreshed,
rejuvenated. The slave soon came to expect my visits,
came to take pleasure in my violent lust. Though cowardly as ever—
hang-dog, feather-voiced, as stooped of shoulder as Pelias at his most
obsequious—she began to throw me sidelong glances,
for all the world like a litter-runt bitch in heat. When she found me
alone in a room, she would come to me softly, seductively touch
my arm, impose her scent on me. Sometimes even
when Medeia was near, whose eyes missed nothing, the wretched slave
would call to me down the room with her foxy eyes. I gave
her warning. I was not eager to lose her—those great fat breasts
dangling above me, glowing in the moonless night. She refused
to hear. I gave commands; she vanished. I waited for remorse;
it failed to arrive. I felt, if anything,
nobler, more alive than before. I soon took other women,
choosing—from slaves, from noblemen's wives—more carefully,
women of taste and discretion. Even so, Medeia learned;

flashed like a dragon, an electric storm. I pretended to end
such pleasures. But I'd grown addicted, in fact. I'd learned the secret
of godhood. In lust alone is mankind limitless,
as vast as Zeus. Who hasn't hungered to live all lives,
pierce the secrets of the swan, the bull, the king, the captive,
close all infinite space in his arms? Such was my desire,
my absolute of hunger. I remembered the Sirens' song.
    "Meanwhile, word got abroad that Medeia had curious powers.
I'd known, of course, it was only a matter of time. Who learned
her secret first, I have no idea. She had visitors,
impotent old men, young women with barren wombs. They'd arrive
at the palace on flimsy pretexts, would tour, do the honors to Pelias,
and eventually vanish with Medeia. I did not comment on it,
though I knew in my bones we were moving toward dangerous waters.
                                                             "I had
at this time troubles more immediate. Our land has been
divided since time began by the sacred Anauros River.
In certain seasons a man or a team of oxen could ford it,
but whenever the river was in spate, the kingdom became, in effect,
twin kingdoms: if the people were starving on one side, and corn and cattle
were plentiful over the opposite bank, the starving died
while the oversupply of their immediate neighbors corrupted. Old Argus,
at a word from me, had solved that problem, and in the same stroke
transformed the very idea of the river. He would cut a wide channel
where ships could pass, carrying the crops of the midland to the sea
and foreign goods inland. So that men could cross it, in any season,
he'd devised, with the help of Athena, the plan of an ingenious bridge
that could span the torrent yet swing, by the force of enormous sails
and waterwheels, so that even the loftiest vessel might pass.
I had no doubt the assembly would quickly agree.
                                        "By some cruel
warp of fate, Pelias appeared at the assembly on the day
the plan was first introduced. Who can say what crackpot fears
assailed the man? Mixed-up memories of the oracle,
which involved the river, or his well-known grudge against all things daring—
the fear that had driven him to tear down Hera's images once,
his coward's terror of acts of will . . . Whatever the reason,
he opposed me. He shook like a tree in high wind. He cajoled, whined, whimpered.
Now ashen, now scarlet, he appealed to the gods, the fitness of things,
to tradition, to unborn generations, to all-hallowed patriotism.

I was stunned, furious. I came close to telling him the truth: he ruled
by my sufferance. When he tipped his head at me, pitiful, appealing for tolerance
of an old man's harmless whim, my rage grew dangerous.
I could feel the muscles of my cheek jerking. I hid them behind
my hands, pretending to consider his words, and by force of will
as great as I'd used when I talked with Aietes, Lord of the Bulls,
I closed the assembly for the day. We would speak of the matter again.
    "That night, standing by the balustrade, I thought about murder,
my heart bubbling like a cauldron. My wrath was absurd, of course.
I would win. I had no doubt of that. But the wrath was there.
I did not hide it—least of all from Medeia. I half
resolved in my mind to depose the old man at once, without talk
or ritual. But in the end, I fought him on the floor of the assembly,
as usual, polite, eternally reasonable,
revealing my anger to no one, or no one but Medeia. That was
my error, of course. The lady of spells had schemes afoot.

    "It seems the old man's daughters had learned of Medeia's skill
and had come to her. Pitifully, timid heads hanging, eyes streaming,
their long white fingers interlaced in lament, they begged for her help.
They spoke of the figure their father cut once—how all Akhaia
had honored him—and how, now, crushed by tragic senescence,
he was less than a shadow of his former self. The eldest wept,
grovelling, reaching to Medeia's knees. 'O Queen,' she wailed,
'child of Helios, to whom all the secrets of death and life
are plain as the seasons to the rest of us, have mercy on Pelias!
We have heard it said that by your command old trees that bear
no fruit can be given such vigor of youth that their boughs are weighted
to the ground again. If there's any syllable of truth in that,
and if what you do for trees you can do for a man, then think
of the shame and sorrow of Pelias, once so noble! Whatever
you ask for this great kindness we'll gladly pay. Though not
as wealthy as those you may once have known in gold-rich Kolchis,
with its floors of mirroring brass, we three are princesses
as rich as any in Akhaia, and gladly we'll pay all we have
for love of our heart's first treasure.' Medeia was pale and trembling.
They could hardly guess, if they saw, her reason. She rose without a word
and crossed to the window and the night. They waited. The thing they asked
was not beyond her power. Nor was it beyond the power
of another talented witch, should she refuse. She breathed

with difficulty. The daughters of Pelias stretched their arms
beseeching her mercy. The youngest ran to her and kneeled beside her
clasping her knees. 'Have pity, Medeia.' The queen stood rigid.
Her head was on fire; familiar pain groped upward from her knees.
At last she whispered, 'I must think. Return to me tomorrow night.'
And so they left her. She threw herself on the bed headlong,
blinded, tied up in knots of pain. She wept for Apsyrtus,
for Kolchis, for her long-lost handmaidens. She wept for the child
betrayed by the goddess of love to a land of foreigners.
She slept, and an evil dream reached her.
                                    "The following night
when the daughters of Pelias returned to her, she promised to help them.
They'd need great courage, she said, for the remedy was dire. They promised.
She gave them herbs and secret incantations. When the foolish princesses
left her room, she crept, violently ill, from the palace
and fled to the mountains, her teeth chattering, her muscles convulsing.
Vomiting, moaning, breathing in loud and painful gasps,
she crawled to the old stone table of Hekate and danced the spell
of expiation for betrayal of the witch's art.

                                    "On the night
of Pelias' birthday, the palace was a-glitter with torches, and all
the noblest lords of Argos were present for the annual feast.
The old man kept himself hidden—some senile whim, we thought,
and thought no more about it, believing he'd appear, in time.
There were whispers of a great surprise in the offing. We laughed and waited.
We gathered in the gleaming, broad-beamed hall,
lords and ladies in glittering attire, Medeia beside me,
wan, shuddering with chills, yet strangely beautiful. I remembered
the glory of Aietes as first I saw him, and the dangerous beauty
of Circe, with her green-gold eyes. Then a rumble of kettledrums,
the jangle of klaxons and warbling pipes, and like lions tumbling
from their wooden chutes, in came the slaveboys bearing trays—
great boats of boar, huge platters of duckling and pheasant and swan—
a magnificent tribute to Pelias' glory and the love of his people.
Trays came loaded with stews and sauces, white with steamclouds,
and trays filled with ambled meat. Then came—the princesses rose—
the crowning dish, a silver pancheon containing, we found
when we tasted it, a meat so exotic no man in the palace,
whatever his learning or travels, would dare put a name on it.

We dined and drank new wine till the first light of dawn. And still
no sign of Pelias. The princesses, strangely excited, their ox-eyes
lighted by more than wine, I thought, assured us he was well.
And so, at the hour when shepherds settle on pastures become
invulnerable to predators, shielded by Helios,
the guests turned homeward, and we of the palace moved, heavy-limbed,
to bed. We slept all day, Medeia on my arm, trembling.
When the cool-eyed moon rose white in the trees, I awakened, thinking,
aware of some evil in the house. I went to the room of the children.
They were sleeping soundly, the slave Agapetika beside them. I turned back,
troubled and restless, molested by the whisper of a fretful god.
The moment I returned to our room, the princesses' screams began.
Medeia lay gazing at the moon, calm-eyed. I stared at her.
'They've learned that Pelias is dead,' she said. The same instant
the door burst open, and a man with a naked sword leaped in,
howling crazily, and hurtled at Medeia. I caught him by the shoulder,
my wild heart pounding, and threw him off balance—in the same motion
snatching my sword from its clasp by the headboard and striking. He fell,
his head severed from his body. Now the room was clamoring with guards,
babbling, shouting, the children and slaves in the hallway shrieking,
the room a-sway in the stench of blood. I snatched up the head
to learn who'd struck at us. For a long moment I stared at the face,
scarlet and dripping, the eyes wide open. Then someone said,
'Akastos!' and I saw it was so. While the palace was still in confusion,
we fled—snatched the children, our two oldest slaves, and, covered by darkness,
sought out the seaport and friends; so made our escape.
                                            "So ended
my rule of the isle of Argos. For all our glory once,
for all my famous deeds, my legendary wealth, I became
an exile begging asylum from town to town. I became
a man dark-minded as Idas, whimpering in anger at the gods,
glancing back past my shoulder in fear. For a time I lost
all power of speech—I, Jason of the Golden Tongue.
The child of Aietes was baffled by the troubles befallen us.
Why had we fled? Was I not the true, the rightful king
of Argos, Pelias a usurper, as all men knew? Had I not
done deeds no king of Argos had done before me?—not only
capture of the fleece, but temples, waterlocks, rock-firm law?
Like a mute, more crippled than stuttering Pelias, I roiled my tongue
and strained at the cords of my throat, but sound refused me. When I closed

my eyes, I saw Akastos. Though I travelled from temple to temple,
no priest alive could assoil me.
                              "And then one morning, groaning,
the walls of my skull on fire with evils, I found I could say
his name. *Akastos! Akastos, forgive me!* I felt no flood
of peace, no sudden sweet purgation. But I learned a truth:
I'd loved him, and I learned I was right in my rule of Argos. Yet right
to escape, save Medeia from the citizens' rage. I'd made Medeia
promises. For love of me she had left her home,
the protection of kinsmen, and managed the murder of a brother she loved,
and outraged all that's human by arranging the patricide
of Pelias' foolish daughters—and then that cannibal feast,
everlasting shame of Iolkos. I understood that her mind,
whatever her beauty and intelligence, was no more like ours—
the minds of the sons of Hellas—than the mind of a wolf, a tiger.
I owed her protection and kindness, and I meant to pay that debt.
But in promising marriage—if marriage means anything more than the noise
of vows—I spoke in futility. If earth and sky
are marriage partners, or the land and sea, or the interdependent
king and state—if Space and Time are marriage partners—
then Medeia and I are not.
                              "In the hills above Iolkos
I watched Medeia at her midnight rites. I've told you the effect.
I was wide awake as a preying animal—as charged with power
as I'd felt as a boyish adventurer sailing with the Argonauts.
Though I slept no more than a jackal on the hunt, I awakened refreshed,
scornful of Pelias and his idiot daughters, at one with Akastos
riding his war-cart as I rode the clattering state. I could do
the same by the meat of women: shuck off obscurities,
considerations, the labored balance of the pondering mind.
A great discovery! Though I meant the state to be reasonable,
I need not famish the animal in me, put away the past,
the chaos of a hero's joys. And so, as a foolish shepherd
brings in wolf pups, dubious at first, and runs them with the sheep
for experiment, gradually learning their queer docility,
and so progresses in his witless complacence to the night when—stirred
by a minor cut, a droplet of blood that for wolves rolls back
the centuries—he hears a bleating, and rushes to find
his herd destroyed, the fruit of his labors in ruin—so I
a foolish king, let passions in, the divinity of flesh.

Gradually lessening my reason's check, I freed Medeia,
agent of my own worst passions; I granted a she-dragon rein.
Screams in the palace, the sick-sweet smell of blood. I saw,
once and for all, my wife was her father's child, demonic.
There could be no possibility now of harmony between us;
no possibility of marriage. We must either destroy each other—
struggling in opposite directions for absolutes, thought against passion—
or part. And there, for a moment, I left it. By arduous labor
I won back the power of speech, won back the control of my house.
Not all my hours on the *Argo* required such pains. So now,
prepared to deal with the world again, prepared to make use,
as the gods may please, of difficult lessons, I bide my time
in exile, caring for my sons and Medeia.
                              "I claim, with conviction,
I haven't outlived all usefulness to the gods. All those
who scorn just reason and scoff at the courts of honest men,
men whose ferocious will is revealed by calm like the lion's—
those who scorn, the gods will deafen with their own lamentations;
their proud pinnacles the gods will shatter and hurl in the ocean
as I myself was torn down once for my foolishness
and cast in the trackless seas. Or if not the gods, then this:
the power struggling to be born, a creature larger than man,
though made of men; not to be outfoxed, too old for us;
terrible and final, by nature neither just nor unjust,
but wholly demanding, so that no man made any part of that beast
dare think of self, as I did. For if living says anything,
it's this: We sail between nonsense and terrible absurdity—
sail between stiff, coherent system which has nothing to do
with the universe (the stiffness of numbers, grammatical constructions)
and the universe, which has nothing to do with the names we give
or seize our leverage by. Let man take his reasoning place,
expecting nothing, since man is not the invisible player
but the player's pawn. Seize the whole board, snatch after godhood,
and all turns useless waste. Such is my story."
                              So Jason
ended. The kings sat hushed, as silent as the goddesses.

19

Kreon sat pondering, propped on his elbows, eyebags puffed,
protrusive as a toad's, the table around him as thick with flowers
as a swaybacked bin in the marketplace. He remembered himself,
at last, and rose. Still no one spoke. Athena, standing
at Jason's back, was smiling, serene and wild at once,
majestic as the Northern Lights. Beside her Hera stood
with hooded eyes, awesome in the flush of victory—
for I could not doubt that Athena and she had won. The goddess
of love, by Kreon's virginal daughter, was wan and troubled,
her generous heart confused. I was tempted to laugh, for an instant,
at how easily they'd confounded her—those wiser goddesses,
Mind and Will. But Aphrodite's glance at Jason
stopped me, filled me with sudden alarm.
The hunger in Aphrodite's eyes—
hunger for heaven alone knew what—
consumed their wisdom, made all the mechanics of Time and Space
foolish, irrelevant. Beyond the invisible southern pole
of the universe her feet were set. Her reach went up,
like the carved pillars of Kreon's hall (vast serpent coils,
eagles, chariots, fish-tailed centaurs), writhing to the darkness
beyond the star-filled crown of Zeus. Kreon, half-giant,
his head drawn back, one eye squeezed shut, addressed the sea-kings,
lords of Corinth and sons of lords:
                                    "My noble friends,
princes gathered from the ends of the earth, we've heard a story
stranger than any brought down in the epic songs, and one
more freighted with troublesome questions. As you see, the hour is late,
and the day has been troubled by more than Jason's tale. It therefore

seems to us fit that we part till tomorrow morning, to reflect
in private. Let us all reassemble to pursue by the light of day
what brings us together here." He paused for answer, and when no one
spoke, he bowed, assuming assent, and prepared to leave.
He reached for Pyripta's hand and raised her to her feet; then, pausing,
he glanced at Jason, saying, "Would you care to speak, perhaps,
with Ipnolebes before you go?" He was asking more than he spoke
in words, I saw, for Jason frowned, reluctant, then nodded.
And so they left the central table, Kreon and his daughter
and Aison's son. And now all the wide-beamed hall arose,
sea-kings murmuring one to another, and slowly made way
to the doors. I pushed through the crowd to keep my eye on Jason.
The sea-kings looked at me, puzzled, perhaps amused. They seemed
to think me, dressed so strangely, some new entertainment. None
addressed me. On the dais, the goddess of love had vanished. I searched
the room, my heart in a whir, to discover what form she'd taken.
I saw no trace of her.
       Then we were standing in a shadowy chamber,
plain as a cavern, where slaves moved silently to and fro
with sullen, burning eyes. There Ipnolebes stood, alone,
quietly issuing commands. Since the time I'd seen him last
he was a man profoundly changed. His skin was ashen, his eyes
remote, indifferent as a murdered man's. When Jason approached him,
the black-robed slave gazed past him as though he were a stranger. Old Kreon
rubbed his jaw, looked thoughtful, keeping his distance. In his shadow
Kompsis stood, the violent red-headed man who'd attacked
them all when the goddess Hera was in him. By the calm of his eyes,
I thought she had entered him again, but I was wrong. It was
another goddess—as deadly as Hera when the mood was on her.
   The son of Aison bowed to the slave and touched his shoulder
as he would the shoulder of an equal he wished to console. For all
his cunning, for all the magic of that golden tongue, he could find
no words. It was thus the slave who broke the silence. He said,
"You knew him, I think—Amekhenos, Northern barbarian
who thought himself a prince in spite of the plain evidence
of welts and chains."
        "I knew him, yes."
           "You could have prevented,
if it suited you . . ."
      But Aison's son shook his head. "No."

His voice was heavy, as weary as the voice of an old, old man.

Ipnolebes sighed and still did not swing his eyes to Jason's.
"No. It was not, after all, as if you'd sworn him some vow.
There are laws and laws, limitless seas of extenuation
eating our acts. Otherwise no man alive would grow old
maintaining, in his own opinion, at least, the shreds and tatters
of his dignity." He forced out a ghastly laugh. "Who am I
to judge? And even if you had, so to speak, let slip some vow,
many years ago—" He paused, wrinkling his brow, having lost
the thread. "There are vows and vows," he mumbled. "I merely say . . .
I merely say . . ." He broke off with a shudder and turned
his face. "I find no fault in you," he said. "Good night."
Lips stretched taut in a violent grin, he stared at Jason.
They spoke no further, and finally Jason withdrew. Old Kreon
followed him, Kompsis at his side. I hurried behind them. In the hall
that opened on the great front door with its thickly figured panels,
its hinges the length and breadth of a man, the old king bowed,
without a word, and they parted. The short, red-bearded man
accompanied Jason, walking out into the night. I kept
to the shadows, following behind.   At the foot of the palace steps
red Kompsis paused, and Jason reluctantly waited for him.
"You amaze me, Jason." He folded his beefy hands and smiled,
malevolent. "The hanged boy was a friend of yours."
Jason said nothing. "He was, I think, the son of a king
who defended the *Argo* from ruin by northern barbarians.
He was a mighty chieftain, at that time.
But later, his luck abandoned him.
His palace fell to marauders from the South. He himself, though old
and cunning as a dragon, was driven to the hills and there surrounded
by Danaans and slain, still clinging to his two-hand sword. His head
they hacked from his shoulders and threw in the river, and all his animals,
horses and dogs, they slaughtered, in scorn of the habit of the Kelts;
and his son in scorn they christened Amekhenos. Shackled as a slave,
for all his angry pride, they brought him to Corinth. Here Kreon
bought him, believing he could tame that wolfish heart." To all this
Jason listened in silence, his eyes on the ground. Red Kompsis
laughed, but his voice was violent, his body hunched. He said:
"He recognized you at once, of course. At the first chance,
he spoke with you. I saw your look of bewilderment.

You'd heard that voice before somewhere,
but you couldn't recall it. Faces, voices, they don't last long
in the snatching brain of Jason." He laughed again. "You would
have remembered him soon enough, I think, if you'd needed his aid.
But the shoe was on the other foot. He was not a man to press
for favors owed to his house. Though a single word from you
to Kreon—fond as he is of his mighty adventurer—
would have freed that prince in the same instant, you kept your peace.
Because of bad memory." He leaned toward Jason fiercely. "—Because of
shallowness of heart. I name it its name! Your every word
reveals your devilish secret!
                    "—Very well, you forgot his name.
He must seek his freedom by other means. And so escaped,
slipped—incredible!—even past sleepless Ipnolebes' eyes.
We know better, of course. You saw his rage. For once in his life
the old man chose to blink. —But whatever his barbarous courage,
whatever the cunning of his savage Keltic brain, no slave
escapes from the gyves of Kreon. And so he was missed, and hunted,
and eventually found in—incredible again . . ."
                            "I know. That's enough!"
Jason broke in without meaning to. He stood tight-lipped,
saying no more. Red Kompsis laughed,
swollen with righteous indignation, godlike scorn.
                            "—was found
in the chief ship of the Arenians, in command of a man
you once knew well—mad Idas, son of Aphareos.
Surely it did not escape the wily Jason's mind
that something, somewhere, was amiss! Why would Idas, for all his famed
insanity, give help to a perfect stranger, a dangerous
Kelt? All the crew was arrested, the runaway slave was hanged,
and still from Jason not a syllable. Though all the harbor
churned up seething in fury at Kreon's tyranny—
grizzly, base-born seadogs with no more nobility of blood
than jackals—still the golden tongue was silent. You can
explain, no doubt. The golden tongue can explain away
the moon, the sun, the firmament, explain away birth
and death, not to mention marriage—leave all this universe pale
as mist." So he spoke, lips trembling with anger, and while he spoke,
the sky grew darker, glowering and oppressive. I understood
it was no mere mortal whose anger charged the night, but the wrath

of a goddess whose power was rising. The Father of Gods had withdrawn
his check on her. The houses of heaven had changed.

                                                  Then quietly
Jason spoke, his gaze groundward. He stood like a spur
of rock when gale winds pound it from all directions and trees
roll crazily, torn up by the roots. "It seems an easy thing
to claim a man should react like a loyal dog, leap out
fangs bared, whatever the attacker, and die at the swipe of a club,
true to the last to his instincts. I cannot defend myself
from the charge that I haven't behaved like a loyal dog—except
that once, by the leap of instinct, I killed my cousin. I might
have saved the slave, as you claim, by a careful word or two
to Kreon; I might by a well-framed speech have rescued Idas
and all his men from prison. I might. You know well enough
the risk. Old Kreon's a stubborn man. He does not like
his judgment doubted or his will crossed. Be sure, if I'd won
those favors from him, I'd then and there have exhausted the old man's
love of me. Whatever good I might hope to do
for all the enslaved, for all my friends, for future generations,
that good I'd have traded for an instant's sweet self-righteousness.
Though all the harbor rose up in rage at an immoral act—
a thousand, three, five thousand men?—I do not find
that the evil deed was rectified, or the sentence undone.
A good man out of power is worth
a pine-seedling in the Hellespont!
Such are the brutal realities, my friend.
Do not be such a fool, Kompsis, as to think man's choice
lies between evil and good. All serious options are moral,
and all serious choices inherently risky, if not,
for the heart that's pure, impossible." So Jason spoke,
and I could not doubt, listening in the shadow of the colonnade,
that his words came not from guilt but from honest intent. His heart
was heavy, his purpose firm. But the god in human shape
was scornful. Kompsis grinned, his eyes like thunder blooming
in the low, black night. "However, the house you owed your life
hangs motionless there in the marketplace, food for crows. Consider:
No grand law will preserve your state if fools succeed you;
and every line comes down, soon or late, to fools. Create
the noblest constitution the mind of man can frame:
eventually fools will crumple it. You plan for the splendid

future, though decay is certain; and you let the present rot
though a single word could cleanse it. Do as you must. I warn you,
heaven is against you. Trouble is coming to the man who builds
his town on blood, or founds his kingdom on crimes unavenged.
Like a shepherd rescuing a couple of legs or a bit of an ear
from the lion's mouth, you salvage justice murdered." As Jason
turned in fury, his blood in his face,
the last man living to be tricked by the jangle of rhetoric,
he saw that the stones where Kompsis had stood were bare, and knew
he'd spoken with a god. His cheeks went white, as if lightning-struck,
and his muscles locked in rage and frustration. "It's the truth," he shouted.
He lifted his face to the midnight sky, his features anguished,
and raised his fists. He seemed to struggle for speech. The cords
of his throat stood out and his temples bulged. Then suddenly
from his chest came the bellow of a maddened bull. "I've been cheated enough!
I've told you nothing but the truth!" So he raged, then clutched his head
as if shocked by searing pain. The sky was silent.

                                                    Later—
it was nearly dawn—I saw him in the windswept temple of Apollo,
hissing angrily, on his knees before the seer. The blind man
listened in silence, his filmed eyes wandering, out of control.
"The gods are many. Who knows how many? They endlessly contradict each other
          like aphorisms.
Tell me what to fear!
I've honored the gods both known and unknown, emptied my coffers on temples,
          images, hillside shrines. Not from conviction—I grant that too. Is a man
          made holy by boldfaced lies?
There was a time I believed that the skies could open, make horses stagger,
the soldier throw up his arms in fear. I believed, in fact,
I'd seen such things. But the world changed, or my vision changed.
What possible good in denying the fact? I could see no proof
that Hypsipyle was evil, whatever the magic of Argus' cloak,
tradition-trick, subtle distorter of patent truth
not, in itself, allegorical.
I saw when we beached at Samothrace
and watched the mysteries, how man's mind
(Herakles swelling to what he believed was a god-sent power)
was all that the mind could be sure of, how even my own conversion
if such it was, had no sure cause in the universe.

And so descended from death to death;
learned on the isle of the Doliones
the fallacy of faith in technique and faith in perception; learned
by the death of Hylas and loss of Herakles—the stupid and yet unassailable
        assertion of Amykos—
old murderer—and the deadly confusion in Phineus' heart—
the fundamental absurdity of the world itself, mad gods in all-out war. I did not
shrink from these grim discoveries. Neither did I whine, renounce
my quest, though I knew no reason for the quest. I slogged on
toward Kolchis. What reason could hammer no justification for,
I justified by groundless faith. Slog on or die,
abandon hope—the hope of eventual clarity.
Those were the choices. I bowed to the gods I could not see—
or could not trust if I happened to see them, as I saw Apollo,
striding, astounding, when we'd rowed our blood to a state of exhaustion—
bowed because life unredeemed by the gods would be idiocy,
bowed, yet refused to lie, claim to see things invisible.
Let the future judge me. I give you my grim prediction, seer:
Famine is coming, deadliest of droughts.
Mankind will stagger from sea to sea, from north to east,
seeking the word of some god and failing to find it.
                              "But yes,
I bowed, dubious, true to my nature yet granting its limits.
What more can heaven demand of a man?
Tell me what to fear!
I've walked, cold-bloodedly honest, to the rim of the pit. I've affirmed
justice, compassion, decency. When granted power
I've used it to benefit man. I've fiercely denied that life
is bestial—having seen in my own life the leer of the ape.
Yet the sky turns dark, and gods threaten me. If the universe
is evil, then let me be martyred in battle with the universe.
If not, then where am I mistaken?"
                         In silence, the seer of Apollo
stretched out his arms to Jason, touching his shoulders. The night
hung waiting. "Lord Jason, you ask me to speak
as a court counsellor, a prince of wizards, a philosopher versed
in the subtleties of old, cracked scrolls. Such things I cannot be.
Though you teach horned owls to sing, by your cunning, or make lambs laugh in
        the dragon's nest,
I can speak only what Apollo speaks.

I can say to you:

The man of high estate will be tinder,
his handiwork a spark.
Both will burn together,
and none will extinguish them."

"Explain!" Jason said. But the seer would say no more.

In her room,
Pyripta, princess of Corinth, wept. The words of Jason
had changed her: for all the smoothness of her face, the innocence
of her clear eyes, the tale had aged her, filled her with sorrow
beyond her years. She clung to her knees, sobbing in the bed
of ivory, and prayed no more for purity of spirit
but mourned her loss. The princess had learned her significance.
She spoke not a word; but I saw, I understood. No hope
of clinging now to childhood, the sweetness of virginity.
Let shepherds' daughters worship in the groves of the huntress! She was
a wife already, sullied with the knowledge of compromise,
faults in nobility, flickering virtue in the flesh-fat heart.
She knew him too well, the husband each tick of the universe
brought nearer, whatever her wish. She was no fool. Admired
the courage of his mind. But she could not walk in bridal radiance
to a future unknown and clean, the gradual discovery of a past
sacred, intimate, hallowed by slow revelations of love.
Yet knew, because a princess, that she would walk, wear white;
knew she would serve, covenant of Corinth, accept the bridegroom
chosen for her, for the city's sake. Perhaps she loved him.
It had nothing to do with love, had to do with loss. Her loss
of the limitless; descent to the leaden cage of enslaving
humanity. Joy or sorrow, no matter. Loss.
    The dark-eyed slave at her bedside watched in compassion and grief
and touched Pyripta's hand. "The omens are evil," she said.
"Resist this thing they demand of you. The city is troubled,
the night unfriendly, veiled like a vengeful widow. Men talk
of fire in the palace, wine made blood." The princess wept,
unanswering. I understood her, watching from the curtains.
I remembered the tears of Medeia, lamenting her childhood's loss.
By the window another, a princess carried in chains out of Egypt—

278

eyes of an Egyptian, the forehead and nose and the full lips
of the desert people—whispered softly, angrily to the night:

> *"Increase like the locust,*
> *increase like the grasshopper;*
> *multiply your traders*
> *to exceed the number of heaven's stars;*
> *your guards are like grasshoppers,*
> *your scribes and wizards are like a cloud of insects.*
> *They settle on the walls*
> *when the day is cold.*
> *The sun appears,*
> *and the locusts spread their wings, fly away.*
> *They vanish, no one knows where."*

At the door one whispered—a woman of Ethiopia,
who smiled and nodded, gazing at the princess with friendly eyes:

> *"Woe to the city soaked in blood,*
> *full of lies,*
> *stuffed with booty,*
> *whose plunderings know no end!*
> *The crack of the whip!*
> *The rumble of wheels!*
> *Galloping horse,*
> *jolting chariot,*
> *charging cavalry,*
> *flash of swords,*
> *gleam of spears . . .*
> *a mass of wounded,*
> *hosts of dead,*
> *countless corpses;*
> *they stumble over the dead.*
> *So much for the whore's debauchery,*
> *that wonderful beauty, that cunning witch*
> *who enslaves nations by her debauchery,*
> *enslaves the houses of heaven by her spells!"*

Another said—whispering in anger by the wall, cold flame:

> *"Are you mightier than Thebes*
> *who had her throne by the richest of rivers,*
> *the sea for her outer wall, and the waters for ramparts?*

Her strength was Ethiopia and Egypt.
She had no boundaries.
And yet she was forced into exile, sorrowful captivity;
her little ones, too, were dashed to pieces
at every crossroad;
lots were drawn for her noblemen,
all her great men were loaded with chains.
You too will be encircled at last, and overwhelmed.
You too will search
for a cave in the wilderness
refuge from the wrath of your enemies."

On the dark of the stairs an old woman hissed, her wizened face
a-glitter with tears like jewels trapped:

"Listen to this, you cows of Corinth,
living on the mountain of your treasure heap,
oppressing the needy, crushing the poor,
saying to your servants, 'Bring us something to drink!'
I swear you this by the dust of my breasts:
The days are coming
when you will be dragged out by nostril-hooks,
and the very last of you goaded with prongs.
Out you will go, each by the nearest breach in the wall,
to be driven to drink of the ocean.
This I pledge to you."

So in Pyripta's room and beyond they whispered, seething,
kindled to rage by the death of the boy Amekhenos,
or troubled by some force darker. For beside Pyripta's bed
there materialized from golden haze the goddess Aphrodite.
Sadly, gently, she touched Pyripta's hair. Then the room
was gone, though the goddess remained, head bowed. We stood alone
in a pine-grove silver with moonlight. I heard a sound—a footstep
soft as a deer's—and, turning in alarm, I saw a figure
striding from the woods—a youth, I thought, with the bow of a huntsman
and a tight, short gown that flickered like the water in a brook. As the stranger
neared, I saw my error: it was no man, but a goddess,
graceful and stern as an arrow when it drops in soundless flight
to its mark. Aphrodite spoke: "Too long we've warred, Goddess,
moon-pale huntress. I come to your sacred grove to make

amends for that, bringing this creature along as a witness,
a poet from the world's last age—no age of heroes, as you know,
and as this poor object proves. Don't expect you'll hear him speak.
He's timid as a mouse in the presence of gods and goddesses;
foolish, easily befuddled, a poet who counts out beats
on his fingers and hasn't got fingers enough. But he understands Greek,
with occasional glances at a book he carries—in secret, he thinks!
(but the deathless gods, of course, miss nothing). He'll have to do."
The love goddess smiled almost fondly, I thought. But as for Artemis,
she knew me well, stared through me. The goddess of love said then:
"I come to you for a boon I believe you may gladly grant
when you've heard my request. Not long ago
a murderer buried his victim in secret, in this same grove
sacred to the moon. As soon as the body was hidden, he fled
with the woman he claimed to love, Medeia, the daughter of Aietes.
I protected them—their right, as lovers. But now the heart
of the son of Aison has hardened against his wife. He means
to cast her aside for the virgin Pyripta, daughter of Kreon
of Corinth. So at last our interests meet, it seems to me.
Forgive me if I'm wrong, chaste goddess. I can see no other way
than to throw myself on your mercy, despite old differences.
Set her against him firmly, and I give my solemn pledge,
I'll turn my back on the daughter of Kreon forever, no more
stir love in her bosom than I would in the rocks of Gaza. Just that,
and nothing more I beg of you. Charge Pyripta's mind
with scorn of Jason, and even in Zeus's hall I'll praise
your name and give you thanks." So the goddess spoke. And Artemis
listened and gave no answer, coolly scheming. I did not
care for the glitter of ice in the goddess of purity's eye,
and I glanced, uneasy, at the goddess of love. She appeared to see nothing
amiss. Then Artemis spoke. "I'll go and see." That was all.
She turned on her heel, with a nod inviting me to follow, and strode
like a man to the place where her chariot waited, all gleaming silver.
As soon as I'd set one foot in it, we arrived at the house
of Jason. The chariot vanished. I was down on my hands and knees
in the street. I got up, dusting my trousers, and hurried to the door.
No one saw me or stopped me. I found, in Medeia's chamber,
Artemis—enormous in the moonlit bedroom, her bowed head
and shoulders brushing the ceiling beams—stooped at the side
of Medeia's bed like an eagle to its prey. "Wake up!" she whispered.

"Wake up, victim of the mischief god! Seek out thy light,
sweet Jason, life-long heartache! You are betrayed!" Medeia's
eyes opened. The goddess vanished. The moonlight dimmed,
faded till nothing was left but the glow of the golden fleece.
The slave Agapetika wakened and reached for Medeia's hand.
Medeia sat up, startled by the memory of a dream. She met
my eyes; her hand reached vaguely out to cover herself
with the fleece. I remembered my solidity and backed away.
"Devil!" she whispered. In panic I answered, "No, Medeia.
A friend!" She shook her head. "I have no friends but devils."
And only now understanding that all she'd dreamt was true—
as if her own words had power more terrible than Jason's deeds—
she suddenly burst into tears of rage and helplessness.
She tried to rise, but her knees wouldn't hold her, and she fell to the flagstones.
I said: "I come from the future to warn you—"

My throat went dry.
The room was suddenly filled, crowded like a jungle with creatures,
ravens and owls and slow-coiled snakes, all manner of beings
hated by men. In terror of Medeia's eyes, I fled.

20

On the palace wall, in his blood-red cape, the son of Aison,
arms folded, gazed down over the city of Corinth.
He knew pretty well—Hera watching at his shoulder, sly—
that he'd won, for better or worse—that nothing Paidoboron
or Koprophoros could say would undo the work he'd done
or open the gates of Kreon's heart or the heart of the princess
to any new contender. He smiled. On the palace roof
behind him, a raven watched, head cocked, with unblinking eyes.
For reasons he scarcely knew himself, Jason had avoided
his home today. It was now twilight; the light, sharp breeze
rising from stubbled fields, dark streams, fat granaries,
brought up the scent of approaching winter. There would come a time
when Medeia would rise and insist upon having her say. Not yet.
Though light was failing, the house, lower on the hill, was dark
save one dim lamp, dully blooming—so yellow in the gloom
of the oaks surrounding that it brought to his mind again the fleece
old Argus wove, and the obscure warning of the seer.

         The vision
blurred; I hung unreal. Then, crushed to flesh once more,
my swollen hand brought alive again to its drumbeat of pain,
I stood—dishevelled as I was, my poor steel spectacles cracked
and crooked—in the low-beamed room of the slave Agapetika,
hearing her moans to the figure of Apollo on the wall. Her canes
of gnarled olive-wood waited on the tiles, her stiff, fat knees
painfully bent on the hassock before the shrine.
         She wailed,
whether in prayer or lament, I could hardly tell: "O Lord,

would that an old slave's wish could wind back time for Medeia
and she never beguile those dim, too-trusting daughters of Pelias,
who slaughtered their father; or would that Corinth had never received them,
allowing a measure of joy and peace, pleasure in the children,
Medeia still loved and in everything eager to please her lord,
her will and his will one, as even Jason knew,
for all his anger, bitterness of heart. The loss of love
makes all surviving it blacker than smoke at sunrise. What once
was sweet is now corrupt and cankered: our Jason plans
heartless betrayal of his wife and sons for marriage with a princess.
And now in impotent rage and anguish, Medeia invokes
their oaths, their joined right hands, and summons the dangerous gods
to witness the way he's rewarded her life-long faithfulness.
Worse yet, she curses old Kreon himself, and Kreon's daughter,
howling her wild imprecations for all to hear. In her rage
she refuses to eat, sacrificing her body to grief
as she sacrificed her home, her kinsmen, her happiness
for Jason's love. She wastes in tears; she cries and cries
in such black despair that her sobs come welling too fast for Medeia
to sound them. She lies stretched wailing on the stones and refuses to lift
her eyes or to raise her face from the floor. To all we say
she's deaf as a boulder, an ocean wave. She refuses to speak—
she can only curse her betrayal of her father, murder of her brother,
death of her sister Khalkiope, through Aietes' rage—
for all of which she blames herself alone, as if
no one before her had ever betrayed on earth. She takes
no joy anymore in her sons: her eyes seem filled with hate
when she looks at them. It shocks me with fear to see it. Her mood
is dangerous. She'll never submit to this monstrous wrong.
I know her. It makes me sick with fear. Let any man rouse
Medeia's hate and hard indeed he'll find it to escape
unmarked by her."

            Agapetika opened her eyes in alarm,
straining—grotesquely fat, feeble—to turn her head
for a view of the door at her back. In the hallway, the old male slave
and the children approached, the two boys squealing and laughing, the old man
shushing them. She slued clumsily, inching around
on the hassock to watch them pass. The old man paused, looked in,
his lean face drawn and crabbed. The eyebags drooping to his cheeks
were as gray and wrinkled as bark. He whispered, "What's this moaning

that fills all the house with noise? How could you leave your lady?
Did Medeia consent?"

                She shook her head, lips trembling, tears
now brimming afresh. "Old man—old guardian of Jason's sons—
how can the troubles of masters not soon bring sorrow to their slaves?
I've left her alone for a little to grant my own grief vent."

    He turned his head, as if looking through walls to Medeia's room.
"No change?" he asked. She covered her face. "No change," she said.
"My poor Medeia's troubles have scarcely begun."

                      The old man
narrowed his eyes. Then, hoarsely: "Poor blind fool—if slaves
may say such things of masters. There's reason more than she knows
for all this woe and rage."

            Agapetika inched around more
to stare at the man in fear. "What now?" she exclaimed. "Sir, do not
keep from me what you've heard."

                He shook his head. "No, nothing.
Vague speculation. Mere idle talk." The twins had run on—
romping to their room, indifferent and blind to misery—
and his eyes went after them, grudging. The whole afternoon they'd kept him
plodding with hardly a rest. At the crest of every hill
his old heart thudded in his throat, and his brains went light, so that
to keep his knees from buckling he would stretch out his hands to a tree
or ivied gatepost, coughing and gulping for air. In the park
high above seacliffs, he'd met with a fellow slave, a servant
in Kreon's palace, and there, where leafless ramdikes arched
past hedges still bright green—where the sky, the distant buildings,
highways and bridges were as drab as in winter despite the glow
of lawns grown rich and lush, deceived by late summer rain—
he'd heard this newest catastrophe. He revealed it now,
compelled by the old woman's eyes. He said: "The palace slaves,
who know the old king's purposes sooner than Kreon himself,
are certain the contest's settled already, as though no man
had spoken in all this time but Jason alone."

                        "Then our fears
are realized," the old woman said; "no hope of escape!"

    "There's more," he said, and avoided her look. "In the palace they say
the king is resolved to expel our mistress and her two sons
from Corinth. He thinks it a generous act, considering her powers
and her sons' inevitable position as royal pretenders. I cannot

say all this is true. But I fear it may be."

"And will
our Jason allow such things?" the old woman asked. But already
she saw that he might. She whimpered, "Though he and Medeia are at odds,
surely he hasn't forgotten so soon what pain she suffered,
torn long ago from her homeland and dearest friends! Though he needs
no friends himself, quick to win facile admirers, thanks
to that dancing tongue, and at any rate more pleased, by nature,
with work than with love—like Argus, like the god Hephaiastos,
a creature sufficient to himself, his heart all schemes—surely
he knows our lady's needs! She might have been queen, herself,
of all dark-forested Kolchis, had her fate run otherwise;
she might have had no more need than he of enfolding arms,
shield against darkness and senselessness. He robbed her of that—
became himself her homeland, father, brother and sister,
her soul's one labor and religion. Can he dare make all that void?—
by a fingersnap make all she's lived an illusion? Can he turn
on his own two children, change them to shadows, to nothing, as though
they'd no more solid flesh than a glimmering wizard's trick?"

As if to himself, the old man said, "The familiar ties
are weaker now. He's no more a friend to this gloomy, crumbling
house. —Say nothing to Medeia."

Just then, beside him at at the door,
the twins appeared and looked in, curious, no longer laughing,
coming to see what was wrong. The woman cried, "Children, behold
what love your father bears for you! I will not curse him—
my master yet—but no man alive is more treasonous!"
The male slave scowled. "Let the children be, mere eight-year-olds,
what have they to do with treasons? As for Jason, what man
is better, old woman? Now that you're old, look squarely at the world.
All men care for themselves and for nobody else. All men
would joyfully swap away sons for the pleasures of a new bride's bed."
She was still, looking at the children. At last, with a heavy sigh:
"Go, boys, play in your room. All will be well." And then
to the attendant: "You, sir, keep them off to themselves, I beg you.
Take them nowhere in range of their mother in her present mood.
Already I've seen her glaring at the children savagely,
threatening mischief. She'll not leave off this rage, I know,
till she's struck some victim dead. I pray to the gods her wrath
may light among foes, not friends."

From deeper in the house then came
a wail deep-throated and wild as the cry of a jungle beast.
My veins ran ice and I jerked up my arm to my face. A shock
of pain flashed through me, innumerable bruises, and I nearly revealed
my hiding place in the shadow of the black oak bed. The slaves
listened to Medeia's wail as if numbed. When the old woman
could speak, she said: "Go to your room now quickly! Be wary!
Do not provoke that violent heart! Hurry! Go swiftly!
The soul of her father is alive in her. This gathering cloud
of tears and wailing will enkindle soon far stormier flashes.
A spirit like hers, headstrong and bitterly stung by affliction—
what wild and reckless deeds may it not dare thunder on us?"
I glanced at the garden, my eyes in flight from the anguish of the house,
and my heart leaped. There stood the goddess Artemis, tall
as a stone tower, watching with burning eyes.

And then
the sea-kings were gathered around me, Jason on the dais, with Kreon,
and the princess rigid in her silver chair. The whole wide hall,
so it seemed to me, was a-gleam with the light of Artemis.
   Paidoboron spoke, dark-bearded king
of barren moraine, debris of glaciers, in his gloomy eyes
the stillness of tideless seas. The assembled kings sat hushed.
At a dark door far from the dais, the slave Ipnolebes watched,
his hand on the shoulder of a boy.

"Think back," Paidoboron said,
"on the days of old." His voice had nothing alive in it—
the voice of a clockwork doll, some old, artificial monster—
and his slow, mechanical gestures enforced the same effect,
mockery of life. "Think over the years and down the ages."
He pointed as if to the darkness of endless corridors.
"Nation on nation the gods have raised up, then crushed again.
Again and again the bow of the mighty the gods have broken,
and the feeble and oppressed they have girded with strength. No law of the stars
is surer than this: Empires shall rise and fall forever
till the day of the earth's destruction. The cities of the strong will burn
and the bones of the master be hurled on the smouldering garbage mounds
beyond the city's gates. Then he who was weak shall be robed
in zibelline, and in place of his shackles
the greaves of a warrior king, and his slaves
shall be splendid nobles of the age just past—

288

till he too falls to the jackals." He paused, looked hard at Kreon.
"Has it not yet struck you, Corinthian king? Though you watched Thebes burn
with your own two eyes—great Thebes whose outer walls were oceans,
whose kingdom's heart was all Ethiopia and Egypt,
city of Kadmos the Wanderer, noblest of dragon slayers—
have you never been struck by the deadly regularity
with which, like suns, great kingdoms rise and fall? Is all this
accident? To the ends of the world the rubble stretches,
the scattered orts of banquets, the fumets of chariot-horses,
fortresses ruined, thrones, the occamy spangles of once-
proud concubines. All human tongues record the same
in their legendry: the dark agonals of kings. And still
man's heart inclines to power, to the wealth and ease, rich art,
fine food, of the demon city. But I tell you the truth: the earth
at our feet cries out its curse on that tumorous growth. In the shade
of walls, earth dies; it stiffens, trampled by sandals, and cracks.
The city's wealth cries softly to marauders in the night, like a whore
at the jalousie. Her mounds bring plagues, her discharge insects,
dry rot, rats. Still the city grows, dark lure of ambition,
hunger of the exiled spirit, abandoned forever by the stars,
for the wombsoft slosh of fat. The corpus of law grows bloated
like a corpse recovered from the sea; and those who enforce the law
grow cynical and rich, foxy, wolfish, beyond inculpation
by any man, till all but frampold devils are shackled
in chains. Then like a thigh-wound festering, the city overflows
her battlements and coigns—robs all the land surrounding for victuals,
chops green-forested mountains for timber, quogs out quarries,
to heave up monuments worthy of the devastating power of her kings,
tombs for the slyest of her paracletes, the most celebrated
of her enemy-smashers, deified dragon-men—sky-high houses
staddled on broken-backed slaves. Consumes the land, the clouds;
builds ships for trade, extends her scope; finds conquest cheaper,
more durable. And so that hour arrives at last
when the city, towering like a mammoth oak—great shining bartizans,
pennons of crimson and gold like leaves in autumn on her high-
spired parapets—an oak majestic in its ignorant pride,
rotten at the core—shudders suddenly at an odd new wind,
and trembles, incredulous, shaken by the gale of exploited men's howls,
and to all the world's astonishment, siles down. So it's gone
for a thousand, thousand years, and so it will continue.

"You may say,
'Nevertheless, there is good in cities: Where else can men
support great art? The complexity of music, the intrinsicate craft
of poetry? Who else can pay for architecture,
the gifts of science, ennobling pleasure of philosophy?'
I answer this: To a hungry man, all food is food,
sufficient to his need. Trembling with weakness, he does not ask
for meats denatured by subtle rocamboles. But the man well-fed,
as short of breath as a boar at the trough, dull-headed with wine,
bloated on the blood of his workers' children—that man has tastes
more particular: not taste for food but for taste itself.
An art has been born. So the poet whose hunger is simply to speak—
tell truths, right wrongs—what need has he for the lipogram,
for colors of rhetoric, antilibrations of phrase on phrase?
Only to the fool who believes all truths debatable,
who believes true virtue resides not in men but in eulogies,
true sorrow not in partings but in apopemptic hymns,
and true thought nowhere but in atramentaceous scrollery—
only to him is elegant style, mere scent, good food.
The city, bedded on the sorrows of the poor, compacts new sweets
to incense the corpse of the weary rich.
                              "—And as for science,
cure my disease and I'll thank you for it. Yet I do not think
you mix your potions and juleps for me. By the ebony beds
of the old loud-snoring mighty you wring your hands and spoon out
remedies—dole out health for the coin of convalescent spiders
in a kingdom of hapless flies. For the spider, health itself
becomes not need but taste, where the treatment of fevers and chills,
chapped lips, a slight but debilitating dryness of the palate while eating
cake, are men's chief griefs. So it is with all the arts;
so even Queen Theology turns a casual amusement
for the pornerastic sky- and earth-consumer, a flatulence
past the power of all man's remedies. Such is my judgment.
I may be in error—a man as remote from the bustlings of cities
as a stylite praying in his cloud. Refute these doubts of mine,
prove that the moral and physical advance of the citified man
outruns the sly proreption of his smoking garbage dumps,
or the swifter havoc of his armies, and I'll speedily recant. Meanwhile,
the past of the world is what it is—read it who likes.
As for the present, I can tell you this, by the sure augury

of stars. The minarets of Troy will burn—vast city of tradesmen
buying and selling, extorting and swindling, callipygious peacocks
whose splay touches even the jade traffic. And out of its ashes
will come new cities, and new destructions—a pyre for the maiden
who now rules white-walled, thundering Carthage, and afterward a city
on seven hills, a seat of empire suckled by she-wolves,
mighty as Olympos itself. But that throne too will fall.
And so through the ages, city by city and empire by empire,
the world will fall, rebuild, and fall, and the mistake charge on
to the final conflagration. I will tell you the truth: the mistake
is man. For his heart is restless, and his brain a crisis brain,
short-sighted, mechanical, dangerous. And the white-loined city
is man's great temptress: hungry for comfort at whatever the cost,
hungry for power, hydroptic-souled, conceiving dire needs
till the last of conceivable needs is sated, and nothing remains
but death; and desiring death. There's pride's star-spangled finale!
The fool who says in his heart 'There is no God' makes God
in his own image, and God thereafter is Corinth, or Carthage—
a sprawling bawd and a maniac—a brattle of voices
in one sear skull—a tyrant terrified by shadows. If gods
exist, they must soon overwhelm that whore—for their weapons, barns
of famine. They will send sharp teeth of beasts, and the venom of serpents;
lay bare the beds of seas, and reveal the world's foundations.
The earth will wither, polluted beneath its inhabitants' feet,
and the false god made in the image of man will lie slaughtered.

                                                        "But the man
who submits to the gods and abandons himself, refuses his nature,
who turns from the city to the rocks and highground—by mastery of his heart
denies the lust to rule and oppress, the fool's-gold joy
of the sophisticate—to him the gods send honey of the cliffs
and oil from the flinty crag. Like eagles caring for their young,
the gods will spread their wings at the rim of the nest to hold him
and shore him safe in their pinions.

                                "This heaven requires me to speak.
No one requires you to hear me, or understand."

                                                With that
the tall, black-bearded Northerner ceased and stiffly sat down,
and he glared all around him like a wolf. He was, it seemed to me,
eager to be gone, the labor the stars had demanded of him
finished. The sea-kings glanced at each other

and here and there men laughed discreetly, as if at some joke
wholly unrelated to Paidoboron's speech. The Argonaut's face
was expressionless, Pyripta's baffled. Old Kreon at last
stood up, enfeebled giant. He rubbed his hands together,
hesitant and thoughtful, and pursed his lips. With a solemn visage
and one eye squeezed tight shut, the king of Corinth said:
"I'm sure I speak for every man in this room when I say,
true and straightforward Paidoboron, that we're deeply grateful
for the message you've brought us, distressing as it is.
You've made explicit, it seems to me, the chief implication
of Jason's tragic story: we're fools to put all our faith
in fobs and spangles no firmer than the heart of man—satisfactions
of animal hungers, or the idealism of the dim-brained dog.
I have seen myself such mistaken idealism:
the fair white neck of Jokasta broken for a foolish prejudice,
she who might, through her people's love, have saved mad Thebes.
As we talk, with our usual flippancy, of kingdoms and powers,
you bring us up short; you recall us to deeper purposes.
If our hearts are disturbed—as surely all sensitive hearts must be
by much you say—we thank you profoundly nonetheless."
So saying, he clapped, bowing to Paidoboron, and quickly, at the signal,
all those sitting at the tables clapped—and even Jason.
How could I blame them? His rant was, after all, outrageous—
his presumption flatly intolerable. Step warily
even with the noblest of prophets—baldhead Elisha who once
when his dander was up, had the children who chanted songs in scorn of him
eaten alive by bears. What can you say to the wild-eyed
looney proclaiming on Fillmore Street,

THE END OF THE WORLD
IS AT HAND!
REPENT!   ?

Throughout the hall, the applause swelled,
and Paidoboron sat fuming, scornfully silent.

At length
Koprophoros rose. Those nearest me frowned to hush my mutterings,
and I hushed. The Asian spoke, great rolls of abdomens
and chins, his long-tailed turban of gold and snow-white samite
splendid as the ruby that glowed on his forehead like an angry eye.
His tone was gentle, conciliatory. He opened his arms

and tipped his head like a puppet, profoundly apologetic
but forced by simple integrity to air his disagreement.
He said:

"Your Majesties; gentlemen:

"Imagine I approach a stranger on the street and say to him, 'If you
please, sir, I desire to perform an experiment with your aid.' The stranger
is obliging, and I lead him away. In a dark place conveniently by, I strike
his head with the broad of an axe and cart him home. I place him, buttered
and trussed, in an ample oven. The thermostat reads 450°. Thereupon I go
off to play at chess* with friends and forget all about the obliging stranger
in the stove. When I return, I realize I have overbaked my specimen, and
the experiment, alas, is ruined." He made himself seem a man unspeakably
disappointed. Then, eyes wildly gleaming, he dramatically raised an index
finger.

"Something has been done wrong. Or something wrong has been done."

He smiled. His enormous eyes squeezed shut, relishing the juices of his
cunning wit. The sea-kings smiled with him. At last, with a gesture:

"Any ethic that does not roundly condemn my action, I'm sure you'll
agree, is vicious. It is interesting that none is vicious for this reason. It is
also interesting that no more convincing refutation of any ethic could be
given than one which reveals that the ethic approves my baking the obliging stranger." He tipped his head, smiled again.

"That, actually, is all I have to say, but I shall not desist on that account.
Indeed, I shall commence anew.

"The geometer"—he gestured—"cannot demonstrate that a line is beautiful. The beauty of lines is not his concern. We do not chide him when he
fails to observe uprightness in his verticals, when he discovers no passions
between sinuosities. We would not judge it otherwise than foolish to berate
him for neglecting to employ the methods successful in biology or botany
merely because those methods deal fairly with lichens and fishes. Nor do
we despair of him because he cannot give us reasons for doing geometry
which will equally well justify our drilling holes in teeth. There is a limit,
as ancient philosophers have said, to the questions which we may sensibly
put to each man of science; and however much we may desire to find unity
in the purposes, methods, and results of every fruitful sort of inquiry, we
must not allow that desire to make mush of their necessary differences.

"I need not prove to you by lengthy obs and sols, I hope, that no ethical
system conceived by man can explain what is wrong in my treatment of the

* Greek, *zatrikion*.

293

obliging stranger. It should be sufficient to observe how comic all ethical explanations must sound.

"Consider:" (Here he gestured with both hands.)

"My act produced more pain than pleasure.

"Baking this fellow did not serve the greatest good to the greatest number.

"I acted wrongly because I could not consistently will that the maxim of my action become a universal law.

"God forbade me, but I paid no heed.

"Anyone can apprehend the property of wrongness sticking plainly to the whole affair.

"Decent men remark it and are moved to tears."

(Everyone was laughing.)

"But surely what I've done is just as evil if, for instance, the man I have wronged was tickled to laughter the whole time he cooked." Koprophoros looked puzzled, slightly panicked in fact. "Yet it cannot be that my baking the stranger is wrong for no reason at all. It would then be inexplicable. I cannot believe this is so, however."

He pretended to be startled by illumination.

"It is *not* inexplicable, in fact. It's *transparent!*"

He paused and formally shifted his weight as a writer shifts paragraphs. With a gesture, he said: "All this, I confess, must seem an intolerably roundabout approach to the point I would like to make to you. The point is simply this. Our hyperborean friend has put forward two simple assertions: that cities are by nature evil, and that the feelings of men—the feelings responsible for the creation of cities—are to be rejected in favor of the noble attitudes of gods—attitudes we cannot experience, as human beings, except as we are informed of them by visionaries like Paidoboron, men who are, for mysterious reasons, infinitely our superiors." He bowed solemnly, with an appropriate gesture, in Paidoboron's direction, then looked straight at me and, for no fathomable reason, winked. He continued:

"You can see, I'm sure, gentlemen, what troubles me—or rather, the many things troubling me. I'll gladly trust an algorist like Paidoboron to tell me most minutely and precisely of sidereal eclipses, 19 year cycles, storms on the surface of Helios, or the lunar wobble. But even if I could grant in theory (as I'm reluctant to do) that the stars send moral advice to me, I wonder, being a stubborn sort of person, what the stars' apogees and perigees—stiff and invariable tracings of geometry, if I'm not mistaken—can have to do with my moral behavior. How, that is, does an astral apogee come to know more about upright action than a vertical line or the loudest physically possible thump? Again, I'm puzzled about the mathematics of why I should turn against human nature when every man here in this room condemns me for my manner of dealing with the stranger—whom you hardly knew!" Gesture. "Indeed, I can think of no one who would settle down soberly to cook a man, discounting the benighted anthropophagi, but a zealot of religion.

"I suggest that we may have been somewhat maligned—that cities, in fact, are a complex expression of the very attitudes involved in your hearty condemnation of me for the way I employ my oven. I suggest that the faults in city life, which Paidoboron points out, are the sad, accidental side-effects of a noble attempt—indeed, a magnificent achievement—which ought not to be washed down the gutter with the unwanted baby in impulsive haste." He slid his eyes up, ironically pious, and delicately tapped his fingertips together.

"Let me assume you agree with me in this. Then our question becomes, 'What kind of rule is most likely to make man's noble and social attempt successful, keeping unfortunate side-effects to the barest possible minimum?' Jason has given us some pointers in this matter. He argues, if I've rightly understood him, that the first principle is simply this: Balance a steadfast concern for justice with unfailing common sense, an intelligent use of alliances, a capacity to change as situations change. And his second principle would seem to be: Sternly reject all emotional urges, let the abstract, calcifying mind wrap the wicked blood in chains—if it can. If it can! For all man's nature, save only his god-given mind, is a fetid and camarine thing, unfit to fish or swim in. So he tells us. Is he right? Is a Philosopher King conceivable who is not an old madman like Amykos?

"Let me ask you to join me for a minute or two in pondering these opinions. Begin with the second.

"No decent man, no man of sober judgment, I venture to say, can fail to be moved to tears of profoundest sympathy by the process which led to Jason's rejection of physical desires. We might of course argue, if we wished to be abusive, that from start to finish the problem revealed in Jason's story is not physical desire but unsound assessment. Which of us here— I do not mean to be unduly critical—would stake all he had on a priestess of Hekate, that is, a witch?—even promising marriage and everlasting praise of her virtue! Which of us, seeing his beloved wife in a very crucible of fiery pain, would creep unfeelingly into a slavegirl's bed? And which of us here would entertain for a moment the notion that revealing his deepest hostilities to a woman for whom murder is as easy as mumbling six words of Sumerian at midnight, or thirty seconds with a few venene herbs, a sorceress for whom all grammary begins with the abrogation of commoners' morals, embrace of the deep's hyphalic causes—which of us, I say, would imagine that such revelations could be wholly innocuous? But to focus on trifles of this kind obscures the darker issue." He gestured all trivialities away.

"Lord Jason's theory—an extremely popular one these days, it seems to me—is that mind and body are by nature, and in principle ought to be, totally divorced, an opinion we may trace in Jason's thought to the punch-addled king of the Bebrykes—not that it matters. An opinion that existence precedes essence. —Don't laugh too quickly! The most outlandish cacodoxy can take on the seeming solidity of stone if its argument is given with sufficient flourish—a proper appeal to our delight in symmetry, with pedal tone notice of our universal dissatisfactions, cut off from Nature by our conscious choice to eat Mother Nature's bears and apples (King Oidipus' problem in its oldest disguise), cut off till we doubt that we're anything at all but our hearts' sad swoons and deliquiums. *I think, therefore I am not,* is the gist of the argument. If I can think about a thing, I am *not* that thing, the argument goes, if only because *subject* is one word and *object* is another and therefore there must be two things involved, not one. And since I can in solemnly spectable fact stand back and think about even my mind, it must be the case, however befuddling, that I-who-think am not even my mind: I am emptiness! My consciousness is a firmly established prison wall between myself and all Nature, even my own. A terribly depressing thought, I grant you. But the cave to which we've wandered has even darker places. Since my consciousness depends upon words, formal structures, the reality outside me is what it is because of the words I frame it in —in other words, there's no possibility whatsoever of perceiving the objective truth of anything, there is only *my* truth: *my* understanding of what words and the objects they grope toward mean. The tiger's rays are my mind's illations, his tectonics the hum of my braincells." He gestured.

"I suggest to you, gentlemen, that however my personal vision may construct the hungry tiger, however boldly I assert (as my scrupulous logic may require) that the tiger I sense is not really there, the tiger will eat me, and I've known it all along, whatever my logic may asseverate. I suggest, in short, that Jason's theory is a deep-seated lie: I do *not,* in fact, think merely with my mind. If I did, I could not explain to myself why you hate me for cooking the stranger. I suggest that philosophers, whose chief business is to think things through, not slog on by faith, like the rest of us, make dangerous, nay, deadly kings. Ideas quite harmless in the philosopher's attic, mistaken opinions which time can easily unmask, can turn to devouring dragons if released on the world.

"What I claim, with respect to Jason's idea—though I do not pretend to prove my claim, being no true philosopher myself but only a man philosophically equipped to defend himself against philosophers—is that man is whole, his passions as priceless as his crafty mind, and mysteriously connected, if not, indeed, identical—so that rejection of the body is a giant step toward madness. If evil actions are transparently evil, the reason is that I can feel them as surely and concretely as I feel a cow or a pang of love. That, I suspect, and nothing baser, is the reason we make cities. Not to flee raw experience of Nature, but to arrive at it, to escape the drudgery of hunting and gobbling so that when we sit down to supper we can take our time and notice it. Show the crude country singer the noblest achievements of our epic poets, and he'll shame all critics in his praise of it." He looked at me again, and again winked. I looked around in alarm and embarrassment. He continued: "The crude balladeer King Paidoboron praises—where are his verses most quoted and loved? In the city, of course. There, there only, have clodpate mortals the time and experience to perceive and appreciate artlessness, or be moved by plain-brained message.

"But I was speaking of Jason." Gesture. "He would curb the flesh in iron chains, deny all passions for the common good. I ask you one question. Can a man make laws for other men if he's purified out of his blood all trace of humanness? I can say to god-struck Paidoboron, 'I disagree,' and no one is overmuch offended by it. But let him constrain me by inflexible laws to behave and frame my affirmations exactly as he does, and you know very well what the upshot will be. Let the tyrant gird his loins and cement his alliances, because make no mistake, I am coming for him!

"Though I've no intention of crushing light-winged opinions into staggering and groaning legislation, I have opinions of my own that I value as dearly as Jason does his—and between you and me and the gatepost, I think mine more tenable. I celebrate the flesh unashamedly: I watch and guide it with mind as a doting mother does her child. I celebrate dancing and the creation of images and uplifting fictions; I celebrate, among other bodily sensations, health and wealth and power, which does not mean I'm unmoved by sickness and poverty and weakness. Search high and low through this moaning world, you'll find no man's illachrymable but the man of stern theories, the ice-cold slave of mere intellect, donzel with a ponderous book, or six loosely knotted opinions he's fashioned to a whip. Don't tell *me*, when you speak of such men, of their liberalism.

"So much for that. Return to Jason's more important principle. He

claims we should balance idealism with pragmatic awareness of the changing world. No man of sense would deny the point." He gestured wearily.
"But gentlemen, consider. As once all the princes of Akhaia rallied around
Jason for pursuit of the golden fleece, so now all the princes have rallied
around King Agamemnon, to avenge the ravishing of Helen by Paris of
Troy. The morality of the war may be right or wrong—I take no stand—
but one thing seems certain: when the Trojan war is won or lost, those
princes who bravely stood together to fight it will emerge a league as powerful as any the world has ever seen. How is it that Jason—given his theory
of power by alliance—sits here in comfort, drinking Kreon's wine—
though a man no older than Hektor, I think, and no less wily than Odysseus
—when the men he'll need to ally himself with, if he ever achieves a position as king, are wading knee-deep in dear friends' blood toward Troy?
Not that I mean to criticize unduly. I express, merely, my puzzlement. He
has given us difficult and complex reasons for believing what we all believe
anyway, as surely as we believe, for no explicable reason, that we ought
not to bake harmless strangers in our ovens—yet he seems to me not to live
by them. The matter needs clarification."

   He smiled, waiting. I saw that the Asian was serenely certain
he'd carried the day. I was half-inclined—even I—to believe it,
though I knew the whole story. Athena herself looked alarmed, in fact,
uncomfortably watching at Jason's side. Above all, Kreon,
it seemed to me, was shaken in his faith. Though no one had doubted
that Jason's victory was settled from the start, Koprophoros' words
had shattered the old man's complacency as a few stern blows
of Herakles' club could loosen trees. He stared with eyes
like dagger holes at Koprophoros. He seemed to be seeing for the first time
the wealth and splendor of the Asian's dress, white and gold impleached,
majesty and taste unrivalled in Akhaia. He seemed to grasp
the remarkable restraint of that master of tricks. Though he might have astonished
the hall with a battery of startling illusions, and dazzled the wits
of the sea-kings with bold transformations and vanishings no one—no mortal,
not even the wily Medeia—could match (for Koprophoros' skill
as an illusion-maker was known far and wide) he had used no weapon
but plain argument, and by that alone had made Jason appear
a fool. As the hall sat restlessly waiting, Jason drew shapes
with his fingernail on the tablecloth, deep in thought. At last,
the king turned to him, evading his eyes, and asked, his voice
almost a whisper, toneless except for a hint of irritation:
"Would you care to offer some comment, Jason?" He smiled too late,

and Jason saw it, and returned the smile; and the whole room knew
that instant that Jason would win.
                                   He let a long moment pass,
then rose, head bowed, regally handsome and, you would have sworn,
embarrassed as an athlete praised. With an innocent openness
that no mere innocent boy could match, he said, "I confess,
Koprophoros is right." He smiled, not harmed in the least by that;
glad to be instructed. "I've admitted already that my judgment was faulty,
though by no means consistently so, I hope. (That you must decide.)
And Koprophoros would be right, too, if I claimed, indeed,
what he seems to believe I claimed. I've spoken
of marriages just and unjust: the king and state, the gods
and nature, mind and body. I meant no attempt to split off
mind, as if body and mind were not one—as surely as Orpheus
and Eurydike were one, while they lived, and are one even now
in the cool and dark of the Underworld—or as Theseus
and Hippolyta are one. The world is rife with inadequacies—
imperfect creatures starving for completion. To survive at all,
weakling must fadge with weakling, and out of that marriage win strength.
Not all unions are therefore holy. The blazing trumpet-vine
clinging to the elm may drive the branches of the tree toward light,
leaning on the strength of the tree for its own expansions; but at last
both fall together. We therefore prudently hack down the vine
in its earliest stages, and tear up its underground tubers and burn them.
I intended no more than that when I spoke.
                                   "As for the business
of Troy—" He paused, looked straight at the Asian, then down, much troubled,
for all the world like a man betrayed by an old, old friend,
and confounded by it. He said at last, too softly for many
in the hall to hear, "I cannot fathom his attacking me with that.
I'm an exile, a man with no army to lead and no leader willing
to take me with his troops, though I've formally pleaded and sworn with oaths
that no past glory of mine would impede his leadership.
Koprophoros knows all that. I told him myself. Why he now
forgets it, and twists my misfortune to shame . . ." His voice trailed off.
    When, little by little, they grasped the force of what he was saying,
the kings were astounded. Those in the back who'd missed what he said
whispered to be told. Shock at Koprophoros' treachery rolled
to the outer walls like a wave. Only three in the room—Koprophoros,
Jason, and I (for all that Artemis knew, I knew)

were aware that—for all his wounded but forgiving innocence
(army or no army, lord or no lord)—Jason had spoken
a cold-blooded lie. He'd told Koprophoros nothing of the kind.
The effect of the lie was immediate and deadly, as he knew it would be.
Not a man there had one single word of good he could say
for Koprophoros.
                        (So once King Arthur, playing the demonic
Other King, understood that to lose the game meant death,
and with powerful fists he ground the chessmen of gold to dust
and smashed the board. In horror the Other King reached out wildly,
and, the same instant, vanished. So Jason too refused
to play the game—he who had played so many for so long.
What was I to think?)
                        Kreon rose, politician to the last.
As if he'd seen nothing, as if merely finishing one more evening
of banqueting, he thanked all who'd spoken and, pleading the lateness
of the hour, dismissed the assembled kings to their beds. As they left
the kings talked earnestly, bending to one another's ears. With Koprophoros,
no one exchanged a word. He gazed at the floor, furious
and smiling, torn between anger and rueful admiration.

                                                    In his room,
Ipnolebes watching like a man turned stone, old Kreon talked,
pacing, wildly gesticulating as his slaves undressed him.
"There it is, you see. Right from the start!" His bald head gleamed
in the candlelight. His shadow leaped up, stretched on pillars,
the shadows of the slaves reaching out to him like ghostly enemies
clutching at his life. He paused, hiked up one foot to relinquish
a sandal, then paced again, short-legged. "We two know better,
you and I," he said, "than to lay our bets on wealth alone,
honor like Jokasta's, genius like that of—" Ipnolebes watched
like a wolf; said nothing. The king prattled on. Ipnolebes' eyes
fell shut, his spirit more fierce than a god's. "There is no anger,"
the voice of the moon-goddess whispered in my ear, invisible beside me,
"more deadly than a slave's." She laughed, aloof. "*There* lies the evil
in tyrannous oppression. It ends in the gem-pure fury of the man
who has tolerated the intolerable, no longer loves
himself or anything living." I observed that the rest of the slaves
were the same, as if Ipnolebes' emotion, ravaged and inhuman,
inwardly burning like a coal that appears (at first glance) ash,

had crept into all their veins through the shadowed, impotionate air.
He broke in abruptly: "Suppose your magnificent Jason was lying."
Kreon, in his nightcap, fat arms stretching to receive his nightgown,
seemed not to hear him at all.

In the wide-beamed banquet hall,
dark and abandoned except for one figure, moonlight fell—
cold shadow of Artemis—mottled on the tables and floor. A slavegirl,
servant of Pyripta, watched in the shadow of the doorway as the man
who remained, though the others had left, paced musingly back and forth.
She watched for some while, then hurried to her mistress to report what she'd seen.
Quickly, silently, the princess arose, her heart pounding
like a drawn kestrel's, and, moving more softly than a huntress in the night,
she went to discover for herself if the message were true. Alone,
her quick mind rushing more swiftly than her small and silent feet,
she entered the hall where Jason paced. He saw her coming
and paused, his eyes averted from the shimmer of her gown. She spoke
in a whisper, a-tremble with the thought that she might be discovered with him,
a-tremble with the thought that she might say more than she ought to say.
Speaking, she half by accident reached out shyly for his hand.
"My lord, what can this mean, that you stay when all others have gone,
pacing the floor like a man tormented by doubts? Though we've asked you
on many occasions to stay with us here, you have always refused us,
insisting on duties elsewhere. So now you make me fear
that my father and I have offended you, stirred up some cause
for grief you can neither suppress nor, because of your well-known kindness,
reproach us with. Or perhaps your heart is still troubled by the cruel
and shameful behavior of Koprophoros. If it's so, let me soothe you
with my father's own words not an hour ago: There's no man in Corinth
not shocked to the soles of his feet by that fat swine's treachery."
As she spoke, her fears melted, and she gazed at him only with tenderness,
like a loving sister. She was unaware that her servant had gone
to Kreon, propelled by duty perhaps, perhaps by cruelty,
and told of Pyripta's meeting with Jason in the moonlit hall.
As fast as his feet would carry him, the king ran down
and now stood, barefoot and in sleeping dress, peeking from the doorway,
slyly observing their mutual temptation and blessing heaven
for his rare good luck.

He held her hand, aware of her virginal
fear of him, and answered softly, "Princess, you need not
frighten yourself with such gloomy thoughts. If I tell you the truth,

301

I remain here for no other reason than pleasure in the place." He smiled,
looked down at her. "But now—you're right—I must go find some bed.
Forgive me for giving you a moment's alarm." He had not missed,
I knew by his half-checked smile, the fact that she spoke in a whisper,
not sorry to be caught here alone with him. Nor did he miss
her searching look now, desire she newly understood. He met
her gaze and, after a moment, kissed her. Her hands moved hungrily
on Jason's back. The pillared room hung frozen like a crystal
in the light of the vengeful moon. The princess whispered in his ear.
He frowned, as if torn, and studied her, and could give her no answer.
The hall gleamed dully. She whispered again, sweet blue-eyed princess,
with the voice of a child, a curious droplet of moonlight shining
on her forehead. And again he gave no answer, but held her in his arms,
looking at her, listening thoughtfully, biding his time.

2 1

The oak where I clung with my eyes tight shut like a terrified lizard,
bruised and battered, kicked like old rubbish from pillar to post,
went flat suddenly in the screaming gale, and I lost my hand-hold—
I pressed up closer and hunched my back, but there was nothing to cling to.
The rough-barked tree became a road of stone on a steep rock mountain,
endless—the labor of emperors—but humbled by pebbles,
cluttered at the sides with bramble bushes and with shining scree.
And now all around me a slum lurched up till it blocked out the darkness—
or became the darkness—staggering, skewbald. No longer did the wind
come raging like a lion at the canyon mouth, or dancing, as if
under pines and cedars, or flying swiftly, whistling and wailing,
spluttering its anger, or crashing like thunder, whirling, tumbling
in confusion, shaking rocks, striking trees—no longer was the wind
so godly, nor the night so godly that sent it; but rattling it came,
wheeling, violent, from wynds and alleys, poking in garbage cans,
stirring up the dust, fretting and worrying. It crept into holes
and knocked on doors, scattered sand and old plaster, swirled ashes,
muddled in the dirt and tossed up bits of filth. It sidled
through tenement windows, crept under double- and triple-locked doors
of furnished rooms. I huddled, raising my collar against it,
clamping my lips against street dust and holding my poor battered hat on.
    And then all at once I was lurching in a rickety vehicle
through streets so crowded the horses pulling had nowhere to move—
fat black warhorses with ears laid flat and with steep-rolling eyes,
snorting and stamping irritation at the crowd, but obedient to the driver.
Staring at his back, I knew by the tingle at the nape of my neck
that I'd seen him before and should fear him. He turned his head and I saw
his thick spectacles and smile—my mirror image, my double!

With the crowd packed tight around us, I had nowhere to flee.

Despite
the ragged, churning horde, the chariot was making some headway.
It rolled in silence, the wheels climbing over small stones, bits of rubble,
as if struggling onward with conscious effort, the driver never swerving
to the left or right, like stoop-shouldered, cool-eyed Truth in a frayed
black coat and hat. We ascended a hill made strange by haze,
its upper part not dazzling, exactly, its lower region
not exactly obscure—dimly visible, impossible to name,
changing, shadowy, deep as the ancestor of all that lives,
awesome and common. The chariot wheels seemed to move in old ruts;
the wind, the smell of the horses, the writing on the chariot walls—
hieroglyphs smoothed down to nothing, as if by blind men's fingers—
had all a mysterious sameness.

"You're enjoying your vision?" he said
and smiled again, showing all his teeth.
"The strangest vision that ever was seen in this world," I said.
He laughed. "No doubt it seems so," he said. "So each man's vision
seems to him. And no doubt it seems a profound revelation?"
"Yes indeed!" I said, inexplicably furious. He grinned, tipped his hat,
icily polite. Then, seeing my swollen hand, he remarked,
"The vision has rules, I hope?" He smiled. "It's not one of those maddening—"
"Certainly not!" I said. "It's an absolute tissue of rules,
though not all of them, of course, at *this* stage—" "Yes, of course, of course."
He seemed both myself and, maddeningly, my superior,
and deadly. He tapped his chin. "So you're piercing to the heart of things."
"Exactly," I said. He beamed. "Excellent! —And there's something there?
The heart of the matter is not, as we've feared . . ." He smiled, mock-sheepish.
I tried in panic to think what it was that it was teaching me,
and my head filled with ideas that were clear as day, but jumbled—
images that had no words for them. Somewhat disconcerted,
I concentrated, clarifying what I saw by explaining
to the stranger as I looked. And now suddenly things grew much plainer.
I now understood things never before expressed—inexpressible—
though everywhere boldly hinted, so plain, so absurdly simple
that a fool if he learned the secret would laugh aloud. I saw
three radiant ladies like pure forms gloriously bright—three ladies
and one, as separate roads may wind toward one same city,
or one same highway be known by separate names. The floor
of the chariot extended to the rims of the universe, wheeling away

305

like a rush of silver spokes devised by the finest of a rich king's
silversmiths, a man so devoted that he never looks up,
and never considers the value of his work, but with every stroke
proclaims the majesty of silver as the wings of an eagle praise wind.
There the three ladies danced like dreams in the limitless skull
of the Unnamable. And the first held a book with great square pages.
Her name was *Vision,* and her tightly woven robe was *Light.*
The second lady held a wineglass to me and smiled at my shyness,
and when I saw her smile I remembered I'd met her a thousand times,
in a thousand unprepossessing shapes, and my heart was as glad
as the heart of a lonely old man when he sees his son. Her name
was *Love,* and her robe was *Gentleness.* The third bright dancer,
nearer than the rest and so plain of face that I laughed when I saw her,
was lady *Life,* and her attire was *Work.* They danced, and their music—
one with the dancers as a miser's mind grows one with his guineas
or the soul of a man on the mountain and the soul of the mountain are one,
subject and object in careful minuet—was *Selflessness.*
I stared dumbfounded at the universal simplicity
and the man at my side stared with me, unconvinced. The whole wide vault
of the galaxies choired, rumbling with the thunder, what *Life* sang (Give),
and *Love* (Sympathize), and *Vision* (Control).
                              I laughed, and the sound
was a quake that banged through the bed of Olympos (the stranger vanished
like a shadow at the coming of a torch), and *Love* was transformed to Aphrodite,
Vision to Athena, and *Life* to Queen Hera in an undulant cloak
of snakes. I shrank in dismay—all around me to the ends of the vision,
the numberless, goggle-eyed gods. Beside me in the palace, a voice said,
"Calm yourself!" and a hand touched me. "Goddess!" I whispered,
for though she remained no clearer to my sight than the morning memory
of a dream, I knew her, and at once I was filled with an eerie calm
as gentle as the calm of sleeping lovers or the solemn stillness
of wrecked and abandoned towns. The goddess said, "Listen!" and raised
her shadowy arm to point.
                    On his high throne Zeus sat motionless,
cold and remote as the Matterhorn, his right fist raised
to his bearded chin. His left hand rested on the hand of the queen
on the throne beside him. The beams of his eyes shot calmly to the heart
of the universe, and he did not shift his gaze when the goddess
of love came forward and kneeled at his feet, surrounded by her host
of suivants—gasping old men still crooked with lust, drooling,

winking obscenely, their flies unbuttoned; middle-aged women
with plucked eyebrows, smiling serenely past cocktail glasses,
with eyes artificially eyelashed and slanted, and propped-up bosoms
exuding the ghostly remains of whole nations of civet cats;
young lovers crushed-to-one-creature as they staggered down crowded streets
lunging through fish-smells and sorrow, from bed to bed.
                                        Aphrodite
lifted her hands, dramatic, and cried, "O mighty Lord,
hear the prayer of your sorrowful Aphrodite! I've waited,
faithful as a child, remembering your promise. In this same hall
you swore that Jason and Medeia would be known forever as the truest,
most pitiful of lovers, saints of Aphrodite. Yet every hour
their once-fierce love grows feebler, turning toward hate. Queen Hera
revels in my shame, egging him on toward betrayal in the hall
of Kreon, and Athena bends all her wit to dredging up excuses
in his fickle heart for trading Medeia for Pyripta. If all
you promised you now withdraw, you know I'm powerless to stop you;
but understand well: fool though you think me—all of you—
you'll never fool me twice with your flipflop gudgeon-lures."
The love goddess closed her lovely fists at her sides, half rising,
and with bright tears rushing down her cheeks, exclaimed:
"I'll throw myself in the sea! Take warning! We gods may be
indestructible, but still we can steal death's outer semblance,
stretched out rigid and useless in the droppings of whales." At the thought
of dark desolation at the slimy bottom of the world, the goddess
was so moved she could speak no more, but sobbed into her fingers, shaking,
and her worshippers bleated in chorus till the floor of the palace was slick
with tears. But Zeus, like an old quartz mountain, was visibly unmoved.
"I've promised you what I've promised," he said. "Be satisfied."
   "But that's not all," she said, eyes wide, a bright blush rising
in her plump cheeks. "I find I'm mocked not only by Hera
and Athena, but even by Artemis—she who claims to be
so pure! I begged her, like a suppliant, to charge the spirit
of Kreon's daughter with a fiery love of chastity.
And what did the cruel and malicious thing do? Went straight to Medeia
to stir up strife in marriage! Let Artemis explain to the gods
her purpose in this, and by what right she behaves so horribly."
   Zeus said, "If Artemis wishes to speak let her speak." But the goddess
at my side said nothing. "Then I will speak," said Zeus crossly,
disdaining to shift his glance to tearful Aphrodite. "The fire

of zeal has never had a purpose. It is what it is, simply,
and any ends it may stumble to it's indifferent to.
As for Medeia, make no mistake, nothing on earth
is more pure—more raised from self to selfless absolute—
than a woman betrayed. For all their esteem, immortal gods
follow like foaming rivers the channels available to them.
Enough. Annoy us no more, Goddess." She backed off, curtsying,
glancing furtively around to see who might be snickering at her.
    And now gray-eyed Athena spoke, the goddess of cities
and goddess of works of mind. In her shadow professors crouched,
stern and rebuking, with swollen red faces and pedantic hearts;
lawyers at the edge of apoplexy from righteous indignation;
poets and painters with their pockets crammed full of sharp scissors and knives;
and ministers cunning in Hebrew. With a smile disarming and humorous—
but I knew her heart was troubled—she said, "Father of the Gods,
no one has firmer faith than I in your power to keep
all promises—complex and contradictory
as at times they seem." She glanced at the goddess of love and smiled,
then added, her tone too casual, I thought, and her teeth too bright,
"But I cannot deny, my lord, that my mind's on fire to understand
how you can hope to keep this one, for surely your promise to me,
that Jason shall rule in Corinth, must cancel the opposing promise
that Jason will cleave to Medeia. I beg you, end our suspense
and explain away this mystery, for my peace of mind."
    For the first time, the beams of the eyes of Zeus swung down
and he met the gaze of his cunning child Athena. He said,
his voice dark beyond sadness, "By murder and agony
on every side, by release of the dragons and the burning of Corinth,
by shame that so spatters the skirts of the gods that never again
can any expect or deserve man's praise—by these cruel means
I juggle your idiot demands to their grim consummation." So he spoke,
and spoke no more. The goddesses gazed at each other, aghast,
then looked again, disbelieving, at Zeus.
                                    It was Hera who spoke,
queen of goddesses. "Husband, your words cut deep, as no doubt
you intend them to. But I know you too well, and I think I know
your disgusting scheme. You told us at the time of your promises
that our wishes were selfish and cruel. In your bloated self-righteousness,
you imagine you'll shock us to shame by these terrible threats, pretending
we've brought these horrors on ourselves. My lord, we're not such children

as to tumble to that! The cosmos is fecund with ways and means,
and surely you, who can see all time's possibilities—
such, if I'm not mistaken, is your claim—surely you could find
innumerable tricks to provide us with all we desire, without
this monstrous bloodbath and, at last, this toppling of the whole intent
of our three wishes. O Master of Games, I remain unpersuaded
by your floorless, roofless nobility. You want no more or less than *we* do:
triumph and personal glory. It's to spite us
you do these things. Like the spiteful bigot who dances in the street
when the brothel burns and the wicked run screaming and flaming to the arms
of Death, you dance in your hell-cavern mind at the terrible sight
of hopes-beneath-your-lofty-dignity shattered, proved shameful.
Well I—for one—I'll not bend to that high-toned dogmatism!
Bring on your death's-heads! Kindle your hellfires! Unleash the shrieks
of humanity enraged! Prate, preach, pummel us! I'll not be fooled:
from rim to rim of the universe, all is selfishness and wrath."
So saying, she struggled to free her hand from the arm of the throne
and Zeus's grip, but his hand lay on hers as indifferent and heavy
as a block of uncut stone. Then Hera wept. And before
my baffled eyes her form grew uncertain, changing and shadowy,
as if hovering, tortured, between warring potentials, and one of them
was *Life*. I remembered Phineus.
Gently and softly
Athena spoke. Her eyes were cunning, watching her father
like a hawk. "My lord, your words have upset us, as you see. If we speak
in haste, our words not carefully considered, I'm sure your wisdom
forgives us. Yet perhaps the queen of goddesses is right after all
that there may be some way you've missed that could lead to a happier issue—
satisfaction of our wishes without such deplorable waste."
"There's none," said Zeus. She glanced at him, sighed, then began again.
"Perhaps now—knowing what our wishes entail—we might modify them."
She glanced at Aphrodite. The goddess of love with a fiery glance
at Hera said, "It was you—you two—if you care to remember,
who begged me to *start* this love affair. But now, just like that,
I'm to turn my back on it. 'Run along, Aphrodite, dear,
you've served your purpose.' " She stretched out an arm to Zeus. "I ask you,
would *you* put up with such treatment? Am I some scullery-slave,
some errand runner? What have they ever done for me?" Zeus sighed,
said nothing. Athena pleaded, "But what are we to do? Am I
to grovel at the sandals of this cosmic cow? And even if I did,

would Hera do it?" The queen of goddesses flashed, "Don't be fooled!
If tragedy strikes, there's no one to blame but Zeus!" Then they waited,
leaving the outcome to Zeus. He stared into space. At last
he lowered his fist slowly from his chin. "Let it be," he said.
From wall to wall through the infinite palace, the gods gasped,
and instantly all the earth was filled with the rumble of dragons
growling up out of the abyss, all the oldest, gravest of terrors
from the age before hunters first learned to make peace with the bear they killed,
the age when the farmer in Eden was first understanding remorse
for the tear he made in Nature when he backed away, became
a man, devourer of his mother and bane of his father, his sons,
outcast of all Time–Space—Dionysos' prey, and scorn
of the endlessly fondling, fighting baboons. All progress, like the flesh
of the sick old trapper in the lair of his daughters, those dragons rose,
like violent sons, devouring. The sky went black with smoke.
"No!" I whispered, "it mustn't be allowed!" The goddess said nothing.
I grew more excited. I would do something foolish in a moment, I knew,
but the knowledge failed to check me. I snatched off my glasses and whispered,
"Where are those others, those three goddesses who danced? They must help us!"
"They're here," she answered, "but obscured, weighed down." She nodded
        at the three
by Zeus's throne, and I saw that it was so: *Vision* burned dimly,
like a hooded candle, in Athena's eyes, and *Love* flickered
in Aphrodite's, and *Life* fought weakly, like a failing blush,
in Hera's cheeks. "But *you*," I said then, my excitement rising,
"you, Goddess of Purity and Zeal—surely you at least
are one and unchangeable! Your power could save us, yet here in the house
of the gods, you're silent as stone." Then, horribly, before my eyes—
no surer than anything else in my vision's deluding mists—
the shadowy figure altered, became like a heavy old farm-wife,
sly-eyed, smiling like a witch. She croaked: "Come, see me as I am.
The crowd of the living are phrenetic with business. I alone am inactive.
My mind is like a dolt's. All the world is alert; I alone am drowsy.
Calm like the sea, like a high wind never ceasing. All the world
is tremulous with purpose; I am foolish, untaught.
Tentative, like a man fording a river in winter;
hesitant, as if fearful of neighbors; formal like a guest;
falling apart like thawing ice, as vacant as a valley. . . ."
I stared in amazement, though a moment's reflection would have shown me
        the truth:

even the goddess of purity and zeal had her earthen side,
sodden and selfish, determined to endure, outwitting the world
by magically becoming it. The two moon-goddesses, Artemis and Hekate,
were secretly the same.

I turned, despairing

of the purity drowned in that warty, flat-headed lump. But the farm-wife
reached to me, checking my impulse to flee, and argued with me further,
queerly indifferent herself, I thought, to the argument.
Her few teeth were like a dog's; her withered hands were palsied.
" 'On disaster,' the brave and ambitious say, 'good fortune perches.'
But I say, 'It is beneath good fortune that disaster crouches.' "
She leered again, and by a gesture incredibly simple and subtle—
no more, perhaps, than the slightest perceptible movement of her eyes—
she suggested a huge and obscene bump and grind. She cooed, eyes closed,

> *"The further one goes*
> *the less one knows*
> *for hustle and bustle,*
> *for hustle and bustle;*
> *Therefore the wise man moves not a muscle."*

She chuckled, foolish and apologetic, and I determined to waste no more
      time on her.
Reckless and honest as a madman, I burst
through the seething ocean of gods to Zeus's feet, where Apollo,
shining like the mirroring sea, sat tuning his lyre for a song—
gentle Apollo with the dragon tusks of Helios.
"Stop!" I cried out—and all motion stopped, even the movement
of Apollo's sleeve in the gentle cosmic wind. I shouted,
angrily slamming my right fist into my left-hand palm,
"I object! This palace is a mockery! The whole creation
is a monstrous, idiotic mockery! The silliest child on his mother's knee
knows good from evil, selfishness from love." Nothing stirred, no one moved.
I turned around, gazed at the gods stretching out in all directions from the throne,
and my soul was filled with amazement and ecstasy at my power to instruct
      and lecture them.
I stretched out my hands like a preacher addressing multitudes, and I felt aglow
like a winter sun. "If the truth is so clear even dogs can see it, how dare the gods
be baffled and befuddled, raising up time after time mad idiots to positions of power,
filling the schools with professors with not one jot or tittle of love for the things

they pretend to teach; filling the pulpits with atheists and cowards who
      put on their robes
for love of their mothers, merely; and filling the courts with lawyers indifferent
      to justice,
the medical schools with connivers and thieves and snivelling,
      sneaking incompetents,
the seats of government with madmen and bullies—all this though nothing
      in the world is clearer
than evil and good, the line between justice and unselfishness (the way
      of the decent)
and cowardice, piggish greed, foul arrogance, the filth-fat darkness of the
      devil's forces!"
As I spoke, declaiming, making existence as clear as day—
saying nothing not spoken by the noblest of poets and sages since time
began (and I said far more than I've set down here, believe me—
revealed to the gods all the wisdom of the Hindus, the secret rediscovered
by Schopenhauer, how man must perceive that the spirit in himself
is a spark of the fire that's in all things living, so that hurting another
means hurting himself; told them how Jesus was angry at the tomb
of Lazarus, how the awesome Tibetan *Book of the Dead*
has a lower truth and a higher truth; told them of the poetry
of Chaucer and Shakespeare, Homer and Virgil, Chia Yi and Tu Fu,
and the anonymous Kelts—*The hall of Cynddylan is dark tonight,*
without fire, without candle. But for God, who'll give me sanity?—
all this and more)—as I spoke I felt more and more filled with light,
more filled with the strange and divine understanding of the mystery of Love
that Dante spoke of in his *Paradiso,* all the scattered leaves
of the universe gathered—*legàto con amore*—and as I spoke, I seemed
to rise without effort, like an eagle with his wings spread wide on an updraft
past Zeus's shins to his bolt-square knees, past his belly and chest
(still gesturing, lecturing, compressing all life to the burning globe
of a family knit by unalterable love—my own humble family,
for where but in a wife, after twenty-one years of loyalty and faith,
sorrows and shocks that would shake down mountains, and a joyous holiness
that theory and defense leave empty and foolish as program notes
or the weight in ounces of a lily at twilight—where else can a man
learn surely of things inexpressible?), and I rose to the very
brow of Zeus, high above drifting haze, above life,
and stopped mid-sentence. I gazed all around me in alarm.

                                                    I was standing

on a mountain, miles past the timber, a place cased thickly in ice,
snowdust everywhere like fire in a furnace. My shoes were frozen,
my fingers were blue. "Goddess!" I howled. The old fat farm-wife,
whiskered like a goat and as dull of eye as a child without wits,
came smiling toward me like a ship's prow sliding out of mist. She stood
and looked at me awhile with her drooling grin, then turned her back
and squatted, inviting me to ride. I climbed on. Immediately I seemed
much warmer. As we started down she sang a foolish sort of song,
its music vaguely like an echo of Apollo's tuning of his harp:

> *"On Cold Mountain*
> *The lone round moon*
> *Lights the whole clear cloudless sky.*
> *Honor this priceless natural treasure*
> *Concealed in five shadows,*
> *Sunk deep in the flesh."*

We came down to the clouds, then down to the timberline;
came to a view of high villages—goatsheds, barns on stilts.
We came to a river. The foul witch sang:

> *"When men see old Lill*
> *They all say she's crazy*
> *And not much to look at—*
> *Dressed in rags and hides.*
> *They don't get what I say*
> *And I don't talk their language.*
> *All I can say to those I meet:*
> *'Try and make it to Cold Mountain.*
> *Hmmmmm.'"*

My double appeared at the door of a cowbarn, pulling at his hatbrim.
"I think your vision has no rules," he said. "Mere literary scraps.
The *somnium animale* of a man who reads too much.
I see traces of a fear that literature may be nothing but a game,
and stark reality the chaos remaining when the last game's played."
What could I say to such cynicism? My heart beat wildly
and I jumped from the old woman's back to snatch up a handful of stones.
He saw my purpose—my double, or whoever—
and clutching the brim of his hat in one hand he went limping for the woods.
"*Is nothing serious?*" I yelled, pelting him. He squealed like a pig.
He was gone. I wrung my fingers, whispering, *Is nothing serious?*
The goddess had vanished. "*Sirius! Sirius!*" the dark trees sang.

22

"Let it be," the deep voiced thunder rumbled, beyond tall pillars,
beyond tall oaks like skeletal hands still snatching at nothing
in the cockshut sky. They lighted the torches, for the day had gone dark
prematurely, grown sullen as a nun full of grudges. King Kreon rose,
stretched out his hands for silence, but the flashing sky boomed on,
drowning his announcement, drowning the applause of the assembled sea-kings.
Then Jason rose, smiling, and spoke—gray rain on the palace grounds
pounding on flagstones and walls, filling lakes with activity, drumming
on the square unmarked tomb of the forgotten king—and the crowd applauded,
rising to honor him as he reached for the hand of the princess. She rose,
radiant with love, as joyful as morning, all linen and gold,
flashing like fire in the light of the torches, her glory of victory.

    In the vine-hung house below, the fleece lay singing in the gleam
of candlelight, and the women gathered as seamstresses stared
in awe at the cloth they must cut and sew. To some it seemed
they might sooner cut plackets in the land itself, make seams in the sky,
for the cloth held forests whose golden leaves flickered, and extensive valleys,
cities and hamlets, overgrown thorps where peasants labored,
hunched under lightning, preparing their sheds for winter. Among
the seamstresses, the daughter of Aietes walked, cold marble,
explaining her wishes, not weeping now, all carriers of feeling
closed like doors. It seemed to the women gathered in the house
no lady on earth was more beautiful to see—her hair spun gold—
or more cruelly wronged. When the scissors approached it, the cloth cried out.

    That night there was music in the palace of Kreon—flourishes and tuckets
of trumpets, bright chatter of drums. In the rafters, ravens watched;

in the room's dark corners, fat-coiled snakes, heads shyly lowered,
drawn by prescience of death. Tall priests in white came in—
white clouds of incense, hymns in modes now fallen to disuse
mysterious and common as abandoned clothes. In the lower hall
a young bull white as snow, red-eyed, breathed heavily, waiting
in the flickering room. His nose was troubled by smells unfamiliar
and ominous, his heart by loneliness and fear. He watched
human beings hurrying around him, throwing high shadows on the walls.
One came toward him with a shape. He bellowed in terror. A blow,
sharp pain. A dark mist clouded his sight, and his heavy limbs fell.

Medeia said now, standing in the room with her Corinthian women,
no jewel more bright than the fire in her eyes, no waterfall,
crimsoned by sunrise but shining within, more lovely than her hair,
her low voice charged with her days and years (no instrument of wood
or wire or brass could touch that sound, as the singer proves,
shattering the dome of the orchestra, climbing on eagle's wings,
measured, alive to old pains, old joys, in a landscape of stone-
cold hills, bright flame of cloud), "I would not keep from you,
women of Corinth, more than I need of my purpose in this.
If my looks seem dark, full of violence, pray do not fear me or hate me,
remembering rumors. I am, whatever else, a woman,
like you, but a woman betrayed and crushed, fallen on disaster."

Silence in the palace. And then the sweet shrill-singing priest,
his soft left hand on Pyripta's, his right on Jason's. When he paused,
a flash of lightning shocked the room, and the room's high pillars
sang out like men, an unearthly choir. Deaf as a stone,
the priest held a golden ring to Pyripta, another to Jason.
The towering central door burst open, as if struck full force
by a battering ram. Slaves rushed to close it. A voice like the moan
of a mountain exploding said, "No, turn back!" But the panelled door
was closed. And now the floor spoke out, roaring, "No! Take care!"
There was not one man in the hall who failed to hear it. I saw them.
But Jason and the princess kissed; the kings applauded. His eyes
had Hera in them, and Athena. And old King Kreon smiled.

Medeia said: "Now all pleasure in life is exhausted.
I have no desire—no faintest tremor of desire—but for death.
The man I loved more than earth itself, his leastmost wish

the wind I ran in, his griefs my winters—my child, my husband—
has proved more worthless than the world by the darkest of philosophies.
Surely of all things living and feeling, women are the creatures
unhappiest. By a rich dowery, at best—at worst
by deeds like mine—we purchase our bodies' slavery, the right
to creep, stoop, cajole, flatter, run up and down,
labor in the night—and we say thank God for it, too—better that
than lose the tyrant. You know the saw: 'No wise man rides
a nag to war, or beds a misshapen old woman.' Like horses
worn out in service, they trade us off. Divorce is their plaything—
ruiner of women, whatever the woman may think in her hour
of escape. For there is no honor for women in divorce; for men
no shame. Who can fathom the subtleties of it? Yet true it is
that the woman divorced is presumed obscurely dangerous,
a failure in the mystic groves, unloved by the gods, while the man
is pitied as a victim, sought out and gently attended to
by soft-lipped blissoming maidens. Then this: by ancient custom,
the bride must abandon all things familiar for the strange new ways
of her husband's house, divine like a seer—since she never learned
these things at home—how best to deal with the animal she's trapped,
slow-witted, moody, his body deadly as a weapon. If in this
the wife is successful, her life is such joy that the gods themselves
must envy her: her dear lord lies like a sachet of myrrh
between her breasts. In poverty or wealth, her bed is all green,
and her husband, in her mind, is like a young stag. When he stands at the gate,
the lord of her heart is more noble than the towering cedars of the east.
But woeful the life of the woman whose husband is vexed by the yoke!
He flies to find solace elsewhere; as he pleases he comes and goes,
while his wife looks to him alone for comfort.

                                                                      "How different your life
and mine, good women of Corinth! You have friends, and you live at your ease
in the city of your fathers. But I, forlorn and homeless, despised
by my once-dear lord, a war-prize captured from a faraway land,
I have no mother or brother or kinsman to lend me harbor
in a clattering storm of troubles. I therefore beg of you
one favor: If I should find some means, some stratagem
to requite my lord for these cruel wrongs, never betray me!
Though a woman may be in all else fearful, in the hour when she's wronged
in wedlock there is no spirit on earth more murderous."

   So she spoke, staring at the outer storm—the darkening garden,

oaktrees and heavy old olive trees twisting, snapping like grass,
in the god-filled, blustering wind. The hemlocks by the wall stood hunched,
crushed under eagres of slashing water. When lightning flashed,
cinereal, the shattered rosebushes writhing on the stones in churning
spray formed a ghostly furnace, swirls of heatless fire.
No torches burned by the walls of the palace above, and the glow
leaking from within was gray and unsteady, like a dragon's eyes
by a new stone bier in a cluttered and cobwebbed vault, a stone-walled
crowd set deep in the earth. In the roar of the storm, no sound
came down to the room where Medeia stood with her seamstresses,
no faintest whisper of a trumpet, but like a vast sepulchre,
a palace in the ancient kingdom of Mu sunk deep in the Atlantic,
the great house loomed, the hour of its trouble come round. The women
gazed in sorrow at Medeia. "We'll not betray you," one said.
Some, needles flying on the golden cloth, were afraid of her,
the room full of shadows not easily explained. And some shed tears.

So through the night they sewed, minutely following the instructions
of Aietes' daughter. And sometimes among the eleven a twelfth
sat stitching, measuring, easing seams—a fat old farm-wife
with the eyes of a wolf—the goddess of the witchcraft, Hekate.

And so through the night in the palace of Kreon the revels ran on,
the slave in black, Ipnolebes, watching with eyes like smoke.

Thus swiftly, shamefully married—or so it seemed to many—
the lord of the Argonauts turned on his children and wife, his mind
supported by high-sounding reasons and noble intentions. Near dawn,
when the storm had grown steady, prepared to continue for days, it seemed,
the lord led his bride to the marriage bed—a cavernous room
scented like a funeral chamber with flowers and crammed wall to wall
with the gifts of Kreon, his vassals and allies. Strong guards, black slaves,
took posts by the door to protect the pair from impious eyes,
and kings melodious with wine sang the hymeneal.
                                                         Then I saw
on the lip of Corinth's harbor—high and dry on logs
and sheltered from the storm by a long dark barn—the proud-necked *Argo,*
blacker than midnight, on her bows a virl of gleaming silver
like the drapery carved on a casket's sides. It loomed enormous
in the barn's thick night, oars stacked and roped on the rowing benches,

sails rolled below—all waiting like a gun. White crests of waves,
plangent as the roaring storm, came climbing the steep rock slope
calling the ship out to sea. I could feel in my bones, that night,
that the *Argo* was alive, though sleeping—the whole black night alive,
like a forest in springtime watching for the first grim stirring of bears.

   Then gray dawn came—the Corinthian women sewed on in silence,
Medeia like marble, in her thirst for revenge hydroptic, as if bitten
by the dispas serpent whose fangs leave a thirst not all the water
in the world can quench. Her heavy old slave Agapetika prayed
at the shrine in her room, stubbornly, futilely urging her will
'gainst Fate's rock wall. The male slave fed the children, keeping them
far from their mother, his mind abstracted, his stiff, knobbed fingers
automatic, even his reproaches automatic, holding those quarrelsome
voices to a whisper—for something of the crepitating anger in the house
had reached their sleep, had filled them with suspicions and obscure fears,
so that now, whatever the old man's labors, there were sharp cries of "Stop!"
and "Hand it back to me!" If Medeia heard them, she revealed no sign.

   In the palace, though he'd hardly slept, the Argonaut opened his eyes,
suddenly remembering, and raised up in his bed, leaning on an elbow,
to gaze through arches eagerly, as he'd gazed in his youth
to the north and west on some nameless island, hoping for a break
in the stretch of bad weather that pinned him to land, the black ship hawsered,
dragged half its length up on shore for protection from the breakers' blows.
Rain was still falling, the mountains in the distance as gray as the sea,
the sky like a corpse, bloodless, praeternaturally hushed. He must wait
for the king to rise, wait for old Kreon in his own good time
to relinquish the sceptre. There were things to be done—mad Idas and his men
wasting in the dungeon—a dangerous mistake indeed, he knew,
the fierce brother watching from a hundred miles off, with motionless eyes.

   Above, Kreon was awake, old man who never slept.
He stood at the balusters, peering intently at the city as his slaves
powdered and patted him, dressed him in the royal attire he'd wear
this morning for the last time. They put on his corselet of bronze,
his glittering helmet, his footguards and shin-greaves, finally his gauntlets,
and over his bronze-armed shoulders they draped his purple cloak,
and they placed in his hand his jewel-studded sceptre. Then, armed
as well as a man can be against powers from underground,

the king descended to the hall where his counsellors and officers waited,
and tall guards stiffly at attention, hands on sword-hilts. He eyed
his retinue, sullenly brooding, and gave them a nod. Then, chaired
by slaves, canopied from rain, he went down to the dark house of Jason.

She came to meet him at the gate. The old man feared to go nearer,
finding her dressed all in black, her eyes too quiet. The rain
drenched her in a moment; she seemed to be wholly unaware of it.
He raised his sceptre, a protection from Almighty Zeus against charms
and spells.
                In the presence of nobles, in the lead-gray rain, he said:
"Woman whose eyes scowl forth thy dangerous rage against Jason—
daughter of mad King Aietes—I bid thee go hence from this land,
exiled forever, and thy two sons with thee. Neither find excuses
for tarrying longer. I've come here in person to see that the sentence
is fulfilled, and I'll not turn homeward again till I see thee cast forth
from the outer limits of my kingdom."
                                        So he spoke, and Medeia stared
        through him,
her spirit staggering, but her body like a rock. "Now my destruction
is complete," she whispered. "My enemies all bear down on me
full sail, and no safe landing-place from ruin." But at once,
steeling herself, only the tips of her fingers touching
the vine-thick gatepost of stone for steadiness, Medeia asked:
"For what crime do you banish me, Kreon?"
                                            "I fear you," he said.
"I needn't mince words. I fear you may do to my child and throne
some mischief too terrible for cure. I have reason enough for that dread.
You are subtle, deep-versed in evil lore. Losing the love
of your husband, you are much aggrieved. Moreover, it's said you threaten
not only vengeance on your husband but also on his bride and on me.
It's surely my duty to guard against all such strokes. Far better
to earn full measure of your hatred at once than relent now
and repent it hereafter." Though his words were stern and his lower teeth
laid bare, I could see no hatred in him. His fear of the woman
was plain to see, yet he seemed more harried than wrathful.
                                                        She said:
"Not for the first time, Kreon, has gossipping opinion wronged me
and brought me shame and agony. Woe to the man who teaches
arts more subtle than those of the herd! Bring to the ignorant

new learning and they judge you not learned but a dangerous trouble-maker;
and both to those untaught and to those who pretend to learning,
mouthing obfuscating phrases with no more ground in them
than tumbling Chaos, the truly learn'd seem an insult and threat.
So my life proves. For since I have knowledge, some find me odious,
some too stickling and, indeed, a wild fool. As for you, you shrink
for fear of powers you imagine in me, or trust out of rumor,
and punish me solely on the chance that I might do injury."
She stretched her arms out, ten feet away. Beaten down by rain,
a woman who seemed no more deadly than a child, she cried out, imploring,
"Kreon, look at me! Am I such a woman as to seek out quarrels
with princes merely from impishness? Where have you wronged me?
You have merely given your daughter to the man you chose. No, Kreon,
it's my husband I hate. All Corinth agrees you've done wisely in this.
How can I grudge you your happiness? Then prosper, my lord!
But grant me continued sanctuary. Wronged though I am,
I'll keep my silence, and yield to Jason's will, since I must."

   He looked at her, pitying but still afraid. And at last he answered,
"You speak mild words. Yet rightly or wrongly, I fear even now
that your heart in secret may be plotting some wickedness. Now less than ever
do I trust you, Medeia. A cunning woman betrayed into wrath
is more easily watched than one who's silent. Be gone at once.
Speak no more speeches. My sentence stands. Not all your craft
can save you from exile. I know you firm-minded and my enemy."

   Medeia moved closer, pleading in the steadily drumming rain,
stretching her arms toward Kreon. "By your new-wedded child," she said . . .
"You're wasting words. I cannot be persuaded."

                              "You spurn me, Kreon?"
"I feel no more love, let us say, than *you* feel for *my* family."
"O Kolchis, abandoned homeland, how I do long for you now!"
"There's nothing more dear, God knows, unless it's one's child, perhaps."
"Gods, what a murderous curse on all mankind is love!"
"Curse or blessing, it depends."

                         "O Zeus, let him never escape me!"
"Go, woman—or must whips drive you? Spare me that shame!"
"I need no whipping, Kreon. You've raised up welts enough."
"Then go, go—or I'll bid my menials do what they must."
"I implore you—"

               "You force me to violence, then?"

                                    "I will go, Kreon.

It was not for reprieve I cried out. Grant me just this: Let me stay
for one more day in Corinth, to think out where we may flee
and how I may care for my sons, since their father no longer sees fit
to provide for them. Pity them, Kreon! You too are a father."
    The old man trembled, afraid of her yet; but he feared far more
the powers he'd struggled against all his life, laboring to fathom,
straining in bafflement to appease. He said: "My nature is not
a tyrant's, Medeia." He pursed his lips, picking at his chin
with trembling fingers. "Many a plan I've ruined by relenting,
and some I've ruined by relenting too late. The gods riddle us,
tease us with theories and lure us with hopes into dragons' mouths.
With Oidipus once, gravely insulted, threatened with death
on a mad false charge, I held in my wrath when by blind striking out—
so the sequel proved—I'd have saved both the city and a dearly loved sister.
Yet with Oidipus' daughter I proved too stern, refused all pause
or compromise, and there, too, horror was the issue. I will act
by Jason's dictum, trusting to instinct and hoping for the best,
expecting nothing. Though I see it may well be folly, I grant
this one day's stay. But beware, woman! If sunrise tomorrow
finds you still in my kingdom, you or your sons, you will die.
What I've said I'll do; have no doubt of it."
                                        So saying, he departed,
ascending the hill through fire and rain. She returned
to her house, and the women of Corinth at the door made way for her.
    Indoors, the slave Agapetika waited, gray, weighed down
by grief. She said, "No hope for us," then, weeping, could say
no more. Medeia touched her, her eyes remote. She said,
grown strangely calm again, "Do not think the last word
has been said—not yet! Troubles are in store for the newlyweds,
and troubles for the wily old marriage-broker. Do you think I'd grovel
in the rain to that foolish old man if not for some desperate purpose?
Never have I spoken to Kreon before or touched his hand. But now
        in his arrogance
he grants me time to destroy him and all he loves. And that
I will—and all I have loved myself." Her lips went white.
"Never mind," she whispered to herself. "Never mind."
                                        "Medeia, child,"
the old woman moaned, eyes wide.
                            The daughter of Aietes turned,
and struck like lightning: "Go from me! Leave this house! Go at once!

322

Live in fields, old ditches! Never let me see you!'' The Corinthian women
stared, astounded, and no one spoke. The slave backed away,
unsteady and shaking, retreating from the room, and in her own room fell
like a plank breaking, to groan on her bed. No one dared comfort her.

Medeia said, as if drained of emotion—the tears on her cheeks
independent of her mind and heart, mechanical as stars turning—
"Go to her, one of you. Tell her I repent. My war is not
with women, sad fellow-sufferers.'' She closed her eyes.
"Do not think I don't love that old woman. I have dealt with her
more gently than I can with those I love far more.'' And then,
suddenly whispering in panic and squeezing her blue-white hands:
"Suppose them slain. What city will receive me? what friend give refuge?
None. So I still must wait, for a time, conjure some tower
of defense. That too I can manage, yes. By the goddess Hekate,
first and last friend welcome to my hearth, not one will escape me.
Your new tie, husband—my soul's grim fire, familiar heartache—
you'll find more bitter than the last. You've proved your cruelty.
Prepare for mine! You'll e'er long find your sweet bedfellow
a lady Hades himself might prove reluctant to fold
in his arms. So I pay you for mocking derision of a princess born
of the mightiest king on earth, a child of the sun-god's race!''

Then she left them, fleeing to her room to put on dry clothes,
preparing in outer appearance for a secret and deadly role.
The sewing women took up the golden cloth once more,
their hearts quaking, too sick with sorrow and fear to speak.
Their needles raced, in the corner Hekate in a long black shawl,
sly-eyed and heavy, whiskered like a peasant,
and each whipstitch she sewed would prove a shackle for the bride
who smiled now, gazing in her mirror, in Kreon's palace. The shadow
of Hekate, rocking on the wall, became a second ghost,
the black, horned god himself in the service of Medeia.

When Jason
learned, by questions to the slave Ipnolebes, what Kreon had done,
he was filled with alarm—no less by the spiteful gloating the slave
could scarcely hide than by knowledge of his wife. But he bided his time,
watching the fiery rain, apprehensive, knowing well enough
that the weather bore some message in it. He knew beyond doubt
he was caught up now in a race against time. He could hardly guess
in which direction the danger lay, couldn't even be sure
how grave it was; but he knew he must be in command when she struck—

or best, get control before she struck—must stand in position
to counter her, issue commands to protect them all.
Yet he could not press; he dared not even suggest that the sceptre be
        granted to him
for fear that even now the king might repent
and everything be lost. He remained with Pyripta, smiling like a bridegroom,
stroking her cheeks and throat, lightly kissing her eyelids, feigning
the adoration he must wait for a calmer time to feel.
The princess talked, pouring her pleasure in her new husband's ear—
talked as she never had talked before, and sometimes broke off
to laugh at her chatter, yet believed his assurance and chattered still more.
She had not known how much she loved him. With a frightened look
she asked of his life with Medeia. He smiled and gently kissed her,
silencing her. "You demand too much," he said lightly, his mind
racing down other, far darker lanes. "We have sons," he said.
"You must understand . . ." But catching the anger and jealousy flashing
in her glance, he swiftly and easily guided her elsewhere. I watched,
protected by a mist from their seeing me, and my heart was divided,
loyal to the woman on the hill below, yet to Jason too,
for he meant no harm, only good for them all, though all he was doing
was false and tragically harmful. Again and again I felt
on the verge of speaking to warn him, but each time fear kept me silent.
The new solidity the gods had given was no great advantage,
I knew to my sorrow. It seemed unlikely that empty shadows
could harm me, or dreams turn real. Yet how could I doubt those bruises,
that stabbing pain in my poor right hand, or my spectacles' ruin?
I constructed theories. Haven't there been cases, I said to myself,
when men fell down stairs while sleep-walking, and with broken backs
dreamed on, explaining the pain by imagined giants? And might
some action of mine inside this dream not trigger repercussions
wherever it is that I really am? So I labored, guessing,
and what was true I had no way of knowing, the rules of the vision
kept hidden from me, however I strained to grasp them, sweating,
and I kept my cowardly silence despite all nobler urges,
huddling in protective mist.

                    At noon, at the midday feast,
his waiting ended. In the presence of kings, high priests in attendance,
the goddesses Hera and Athena behind him (I alone saw them—

their look triumphant and wary at once, Aphrodite glaring,
furious at Jason for the love he feigned, scornful of her power),
Kreon—with an endless rambling speech—allusions to Oidipus,
Jokasta, Antigone—transferred his sceptre and power to Jason.
Great lords of Corinth unfastened the cloak from the old king's shoulders
and draped it on Aison's son, its wide flow covering the cape
Argus had made at Lemnos. Attended by lords, he took
the central chair on the dais. His kingship was ratified by vows
to Zeus and Hera and the chief gods of the pantheon,
such vows as no man on earth would break. And high in the rain
some saw Zeus's eagle, they thought, though others thought not.
The assembled kings, his equals, came to him, confirming alliances
promised to Kreon in the past, and one by one they bowed to him,
taking his hands, and bowed to Pyripta beside him, his queen.
Again there were drums and trumpets, and slaves poured wine.

                                                    And then
a thing so strange took place that no one felt certain, afterward,
whether it had happened or not. All in gold, the Asian, Koprophoros
stood before Jason, solemn. He bowed to the ground in the fashion
of the Orient, then bowed to Pyripta in the same manner.
When he spoke, his voice was as deep and soft as the slow thundering
of far-off rainclouds, a voice so changed I was filled with alarm.
"So the game is ended at last, good prince," he said, and smiled.
"All you were robbed of in life, you have now back in hand, though opposed
by more than you dreamed." He turned to the kings around him. "Let men
report it to the word's last age that once, in a place called Akhaia,
a man, by cunning and tenacity, out-fought the gods
of the Underworld for a city and princess, though the gods of Death
were granted their prey in advance by fate. Yet lose they did,
for the moment, playing too lightly—as the mighty will do sometimes.
But fate, after all, is inexorable, whatever man's power.
The dagger blade has already cut deep in the shimmering veil;
the dream is nearly done. Fear now no god, Jason.
Fear things human, and infinitely more terrible.
He smiled his scarcely perceptible smile. "If my words seem strange,
ponder them after I'm gone. And so, good-day." With that
he tapped the stone floor lightly with his foot. In a flash, where he'd stood
there loomed an enormous serpent whose wedge-shaped head struck the roof
and whose coils were thicker than an ancient oak—a female serpent
obscenely bloated with eggs; and I thought of Harmonia,

noblest of queens, transformed by the Master of Life and Death
to Queen of the Dead. She vanished.

                       While the hall still stared, dumbfounded,
Paidoboron bowed to the throne. His words were stern and brief:
"Now all escape is sealed." And immediately he, too, vanished,
and there in his place stood a dragon who filled all the palace with fire,
and his scales were like plates of steel. Each nail on his saurian claws
was longer than a man, and his two bright fangs were massive stalactites,
children of the world's first cave. Then the dragon too was gone.
    Kreon, pale as a sea-ghost, clutched at his chest, shaking,
and even Jason was trembling. The nobles around him swore
it was Hades himself he'd contended with, or his surrogate, Kadmos,
man-god ruler of the dead. They swore that Death and his wife
had come for their sport and had made long-winded mockery
of Kreon's fears and Jason's desires and the hopes of the sea-kings,
the whole fierce struggle a sardonic joke. The princess suddenly
cried out, waking from a vision. But at once, though his throat was working
and dark blood rushing to his face, the son of Aison seized
his new bride's hand and calmed her. When his tongue would work, he said,
"Don't be afraid! I swear all this terror will prove some trick
of Medeia's. If not, you've heard what the two ghosts say: The gods
have retired from the conflict. It's now no more than mere human craft
we must guard against. —Yet I'm certain it's only as I said at first,
some heartless illusion by Medeia, designed to terrify us."
At once they believed him, for surely the gods play no tricks so base,
not even the gods of the Underworld. So they told themselves,
and so, little by little, their calm was restored. His thick fear
hidden in the deepest, darkest of abditoriums,
Jason spoke lightly, driving out shadows as, long ago,
he'd lightened the hearts of the Argonauts when hope seemed madness.
He praised King Kreon's long wise rule and swore to uphold
his principles, and praised his visitors and vassals. Of those things
nearest his heart—Idas in the dungeon, his own wife and children
banished—he spoke not a syllable, biding his time. His eyes
moved, as he spoke, from rafter to rafter through Kreon's hall,
secretly watching omens, a silent invasion: ravens.

23

Dressed exactly as he always dressed, not in regal array
but hooded and wrapped against rain—for it still fell fierce and fiery—
Jason went down, alone, to the vine-hung house where Medeia
and the Corinthian women sewed. He rang the great brass ring
and waited, restless but patient. At last the male slave came
and, seeing his master, said he would bring out Medeia. He returned
to the house, and after a time the princess of Aia came out.
She stood in the shelter of the rainwashed eaves, and he called to her
and asked her to unlock the high, wide gate. Medeia said only,
"Speak from there." He seized the bars of the small window
in the gate and called, "You prove once more what I should have remembered:
a stubborn disposition's incurable. A home here in Corinth
you might have yet if only you'd endure old Kreon's will
with at least some show of meekness. But no, you must hurl wild words.
So you're banished—thrown out of Corinth as a dangerous madwoman.
And rightly, no doubt. Not that I too much care, for myself.
Rail all you please at vilest Jason. Often as the old
man's fear of you rose, I struggled to check it. I would have had
you stay. But still in your obstinate folly you must curse and revile
the royal house; so it's banishment for you—and lucky no worse.
But despite all that, more faithful than you think, I've prevailed so far
as to see that you'll not lack gold or anything else in exile.
Hardships enough you'll suffer with your sons. So for all your hatred,
take what I give you, Medeia."
                              When first he began to speak
she listened with anger locked in, as if, despite her fury,
she intended to answer with restraint; but as Jason continued, speaking
of Kreon as king (I realized now with a shock that she knew

all that happened in the palace, informed by black-winged spies)
her fury broke from its prison. She screamed, "O vile, vile, vilest!
Rail I may well! Do *you* come to *me—to me, Jason?*
This is no mere self-assurance, no manly hardihood.
It's shamelessness! And yet I'm glad you've come, husband.
I do have one joy left, and that's berating you.
As all Akhaia knows, I saved your life. I helped you
tame those fiery bulls and sow that dangerous tilth.
The snake wreathed coil on coil around that cursèd fleece
I put to sleep for you. I fled my father and home,
arranged my brother's death and later King Pelias' death,
at his own children's hands. Such deeds I've done for you,
and yet you trade me away like a worn-out cow for a heifer,
though I bore you sons. If you'd still been childless, I might perhaps
have pardoned your wish for a second wife. But now farewell
all faith—for this you know in your soul: You swore me oaths.

   "Come, let me ask you questions as I would a friend. Where should
I turn? To my father's house? To Aia? You know well enough
how they love me there—kinsmen I betrayed for you. Shall I go
to the Peliad sisters? Perhaps we can all have a good laugh now
at that monstrous birthday party. You see how it is: by those
who loved me at home I am now hated; and those who least
deserved my wrath, I have turned to foes—for you."

                                                He listened,
hands on the gatebars, his head bent. When her rantings ceased,
he said—not troubling to shout against the rain—"Again and again
you've preached all that, and again and again I've allowed it to pass,
though surely it's true that I need thank no one but the goddess of love
for the services you mention. But let that be; I find
no fault with your devotion. And as for the marriage you hate,
I say again what I've said before: with calm dispassion
I made that choice, and partly for you and my sons. No, hear me!
Not out of loathing for your bed, Medeia (the thought that galls you)
and not through lust for a new bride or for numerous offspring—
with the sons you've borne me I'm well content—but for this alone
I've made my choice: to win for my family, my sons and you,
such safety and comfort as only a king can be sure of. My plan
is wise enough; you'd admit it if it weren't for your jealousy.

   "But why do I waste my words on you? When nothing mars
your love, you imagine you're queen of the planet. But if some slight shadow

clouds your happiness, the best and fairest of lots seems hateful,
and the finest of houses a shanty in a field of thorntrees."

At this
Medeia grew angrier still, tied hand and foot by arguments,
as usual, and straining against the injustice like a penned-
up bull. I could have told her the futility of trying to fight
by Jason's rules; but they looked—both of them—so dangerous,
and the surrounding storm was so violent, such a fiery menace,
I kept to my safe hiding place in the dark, thick vines.
She said: "If you were not vile, as I've claimed—if all these things
you say to me weren't shameless lies—you'd have asked straight out for consent
to your plan, not slyly deceived me."

He laughed. "No doubt
you'd have helped me nobly, since even now your jealousy rages
like a forest fire."

"It was not *that* that stopped you. I am
a foreigner, and middle-aged. I cease to serve
your pride."

His square fists tightened on the bars, and I could hardly blame
his anger at the woman's unreasonableness. Though his jaw-muscles twitched,
he still spoke gently: "Medeia, lady—"

At the word, her face
went white, her emotion like crackling fire. "Go!" she screamed.
"Run, drunken lover! You linger too long from your new bride's chamber.
Go and be happy! May your marriage soon prove a pleasure you'd fain
renounce." Then, sobbing, she fled into the house. He turned heavily
and made his way back up the worn stone steps to the palace.

Not long
did she weep in her fury at Jason. In her room, the oak door closed
on the sewing women, she gathered from secret places her herbs
and drugs, and above all the coriander for conjuring.
Taking a ring she had lately received from a wealthy king
named Aigeus, father of Theseus—a man who'd travelled
from a distant land for theurgic cure of his sterility—
she placed the ring on a silver dish and murmured his name.
Soon the bejewelled ring began to move. When it came
by its own energy to the rim of the dish, the gate-ring clanged,
and Medeia called to have Aigeus shown in. He arrived with a look
befuddled and amused, unable to think for the life of him
what had brought him here in such weather. Soon she had told him all

her tragedy, and old King Aigeus, kindest of men, was promising
sanctuary in his own far-distant land. He said,
pulling at his beard with his wrinkled hands, "But come, King Kreon
banishes you, and Jason allows it? Most base! Most base!"
   "His voice protests," she said, "yet he thinks it best to endure it."
   "Shameful!" King Aigeus said, and again offered sanctuary.
   "Perhaps if you'd swear a solemn oath to me—" she began.
   "You mistrust me, child? Tell me what fear still troubles you."
   She touched his two hands. "I trust you, but the house of Pelias hates me,
and Kreon as well. Bound by oaths, you could never yield me
if ever they came to drag me from you. Bound by mere words,
not solemn oaths, you'd have no defense and would yield to their summons
perforce. They are powerful kings, my lord."
                                          He stared above
her head, mumbling: "What need for such far-sighted prudence here?"
But at once he said, "I'll do as you wish, Medeia. Name
your gods."
                    She said: "Swear by the earth below, and the sun,
my grandfather, and the whole vast race of the deathless gods . . ."
   "To perform what?—or resist what?"
                                          "Never yourself
to expel me from your land or willingly yield me to enemies
so long as you still bear life."
                          He said: "By the firm earth,
by the sun's light, and by all the gods, I swear all this,
and if I fail to abide by my oath, may the gods send down on me
the doom reserved for sacrilege."
                          Medeia nodded,
clasping his hand. "Go thy way with my blessing," she said,
"I'm fully content." Aigeus descended to the street, his heart
grieved for Aietes' daughter, and full of uneasiness.

   Down by the water in the sail-tent slum there were angry stirrings,
huge men moving from fire to fire, hunkering for warmth
in the roaring storm, and grimly exchanging the latest news.
There lay a new ship there, I saw—a long, gray warship.
I kept my distance, my right hand darkly swollen and throbbing
from our last encounter. Gradually, in their restless shifting
I began to see patterns, some plan taking shape. A few at a time,
from various parts of the wide, tented harbor, the sailors began

to move through the rain into Kreon's city. They paused at the doors
of shops, smiling in from beneath drenched hoods. They called out to children,
gave greeting to snarling curs at the mouths of alleys, and so
by imperceptible stages surrounded the palace, toward nightfall,
taking positions, like lengthening shadows, then vanishing.

In the vine-hung house, the work of the women was finished now—
a delicate robe and wreath of gold, the most splendid attire
that was ever seen on earth. Medeia's fingers traced
the invisible seams; her eyes drank in the boundless landscape
figured in the cloth by Argus' art. She said: "Now, women,
my revenge is near at hand. I'll tell you the whole of my purpose,
though not much pleasure will you take in what I tell. I will go
to Jason tonight with his precious sons, and when he receives us,
I'll speak soft words, claiming I've come to understand, myself,
that his plan is wise and just. Then gently, with passionate tears,
I'll entreat that my sons may remain in Corinth, though I may not,
and beg that he grant them permission to carry my gifts to the princess
to soften her heart and her father's. If the lady accepts these presents—
this gown and wreath of gold—and if she dresses in them,
she'll die horribly, and all who touch her, for with fell poisons
the cloth will be anointed. And now the darkest part.
If Jason, in a futile attempt to save his dying princess,
touches the girl and dies himself, my revenge is ended,
even in my heart. I'll carry him away in a dragon chariot
conjured out of ashes, and bury his remains in a tumulus befitting
a prince so noble; and I'll weep and lament as I would if he'd died
for me, and I'll honor his memory. But if Jason lives,
having watched his princess die, having taken no risk for her,
held back by prudence—Jason to the last the invincible sea-fox—
thus will I bring down ruin upon him: I'll murder his sons."
The Corinthian women all cried out at once, but Medeia said quickly:
"Nothing can save them. I've sworn with solemn oaths to do all
I've said. I will wreck the house of Jason to the last beam,
then flee the ground of my dear children's blood. So be it.
Flee and live on for what? you may ask. No home, no country,
no refuge from grief . . . Nevertheless, live on I will,
stripped of illusions, apparent joys, false, foolish hopes,
my teeth bared to the blackness on every side, like poor
mad Idas, who knew from the beginning. Feeble and poor of spirit

let no one think me, nor indolent, taking the world as it comes.
Say that Medeia was of use to friends and to enemies dangerous,
sure as the seasons, remorseless as nipping, back-cracking cold."
   Timidly then one woman spoke: "Medeia, lady,
all of us here love justice, surely, and would willingly help you,
betrayed as you are. But this! All the laws of gods and men—"
   "I forgive your words of censure. You're not as wronged as I am."
   "And can you find it in your heart to kill your children, Medeia?"
   "I can find no other way to bring my husband down."
   "Making yourself, in the same stroke, the unhappiest of wives!"
   "Yes. But the vow is sworn. All future words are waste."

   And so, attended by her two old slaves, her hands closed firmly
on her children's hands, Medeia walked that night through the violent storm
          to the palace
of Kreon—now of Jason. They waited
while guards went in for instructions. Old Kreon shook with fright,
his small eyes widened, convinced that his house must be filled to the beams
with devils, with Medeia so near. But Jason persuaded him at last
to allow the party entrance—for, better to know her mood,
attend to her threats, if she made any, than seek to guard
'gainst possibilities as ubiquarian as air. The guards
went out; old Kreon and his daughter left the hall, retiring
for safety, at Jason's request, to their separate chambers.
                                        And now
the carved door opened again, and there Medeia stood,
her two young sons beside her, clinging in fright to her hands.
She shook back her hood without touching it—a gesture graceful
and accidentally defiant. Her hair came blazing into view,
bright as the sun, and the kings were hushed by awe. She went
to Jason, leading his children, and in front of his chair she kneeled
like a suppliant. The two old slaves stood near.
                                        She said:
"Jason, I entreat you, forgive those words I spoke in anger.
You must bear with me in my passionate moods, for was there not
much love between us once? I've been reasoning through your claims,
my brain less feverish now, less egomaniac—
less like my poor mad father's—and I see that your plan is right.
I chide myself: Why this madness, Medeia? Why this anger
at the land's rulers, and the lord who acts for your own good

and the children's? Why this sorrow? Is heaven not once again
proved kind? Have you forgotten, woman, that the four of you
are friendless exiles bound to fight in whatever way
you can for survival? So, by stages, I've come to myself
and have seen how dangerously foolish I was. So now I've come
to grant my approval of all you've done, and to beg your forgiveness.
It was I myself who was wrong; you were not. I should have shared
in your plans and lent you aid; I should have countenanced
the match and ministered joyfully to your bride. But we are
as we are—I will not say evil, but—women. You were wise, as always,
refusing to vie with me, matching folly against folly. My spirit
is saner now. I yield to you and confess, I was wrong."
Then, to the children: "Sons, speak to your father. Be reconciled.
Let this terrible battle between dear friends be ended."
Weeping, she raised their hands to Jason's knees, and Jason
took them, clasping them fondly, his eyes full of tears. No wonder
if his heart refused, that instant, to believe it treachery.

He said:

"Lady, most noble of all women living, I praise you now
beyond all praise in the past. And I gladly excuse your anger.
Small wonder if a woman's wrath be kindled when her husband turns
to another wife. But now your mood's more sane, and you
perceive, though late, where our welfare lies. And you, my sons,
away with these tears! For I dare to hope—the gods willing—
you'll be rich and powerful yet in Corinth. Grow strong! Leave all
the rest in your father's hands. May I live to see you reach
the prime of youthful vigor, envy of my enemies!"
He paused, studying Medeia. "Why these fresh tears?" he said.
"Why this turning away of your face?"

"It's nothing," she said.
"My heart was brooding on the children."

"But why in such terrible sorrow?"
"I bore them. And when you prayed just now that they reach their prime,
a sad foreboding came over me, a fear of the future."
He looked at her, his face thoughtful and sorrowful at once.
"Take heart, Medeia," he said. "They shall not lack my protection."
She nodded. "I will, husband, and will not mistrust your words.
—But of that which I came here to say I've said only a part, my lord.
Let me say now the rest: Since it's Kreon's will that I
be banished—and I grant that's best, vexatious to Kreon's house

and to you—I will go into exile. But as for our two dear sons,
I beg you, let Kreon not banish them, nor banish them yourself,
since you've won more power in this hall than you like to admit.
          Let them live
in Corinth, reared in the palace, so that no one may doubt the right
you've promised them."
                    "I doubt I have power sufficient to move him
so far, Medeia," he said, "though I may have such power in theory.
And yet I'll try."
                "Let your bride entreat him, for surely then—"
  "I will, yes." He thought about it for a moment, frowning.
"I may persuade her."
                    "You will, if the woman's like other women.
And I'll help you, Jason. I'll send our children with gifts for her,
a golden gown and wreath so beautiful no living mortal
has seen their match." She turned to the slave Agapetika
and took those gifts from the old woman's hands. The old woman's eyes
threw a wild appeal to Jason, but she could not speak, her tongue
turned stone by Medeia's spell. Medeia said, "She'll be blessed
a thousandfold, winning you, most splendid of heroes, for her spouse
and dowered with treasures from Helios." And then, to her sons:
"Children, take these gifts in your hands and carry them to her
as your father directs. They're gifts no woman could refuse."
                                              But Jason
held back in fear, having recognized the cloth. He said,
casting about for some stratagem by which he might be
more sure of her, "No, wait, Medeia! Why cast away
this finest of treasures?—for surely that cloth is the fleece from Aia.
The princess has robes and gold enough. Keep it for yourself,
a sure protection from hardship and suffering in exile. If my bride
esteems me at all, she'll prize my wish beyond any mere treasure."
  Medeia said, "My lord, I have not chosen lightly
these gifts I bring." Sadly, solemnly, she met his eyes.
"How is a woman to prove to the man she's given her life
that, following his wish, she renounces all earthly claim to him?
This cloth was, to me, chief proof and symbol of our steadfast love.
Giving it away—that which I prize beyond all other wealth—
I give you away, my husband, and all our past together,
for our sons. To me, it's a gift no less than Khalkiope gave
for hers. Do not shame me, or reduce me to insignificance,

by refusing this queenly gesture. I'm left with no other I can make.
You know me, Jason. Have mercy on my pride. I'd give my life,
not merely gold, to save my sons from banishment."

Then Jason believed her, and, placing the golden gown and wreath
in his two sons' hands, he said, "Wait here, and we'll test the power
of your gifts at once," and he rose to lead them to Pyripta's room.
Medeia said, "Children, speak bravely when you meet with your father's new bride,
my mistress now, and beg her to save you from banishment.
And don't forget: with her own hands she must receive our presents.
Hurry now, and the gods be with you! Return to me soon
with the news I'm eager to hear."

Then the children left with Jason,
the old male slave attending. The sea-kings watched them leave,
no man daring a whisper. In time they returned again,
and Jason said, "You've done well, Medeia. Your sons are spared.
The royal bride has received your gifts with gracious hands.
Henceforth I hope for peace between our family's branches."
He studied her, baffled despite all his years of knowledge of her,
his mind clouded by the thought that the fleece was still with him, his curse.
"Why so distraught?"

"A pain, my lord."

"Such moans seem strange
when I bring you joyful news."

She covered her eyes, groaning.
He said, now deeply troubled, "Can there be in what you've done
some harm still undetected?"

"I was thinking of the past," she said.
"I loved you, Jason. I would have thought even a man might grieve.
But now we'll go. All I came for is done." With her slaves and children
she moved like one in a nightmare toward the door. With his eyes
he followed them. After they left, he turned slowly,
his heart racing, back toward Pyripta's room. He knew
he'd missed something, but for all his cunning, he couldn't guess what,
or whether the things were already accomplished or just now beginning.
His heart was filled with fear, suddenly, for Medeia's life,
as her boundless rage turned inward. He could feel now all around him
a rush, as if Time had grown sensible, and volcanic.

Below,
far ahead of the old, tortuously moving slaves,
Medeia hurried with the children, bending her head against the rain,

rushing downward through lightning, her two sons crying in alarm
and pain at the speed with which she dragged them homeward. Medeia
wailed aloud, her tears mingling with the hurrying rain,
her voice feeble in the ricochetting boom of thunder:
"No! How can I? Farewell then all insane resolves!
I'll take them away with me, far from this fat, corrupting land.
What use can it be—hurting my sons to give Jason grief,
myself reaping ten times over the woe I inflict? I won't!
That too has a kind of victory in it: he wrecks my life,
tears it to shreds, and with furious calm I allow him his triumph,
trusting in the gods' justice hereafter, the fields where the meek
are kings and queens, and the powerful on earth are like whipped dogs.
There's *moral* victory!" But she threw back her hair with a violent head shake
and clenched her teeth. "—So any craven slave will tell you,
smiling at his coward's wounds, whimpering to the gods. Shall I make
my hand so limp, my waste so trivial? —But no, no, no!
Repent, mad child of Aietes! Though a thousand curses rise
like stones turned judges in the wilderness, all justifying
in one loud cry your scheme, yet this alone is true:
If you strike for pride, for just and absolute revenge, the stroke
is wasted; for who will call it pride or justice, from you?
'Her father was mad in the selfsame way and to the same degree,'
they'll say, and they'll wrinkle their broad Akhaian brows and wipe
cool tears away. Dear gods! Even as an instrument of death
they've made me nothing, meaningless! And yet though Jason
robs me even of human free will—takes from me even
my soul's conviction of freedom—I still can give pain. Even now,
crowned by the wreath, swathed in her golden robe, his bride
is perishing. I see it in my heart. You've served me well, good sons.
One more journey I must send you on, now that we're home.
Run in! Go quickly! I'll follow you soon." She opened the gate
and clung to it, weeping. The boys went timidly in toward light.
But for all her wailing, her mind was not for an instant deflected
from what she was seeing. For her witch-heart saw it all, from the beginning:
    Before she was aware that his sons were with him, the princess turned
with an eager welcoming glance toward Jason. But then, drawing
her veil before her eyes, she turned her white cheek away,
loath to have them come near. The children paused, frightened,
but Jason said quickly to the princess, "Do not be hostile to friends.
Forget your anger and turn your face toward me again.

Accept as loved ones all whom your husband holds dear; and accept
their gifts—worthy of a goddess—look! Then plead with your father
that he soften toward these children and excuse them—for my sake, Pyripta."
The princess, seeing that golden gown, could resist no longer
but yielded to his will, and gladly. And scarcely had Jason left
with his children and their old attendant, than the princess put on the new dress
and circled her hair with the golden wreath. In her shining mirror
she ranged her locks, smiling back at the lifeless image,
then rose from her seat and around the room went stepping, half-dancing—
her blue-white feet treading delicately—Pyripta exulting,
casting her eyes down many a time at her pointed foot.

But now suddenly the princess turned pale, and reeling back
with limbs a-tremble, she sank down quickly to a cushioned seat—
an instant more and she'd have tottered to the ground. An old black handmaid,
thinking it perhaps some frenzy sent by Pan, cried out
in prayer. Then, lo, through the bride's bright lips
she saw white foam-flakes issue—saw
her eyeballs roll out of sight, no blood
in her face. Then the slave sent out a shriek far different from the first.
At once, one slave went flying upstairs to Kreon's chamber,
another to Jason to tell him the news. The whole vast house
echoed with footsteps, hurrying to and fro. Before
a swift walker with long, sure strides could have paced a furlong
she opened her blue eyes wide from her speechless agony
and groaned. From the golden chaplet wreathing Pyripta's head
a stream of ravening fire came flying like water down a cliff,
and below, the gown was eating the poor girl's fair white flesh.
She fled crazily this way and that, aflame all over,
shrieking and tossing her hair to be rid of the wreath, but the gold
clung firmly fixed. As she tossed her locks, the fire burned brighter,
and soon all the palace was heavy with the smell of her burning hair
and flesh. She sank to the ground, her throat too swollen for screams,
a dark, foul shape that even her father might scarcely know.
Her features melted; from her head ran blood in a stream, all melled
with fire. From her bones flesh dripped like the gum of a pine—a sight
to silence even the eternally whispering slaves. Lord Jason
stared, rooted to the ground where he stood—nor would anyone else
go near that body. But wretched Kreon, with a wild bawl
threw himself over the corpse, closing his arms around it
and kissing it, howling his sorrow to the gods. "Now life's stripped bare,"

he sobbed. "O, O that I too might die!—these many years
ripe for the tomb, and thou barely ripe for womanhood!"
So old Kreon wept and wailed; and when he could mourn
no more and thought he would raise again his ancient limbs,
he found to his horror that she clung to him as ivy clings
to laurel boughs. The slaves and the guards of the palace stood helpless,
an army of useless friends. The fat king
wrestled with his daughter. When he pulled away with the whole of his strength,
his agèd flesh tore free of his bones. Too spent at last
to struggle further with the corpse or howl in pain, he sobbed,
dryly, resigned to death. The slave Ipnolebes
stood over him, watching with empty eyes. The old king whispered,
"Nothing works! All we've learned is that!" And he died.
Ipnolebes said nothing. Then, all around the room,
the slaves began to whisper again. A sound like fire.

Then Jason covered his eyes with his hands and moaned, for at last
he saw to the end. And then he was running in the wild hope
that still there was time. He flew down the palace steps—no guards
in sight there now—and down through that smoky, endless rain,
the clattering thunder and the sudden bursts of fire out of heaven,
to his own locked gate. He hurled his shoulder against it with the force
of Herakles' club, and the huge bronze hinges snapped like wood.
The Corinthian women inside all ran to the windows in fear,
hearing the racket of his coming. But he came no further. Above
his head, like a hovering lightning shape, Medeia appeared
in a chariot drawn by dragons—beside her, the bodies of his sons.
Squinting, throwing up his arm against that blood-red light,
his throat convulsing till his words were barely intelligible,
he shouted, "Monster! Female serpent abhorred by mankind,
by the gods, and by me—you who could find it in your heart to murder
the children you bore yourself, to leave me childless and broken—
by all the gods in heaven or on earth or under the earth
I curse you! May you live forever in the pain you've brought yourself,
and with every passing day may your sorrow triple, and your mind
grow more unsure, more tortured by doubt of what's happened here,
till nothing is certain but hopeless and endless sorrow."

                                                    Even now—
the proof of her victory gray and inert beside her—she turned
her face from the lash of his words; broken as he was, he knew
her chief point of vincibility: self-doubt, her fear

339

that all she might do on earth was nothing but the afterburn
of her father's mindlessly rumbling, teratical blood. She shouted,
"Curse all you please. You've turned too late to religion, Jason.
Why should the gods pay heed to the curses of an oath-breaker?"
She laughed, terrible and false, a crash of ice. He howled,
"Yield me one thing and go then, free of me forever." She waited.
"The bodies of my sons," he said, "to bewail and bury." But again
Medeia laughed, monstrous in her spite. "Never, my husband!
I'll bear them myself to the shrine of Hera in the high mountains
and there bury them where none who hate me will climb to insult them,
scattering their stones. For the land of Sisyphus I'll ordain a feast
with solemn rites to atone for the blood I've impiously spilled,
then afterward away to Erekhtheus I'll go, and live in protection
of Aigeus, Pandion's son. And you, vile wretch—this curse
I place on you, in the hearing of earth and the burning sun
and the multitudinous gods: May you now grow old alone,
childless and silent, and die at last a shameful death,
crushed by a beam from your own *Argo*. Then, then or never,
shall our marriage end." He listened in silence, his skin burning
from the heat of the sun-god's chariot. He wailed: "Medeia, give back
my sons." But again her reply was, "Never!" Then, turning slowly,
she pointed to the palace. "Burials enough you'll have, I think,
without these, husband." He looked. All the palace was churning fire—
the tapestried walls, the trusses and cantled beams, the doors,
the vaulting roofs. His muscles knotted more tightly than before,
and his mind went wild. "Not *my* work, husband," Medeia said.
"The friends you'd have saved, in your own good time, from Kreon's dungeon
have fashioned keys of their own. I'll bury our children, Jason.
Deal with the dead mad Idas and Lynkeus scatter in their wake!"
More darkly than ever he'd have cursed her then, but his tongue was a stone,
his thick neck swollen as an adder's. With the strength of fifteen men
he seized the great bronze gate he'd torn from its hinges, twisted it,
breaking it free of its latch and lock, swung it around once,
and fired it upward at his wife. The chariot and dragons vanished,
cunning illusions, and the door went planing through the night, arching
upward and away six furlongs, gleaming. All the sky
was alight from the fire in the palace; and now there were more fires burning,
the brothers taking remorseless Argonaut revenge on a king
now dead. Jason could do nothing, kneeling in the cobbled street,
bellowing wordless fury, clinging to his skull with both hands,

340

for the heat of burning Corinth was nothing to the fire in his mind.
Kneeling, his muscular thighs bulging, he swayed and strained
for speech. He'd forgotten the trick of it. And now he grew silent,
became like the focus of the whole world's pressure. The city all around him
roared, full of fire and shouts, alive with people on the run.
And now, as steady and endless as the rain, gray ashes fell.
    Kneeling, furious, no longer sane, Lord Jason grew old.
Before my eyes his skin withered and his hair turned white.
The street became the *Argo*. I shouted in terror for the goddess.
Waves crashed over the gunnels; from the sailyard icicles hung.
And still, like snow, white ashes drifted through the universe,
and above the sailyard, circling, circling in the darkness, the ravens.

24

I stood on an island of flaking shale, where snow lay gray,
in sickly patches; an island barren except for one tree
by a miracle not yet dead, but bare and aging, failing,
the surrounding air so choked and smoky that, for all I knew,
I'd stumbled on the kingdom of Death. From every side I heard,
ringing across what must have been black and sludgy waters,
cracks and explosions, rumblings, shots; the air was filled
with the whine of what might have been engines. I could see, through the
     snow and smoke,
no smouldering fires, no rocket's glare, no proof that the earth
was not, itself, unaided by man, the attacker and attacked.
Holding my right hand—stiff and useless, violently throbbing—
in my left, the collar of my old black coat drawn high to shield me,
I moved with feeble and tottering steps toward the center of the island.
I began to see now there was more life here than I'd guessed at first:
insects struggling in the ice, and sluggish serpents, hissing,
venomous mouths wide open. I kept my distance, and passed.
In every crevasse of that sickened place, there were lean, white gannets
crying forlornly in inconstant, snow-filled brume. I found
a man with a stick walking slowly in front of the entrance to a cave,
turning in slow, stiff circles, as if in search of something.
His beard came nearly to his knees; his ankles were knobby and swollen
from some old injury; he had no eyes. He frowned,
stern and strangely unbent for a man so old, and a hermit.
"Who's there?" he said, and pointed his stick. I struggled to answer,
but no words came. He reached toward me with his square, gray hand
to feel out my features and manner of dress, then shook his head
dully, wearier than ever, and turned his face away,

thinking, or listening to something out on the water. I thought
he'd forgotten my presence; but he said suddenly, "Whoever sent you,
tell them to take you back. Say to them, 'Oidipus thanks you,
but he takes no interest in the future.' Now go." He waved at me gruffly,
not unkindly but impatiently, like a man interrupted.
"Are you gone?" he said. I tried to think how to tell him I was not as
free in my comings and goings as he seemed to think. He said,
"Good, good!" and nodded, thankful to be rid of me.
I said, "I can tell you of Kreon's death." He started, indignant.
But after a moment my words registered,
and he scowled, standing quite still, as if carefully balancing.
"He's dead, then," he said. I said: "A horrible death. I saw it."
He wiped his eyebrows. "Don't tell me about it. Kreon was dead
from the beginning." He mulled it over. "That was the difference between us."
There, to my surprise, he let it drop.

And then

I too heard, breaking through the smoky dark, the queer sound Oidipus
strained to catch: a rhythmic cry and the faint whisper
of oars swinging. He leaned both hands on the crook of his cane.
"More company," he said, and braced himself. A moment later
I saw the *Argo*'s silver fangs come gliding out of darkness,
the long oars swinging like the legs of a huge, black sea-insect,
crusted with ice. The sail was stiff. On the island around us
the ice and dark snow reddened, as if the war had come nearer,
riding in the black ship's wake.

Straight in toward shore she came,

the oars now lifted like wings, and as soon as the keel-beam struck,
down leaped a man in a great brown cape that he swirled with his arm
as if hoping to frighten the night. His icy beard and mane
were wild, his bright eyes rolling. When he saw me he halted and covered
his eyes with both hands, then carefully peeked through his fingers at me.
At last, convinced that the curious sight was no madman's dream,
he bowed to me, then turned and tip-toed over, through the snow,
to Oidipus. He whispered, smile flashing, "My name is Idas,
or so men call me, and I answer to it. Why increase, say I,
the general confusion? Which is, you may say, an immoral opinion."
He glanced past his shoulder to the ship, then whispered in Oidipus' ear:
"I deftly reply, after careful study: 'I burned down the city
of Corinth, sir, in the honest opinion it belonged to a man
who'd sorely grieved me—but found too late that the fellow had left it

to my dear old friend, in whom I was only, at worst, disappointed,
which is not, you'll agree, just cause for destroying an old friend's town.
But what's done is done, as Time is forever inkling at us.
And, being a reasonable man, within limits, I turned my faltering
attention to doing him good. I must make you privy to a secret:
He'd had it worse than I, this friend. He'd lost his lady.
A nasty business. She murdered his sons and reduced him to tatters—
it's the usual story. In the merry words of our old friend Phineus,
'Dark, unfeeling, unloving powers determine our human
destiny.' He was beaten hands-down, poor devil. She made
considerable noise about oath-breaking, and believed herself,
as well she might, since she spoke with enormous sincerity,
which is to say, she was wild with rage. She called down a curse,
that Jason should die in sorrow and failure, on his own *Argo*—
a curse that may well be fulfilled. On our sailyard, ravens perch,
creatures beloved of the master of life and death, Dionysos.
Having struck, she fled to Aigeus' kingdom in Erekhtheus,
which now we seek. Our luck has not been the best, as you see.
Winds play sinister games with us; familiar landmarks
change in front of our eyes, outrageously cunning—no doubt
ensorcelled by Jason's lady. From this it infallibly follows,
if you've traced all the twists of my argument, that we've landed here
to gain some clue to our bearings." He smiled, eyes slyly narrowed,
pulling at his fingers and making the knuckles pop. King Oidipus
with his old head bent as if looking at the ground, said nothing for a time.
At last he said, "Let me speak with this man." Mad Idas bowed.
"Of course! I had hoped to suggest it myself!" He signalled to the ship,
and a moment later Lynkeus jumped down, and after him Jason.
They came toward us. "You must understand," mad Idas said,
"that my friend cannot speak. He was once the most eloquent of orators,
but a secret he suspected for a long time, and continually resisted,
eventually got the best of him and took up residence
in his mouth. Look past his teeth and you'll see it there, blinking like an owl,
huddled in darkness. He's grown more mute than Phlias, who could answer
the anger of the world with a dance. A terrible business."

> The blind king
listened as Lynkeus and Jason approached. When they stood before him,
he reached out to feel first Lynkeus' features, then Jason's. No man
was ever more ravaged—grayed and wrinkled, hunched. Oidipus
dropped his hand to his side again and nodded. "I see

it's broken you, this sorrow. And yet you hunt her." Jason
nodded, a movement almost not perceptible
even to a man with sight, but Oidipus went on, as if
he too had caught it: "The world is filled with curious stirrings.
I feel all around me some change in the wind. I see things,
here on this hyperborean island a thousand miles
from home. I catch queer rumors. Remote as I am, in this place,
from the traffic and trade of man, you're not the first to touch here,
though the change struggling toward life in you is the weirdest of them all.
That much I sense already. Yet what it is your life
is groping toward I've not yet understood. It may come.
It *will* come, I think. I feel myself almost closing on it,
though of course I may not. I set great store by my intellect once;
thought I was wiser than all other mortals." He laughed to himself.
"I answered the riddle of the Sphinx—sat pondering, wringing my fingers,
and suddenly got it, leaped up shrieking, 'It's a man! A man!'
Poor idiot! I thought after that that my crafty eye could pierce
all life's mysteries: Set myself up as a sage, became
(gloating in my prizes—the throne of Thebes, and her beautiful queen)—
became the most foolish of kings, unwitting parody of one
who was truly wise in Thebes, the seer Teiresias,
blinded for sights forbidden—the bosom and flanks of Athena—
as I, too, would be blinded for knowledge not lawful. I now
hold myself in less awe." He smiled. "I have no virtue
except, perhaps, humility. 'Know thou art a man' the god warns—
Apollo, strangler of snakes. And I know it. Smashed to the ground,
to wisdom. With every hair I lose, a desire dies;
with every eyelid flicker, I forget some fact." Abruptly,
remembering the cold and his guests' discomfort, the old man said:
"Come in my cave, good sirs. There's a fire, and stones for chairs."
He led the way, tapping with his stick, and we followed him.
He'd shielded the entrance to the cave with scraps of wood (old crating,
the salvaged planking of ships) till it looked like the shacks you see
by the city dump. But the glittering walls of the cave were warm.
Idas and Lynkeus stirred the coals, found logs to add.
Jason stood quiet as a boulder, white-bearded, staring intensely
at something deep in the fire. Then all but Oidipus sat down.
I sat in the shadow of the others and reached out timidly for heat.
Oidipus tipped down his head, both hands on his cane, his forehead
furrowed like a field. "That was not the least of visits

when Theseus came with his Amazon, after his cruel betrayal
of the beautiful Ariadne, whom Theseus swore he'd praise
forever. He felt no remorse at that. All the world betrays.
The fibers binding the oak together or the towering plane tree
sever, sooner or later; or a life-giving storm from Zeus
turns to an enemy and tears up the tree by its roots. In Nature
steadfast faith is an illusion of fools. So Theseus claimed,
and scorned her, despite all she'd done for him. But later, seeing
how deep that emptiness runs—how the center of the universe
is Hades' realm, where the absence of meaning lies bitter on the tongue
as a taste of alum—he changed his opinion. He fought his way back
to the kingdom of the living and made his own heart a law contrary
to the world's. And at last he subdued that passionate Amazon
by laying plain the deadness at the core, the all-out battle
of dark gods seething, each against all, like atoms. Like you,
a metaphysician to the bone, he knew, that scorner of vows,
the smell of mortality in promises. Without that knowledge
nothing of importance can begin, though knowledge, if it goes no further . . .
The rest is murky. So I saw myself—I, who answered
the Sphinx's riddle and swore by unflagging intelligence
to keep Thebes firm. I was shown soon enough the absurdity
of hopes so overweening. The ground underneath me shifted,
and all I perceived and reasoned about was a mirror trick.
I learned that the way of the universe is dim, unnamable,
shape without shape, image without substance, a dark implication
from silence. . . .
               "And yet it is also true that Herakles was right—
with Herakles too I passed a day—who believed his father
was loving and always near, assuaging torments. (In a world
confused and contradictory, everything is right, and all
potential is real possibility.) By the character of Zeus
as he understood it, he judged all things. When he seized the initiative,
judging for himself, as if Zeus were not there, he was filled with darkness,
loneliness, sorrow, and fear. Many times he fell, by his standard,
and many times climbed back, bellowing, striking all around him
with his wild-man's club. He was wrong, of course, in believing his father
was there, or that Zeus felt concern—one more blind, feelingless power—
but the sorrow and joy in redemption were real enough. So the Trojan
Aeneas thought, who abandoned the woman he loved for duty
and sailed out of Carthage, take it as she might. His voice grew wild,

telling me the story: 'What pure serenity I felt,' he said.
' "Let nobody fool you," I said to the sailors around me in the ship,
"though the mind yaw this way and that, anchorless, the heart can be sure
what's right and wrong, what the gods require. I've proved it myself,
when I turned sternly on selfish desire for that loveliest of queens
who lulled my noble and difficult purpose to sleep, seduced
my lion-ambition with presents and comforts, till I'd half-forgotten
my people's destiny, my arms grown flabby, the back that once
easily carried my father from burning Troy grown frail
and flimsy as a girl's, my mind once keen grown soft with love
and wine and poetry. 'Who can say what's best?' I sighed,
sunk in the softness of Dido's scented bed. But a voice
outside my life and larger than life came urging me onward,
peremptorily ordering 'Up! To Italy!' And now that my legs
stand balanced on the deck of the ship again, I know the truth,
know it by the salt's sharp bite in the spray, by the soul-reviving
pressure of the wind. There is no personal pleasure—none!—
that touches the joy of duty! The man who claims the gods
are remote, indifferent—the man who feels no presence of the gods
in all he does—is a man half dead. They exist; they reveal
their character and will in every leaf and flower. Woe
to the fool who closes his heart to them! His heart will be dark,
his deeds puny and ridiculous!" So I spoke on the ship,
ploughing north toward Italy,' he said. 'But that was before.'
He laughed, furious, when he spoke with me now of his former opinions.
'Stark madness,' he said, and gnashed his teeth, pacing back and forth.
'I could hardly know that as soon as I left her she'd killed herself,
though we saw, three nights out of Carthage, the glow of her funeral pyre.
Not all the magnificent kingdoms on earth are worth the death
of a single beautiful woman—nay, the death of even
a sick old man. When I met her shade I came to my senses,
but understood too late. And with nothing remaining but duty,
I followed duty—followed what once I'd known by feeling,
I thought, as the gods' command. Came no such feelings now.
Turnus dead, my better, but a man in my destiny's way;
Lavinia my wife, a useful ally—her bed no Dido's.
Loveless, friendless. A compromiser for the good of the state,
selfless servant of the gods as a burning stick is servant
to the chilly, indifferent shepherd. Such is the sorrow of things.'
So he spoke, full of anger, longing for death. Nor was it much better

for Ticius, or Lombard, or Brutus, or the others dispersed out of Troy,
obedient to what they imagined the high gods' will. But each,
sick with betrayals, too cynic for love such as Orpheus had,
made his peace, built up weary battlements—for all his scorn
of pride, made his stand of proud banners. And rightly enough. No worse
than Akhilles' way—if Odysseus told me, in that much, the truth.
He would not bend for the pompous bray of civilities, that one!
Would let all Akhaia go down for one woman, his prize of war
whom dog-eyed Agamemnon stole, supported by lordlings,
Akhaians gathered from far and near for a high moral purpose,
they pretended—lying in their teeth. They did not fool the son
of Peleus, raging in his tent and cursing their whole corrupt
establishment. He set his pure and absolute passion
beyond the value of all their chatter of community effort
till Patroklos died, and Akhilles' passion made him hate all Ilium
and battle for Akhaia in spite of himself. He wagered his soul
on love and hate, and let duty be damned. But Priam,
bending in sorrow for his headless, mutilated son, made Akhilles
shudder at last with sanity, crying aloud to the gods.
He too, the gentle and courageous Hektor, was a lover—loved
both justice and the people of his city and house. Constrained to fight
for an evil cause or abandon loved ones, he wiped the lines
from his forehead, gave up on metaphysics, played for an hour
with his son, then put on his armor. So goes the universe,
disaster on this side, shame on that . . . Yet not even these
are trustworthy.
          "For ten long years Odysseus debated,
tossed like a chip by the lunatic gods—not the least of them
the gods in his sly, unsteadfast brain. Defend him as you will,
Odysseus couldn't be certain himself that he truly intended
to make his way back to Penelope. He bounced from wall
to wall down the long dark corridor of chance to that moment of panic
when Alkinoös' daughter found him by the sea and fell
in love with him. Then swiftly that quick brain lied: told tales
of battle with the Cyclops, the terror of Sirens, debasement on the isle
of Circe—fashioned adventures, each stranger than the last, to prove
that all this time he'd had no end but one, return to Ithika
and his dear lost wife. And so, assisted by the wily Athena,
he explained away his drifting and eluded the sweet, light clutches
of Nausikaa—but committed himself to the older, half-

forgotten prison, and there Alkinoös sent him, laden
with gifts on that oarless barque. But though he reached the hall
itself and learned who was loyal to him, he could find no way
to win back his power from the suitors there, fierce men who'd kill him
gladly if he dared to reveal himself. So hour on hour,
disguised as a beggar in his own wide hall, he gnashed his teeth,
watching them eat through the wealth of his pastures and smile obscenely
at his pale-cheeked, ever more beautiful wife; and his hands were tied.
She seemed not to know him (though his dear old dog had died of joy
at sight of him). Yet she it was who suggested the test
of the bow, and placed in Odysseus' hands the one weapon
with which he might make his play. And play he did! Such slaughter
was never seen, not even on the Trojan plains. When it ended,
and the house was cleansed of the stench of blood by sulphur fumes,
his disloyal servants hanged and those proved loyal rewarded,
Odysseus, deserving or not, had his kingdom and wise good wife
and best of sons. Whatever a man could dare to ask
if the world were just and orderly, and the gods kind,
all that and more, he was given.
                    "So it is that the lives of men
confute each other, and nothing is stable, nothing—nay, not even misery—sure.
For that reason I abandoned rule,
and abandoned all giving of advice. If I liked, I could point your ship
in the direction of Aigeus' land, the kingdom of Theseus' father,
or give firm reasons for avoiding the place. But I've little heart left
for tedious illusions—not mine, not even some other man's.
Life is a foolish dream in the mind of the Unnamable.
When he wakens, we'll vanish in an instant, squeezed to our nothingness,
or so we're advised by books. Therefore I devote myself,
for all my famous temper, wrecker of my life, to learning
to forget this life, drifting, will-less, toward absolute nothing,
formless land where all paradox, all struggle, melts.
A man who's been totally crushed by life should understand these things,
a man whose loss has proved absolute. All the more, therefore,
I wonder what reasons Jason may have found—unless, perhaps,
pure rage, after all these years, has still sufficient power
to drive him on, forcing him even now to seek
revenge. You say that the yard on your mast is a roost for ravens.
A dangerous sign; I agree with you. For surely the curse

350

Medeia placed on Jason is there confirmed, death
on the *Argo*. And yet on that selfsame ship he follows her.
But that, I think, is by no means the worst of attendant omens.
In your wake come the groans of unheard-of creatures, and a smell of fire,
and sounds of a vast, unholy war. I need not say
'Turn back in time, have nothing to do with this futureless man,'
for the dullest peasant could give such advice. I ask, instead,
what brings you here? What can it be you've grasped—or what
do you hope for? I am anxious to understand."

Mad Idas held
his hands to the fire, Lynkeus looking sadly through the walls.
Jason waited, struggling against his restlessness. Then Idas said:
"All you've told me I've known from the beginning, though it's taken me years
to grasp the thing that, because I am not like other men,
I knew. As my brother sees with his lynx's eyes more things
than others see, so I, in my madness, am blessed or cursed
with uncommon sight. In every tree and stone I see
the gods warring—not to the death but casually, lightly,
to break the eternal tedium. And I see the same
in human hearts. It filled me with panic once. Not now.
Once, half-asleep with friends who were talking, telling old stories,
and all signs swore that not a man there could work up a mood
for quarrelling, I would feel an estrangement in the man at my side—
fear, mistrust, or some other emotion dividing his heart—
and I'd know if I let myself look I'd discover the same in them all,
no stability in any man, no rock to lean on,
all our convictions, all our faith in each other, an illusion—
reality a pit of vipers squirming, blindly striking,
murdering themselves. Cold sweat would rise on my forehead, and I
would strike out first, their scapegoat; my own. But as time passed
I got over that; came to accept more calmly the darkness
that surrounds and shapes us. I came to accept what you preach to us now,
the voracious black hole at the core of things. I too observed
how fine it would be if Herakles were right—some loving god
attending mankind in every sorrow, demanding merely
total devotion, action conformant to His character.
Since no such god was there, I let it pass—allowed that
Theseus' way was best, faith by despair. But we
had stolen the fleece, we on the *Argo,* and Theseus had not.

351

That was the difference. We'd done the impossible, and never again
would Theseus' way suffice. Then Medeia murdered the sons
of Jason. There's no way up from that. No way, at least,
for Jason himself. For no revenge, however dire,
could have any shred of meaning. You see how it is. No man
could guess such love, such rage at betrayal. She emptied herself.
All the pale colonnades of reason she blew sky-high,
like a new volcano hurled through the heart of the city. So he,
reason's emblem, abandoned reason." He glanced at Jason,
furtive and quick, his mad smile flashing in the light of the fire.
"He abandoned the oldest rule in the world. It's not for revenge
that he hunts Medeia. Move by move they played out the game
of love and power, and both of them lost. What shamelessness,
what majestic madness to claim that it wasn't a game after all,
that no rules apply—that love is the god at the heart of things,
dumb to the structured surface—high ruler of the rumbling dance
behind the Unnamable's dream. And does Jason think, you ask,
that he'll overcome that woman's rage with his maniac love?
Not for an instant! He thinks nothing, hopeful or otherwise:
his will is dead, burned to cinders like Koronis' corpse
on her funeral pyre, from whence the healer Asklepios leaped;
or burned like the Theban princess Semele in lightnings from Zeus,
out of whose ash, like the Phoenix, the god Dionysos rose,
god who first crushed from the blood-soaked earth the wine he brings
to the vineyard's clawing roots. He has no fear any more,
of total destructions, for only the man destroyed utterly—
only the palace destroyed to its very foundation grits—
is freed to the state of indifferent good: mercy without hope,
power to be just. No matter any more, that life is a dream.
Let those who wish back off, seek their virtuous nothingness;
the man broken by the gods—if he's still alive—is free
even of the gods. Dark ships follow us, ghostly armadas
baffled by his choice. Sir, do not doubt their reality.
I give you the word of a madman, they're there—vast lumbering fleets,
some sliding, huge as cities, on the surface, some drifting under us,
some of them groaning and whining in the air. At times his voice
comes back to him, though not his mind, and he shouts at them:
*'Fools! You are caught in irrelevant forms: existence as comedy,
tragedy, epic!'* We let him rave. The end is inevitable.

We sail, search on for Erekhtheus, in an endlessly changing
sea." So he spoke, and ended.
                                        Then Oidipus rose from the fire
and tapped with his cane to the mouth of the cave. He stood a long while
in sad meditation, then pointed the way, as well as he knew how.
The winds had brought them far, far north. It would take them months
to row the *Argo* to warmer seas and the kingdom of Aigeus.
"Go with my blessing," the blind king said. "May the goddess of love
bend down in awe. The idea of desire is changed, made holy."
They thanked him, and Jason seized his hand and struggled to speak.
But Oidipus raised his fingers to Jason's lips and said,
"No matter." Jason bowed, and so they parted. In haste
they mounted the *Argo,* and Idas signalled the rowers. The blades
dug in, backing water, and the black ship groaned, dragging off the shore,
drawing away into darkness and smoke. The night was filled
with explosions and lights, what might have been some great celebration
or might have been some final, maniacal war. Then came
wind out of space, and the island vanished. I was falling, clinging
to my hat. But the tree was falling with me, its huge gnarled roots
reaching toward the abyss. I hung on, cried, "Goddess, goddess!"
In the thick dark beams of the tree above me, ravens sat watching
with unblinking eyes. I heard all at once, from end to end
of the universe, Medeia's laugh, full of rage and sorrow,
the anger of all who were ever betrayed, their hearts understood
too late. At once—creation *ex nihilo,* bold leap of Art,
my childhood's hope—the base of the tree shot infinitely downward
and the top upward, and the central branches shot infinitely left
and right, to the ends of darkness, and everything was firm again,
everything still. A voice that filled all the depth and breadth
of the universe said: *Nothing is impossible! Nothing is definite!*
Be calm! Be brave! But I knew the voice: Jason's, full of woe.
A rope snapped, close at hand, and I heard the sailyard fall,
and ravens flew up in the night, screeching, and Idas cried out.
Oidipus, sitting alone in his cave, put a stick on the fire.
"Nothing is impossible, nothing is definite. Be still," he whispered.
The Moirai, three old sisters, solemnly nodded in the night.

In a distant time I saw these things, and in all our times,
when angry Medeia was still on earth, and the mind of Jason

struggled to undo disaster, defiant of destiny, crushed;
I saw these things in a world of old graves where winecups waited,
and King Dionysos-Christ refused to die, though forgotten—
drinking and dancing toward birth—and Artemis, with empty eyes,
sang life's final despair, proud scorn of hope, in a room
gone strange, decaying . . . a sleeping planet adrift and drugged . . .
while deep in the night old snakes were coupling with murderous intent.

A Note on the Type

The text of this book was set in Intertype
Garamond No. 3, a modern rendering of the type first
cut by Claude Garamond (1510-1561).
Garamond was a pupil of Geoffroy Troy and is
believed to have based his letters on the Venetian
models, although he introduced a number of important
differences, and it is to him we owe the letter which
we know as old-style. He gave to his letters a
certain elegance and a feeling of movement that won
for their creator an immediate reputation and the
patronage of Francis I of France.

*Composed, printed and bound by
the Haddon Craftsmen, Inc.,
Scranton, Pa.
Typography and binding design by
Virginia Tan*